MY HEART'S TRUE DELIGHT

TRUE GENTLEMEN BOOK 10

GRACE BURROWES

DEDICATION

To those with disorders of mood

CHAPTER ONE

"If you are so unforgivably clodpated as to challenge William Chastain to a duel," Ash Dorning said, "I will shoot you in the arse myself, Tresham. And lest you forget, I was raised in the country. My aim is faultless."

"You won't shoot me," Jonathan Tresham replied. "Lady Della would never forgive you for wounding her devoted brother. Besides, I'll need you to serve as one of my seconds."

Ash poured two fingers of brandy from the better stock kept behind The Coventry Club's bar. At this midmorning hour, the cleaning crew had already come through. The room was tidy and deserted, and a perfect place to talk sense into Tresham.

Or try to. He passed Tresham the medicinal tot and poured one for himself. "If you add fuel to the flames of gossip by involving Lady Della's name in a matter of honor, you will be the brother she never forgives. As far as polite society is concerned, the Haddonfield menfolk are her siblings, and your involvement in the situation would only cause the wrong kind of speculation."

Lady Della's mother and Tresham's father had had an affair while married to other people. The tall, blond Haddonfields affectionately referred to the petite brown-haired Lady Della as their changeling, but anybody who took a close look at Della and Tresham side by side would see an uncanny resemblance.

If those people had any sense, they'd speculate silently. Della was fiercely loved by all of her siblings and by any number of relatives and family connections.

Della was loved by Ash, too, not that his sentiments signified.

"Why did she do it, Dorning?" Tresham took his drink to the roulette table and gave the wheel a spin. "Why run off with Chastain? He's a bounder and an inept card player, and worse yet, a rake."

Because Ash was a co-manager of The Coventry Club, he knew exactly what Tresham meant. The more heavily William Chastain lost, the more heavily he drank, and the more heavily he bet. Ash had a fine grasp of probabilities, while Chastain had a fine grasp of the brandy decanter.

"To young men just down from university," Ash said, "Chastain offers a certain shallow-minded bonhomie. He looks the part of the man about Town. He pays his debts, or we'd not let him back in the door." Though how he paid his debts was something of a mystery.

"His damned father must be covering his markers," Tresham muttered. "Last I heard, Chastain was engaged to some French comte's granddaughter, so his papa is doubtless keeping Chastain out of trouble as best he can until the vows are spoken. I really do want to kill him."

So do I. "That won't help. Chastain traveled no farther with Della than Alconbury. If he wants to live, or ever sire children, he'll keep his mouth shut. The whole business will remain a private regret for both parties."

By daylight, the game room looked a little tired, even boring. The art on the walls depicted good-quality classical scenes—scantily clad nymphs, heroic gods—but nothing too risqué and nothing too impressive either. Without the click and tumble of the dice, the chatter of conversation, or the sparkle of the patrons' jewels, the room was simply a collection of tables and chairs on thick carpet between silk-hung walls.

Any Mayfair town house would have been at least as elegant. But that was the point: The Coventry's elegance was comfortably bland, not showy, not distracting. The focus of the patrons was to be on the play and on each other.

Ash's focus was on Della Haddonfield, whom he had given up trying to forget months ago.

"Chastain drinks when he loses, and he loses nearly every time he plays," Tresham said, wandering between the tables. "Sooner or later, he'll drink too much and start wittering on about the elopement with Lady Della. He spent half the damned night with her in that inn, Ash. I should kill him for that alone."

"I know, Tresham,"—*God, do I know*—"but Della apparently went with him willingly. Would her family tell you if that wasn't the case?"

"I have no idea." Tresham perched on a dealer's stool and took up a deck of cards. "I hate this," he said, shuffling the deck with casual expertise. "Chastain is an affront to good society and somebody needs to take him in hand."

Somebody needed to put out Chastain's lights. "Deal me in." Ash took up a stool at the same table. "Has it occurred to you that Della might be smitten with Chastain? She might be heartbroken that Chastain's father interrupted their elopement."

"My wife's theory is that Della chose Chastain because he's nothing more than a handsome lackwit. Della could manage him without looking up from her embroidery hoop. She's an earl's daughter, so Papa Chastain and Mama Chastain would eventually reconcile themselves to the match." Tresham gathered up the cards and set the deck in the middle of the table. "I shall trounce you at cribbage."

Ash produced a cribbage board from the shelf beneath the table. "You don't believe Della is smitten with Chastain?"

"I know she isn't. She once mentioned Chastain to me when I drove out with her. Her tone was less than respectful."

Ash cut for the crib and pulled the low card. "Feelings can change."

"Not those feelings. Della expressed pity for his sire and shared the opinion that Chastain will bankrupt the family within two years of gaining control of the Chastain fortune. She's right."

Play moved along, with the cards favoring Ash. His leading peg was halfway around the board when his brother Sycamore sauntered in, looking dashing and windblown in his riding attire.

"That is the good brandy at Tresham's elbow," Sycamore said, pausing to remove his spurs. "Since when do we give away the good stuff, brother mine?"

Ash picked up his cards to find another double run, his third of the game so far. "We are generous with Tresham because he needed a tonic for his nerves." As had Ash. "I'm beating him soundly."

Sycamore peered over Tresham's shoulder. "William Chastain needs a sound beating. Who's with me?"

Tresham put down his cards. "What have you heard?"

Sycamore could be tactful—about once every five years—and then only out of a perverse impulse to surprise his older siblings.

"Chastain was at his club last night, lamenting that his French bride refuses to cry off, despite the failed elopement with a certain Lady Delightful."

Tresham was on his feet so quickly he knocked his stool over. "I will kill him, slowly, after protracted torture. I will *geld* him and cut the idiot tongue from his empty head. By Jehovah's thunder, I ought to ruin his father for siring such a walking pile of offal."

"If you do ruin him," Sycamore said, taking a sip of Tresham's brandy, "please do it here, so the club gets a bit of the notoriety and ten percent of the kitty."

"Tresham, you *cannot*," Ash said, getting to his feet. "You cannot so much as intimate that Chastain's wild maunderings have any connection to reality or to Della, and you most assuredly cannot strut about all but proclaiming that her ladyship has an illegitimate connection to you."

"But—"

Ash stepped closer. "*No*. Not if you care for her, which you loudly claim to do. The Haddonfields have substantial consequence. They have weathered other scandals. You can be a friend of the family, a cordial acquaintance, but you cannot involve yourself in any manner that makes the situation worse than it already is."

Tresham finished his drink and set the glass on the table with a *thunk*. "I'm supposed to be the sensible one. The role grows tedious. But then, I'm selling most of this club to you two. How sensible was that?"

"Very sensible," Sycamore said. "We're making you pots of money to go with the barrels and trout ponds' worth you already have."

"Della will be a spinster now," Tresham said, and Ash sensed they'd reached the heart of the dilemma. "She's the only Haddonfield yet unmarried. They've all been trying to fire her off—my own dear Theodosia has tried to help—but to no avail. Now Chastain has botched an elopement, and Della will suffer the consequences. Nobody will marry her after this."

"Perhaps she doesn't want to be married," Sycamore said.

"Then why elope with William the Witless?" Tresham snapped. "That was a desperate measure indeed, and now she's to be an old maid."

Ash picked up the discarded brandy glass and shook the dregs into his mouth. "She will not be an old maid. Della is lovely, charming, smart, kind, funny, and quite well connected. You are making too much of a bad moment."

Sycamore sent him a curious look. "This is more than a bad moment. She spent most of the evening in the same bedroom with Chastain at the inn in Alconbury. That news was galloping up and down the bridle paths this morning. I discredited the rumor with laughing disbelief, but it's as Tresh says: Lady Della has had no offers, and Chastain is no sort of prize. The appearances are dire."

If Ash could have beaten himself soundly at that moment, he

would have. Lady Della had quite possibly discouraged many offers while waiting for a proposal from Ash himself.

"The situation is far from dire," he said. "The necessary steps are simple. The Little Season is under way. We will treat Lady Della to a show of support, mustering a phalanx of eligibles to stand up with her. She will carry on as if the gossip is just that. Chastain will learn discretion in a violent school if need be, and come spring, some other scandal will have everyone's attention."

"It's a plan," Sycamore said, in tones that suggested it was a hopelessly stupid plan.

"And if this plan doesn't work?" Tresham asked. "Then may I part Chastain from his tiny cods?"

"If the plan doesn't work," Ash said, "then I will marry Della myself."

Sycamore for once had nothing to say, while Tresham looked mightily relieved. Ash could make this offer because he was sure to a soul-deep certainty that he was the last man Della Haddonfield would ever agree to marry.

∾

"A FAILED ELOPEMENT is not the end of the world, Della." George's tone held equal parts commiseration and good cheer. The commiseration was genuine, while Della took leave to doubt her brother's good cheer.

"We're Haddonfields," he went on, crossing to the decanters on the sideboard. "We get into scrapes. Have a nip for courage."

"No, thank you," Della replied, pacing across the family parlor. "Brandy has quite lost its appeal." Nothing appealed, except a long-term repairing lease at the family seat in Kent. Was that really too much to ask?

If George thought it odd that his baby sister had learned of brandy's restorative powers, he was too dear a brother to remark it.

He was also too much of a Haddonfield male not to partake himself, despite the early afternoon hour.

"You think this is an insurmountable disaster," he said, "the scandal to end all scandals. Do you not recall when I was found kissing a certain earl's son by moonlight in a not-deserted-enough garden?"

"That was passed off as misguided affection, foolishness in the dregs, stupidity and high spirits. Men are allowed to be foolish and regularly are. Ladies are held to a different standard, and by any standard, I have been stupid." Terribly, horribly, dreadfully stupid.

Also unlucky and desperate, not to mention a tad unbalanced.

George took a sip of his drink, his gaze assessing. The old brotherly charm and cajolery clearly weren't working their usual magic. If Della's siblings had paid half a wit of attention, they would have realized charm and cajolery had ceased working on her years ago.

But no, of course not. The older Haddonfield siblings—and they were legion—were all married. The senior Haddonfields were setting up and filling their nurseries at a great rate, wafting about on balmy seas of marital bliss.

And Della was truly, sincerely happy for them.

"Listen to me," George said. "You are an earl's daughter, regardless of your connection to Tresham. You simply sail ahead as if nothing's amiss, give the cut direct to any who intimate otherwise, and in a year or two, this will all be old news."

Della's escapade would not be old news twenty years hence. The Haddonfield menfolk got into scrapes, the ladies did not.

"George, why did you come up to Town?" Hotfoot, and without his wife and children, from whom he was seldom parted.

"Because I missed my siblings?"

"You saw me a month ago." When Nicholas and Leah came up to Town, Della was dragged along with them. When the earl and his countess returned to Kent, to Kent Della did go.

George set his drink on the sideboard and took the place at her elbow. Like every Haddonfield save Della, he was tall and blond, though not as stupendously tall as Nicholas, nor as spectacularly muscular as Beckman. Della had learned to live with being loomed over by her siblings, but today, her patience had run off with her common sense.

"Daniel and Kirsten are preparing to come to Town as well," George said. "Beckman and Sarah won't be far behind. Max and Antonia will probably pop back into London now that harvest is under way. Ethan and—"

"I won't have it." The sick, roiling feeling in Della's belly crested higher. "Tell them all to stay away. For my family to flock to my side only confirms that I've erred badly. That's not simply sailing ahead, George, that's hiding me behind Haddonfield consequence, and it will only make the situation worse."

"You're upset," George said, patting her shoulder, which nearly earned him a demonstration of Della's accuracy with a right upper-cut. "Understandable, but because you're upset, you are not thinking clearly. By this time tomorrow, you'll be glad our siblings—"

"*Do not* tell me what I am feeling, or what I will be feeling." *And do not pat my shoulder as if I were one of Willow and Susannah's dogs.*

The fraternal concern in George's eyes cooled to frank puzzle-ment. "Then you weren't pulling a stunt merely to gain our notice?"

"I *eloped* with William Chastain, George. I didn't drop my parasol in the Serpentine to see which bachelor would soak his breeches fishing it out for me."

George draped an arm around her shoulders, which Della toler-ated. Barely.

"Chastain's a buffoon, Della dearest. What were you really about?"

She'd been trying to prevent a scandal, oddly enough. "Eloping. Trying to free William from a betrothal he never sought." Taking a small risk for a larger reward. Or so she'd told herself. Chastain was a nasty dunderhead, an even greater dunderhead than she'd known.

He'd bungled every possible detail in every possible direction, and she had been an idiot to trust him.

"I can't credit that you truly intended to marry him." George dropped his arm and retrieved his drink. "Men are generally troublesome. I will be the first to admit that, and my perspective is more informed than most. I thought you were merely taking your time, waiting for the right fellow to do the tender-kisses-and-moonlight-strolls bit."

The right fellow *had* offered Della tender kisses and moonlight strolls. Then Ash Dorning had decided he wasn't the right fellow, for reasons Della still could not fathom. Ash would not give a flying fig for Della's irregular antecedents—he and Jonathan Tresham were fast friends and business associates—but something had deterred Ash from paying her his addresses.

"I grew tired of waiting," Della said, and that much was true. "George, would you mind very much if I went up to my room for a lie-down? I've been somewhat short of sleep lately and could use a nap." A hundred years wrapped in Mama's shawl and buried beneath twenty quilts ought to suffice.

"Have your nap, but, Della, you should know that Leah and Nicholas are very concerned. Chastain has already been indiscreet. He hasn't named you specifically, but he's dropped broad hints. The Merryfield ball is Wednesday night, and Leah was making references to a show of strength and putting a brave face on matters. Do you want to know the real reason I came up to Town?"

"The other real reason?"

"To make sure our dear brother Nicholas doesn't call anybody out. Fortunately, Nick is titled while Chastain is a mere baronet's heir. Strictly applied, the rules don't allow for Nick to call out a commoner."

Della sank onto a hassock. "But Tresham is a commoner, Beckman is... And when have any of my brothers played by the rules? George, promise me there won't be any duels. *Please.* I am happy to live out my days in obscurity at the family seat, and nobody need ever mention my name again."

Happy would be a stretch, but contentment might still be possible.

"You deserve better than banishment, Della. Chastain abused your good name terribly, and then his idiot father had to make the situation worse. I could reconcile myself to having Chastain for a brother-in-law, but his parents are not to be borne."

"William's parents might be much of the reason why he is the way he is." *And conversely.*

"You call him William. Do I understand that you would yet marry him, given the chance?"

While George swirled his brandy, Della reflected on plans gone awry, Haddonfields run amok, and William Chastain's innocent fiancée.

"If I say yes, then Nicholas will try to bribe William into crying off his betrothal outright, and I don't want that." Not now, not when the poor woman's family had stood by the agreement to marry despite William's attempt to flee.

George finished his drink and headed for the door. "If you say no, that you won't marry Chastain, then one has to wonder why the hell you ran off with him in the first place. Prepare yourself to face the tabbies at the Merryfield ball, Della. Not for your own sake, but for the sake of the family so bewildered by your actions."

The ball would be a disaster, another way to fan the bonfire of gossip. "I am bewildered too, George," Della said. "Bewildered and so very, very sorry." She'd apologized to Nicholas before setting foot back in his house and to Leah ten minutes thereafter. "George?"

But George had already left and silently closed the door. Della had every intention of slipping up to her room before another sibling could pounce on her, except that raised voices resounded as she passed by the closed library door.

George, who never shouted, was shouting, and Nicholas, the soul of patient consideration, was shouting back. The words *duel* and *family honor* reached Della's ears, along with profanities aimed at William Chastain's cognitive abilities.

Della reversed course, opened the library door, and strode in. Nicholas and George were glowering at each other from within fisticuff-range on the far side of the reading table.

"No duels, Nicholas," Della said. "This is all my fault, and I will pay the price for my folly. Please plan to escort me to the Merryfield ball on Wednesday. When the talk dies down, I will repair to Kent, and you may wall me up in the chapel. First, I will show my face before all of Mayfair and weather the scorn I am due. Then, I will gladly accept banishment. Are we agreed?"

Nick took a step toward her. "But, Della, dearest, you cannot—"

"Agreed," George said.

"Good." She managed to maintain her composure until she was in her room behind a locked door. Only then did she allow the tears to fall.

CHAPTER TWO

"If Chastain walks into this club," Sycamore said, "you will politely walk him right back out again."

Ash smiled for the benefit of the Coventry's patrons, as if Sycamore had made one of his typical witty remarks. "Should Chastain walk through the door, we will both walk him right back out again, politely or not."

The early evening gossip at the Coventry was running in many directions.

Lady Della had been a fool to get into a carriage with Chastain.

Lady Della had been desperate to get into a carriage with Chastain.

Chastain had been quite daring to attempt to make off with an earl's sister.

Chastain could be forgiven for trying to trade an émigré's daughter for an English aristocrat.

In any case, Lady Della, *at her age*, really *should have known better*.

"The betting book at White's already has several wagers," Sycamore said, keeping his voice down in a rare display of tact. "Her ladyship will have a baby by April. Chastain's fiancée will have a baby by April. They will both have babies by April."

Ash was so accustomed to living at a distance from his emotions that he needed a moment to identify the upwelling of violent impulses that Sycamore's recitation produced.

I am angry. In a proper, seething rage. A condition as novel as it was inconvenient. Ash was angry at Chastain, at the malicious talk aimed at an otherwise exemplary young lady, at Della's family for allowing this entire farce to occur, and of course—always—at himself.

"Who?" Ash asked. "Who wrote those wagers in a location that assured all of polite society hears of them?"

"Easier to ask who hasn't put down a few pounds one way or the other. And no, I did not. Babies arrive according to probabilities known only to the Almighty. Besides, you would kill me."

"As scrawny as you are, when the Haddonfield brothers finished with you, there would be nothing left worth killing."

Sycamore—who had left *scrawny* behind a good five years, eight inches, and four stone ago—offered a bland smile. "I abhor violence, Ash."

No, he did not. Sycamore was a fiend in the boxing ring, very likely a result of having six older brothers and a smart mouth. If he were more scientific about his strategy and a bit faster, he would have a prayer of besting Ash in a fair fight. What Sycamore could do with knives was uncanny.

"I abhor gossip," Ash said. "What the hell could Della have been thinking?"

"You are attempting to divine the mental processes of a female," Sycamore replied, snagging a flute of champagne from a passing waiter's tray. "Doomed undertaking for a mere mortal male, much less one with your limited gifts. Whatever Lady Della was thinking, she's supposed to attend the Merryfield ball tomorrow night, and that means one of us must be there as well."

Ash had spent two Seasons studiously avoiding any social gathering where Della was likely to appear. If their paths did cross, they greeted each other cordially and just as cordially ignored each other for the rest of the evening.

Ash timed visits to the family seat in Dorset for when Della was in Town. Della's removes to Kent often coincided with Ash's stays in London.

"You go," Ash said. "I'll handle things here."

"No." Sycamore took a casual sip of his champagne. "I'll stay here. You go. She likes you, and she will need friendly faces around her."

"Your face might be ugly, but it's friendly to most any pretty female." And Della was exquisite.

"Ash, dimwitted and homely though you are, she needs you. You've seen what happens when Mayfair decides to turn its back on a woman. In the receiving line, Lady Della will be served cold civility and that only because her titled brother will glue himself to her elbow. Nobody will stand up with her, nobody will even sit near her at supper save her family, which will only make matters worse. Before the dancing resumes, punch will be spilled on her dress, and that will be a mercy because it will permit her an early exit. She needs *you*."

I am the last man she needs. "I'm returning to Dorning Hall next week, Cam."

"Fine," Sycamore said flatly. "Though winter comes to Dorset and London alike. Scamper away next week, but attend the Merryfields' ball before you pull your annual disappearing act."

As if Ash's disappearing act were limited to once a year. "All she needs are a few eligibles to stand up with her. The talk will die down, somebody else's scandal will come along, and all will be well."

Sycamore aimed a glittering smile at a widowed marchioness who hadn't graced the Coventry since the previous June. Lady Tavistock was a skilled gambler and used her charm and beauty to distract her opponents.

And the dealers. Ash suspected she'd distracted Sycamore a time or two, though not at the card tables.

"Perhaps in addition to your other mental aberrations, you are prone to fantastical thinking," Sycamore said. "Lady Della is all but ruined, unless Chastain reveals the name of some other woman who happened to be bouncing on the sheets with him at the Alconbury Arms when Papa Chastain stormed onto the scene."

Sycamore occasionally landed a solid gut punch in the boxing ring—and sometimes when not in the boxing ring.

"Bouncing on the sheets?"

"'Fraid so. Have a sip of my wine. You have gone all peaky and pale."

Ash took the glass and drained half of it, which was an insult to the vintage. He'd tucked his anger away in its usual mental cupboard. Like a feline determined to get into the pantry, it would scratch and mew and paw at the door, but the lock would hold.

With the rest of his mind, he focused on a solution to Della's situation. "She needs eligibles, a dance card full of them."

"Not full," Sycamore replied. "Full would look contrived. Full would require all the brothers and in-laws and so forth."

The marchioness took up a place beside Mr. Travis Dunwald. She beamed at him, and young Dunwald bowed over her hand. He was quite eligible, a fine dresser, and not much of a gambler. Could not have calculated a probability if every card in the deck save one was face up on the table.

"How much does Dunwald owe us?" Ash asked.

Sycamore named a sum that was probably equal to Dunwald's entire quarterly allowance. He was nephew to a viscount and the old boy's heir. Eligible and solvent were not always near neighbors.

"What about Gower?"

Sycamore named an even larger sum. "What are you up to, Ash?"

"Don't worry, I'll cover the difference from my share of the monthly proceeds. What I am up to is filling Lady Della's dance card."

Sycamore retrieved the half-empty wineglass from Ash's grasp.

"Not a bad idea, especially coming from one of your modest intelligence, but she still needs *you*, Ash."

"No, she does not." Ash reaffixed a friendly smile to his face and began a circuitous approach to the table where Dunwald was trying to pretend he knew his way around a hand of cards.

He didn't, but he could manage a quadrille without falling on his handsome arse, and that was all Della required of him.

~

DELLA ASSURED herself that the receiving line hadn't been too ghastly. Lady Merryfield had been pitying rather than cold, Lord Merryfield had stared at Della's bosom only until Nicholas had cleared his throat. For a hostess to have a nearly fallen woman among her guests would lend cachet to the evening, apparently.

"That wasn't so bad," Nicholas murmured as they waited for the herald to announce them. "You'll see I was right. A few dances, a glass of punch, and some supper, and we can put the whole business behind us."

That had been George's argument as he'd headed off to the ball in his own conveyance, an advance guard scouting hostile terrain. Nicholas was studying the crowd in the ballroom below as a ship's captain watched an approaching gale.

"You needn't worry that Chastain is here," Della said as they advanced toward the steps down to the ballroom. "His father has hauled him off to Sussex, where he's to bide until the nuptials take place."

Nick glanced down at her, his smile faltering. "How do you know that?"

"I just do." Della's lady's maid was friends, cousins, or formerly employed with half the lady's maids in Mayfair. They formed an intelligence network that would have shamed Napoleon's best spies.

The herald announced the Earl of Bellefonte and Lady Delilah

Haddonfield, and the tide of conversation in the ballroom below ebbed to a trickle, then fell silent.

"A new experience," Della said, taking a firmer hold of Nick's arm. "I have rendered all of Society speechless."

She tipped her chin up when she wanted to crawl away on her hands and knees. What stopped her was the certain knowledge that she deserved exactly the reception she was getting, and that only after she'd endured this penance would her family allow her to slink off to Kent.

"Tresham is here," Nick murmured, offering her a smile that did not conceal the worry in his eyes. "George is beneath the minstrel's gallery. Worth Kettering and his lady are right outside the cardroom, and I do believe that's my own dear Valentine Windham beaming at us from near the punchbowl."

Windham was a duke's son and a composer and pianist of some renown. His show of tolerance would be remarked—also seen for what it was, a kindly display toward an old friend's disgraced sister.

"He'll dance with you," Nick said. "If I have to beggar myself commissioning damned string quartets from him, he'll dance with you."

By design, Della had arrived too late for the opening promenade. Lord Valentine led her out for the world's longest minuet. Nick stood up with her for a gavotte. All the while, gossip, talk, and tittering whispers followed her around on the dance floor.

Della was about to excuse herself to run the gauntlet of the ladies' retiring room—the sooner that was dealt with, the better—when Mr. Travis Dunwald approached.

"Lady Della, might I have the honor of leading you out for the quadrille?"

Dunwald's tone was cool. He looked down a patrician nose at Della, as if she were something malodorous stuck to his riding boot. This overture had all the earmarks of a drunken dare made late at night in one of the less reputable gentlemen's clubs.

"She would be honored," Nick said far too heartily. "Wouldn't you, my lady?"

Della saw nothing but disdain in Dunwald's eyes. If she declined, the gossip traveling around the ballroom with the speed of a brushfire would turn into an inferno, and there was all six and a half feet of Nick, trying hard to look cheerful—and harmless.

"I would be honored," Della said, placing her hand on Dunwald's arm.

The quadrille was a long, complicated dance, and in its course, Della came face-to-face with every smirking, leering, cold expression a man's features might wear. She had expected the antipathy of the women. A lady who fell from grace was like a house of contagion, to be avoided by all decent women lest the taint of dishonor spread by association.

But Della had not anticipated the particularly virulent contempt aimed at her by the gentlemen. Their hands grazed the sides of her breasts, their eyes frankly stripped her naked. Her partner for the allemande pretended to stumble such that he happened to get in a bruising squeeze to her derriere.

She did not dance every dance—far from it—but when James Neely-Goodman approached her before the supper waltz, Della had had enough.

She liked James. He was of only average height, and they often danced together because he partnered her well. His father was a baronet, and the family's wealth was vast and respectably ancient.

Even James, though, regarded her as if she'd betrayed him personally.

I can't do this. The thought landed in her mind with the solid substance of irrefutable truth. *I cannot be handled and disrespected and all but spit upon by men who lined up to partner me at cards last week.*

"Lady Della." James bowed shallowly and he did not take her hand. "I beg leave to pay you the honor of asking for your supper waltz."

Pay you the honor. The words were wrong, the tone was wrong. Utterly indifferent, not *even* contemptuous.

"Alas," said a smooth male voice to Della's right, "you are too late, Neely-Goodman. Her ladyship's supper waltz is spoken for."

Della would know that voice in Stygian darkness. "Mr. Dorning, good evening."

Ash Dorning, tall, dark-haired, and lean, made an impressive figure in evening attire. The jewel in his cravat pin exactly matched the striking periwinkle hue of his eyes, and his smile was neither forced nor improper. He and James held some sort of silent male conversation. Ash smiled steadily, James looked askance, raised an eyebrow, then shrugged.

"Enjoy your dance, my lady." He drifted away without bowing.

Della gathered up the tattered remains of her dignity and gazed out across the ballroom. Many people had seen this exchange, and every one of them would wonder what on earth had just transpired.

Della herself had no idea. "You need not spare me a pity waltz, Mr. Dorning. You've avoided me for months, and I am actually a bit fatigued."

On close inspection, Ash looked tired too. His eyes were shadowed, his mouth bore a slight tension. When he'd first distanced himself from her, Della had suspected him of suffering some physical ailment. The Dornings were notoriously robust, though, and months of listening for any scrap of gossip associated with Ash or his club had yielded no support for Della's theory.

He simply did not like her as much as she liked him—as she *had* liked him.

"I saw what happened with Fletcher," Ash said, referring to Della's partner for the allemande. "I saw your quadrille. You will please dance the supper waltz and share the buffet with me. We have a family connection, and you are entitled to my loyalty. Nobody will remark my partnering you."

Couples were moving onto the floor, and the waltz was Della's favorite dance. "I do not want your loyalty, Mr. Dorning. I would rather have your friendship."

His smile remained in place, and yet, his expression grew subtly pained. "You have both, do you but know it. Shall we dance?"

Della had longed desperately for just that invitation from him. A year ago, even a month ago, she would have been delighted to turn down the room in his arms.

"I do not want your pity, Mr. Dorning."

"I do not pity you." He held out his gloved hand.

Nicholas approached, holding two glasses of punch, his expression wary and hopeful. "Dorning, a pleasure."

"Bellefonte, good evening. I aspire to dance the supper waltz with her ladyship."

Nicholas would not plead with Della in public, but he was the head of the family and concerned not only for her but for all the cousins, in-laws, sisters, daughters, and aunties.

"Very well." Della put her hand in Mr. Dorning's. "The honor is mine, Mr. Dorning."

~

"TRY NOT to look as if you're being led to the gallows," Ash murmured. "We are putting on a spectacle. I apologize for Fletcher's unseemly clumsiness."

The introduction began as they reached the dance floor. Della sank into a curtsey, then assumed waltz position. Ash kept a scrupulously correct distance between them, and yet, she was in his arms, gazing up at him with curiosity rather than ire.

That was progress. Toward what, he did not know.

"I suspect Mr. Fletcher was put up to partnering me as part of some drunken wager," Della said.

He owed her honesty, in this at least. "I put him up to it."

Ash moved off with her and was reminded that Della Haddonfield was a superb dancer. Some ladies followed a lead well and were easy to guide. Della needed no guidance. By instinct alone, she matched a man's steps, such that he could think a direction, and she was there with him.

"You need not put anybody *up* to anything for my sake, Mr. Dorning. Was Dunwald your idea too?"

He nodded. "And Neely-Goodman." He braced himself for anger, but Della merely shifted her hand higher on his shoulder, taking a slightly firmer hold of him.

"Are there others?"

"I thought three sufficient to quell the worst of the gossip." He twirled her under his arm on a corner and broke a little piece of his heart as she smoothly came back into his embrace. How long had he dreamed of turning down the room with the lovely Lady Della? How long had he watched as one lucky man after another bowed over her hand and led her out?

Della matched his steps through an intricate pirouette. "I am beyond salvation, Mr. Dorning, though I do appreciate the effort you've made on my behalf. I wonder why you made it."

Because this at least I can do for you. Because I owe you. Because... He tossed aside the answers she would never believe and instead settled for one she would.

"I don't know what you were about with Chastain, my lady, but I know you well enough to grasp that matters did not go as you intended. You would not steal another woman's fiancé. You would not be caught by the groom's enraged father unless you wanted to be caught."

Russet brows drew down, suggesting Della's own family hadn't put together that much.

"Plans sometimes go awry," she said. "Even well-laid plans."

Ash danced her around the entire ballroom and let himself simply enjoy the moment. That the circumstances were miserable and the people watching were completely misreading the situation was of no moment. Ash was waltzing with the only woman to truly catch his eye—and his heart—and that was more consolation than he was entitled to.

"You planned to elope with Chastain," he said as the music came to an end, "and you planned to get caught before the first overnight stop. You did not plan for his idiot father to take so long to catch up with you, or to make such a public display when he did."

And what price had Della paid for her miscalculation? Had she been bouncing on the sheets consensually, struggling against Chastain's advances, something worse?

"My plans went awry," she said quietly. "My plans went badly awry."

The rage locked behind Ash's mental cupboards took on the low growl of a lion.

He led her from the dance floor and remained at her side. The doors to the gallery had been opened, and the line had formed for the buffet. He kept her hand tucked around his arm, the better to prevent her from dashing off to the ladies' retiring room, never to be seen again.

"We all make mistakes, Della," he said. "I've made more than my share." And on some fine and distant day, he might explain to her all the mistakes he'd made with her.

"This damage cannot be repaired, Mr. Dorning. I have made my bed, and I will lie in it alone." She spoke pleasantly, but the bleakness in her eyes belied her tone. "You may return to Dorset with a clear conscience. You've stood up with me for the pity waltz, and everybody will accord you capital-fellow status for your generosity of spirit."

The line shuffled forward. "How do you know I'm returning to Dorset?" Ash kept his voice down, both because everything was too easily overheard in such close quarters and because he wanted to create that fiction that he and Della were having a lovely little chat.

"You have scampered off to Dorset every autumn for the past four years. I've written to you there, but you do not write back."

"And I have appreciated your letters." He had *memorized* her letters. He and Della had a family connection. Writing to him was not quite scandalous, but it had surely been brave. Not answering her letters had been cowardly, though Ash told himself that encouraging her friendship would be unkind.

"I was planning to leave for Dorset next week," he said, "but in light of tonight's developments, I will put off my departure." He tempted fate with that decision, but better to tempt fate than further neglect his honor where Della was concerned.

She moved with him another few steps forward. Ash did not particularly want any glazed ham, stale profiteroles, or mashed potatoes sculpted to look like rows of pigeons. But Della needed to eat, and more than that, she needed to appear in great good health with an entirely normal appetite.

"You need not put off your departure for my sake," Della said, passing Ash two plates. "After tonight's fiasco, I will be allowed to leave Town in disgrace."

"Tonight has been far from a fiasco," he said. "Not quite a triumph, but not a failure. As I recall, you prefer beef to ham."

She sent him a curious look and filled both plates as she moved with him down the line. Della was enduring moment by moment, a skill Ash knew intimately. To a casual observer, her movements would appear relaxed and her expression pleasant.

What a damned painful irony to be sharing a waltz and supper with her and have her participation in those pleasures be out of dire expedience.

"Tonight has not yet descended into abject failure," Della said as they wandered down the gallery in search of a place to eat. "But the dance floor has certainly been purgatory. Where inept sinners go to marinate, which is less than I deserve. What about the terrace?"

Her self-castigation sat ill with Ash, though Society would agree with her. Ash did not know what her true motivation had been, but he entertained the theory that the whole business with Chastain was somehow the fault of one Ash Dorning.

"The terrace will suit," he said, and they found a small table with two chairs along the outside wall of the gallery. "Let's take stock, shall we?"

"Of what?"

"The progress of the battle." He set the plates on the table and held her chair. "You were acknowledged in the receiving line, and nobody has offered you the cut direct." He lingered near her shoulder when pushing in her chair, because in the terrace shadows, nobody would see him stealing a whiff of her honeysuckle perfume.

And because he was an idiot.

Della unfolded her table napkin. "The gentlemen have offered me leers, groping, coldness, and contempt."

"They *what?*"

She glanced around the relatively deserted terrace, pulled off her evening gloves, and draped them across the linen in her lap.

"Fletcher didn't merely stumble. He groped my bum. The quadrille was an exercise in how close a man's hands can come to a woman's breasts without actually touching them. I'm not hungry."

Neither was Ash. He silently promised the lion roaring behind iron mental bars a few rounds at Jackson's. A dozen rounds, in fact.

Which would not help Della one bit. He took off his gloves and put a quarter slice of toast topped with oregano and melted cheddar on her plate.

"Eat something. Please. Fletcher will find his debts at The Coventry are not, alas, forgiven."

Della took a bite of toast. "That was how you inveigled them into dancing with me?"

"Dunwald, Fletcher, Neely-Goodman... They are inept at cards and too proud to admit it. I have tried to explain some basics about probabilities to them, but they disdain my guidance. You have made progress tonight, Della, despite the unforgivable disrespect to your person."

She dusted her hands when she'd finished her toast. "Mr. Dorning, why have you taken it upon yourself to repair my reputation? I am the realm's most spectacular fool for running off with Chastain, and I am prepared to pay for my folly."

Ash was certain Della hadn't expected to pay nearly this high a price, though. Not in her worst nightmares. So what, exactly, had she been about with Chastain?

"All you need," he said, "is to continue as you've gone on tonight. I'll take you driving in the park tomorrow if the day is fair and escort you to the Dickson's Venetian breakfast on Monday. If you keep your chin up, and Chastain remains in Sussex, you can confront the gossips none the worse for your ordeal."

"Why?" Della asked, reaching for another triangle of toast.

He knew what she was asking: Why come to her aid now, when Ash had all but ignored her for months?

He wasn't about to open that barrel of rotten fish. "Why squire you about? Because I thought I could arrange for others to play that role, but the three I recruited tonight made a hash of the business. I'll play the doting swain for a week or two, and then you can break my heart and cast me off."

A fine plan indeed, offering Della a chance at reparation for the bad turn he'd been serving her for months.

"You never cast me off," Della said. "We shared a few harmless kisses, nothing more."

Those kisses had been luscious and unforgettable, also far from harmless. "I don't see the past as you do," Ash said, "but one doesn't argue with a lady. Why not give my plan a try, Della? It can't hurt to have a friendly escort while the gossip runs its course."

Friendly. She'd probably thought of him as a friend at one point and hoped he'd become much more than a friend. So had he, but could she afford to scorn what he offered now?

"I will drive out with you tomorrow if the weather's fair, and I will think about what you propose."

"Excellent. I won't fail you, Della."

She finished his toast without replying, but they both knew what had remained unsaid: I won't fail you *again*, Della.

CHAPTER THREE

"I cannot drive out with you, Jonathan," Della said, "though I appreciate the offer." She received him in the family parlor because he—at least behind the walls of the Haddonfield home—was her family, and she—not that she would admit it—was pathetically glad to see him.

"What you cannot do," he said, closing the door, "is hide. Last night's ball went surprisingly well. You danced exactly enough dances with exactly the right sorts of partners. You did not arrive too late, you did not leave too early. You neither hung your head in shame nor indulged in unseemly arrogance. You might weather this storm, Della, but not if you throw away the luck that's been handed to you."

Ash Dorning had handed her that luck, and he'd done so in a way that trod the line between clever subterfuge and the loyalty of a family connection. If she hadn't loved him already, she'd love him for that alone.

"I am not hiding, and last night did not go entirely well."

Jonathan Tresham, as a duke's heir, a man of substantial means, and a handsome devil, had been considered the matrimonial catch of the decade. He'd ignored the heiresses and blue bloods to marry a widow of modest station and enormous personal merit.

To Della, though, Jonathan was the only brother who shared her brownish hair, the only brother to share a paternal bloodline. He was also her only brother who still labored under the delusion that he could lecture her.

He stalked over to the window, peering out into a garden full of blown roses and tired chrysanthemums.

"Theodosia claims that an initial appearance after falling from grace could not have gone better. Today is a fine day, you appear to be wearing a carriage dress, and my tiger is walking my curricle. Let's be off, shall we?"

"You may take yourself off," Della said. "We have agreed that appearing together in public will only fuel speculation, Jonathan. We have the same mouth, the same chin, the same brows... I appreciate your willingness to show the colors, but you may tell Theodosia that I have refused your escort."

Unlike Della's Haddonfield brothers, Jonathan was hard to read. He could be vastly entertained and look utterly bored. He could be in a violent rage and appear amused. He had a gambler's ability to control his expressions, a skill Della envied him.

"Theo did not put me up to this," he said, pacing between the parlor's floor-to-ceiling windows. "She approved, though. And so what if people talk? I will eventually step into Quimbey's shoes, and you are a Haddonfield by birth. I honestly don't care if people speculate that you and I are related."

Della smiled at him sweetly. "Perhaps, when the good folk of Mayfair tire of pillorying me for running off with Chastain, we can revive their efforts with mention of my bastardy, hmm?"

Jonathan stilled before a bust of Pliny the Elder, to whom he bore a resemblance about the nose. They both had an air of aggrieved masculinity, though Jonathan was of course more imposing.

"I did not deserve that, my lady."

No, he did not, but as was often the case, Della had spoken more sharply than she'd intended. Worry did that to her.

"I'm sorry. I am not myself. Shall I ring for tea?" Ash wasn't due to come by for another twenty minutes, and Della would honestly rather not be alone.

"A cup of tea would be appreciated. How are you, Della?" His tone was brusque, and Della was abruptly weary.

She sank onto the piano bench. "I am overwhelmed. I knew I was embarking on foolishness, but I did not expect to get caught, and I did not expect..." She hadn't expected to be nearly raped, disgraced, then made to—of all things—face down polite society one dance at a time.

"I wanted to call the perishing varlet out," Jonathan said, looking self-conscious. "Ash Dorning talked sense into me, but it was a very near thing."

Him again? Della was surprised, also a little pleased. "Mr. Dorning is taking me driving shortly," she said, getting up to tug the bell-pull twice. "His good sense is one of his most commendable qualities. May I ask you something, Jonathan?"

The door was closed, they had privacy, and Della had been looking for a moment to put this question to her brother for quite some time.

"Ask me anything. If it's within my power, I will see your request granted."

Typical of Jonathan, he thought she wanted a material boon from him, or perhaps a service. What she needed was an answer.

"Have you ever felt as if the entire world is about to end? As if everything you've ever feared, every nightmare you've dreamed, is about to come true all at once?"

He studied her in an unnerving silence. "Yes."

A trickle of relief coursed through Della.

He sank into a corner of the sofa and crossed one booted ankle over the opposite knee. "When Theo refused to marry me, I nearly went mad. I could not make sense of her refusal. I was a ducal heir, not too bad looking, able to provide well for her, and she rejected me out of hand. Given the cards I held, I could not fathom why mine was a losing hand."

This was not the answer Della had sought, but it was still an interesting reply. "What was that like? Being rejected by the one person you thought to give your heart to?"

"Damned awful, pardon my language. Everything I'd strived for —wealth, standing, influence, the respect of my peers—crumbled to dust. I was so overwrought I nearly got drunk."

"You nearly got drunk?" Della had not been raised with Jonathan, had not known of her connection to him for much of her childhood. He was still in some regards a mystery to her.

"I am not a teetotaler," he said, "but as owner of the Coventry, I had to keep my wits about me. I learned to imbibe judiciously. One suggestion I conveyed to both Sycamore and Ash Dorning was that they do likewise as they took over the club."

"How is the club faring?" she asked, joining him on the sofa.

"Quite well, I am both relieved and dismayed to report. Sycamore Dorning has a quality I lack, of charming and commiserating with the patrons, celebrating their wins, recalling which of them has a daughter to fire off or an auntie with gout. Ash has taken on the finances and management of the staff. He sees to the building proper, the inventories, and the collection of debts. He has a natural grasp of numbers, as I do. They are the epitome of the adage that two heads are better than one, and the club is profiting accordingly."

The tea tray arrived, the clock advanced at the pace of a glacier in winter, and Della began to fret that Ash would stand her up.

"If Ash and Sycamore Dorning are such an effective team," Della said, "why does Ash Dorning spend some of the winter at the family seat each year?"

Jonathan took an inordinate time stirring his tea, tasting it, and setting down his cup and saucer."Homesickness, I suppose. London in winter is a dreary, smelly place, and Sycamore likes to travel in the summer. He's taken to Paris like an apprentice seamstress turned loose in a mercer's warehouse. Will you attend the Dickson's Venetian breakfast on Monday?"

Two things had just happened. Jonathan had prevaricated regarding Ash Dorning's winter journeys, and then he'd changed the subject. The little niggle of worry Della felt about Ash possibly forgetting their appointment acquired sharp edges. Was Ash well? Was he hiding a mistress and family in the shires? Was he too fond of the poppy or—

A knock on the door cut short her flight of imagination.

"Come in," she said.

Ash strode through the door, resplendent in riding attire. "My lady, good day. Tresham, stop making a pig of yourself with the biscuits."

Like a wave receding into the sea, Della's anxiety eased. "Mr. Dorning, greetings. Will you share a cup of tea before we depart?"

"I'll have a biscuit," he said, taking the place beside Della on the sofa. "Tresh, what brings you here besides free food and the company of a lovely lady?"

Ash Dorning was so confident, so at ease with himself, and so blasted good-looking. Every time Della beheld him, she fell prey to yearning, and this occasion was no different.

"I came to congratulate Della on weathering the first volley," Jonathan said. "You made a lovely couple for last night's supper waltz."

Ash popped a tea cake into his mouth. "Of course we did. That was the point, also entirely my pleasure. Now we will make a sedate circuit of the park, bold as you please, and doubtless encounter a few sniffy dowagers and malicious gossips. We will ignore them all, won't we, my lady?"

When Ash Dorning smiled that conspiratorial, playful smile, Della could ignore the flames of hell burning beneath her feet.

"We will have a very pleasant time," she said. "We might even go for an ice at Gunter's, seeing as the weather is so mild."

Ash tucked a tea cake into his pocket. "Excellent notion."

Jonathan rose and bowed over Della's hand. "Enjoy the fine weather while it lasts, then." He nodded at Ash. "Winter will arrive all too soon. I'll see myself out."

Della finished her tea. "What was that about?"

"What was what about?"

"'Enjoy the fine weather...' I know Tresham the least well of all my brothers, but he often acts the most obnoxiously fraternal."

Ash rose and extended his hand to her. "He worries. It's hard to worry for somebody and be unable to show that you care for them."

Della put her hand in his. "To the park, Mr. Dorning. I have a skirmish to endure, and you are right. To care for somebody without being allowed to show that caring is a very difficult challenge indeed."

She rose and walked past him, pleased with herself for firing the first cannonade of the day—straight at Ash Dorning's heart.

~

ASH HANDED Della up into his curricle—Sycamore's curricle, truth be told—and mentally kicked himself for stumbling into her gun sights. *To care for somebody without being allowed to show that caring is a very difficult challenge indeed.*

He had hurt her with his show of indifference. He had protected her, but he had hurt her too. The presence of the tiger riding at the back of the vehicle spared Ash from further salvos, but not from the guilt Della's observation engendered.

"Would you like to drive?" he asked.

"I would," she said, taking the reins. "What is your horse's name?"

"This is Sycamore's gelding. His name is Denmark, and he's as sensible as he is handsome."

"Like you," Della said, clucking to the horse.

"You flatter me, my lady."

She smiled, her expression probably for show. They bantered their way to Park Lane and then into Hyde Park itself, where autumn was advancing despite the mild weather. Leaves drifted down from the towering maples and twirled onto the surface of the Serpentine, and a solitary common blue butterfly hovered over the water.

"I love this season," Della said when they'd exchanged nods—

terse, chilly nods, but nods—with three other vehicles. "Everything is relaxing into winter's quiet. All of nature breathes a sigh of relief."

Ash certainly wasn't breathing any sighs of relief. "But everything is dying as well. The days grow short, the nights chilly. Animals with any sense take to their burrows, and the growing season ends. It's a sad time of year."

Della steered the horse around a bend in the path. "But a sweet melancholy, wouldn't you agree?"

"There is no such thing. Shall we walk a bit?"

Della signaled Denmark to stand. "No time like the present, I suppose. If I'm given the cut direct, at least only a few people are on hand to see it."

The tiger stood at Denmark's head, not that such a well-trained equine needed that much supervision, and Ash helped Della down from the curricle.

He loved—*loved*—her physical form. She was small but well curved, feminine perfection on a compact scale. Her energy was palpable, and he loved that too. Della Haddonfield would never spend days in a dark room, silently begging heaven for the motivation to wash.

And she would have a hearty disgust for a man who did.

"This way," she said, twining her arm through Ash's. "The water has a particular scent when the banks are muddy. I prefer the quieter paths."

"You prefer privacy if you're to be given the cut direct, but, Della, I won't allow that to happen."

She tipped her chin up and marched forth. He loved that about her too. What she lacked in stature, she made up for in dignity, so why the hell had she fallen in with Chastain's most undignified scheme?

"Will you tell me why you pretended to elope with Chastain?" Ash asked.

"Will you tell me why you never answer my letters?"

"Fair enough." He walked along while sorting through credible prevarications. "As a younger son, my means until recently have been limited. I did not deserve to engage your affections when such sentiments could lead nowhere."

It took Della all of six paces to return fire. "I have ample settlements, and your prospects have improved dramatically. Your dear brother Valerian has less means than you do, and he married an heiress. Oak has married a well-situated widow. Men without means marry all the time, Mr. Dorning. Besides, a short note informing me that you are still alive and the weather in Dorset has been nasty isn't likely to provoke me to a wild passion. You are an impressive specimen, but not even your allure is that strong."

Ash closed his mind firmly on the notion of Della in a wild passion. "I have answered your question. I did not regard myself as worthy of your affections and behaved accordingly." And that was the truth. "I apologize for any hurt I've caused you."

They rounded a corner in the path and might as well have walked into a remote corner of the New Forest. The bustle and crowds of London were a distant memory, and the loudest sound was birdsong.

"Are you well, Ash?"

Della's question held potential absolution for all the times he'd pretended indifference, and her words held worry—for him. Worry he did not deserve.

"I am in robust physical health, thank you. About Chastain?"

Della picked up the pace. "The less said, the better."

"You went with him willingly?"

She peeled her hand free of Ash's arm and crossed the clearing to a bench sitting in the sunshine.

"I went with him of my own free will," she said, taking a seat. "He wanted out of his betrothal, I wanted to be ever so slightly disgraced. The plan was, after his father caught up with us—which should have happened within five miles of St. Albans—Chastain could go wenching and wagering on his way. I could finally return to Kent, a confirmed spinster who had had a quiet, not-that-close brush with disaster."

The tale was plausible, particularly given the annoyed attitude of Della's posture. She hunched forward, hands braced on the bench, gaze on the lush fall grass.

And she was lying.

Ash came down beside her. "Della, you won't shock me, you won't disgust me, you won't in any way offend me, or reduce my esteem for you, but I must know: Did Chastain hurt you?"

She untied her bonnet and set it on the bench, perhaps to give her time to choose her words. "No duels, Ash. I cannot have anybody fighting a duel over this. Nicholas is a dead shot, and Chastain is merely a dull-witted lout. It's not as if I was as pure as the vestal virgins anyway."

Something heavy and primal shifted inside Ash, bringing with it both a deadly calm and a banked rage.

"I don't care if you comported yourself like White Chapel's most infamous strumpet. According to every immutable law of masculine decency, the lady alone chooses with whom to share her favors. Did he *hurt* you?"

Della took a deep breath, her shoulders lifting and settling. "Chastain was too drunk, but the notion of turning our shared outing into a true elopement had taken hold of his imagination. He had me on the bed and was fumbling about when his father burst in with the innkeeper's wife and two footmen at his side. I was somewhat clothed, also in some disarray."

A woman *somewhat clothed* could nonetheless be raped. "No duel, then," Ash said. "But give me the word, and I will hurt him badly."

She leaned into his shoulder. "You are very dear. Mostly, Chastain frightened me. He's quite strong, and he'd been drinking for much of the day. I don't think he could have *done* anything, but he was intent on trying."

Ash allowed himself to drape an arm around her shoulders and pull her close. "Give me leave, and I will address the slight to your honor, Della. I will bring you his pizzle on a platter. I will cut off his balls and serve them to Willow's dogs. You placed your trust in him, and he not only bungled the whole business, he violated your person."

She curled closer. "No, he did not. He pushed me onto the bed and more or less fell on top of me. Sorting out my skirts defeated his limited coordination, and in another minute I would have applied my knee to his breeding organs."

That was courage talking, the shaky courage of somebody who'd had a near miss. *Applying her knee* would have required that Chastain give her room to aim and fire, and even half drunk, few men would have been that heedless.

"Hold me, please," she said. "Since Nicholas retrieved me from the inn, I have been groped, pinched, and nearly fondled, but nobody... Please just hold me."

Ash obliged, wrapping her in his arms. She fit his embrace like she was made for him, like homecoming and Christmas and every good and dear thing.

"You need never see Chastain again, Della. He betrayed you, but the worst of his schemes failed. You're safe."

She wasn't crying, not that he could tell, but she was resting against him as if winded and weary. "I'm not safe. Not yet. Another few weeks of pretending to be a woman who has committed no serious wrong, and I might be allowed to slink off to Kent."

And I will slink off to Dorset. Again. "That's the spirit. *Noli desperare,* and *once more unto the breach.*"

He remained with her on the bench until she sat up a few precious, torturous moments later. "You won't say anything to Nicholas or Jonathan? About Chastain and the bed?"

"Not a word. You have a leaf..." He untangled it from her chignon. "Better."

She took up her bonnet, but didn't put it on. "Thank you, Ash Dorning."

"For?"

"Asking if Chastain misbehaved." She untangled the bonnet

ribbons, blue satin the same color as her eyes. "He frightened me. I hate that. I hate him. I hate myself for allowing the whole farce to happen."

Ash rose and offered her his hand. When she stood, he took her bonnet, placed it on her head, and did up the ribbons in a loose bow.

"A man who outweighs you by a hundred pounds spent all day getting drunk. He broke his word to you and then menaced your virtue. He and he alone is responsible for what transpired. You did not *allow* anything, Della. Put the notion from your head and toss it into the midden."

They stood improperly close, but Ash was determined to make his point.

Della braced a hand on his shoulder and kissed his cheek. "Thank you. I have missed you so very much, Ash Dorning, but you're here now, and you're still you. I thank you for that."

You're still you. She could not know how those words puzzled and pained him.

She took him by the arm and led him back to the walkway, while Ash marveled at what had just happened. Soon—too soon—he'd remonstrate with her for casual displays of friendship. Soon, he'd talk himself into believing a peck on the cheek meant nothing.

Soon. But as Ash wandered down the leaf-strewn path with Della at his side, the lion in his mind was for once purring.

CHAPTER FOUR

Grey Birch Dorning, Earl of Casriel, was a profoundly happy man. Despite the burden of an old and vast estate, which seemed to ingest money much more quickly than it produced same, despite the tedium of his duties in the House of Lords, despite the little urchin whose damp grasp hopelessly wrinkled his cravat the instant he appeared in the nursery every morning, he was a very happy man indeed.

Particularly when his countess, wearing not one stitch, was draped about his person and in a friendly mood.

"Afternoon naps are so restorative," Beatitude observed. "Why more adults don't indulge, I will never know."

"If we napped any more frequently... Do that again."

She licked his nipple, then blew on it. Then she licked him Elsewhere, a skill at which Beatitude was fiendishly clever, and Grey—being a gentleman, a devoted husband, and all-around good sport—got in a few licks of his own, so to speak, until Beatitude hauled him over her and commenced their favorite shared pastime, *seeing to the succession.*

"Why is it," Beatitude asked around a yawn fifteen exuberant minutes later, "I need a nap to recover from our naps?"

"Because I am a lover without compare, of course."

"And so modest." She smacked his chest gently, shifted off of him, and collapsed against his side with a sigh of happy repletion. "I suspect I am breeding again. More evidence of your masculine prowess."

Grey had wondered when she'd say something. He'd suspected another child was on the way based on the sensitivity of Beatitude's breasts and a certain knowing quality in her eyes. When she was carrying, she was also more likely to choose gunpowder tea over China black or hot chocolate, and the scent of tallow made her bilious.

Grey gathered her close. "You're sure?"

"I've missed my menses three times."

He'd noticed that too, of course. "Do you know why I am such a great lover?"

Beatitude tucked her leg across his thighs. "You are a Dorning male, the best of the lot. Some things are a matter of God-given endowments." She patted his endowment fondly.

"All the *endowments* in the world don't make a man a decent lover, your ladyship. While I will admit to a certain fascination with conjugal intimacies since marrying you, if I acquit myself adequately in bed, that is solely because of the inspiration joining me under the covers."

She kissed his cheek. "I love you too, Grey."

"Are you worried about the baby?" *He* was worried. He would spend the next five months vacillating between desperate anxiety and desperate prayer. All the while, he'd beam husbandly good cheer at his wife and manfully endure the heightened sexual appetite that pregnancy brought out in her.

"I am not worried about the baby in the sense you mean," she said. "I found childbirth uncomfortable, but not the horror I was dreading. I am worried that you are worried about the baby. Another child is another mouth to feed, a son to educate, or another daughter to dower. It's not as if you haven't a few spare brothers to carry on the title should we prove unequal to the task."

She was angling around to some topic or other, being subtle, which Grey's limited, and at present foggy, powers of divination grasped only vaguely.

"I love our daughters," he said, shifting to crouch above her. "*I love you*. If we have ten daughters, I will be ten times more delighted than I am now, which is a physical impossibility. If you decide we're through having children, I will content myself with three and spoil them all terribly when I'm done spoiling their mother to the best of my feeble ability. As long as you love me, Beatitude, we will manage splendidly."

She clung to him for a moment, suggesting he'd bumbled into the reassurances she'd needed. "I do love you, Grey. I just want a healthy baby."

He kissed her nose. "I want a healthy baby and a healthy mama. Let me know when I can share our good news with the rest of the family."

"Give it another month. We're still in the early days."

He shifted to spoon himself around her. "Close your eyes, Beatitude. You've earned your rest."

Grey closed his eyes and spared a moment for a prayer of gratitude—that he was married to this woman, that she was in good health, and that she was his best friend, lover, confidante, partner in mischief, and the mother of his children.

"I had a letter from Ash today," Beatitude said, voice drowsy. "He's put off his return to Dorning Hall for a week or two."

Ash had tried spending the winter in Town. It hadn't gone well, but then, his winters never did.

"Are matters in hand at the club?" Or had Sycamore created some scandal that necessitated Ash remain in London to manage an irate father, offended competitor, or wronged patron?

"Matters at the club go swimmingly, though Lady Della Haddonfield has run into a spot of bother—Ash was delicate on the details—

and Ash will remain in London to afford her an escort from time to time. He expects to be down here in another month at the latest."

Lady Della Haddonfield.

Among both Dornings and Haddonfields, hope had at one time flourished that Ash and Lady Della would make a match. Ash had decided that wasn't meant to be. Grey wasn't sure what Lady Della had decided, but if she was accepting Ash's escort, she was either desperate or very forgiving.

"If he breaks her heart," Grey said, "I will thrash him, mulligrubs notwithstanding."

"And if she breaks his heart?"

Beatitude had the courage to name what other Dornings feared to mention. "Ash always recovers from his doldrums. He'd accept Lady Della's rejection gracefully."

But then what would he do? The family trod a careful line with Ash, neither hovering over him nor abandoning him, but the line moved from year to year, and only Ash knew where it truly needed to be.

Beatitude took Grey's hand and settled it over her breast. "We could go up to Town, Grey. The weather is still fair."

Grey wanted to go up to Town for Ash's sake, of course. He could make suitable noises about voting his seat, though the truly important legislation was usually taken up after Christmas. He could pretend Beatitude wanted to do some shopping, and he could intimate that a summer in Dorset had left him longing for the blandishments of Town.

He hated Town, and Ash knew that.

Ash hated being coddled, as Grey and every other Dorning family member knew.

"We will rely on the dubious strength of Sycamore's fraternal loyalty," Grey said. "He has a way of not pulling his punches with Ash that seems to work. Ash is an adult, and an occasional bout of the blue devils doesn't make him any less so."

In fact, that burden gave Ash a more compassionate outlook on human nature than Grey himself had, too compassionate perhaps.

"You could go to Town without me," Beatitude said, wiggling her hips in a manner that communicated itself directly to Grey's breeding organs.

"Ash would be offended if I galloped into Town simply because he's varying his routine by a few weeks. Who was it that told me to have faith in my brothers?"

Beatitude set up a slow, sweet rhythm. "You could send Willow around to assess matters."

"No, I could not. Willow has puppies on the way. Beatitude, if you insist..."

"You love it when I insist."

He did. He absolutely did. "Oh, very well. I admit it: I adore you. I am yours to command, and I always will be. Have your way with me, you merciless fiend."

So she did. She absolutely did.

≈

"DELLA CLAIMS last week's outing in the park went well," Nicholas Haddonfield, Earl of Bellefonte, said. "I'd like your version of events."

Ash and Della were to leave for the Dickson's Venetian breakfast in ten minutes. He'd arrived early, hoping to spend that much more time with the lady—not with her enormous, blond, glowering brother, who was stalking the Haddonfield guest parlor like a caged hyena.

"Do you imply that your sister is mendacious?" Ash asked pleasantly. "If so, I'd have to invite you to meet me at Jackson's for a few friendly rounds."

Bellefonte had several inches of reach on Ash and would doubtless land plenty of blows, but he wasn't as fast, and he wouldn't punch as hard as Ash. Ash had yet to step into the ring with a man who could match him for speed or power.

"Spare me your friendly rounds, Dorning. Della managed to slip off with Chastain and get as far as bedamned Alconbury. I am her brother, she is under my protection, and I failed her. Forgive me if, because I doubt my ability to keep my sister safe, I am assuring myself of her veracity."

Ah, well then. "You need not be ashamed," Ash said, comparing the time on his pocket watch with the time on the eight-day clock. "Della has more cunning than you give her credit for. With older siblings talking over her and mistaking her diminutive stature for diminutive intelligence, she's had to develop some guile."

Haddonfield's scowl became perplexed. "We don't talk over her."

Where was Della? "The next time you have a family meal, watch how many times she's interrupted and talked over. Watch who asks interesting questions of whom and who is merely supposed to pass the butter on command. I am familiar with this tendency only because Sycamore has complained of the same treatment. He was late to grow into the family height, and the lack of inches and years afflicted him sorely."

"We love Della," Haddonfield said. "We love her especially because..." He looked around, as if the carpet, wallpaper, or furniture had all been changed the previous day.

"You love her because she's a half-sister to some of you and no blood relation at all to others." Including to Bellefonte himself. Nicholas was the product of his father's first union. Della's mother had been the late earl's second wife. The Haddonfield family tree resembled a thorny hedge more than a sturdy oak.

"We love her because she's special," Haddonfield said. "And if you break her heart again..."

"You'll meet me at Jackson's?" Ash had not broken Della's heart. Disappointed her, yes, but broken her heart—God, no. Please not that.

"My countess likes my handsome phiz in its current arrangement," Haddonfield replied. "You are rumored to have lethal speed and a devilish cold temper in the boxing arena."

A soft tread outside the door had Ash putting his watch away.

"One doesn't step into the ring to play pat-a-cake while stripped to the waist, does one?"

The footsteps faded, and Ash found himself the subject of Haddonfield's blue-eyed scrutiny. "Dorning, what exactly are you about with Della?"

"I am about providing her a cordial escort for her next few social outings. I will be seen to gaze longingly after her retreating form, to caress her gloved hand unnecessarily when I walk with her, and to generally lay my heart at her feet—discreetly, of course. She will lead me a bit of a dance, then send me on my way."

Haddonfield wrinkled his nose. "If you're besotted enough to engage in this farce, you're besotted enough to propose in earnest. Why not simply marry her?"

The question hurt worse than a left uppercut at the end of the twentieth round. "Her ladyship and I would not suit."

"The hell you wouldn't." Haddonfield prowled around the piano and stalked up to Ash. "She wrote to you in Dorset. I franked the letters, and I know you never wrote back. She writes to all of our siblings, but Susannah gets twice the mail, because Della hopes your brother Willow will mention something about you to Susannah. Everywhere we go, Della surreptitiously looks for you, and is disappointed to find you not among the guests." Haddonfield leaned closer. "You have made my sister pathetic."

Ash fluffed his lordship's cravat. "Do not, I beg you, refer to Lady Della as pathetic. I would love to go twelve rounds with you, assuming you lasted that long."

The pounding would be glorious, and the recovery days of sheer, righteous hell.

Haddonfield patted Ash's lapel with an enormous paw. "If Della catches sight of you at some damned musicale, she stares out of windows for the next week. If she sees you at a ball, she takes out her embroidery the next morning and sews not a single stitch for hours. Has it occurred to you, Mr. Dunderheaded Dorning, that this whole melodrama with Chastain might have been a ploy to gain your attention?"

A left uppercut followed by a merciless straight right. "Her ladyship was doubtless attempting to earn a respite from her siblings' matchmaking."

Haddonfield straightened. "Meaning she never intended to marry Chastain. My countess suggested as much. So how did the outing in the park truly go?"

Haddonfield was known as an exceedingly genial man, a doting paterfamilias, and kind to children and animals. He was well liked, well connected, and well heeled.

And he—all seventeen stone of him—was afraid for his youngest sister. "The outing truly did go well. Grudging nods, mostly. Lady Caldicott tried for the cut direct, but we were on foot, and I made it a point to occupy the middle of the path and bow over her hand. She relented. Her Grace of Moreland chatted Della up long enough that other people had to notice."

Haddonfield made a face. "That was likely Lord Valentine's influence. He's close to his parents. What did Her Grace and Della discuss?"

"Nothing of any consequence. The mild weather, the relief from summer's heat, the Morelands' harvest, and Her Grace's newest grandchild. Her Grace's generosity was in talking to Della at all."

Haddonfield snorted. "You will not find a randier, more headstrong, and unconventional lot in Mayfair than Moreland's get. I consider Lord Valentine a friend."

"I consider Lady Della a friend." One who was due to make her appearance *now*, please God.

Haddonfield ambled over to a bust of some beaky old Roman and propped an elbow on the philosopher's head. The earl was tall enough that this occasioned an unlordly slouch.

"Would it be so bad, being married to Della?" The question held a wheedling note.

"The query from your perspective ought to be: Would it be so bad for Lady Della to marry me, and I can answer that. Marriage to me is not a fate any woman you care for deserves."

Haddonfield propped his chin on his hand and treated Ash to a slow perusal. "Why? You aren't ugly, you have an income. You are of suitable family, and she's smitten with you."

Because I become insensate with irrational sorrow and indifferent to decency. I become numb to joy and in thrall to despair. I lose days to darkness and weeks to a paralyzing lack of motivation. I become an animal beyond the reach of reason.

"We would not suit, Haddonfield. I esteem Lady Della above all other women and wish only for her happiness, but we would not suit."

Haddonfield looked like he wanted to protest, or perhaps throw a punch or two, but his expression became all smiles when Della strode through the door.

"Darling sister, you brighten the day with your feminine pulchritude. That is a fetching frock."

Della stuck her tongue out at him. "You needn't lay it on so thick, Nicky dear. I dressed so as not to call attention to myself. Mr. Dorning, you are punctual. Shall we be off?"

Della exuded her usual brisk energy, and her smile was warm. Her ensemble was a soft brown velvet dress with red piping that went nicely with her chestnut brown hair. Her eyes, though, gave away a hint of worry.

"The dress complements your coloring," Ash said. "Your brother was only being gallant."

Della wrapped her hand around Ash's elbow. "Which means he's up to something. Nicholas, I will be fine. Mr. Dorning will see to it."

"He had better," Haddonfield said, catching his sister by the arm and kissing her cheek. "Dorning, you will think about what I said?"

"The discussion concluded to my satisfaction," Ash said as Della sent him a curious look. "I regard the subject as closed." Forever, because Ash's ailment was incurable.

Haddonfield smiled, and though he was not related to Della by blood, their smiles bore similar hints of mischief.

"You may regard the subject as closed, Dorning, but you're wrong. You are absolutely, pigheadedly, stupidly wrong. Have a nice time, and, Della..."

"We're off," Ash said before Haddonfield could lecture his sister. "A pleasant day to you, my lord."

Haddonfield saluted with two fingers. "To you, too, Dorning, and you are still wrong."

~

A VENETIAN BREAKFAST so late in the year was a chancy undertaking, but the afternoon sunshine held fair as Della and Ash arrived. Ash helped her down from his town coach, holding her hand a moment longer than necessary before offering his arm.

He was appallingly good at the role of doting swain. Della reminded herself repeatedly that, for him, it was only a role.

"Might you step on my hem?" Della asked him quietly a half hour after their arrival. "I want very much to go home. I thought the whispers and stares would fade, but they haven't."

"If you tuck tail and run," Ash replied, his hand resting over hers, "Nicky dear will want to know why. Then he will discuss the matter with his countess, and she will make her attempt to pry details from you. Then brother George will have a go at you, and did I hear that brother Beckman might nip up from the country?"

And who should be lurking by the buffet tent, but none other than Lady Caldicott, like Cerberus guarding the gates of hell. The little niggle of worry that never entirely left Della in peace threatened to expand into a ball and chain.

"Let's stroll by the river," Ash suggested, changing course. "The day is pretty, and the weather cannot hold."

Della's good luck could not hold. Her Grace of Moreland had rescued the situation in Hyde Park, graciously acknowledging Della and doing so in a public venue. No benevolent duchess appeared among the couples and small groups strolling the Dickson's grounds.

"James Neely-Goodman is here," Della said, steps slowing as she readjusted her shawl. "He'll cut me."

"No, he will not." Ash sounded very confident of his conclusion.

"What were you and Nicholas discussing when I joined you gentlemen?"

"When you rescued me? Let's see... Nicholas was concerned that you were pilloried in the park last week and kept that affront to yourself lest you upset him. His nerves are delicate, I take it."

Della's nerves were delicate. She gave Ash's arm a hard squeeze. "Be serious, please."

"Nicholas feels he's failed you, Della. Your brother adheres to the quaint notion that as the titleholder, it's his job to keep his family safe, and you ended up in harm's way. No matter that you might have intended to end up there, he's ashamed."

"Nicholas feels *ashamed*?" Della stalked off a few paces, when she wanted to kick her brother's handsome backside and hurl imprecations at him. "Nicholas did nothing wrong. I am ashamed."

"You might want to express yourself a little more moderately. Lady Caldicott hasn't taken her eyes off you since we alighted from the coach."

And one could not stick one's tongue out at society's most accomplished gossip. Della resumed her place at Ash's side and tucked her hand around his muscular arm.

"You have distracted me from my query," she said. "What were you and Nicholas truly discussing?"

"Let's have a look at the fish pond, shall we?"

A stinky old fish pond held no appeal whatsoever. Della minced along with her escort, because the fish pond was at least out of earshot of the buffet tent. A little walking path ringed the water, and a folly sat at one end with a view of the house and the nearby river.

"You are concocting a falsehood regarding your discussion with Nicholas," Della said as they began their circuit of the pond. "You are trying to fashion a lie that will be credible, but not too dishonest. A lie that appears to flatter perhaps, while in truth it offers me insult. My family has been serving me such lies since I toddled out of the nursery."

If Ash responded with the predictable platitudes—*my lady, you exaggerate; my lady, if your family prevaricates, they do so to spare your sensibilities*—she would push him into the pond.

"Do they wrap you in cotton wool because you're petite?" Ash asked.

"I arrived to this world sooner than expected, or so my nursemaid told me. The rumors of my fragile health have been greatly exaggerated ever since, but being scrawny did not help."

"You appear quite robust to me, my lady." Ash managed to infuse a hint of deviltry into that observation, but was the flirtation real or for the benefit of Lady Caldicott, scowling at them across the lawn?

"Was Nicholas trying to bribe you to marry me?"

By only the smallest hesitation in Ash's stride did he betray the accuracy of her guess. "Why would your brother do that?"

"Because, as you say, Nicholas feels ashamed, and the antidote to his sense of failure is to find me a husband. You are of suitable station, et cetera and so forth. Ergo, behind a closed door, Nick might explore the subject with all the delicacy of a rhinoceros in a milliner's shop."

"Interesting image. Shall we sit?" Ash nodded in the direction of the folly, a pagoda-like structure that sat eight steps higher than the surrounding terrain.

Della allowed herself to be led up the stairs and settled on a bench with her back to the tent—and to Lady Caldicott. Ash remained on his feet, gaze on the river placidly rolling along some distance away.

"I do not want to treat you as your family treats you," he said. "They mean well, while in effect disrespecting you. You are small but mighty, as the Bard put it, and I esteem you highly."

Small but mighty. Nobody else had called Della that, and yet, she did not feel complimented. "And now you will tell me why we could never suit." If anything could loom as a worse penance than a cut direct before half of society, a lecture from Ash on marital impossibilities could.

Della abruptly wanted to wrap her shawl around her head, hunch in on herself, and have the folly to herself.

"I owe you the truth," Ash said gently. "Keeping it from you only flatters my vanity and creates misunderstandings. I am not a suitable husband for any woman, Della. I never will be."

This wasn't a dramatic declaration, but rather, a tired, oft-visited conclusion. "Do you prefer men?" Even those fellows sometimes married, and the union could often be considered successful. George was a case in point, though Della wasn't sure exactly whose intimate company he truly preferred.

"I enjoy the company of many men," Ash said, "but not in the sense you mean."

What did that leave? "Are you ill?"

"Yes, but my illness is not of the body. I suffer melancholia, though that makes it sound noble and romantic. I turn into... Do you have any friends with this affliction?"

Over the past two years, Della had concocted a long list of reasons why an apparently eligible and interested man might not offer for an eligible and very interested female—a gambling habit, an opium addiction, a family on the wrong side of the blanket, a wife tucked out in the shires, a preference for men, an inability to function sexually, poverty, consumption, an unmentionable disease...

She would never have guessed that urbane, handsome Ash Dorning was afflicted with melancholia.

"I am familiar with the condition in only a general sense," she said. "This is why you spend winters in Dorset?"

"It is. I've tried spending winters in Town. At university, the winters weren't so bad, and sometimes I am felled during the warmer months. May I sit?"

"Of course."

He took the place a decorous one foot away. "The ailment can strike without warning, or it can come over me slowly, day by day stealing my motivation. I never know how long the bouts will last, never know how bad they will be. I liken my condition to being at war. The enemy is out there, always watching, and victory is never assured."

What an appalling analogy, and yet, Della understood it. "I'm sorry."

He brushed a glance at her. "I beg your pardon?"

"I'm sorry this malady afflicts you. Clearly, you endure misery because of it."

He braced his forearms on his thighs and leaned forward. "Everybody around me endures misery because of it. When I am afflicted, I have no appetite and no energy. Shaving is too much of an effort, and bathing is an ordeal. I can lie in my bed for days, Della, a human pit of darkness. My family worries, and I am sick with disgust at myself, but I can't seem to *do* anything save loll about and wish I were different."

Della longed to take his hand, longed to wrap her arms around him and hold him fast.

And to be held by him. Instead, she picked up a trio of acorns from those scattered on the bench beside her and fired them one by one over the railing at a whorl in the bark of the nearest tree.

"Do you contemplate taking your own life?"

He sat up. "I do not. Whatever god has sent me this affliction has also sent me the sliver of rational perspective to remind me that the darkness passes. It always passes, no matter how abjectly terrified I am that it will not. Then I am well for long periods, and my gratitude for those months of normal life is as bottomless as my despair at the other times."

"I don't think of you as abjectly terrified." Just the opposite, in fact. Ash was unfailingly in control of matters, ever competent.

"I hope your good opinion of me is never diminished, Della. I hope you never see me indifferent to my own hygiene, indifferent to day and night, unwilling to leave my dwelling, unable to carry on a coherent conversation. I can sink into rages over nothing and weep for less than nothing. I become a lesser creature entirely, one I hope you never meet."

Della had read about melancholia, but she was more familiar with the literature on hysteria and hypochondria, those being typically female complaints.

"I'm sorry," she said again, marveling at how far appearances could diverge from a person's private reality. "I am just so sorry." She fired three more acorns at the hapless tree five yards off, hitting the whorl of bark hard each time.

"I don't want your pity any more than you want mine," Ash said, regarding the oak she'd made into her target. "I want you to think of me as the charming and witty Ash Dorning, who can be a good friend, an amiable escort, and even a passable flirt, but he's too good a friend to ever expect anything more than that from you."

He offered her a crooked smile and a wink, and Della's heart broke for him. "Do you think you are the only person to battle private demons, Ash Dorning?"

"Of course not," he replied. "But I am determined that my demons remain mine. A wife goes into marriage expecting her husband to provide for her, to make a home with her that's a haven from the miseries of the world. I cannot be such a man, and thus I will not marry."

Della sat beside him in the pretty little folly, her mind taking off in three different directions at once.

Firstly, how would Ash Dorning know what *a wife* expected from marriage? Did all wives carry around the same set of expectations, like a military pattern for a musket? Did Ash see a husband's role as a glorified banker, doling out pin money and placid domesticity in exchange for his wife's marital favors?

How utterly distasteful. Secondly, what if acquiring a wife, a dedicated ally, made battling the demons less of a struggle?

Thirdly, did he expect his spouse would never have a demon or two of her own to subdue? Was marriage only for the perfect and healthy?

Della certainly hoped not. "You have this all sorted in your mind," she said. "I suspect logic would be unavailing should anybody attempt to reason you away from your conclusions."

He seemed amused, the lout. "My conclusions are logical."

Della rose. "No, they are not, but they are your conclusions, and I am the last person to pry away a comforting lie when cold reason could not serve anywhere near as loyally." She descended the steps without Ash's escort, though he followed at a sauntering pace.

"You don't know what it's like, Della." Beneath his amused tone lay a hint of defensiveness.

"You're sure of that?" She took his arm, mostly to keep the appearances friendly, but the discussion had upset her, and when she was upset, she needed to be alone with her thoughts.

"You have doubtless had the blue devils," he said, "a few despondent days. Melancholia is a grief that has no cause, no bottom, and no reliable end. It's an ever-fading twilight that feels eternal and deserved, though you know it's neither."

And he had walked, stumbled, and crawled through this twilight alone, over and over, and was prepared to traverse it alone for the rest of his life.

"I must think on this," Della said. "You have explained much, and I thank you for telling me. I will speak of it with no one, and I do mean no one, Ash. Not my lady's maid, my siblings, or my cat. No one."

A subtle tension left him. "Thank you. When we met... When I kissed you, I was having an extended period of good health. I hoped the melancholia was behind me, but it never is."

"Someday, perhaps it will be, or it won't be as severe. Let's give Lady Caldicott what she's been longing for and allow her to offer me the cut direct, shall we?"

Della took a firmer hold of Ash's arm and marched for the buffet tent.

CHAPTER FIVE

Telling Della Haddonfield about the melancholia hadn't gone as planned, but then, Ash hadn't planned to tell her, ever. Then he'd seen Lady Caldicott, a serpent coiled and ready to strike, and it occurred to him that Della deserved to know the truth.

Della had enemies now, but she also had an ally, despite the fact that he could never be her husband.

Or anybody else's, of course, not that he'd want to be anybody else's.

"You aren't appalled?" he asked as they made their way toward the buffet tent.

"Of course I am appalled," Della replied. "That you should have to contend with this all on your own, that you've carried this burden by yourself for years, that medical science has nothing worthwhile to offer you... You have consulted with physicians?"

"Several."

"And they were generally useless." She stalked along as if the buffet tent were an enemy citadel in need of storming. "Bleedings, tonics, dull books, bland diets, *harp music*. All of it useless, am I right?"

"You are." And why would she know this? "My oldest brother, Casriel, is a talented harper, but his efforts have never had any noticeable effect. When I am at the Hall, it's all I can do on fine days to sit on my balcony and wave back to the children playing in the garden should they take any notice of me."

Della sailed right past Lady Caldicott with a single terse nod. "Does anything help?"

Her ladyship gaped after them, looking like a surprised bulldog. Ash managed a tip of his hat and a smile, but Della was intent on her objective.

"Nothing helps." That wasn't quite true. "Nothing helps for very long. You must be quite hungry."

"I want this ordeal behind us," she said. "Flinging me up before polite society, like a clay target to draw their fire, has grown tedious. You and I have matters to discuss."

Ash would allow Della to discuss them, just this once. She must satisfy herself that his situation was hopeless, and then she would understand that *their* situation was hopeless.

Not that they had a situation.

"Do you want to know what helps?" Ash said. "What temporarily knocks the damned beast back on his haunches?"

"Do you have a name for your beast?" Della asked, taking up two plates and shoving them at him. "Women name their menses, you know. Aunt Betty came to call, that sort of thing."

He accepted the plates. "I hadn't known that." Had not ever wanted to know such a thing and would be unable to forget it.

She gave him a look, assessing, a trifle peevish. "There is much you do not know, Ash Dorning. Tell me how you placate your beast."

"A thorough beating improves my spirits considerably, but only for a short time." He had not meant to say that. Not to a lady, not to anybody. He should have referred to putting up his fives, a few rounds at Jackson's, anything but the bald, pathetic truth.

Della slapped a spoonful of apple compote onto his plate. "Do you mean with riding crops and that sort of thing?"

The tent was all but deserted, an amazing stroke of luck. "What do you know of *that sort of thing?*" Ash asked, keeping his voice down, despite the lack of an audience.

"I have a regiment of older, randy, naughty brothers. The naughtiest of the lot is George, who looks the most angelic. He has explained the English vice to me. I do not entirely understand it. Ham, fowl, or beef?"

Ash did not understand how a lady could discuss sexual games between the vegetables and the cheeses.

"Ham, please," Ash said. "I am a pugilist. A regular at Jackson's. I box."

"And thumping away on another fellow raises your spirits?" she asked, adding some cheese and bread to their plates.

"It's not like that," Ash said. "It's not a friendly round of thumping away. Perhaps we should change the subject."

"No, we should not." Della forked a final wedge of cheese atop his ham. "If I let you get away with changing the subject now, when the discussion has grown interesting, you will think I permit such evasions in the normal course. I do not."

He had expected that Della would be if not disgusted, then at least put off by his mental frailties. That she would look at him differently. Her scrutiny was as intense as ever, and in no regard was Della Haddonfield put off. If anything, she looked determined and curious.

Which cheered Ash, even as it gave him cause to worry. "Let's eat down by the water."

Della collected two glasses of punch and some table napkins and preceded him out the tent's back entrance.

"Tell me about this boxing," she said. "How does it help?"

"It just does."

She cut across the grass to the path that led down to the river. A slight breeze had sprung up, sending fallen leaves dancing across the lawn. Della made her way through the swirling leaves with an unerring sense of forward momentum, and Ash wished for his brother Oak's ability to sketch.

In the coming months, he'd like to remember Della like this. Striding forward, sure of her course, a small vessel confidently navigating open water.

He followed her, letting her choose their bench. Other couples wandered the path along the river, a few had spread picnic blankets. By this time next week, the scene could be pelted with sleet and the river roiling with angry currents, but for today, the weather held.

"What part of the boxing helps?" Della asked, taking a seat and setting her plate in her lap. "Is it the exertion? The male company? The drinking afterward?"

She knew more of boxing than most ladies would admit. Ash considered prevaricating, then discarded the notion. Della might not quail at a diagnosis of melancholia, but his reasons for fighting should give her pause.

"I like the pain," he said. "I am a competent boxer. My strategy is to provoke my sparring partner into hitting me as hard as he can, as often as he can. Afterward, I'm aching and bruised, but my spirits improve. I am more at peace." That his sparring partner usually ended up peacefully unconscious on the floor was lamentable, but those men walked into the ring willingly.

"I always thought there had to be something about fisticuffs I didn't comprehend," Della said, making a sandwich of bread and cheese. "Something that would inspire otherwise rational men to get half naked and pound on each other. George says there's an erotic element to it, but dear George has a rather vivid and focused imagination in some regards."

Ash set his glass of punch on the ground. "An erotic... An *erotic* element? To fighting? He *said* that?"

"You know,"—Della gestured with her food—"stirs up the humors, battle lust being a subspecies of lust generally. Then you and your partner have a jolly pint together, patting each other on the backside and singing dirty songs with your mates. Then you toddle off arm in arm, drunk as lords and in charity with the universe, probably to call upon the nearest bordello."

Now that Ash thought about it, the peace and contentment that followed a good bout in the ring was in some ways similar to a post-swiving glow, as best Ash recalled that rare pleasure. Not that he would admit the similarity out loud to anybody. Ever.

"George needs to learn some discretion," he said. "In any case, a good thrashing settles me down for a time, but the effect is temporary. When I'm in the grip of serious melancholia, the effect is barely noticeable. I regard the pugilism as a flawed preventative or an unreliable palliative. Does George box?"

"He does not. Eat something."

"What did you and Chastain talk about all the way to Alconbury?"

"I will permit you to change the subject, because this gambit will profit you nothing. He rode up top, I rode inside. Thus, I had little warning that he was imbibing the day away until we were in close quarters. I could beat you, you know. Take a crop to you, if that would help. Less dangerous than angering another man." She wrinkled her nose. "I wouldn't mind a chance to admire your manly fundament, if we're being disgracefully honest."

"Why thank you, my lady, but I must decline your generous and entirely inappropriate offer."

She sent him a sidelong grin. "George says one starts gently and that there's an art to wielding a crop on a bare and willing—"

Ash took her hand and applied her sandwich to her mouth. "I will be having a very stern talk with Mr. George Haddonfield. Will you attend the Whitfield musicale on Wednesday?"

Della munched her food. "I suppose I must. You?"

"I will be honored to escort you."

"You don't have to. If George is still in Town, he can take me. Nicholas will, if necessary."

"I shall escort you, and I will enjoy it." To Ash's surprise, he was enjoying himself in that very moment. Della was less conventional than he'd thought her and much harder to shock. "I had not told you of my malady because I did not want you to think less of me. That was selfish. I should have told you the truth sooner lest you think the fault somehow lay with you."

"Friends are honest with each other, Ash Dorning. Good friends are."

She wasn't scolding him, though he deserved a sound scolding. "I will be a better friend in the future, Della, I promise."

She bumped his shoulder. "You'll write back to me?"

"Let's not get carried away."

He did get a little carried away, though he first looked around to make sure nobody was watching. In the manner of a friend, he kissed Della's cheek, and in the manner of a friend, she ignored his overture entirely.

They finished their meal, wandered the grounds for another half hour, and took a cordial leave of their host and hostess.

As Ash handed Della into the coach, he mentally battled the delightful image of a laughing, *friendly* Lady Della applying smart blows with a riding crop to his bare bum.

∼

DELLA CLIMBED INTO THE COACH, willing to call the Dickson's Venetian breakfast a limited success, but for the revelation that Ash Dorning suffered melancholia.

He would be that noble and that clodpated as to endure despair while trying not to burden others. Part of Della wanted to regale him with tales of her own weak moments, but another part of her cautioned restraint. Melancholia could be fatal, despite Ash's assurances that he'd been spared the temptation to take his own life—so far. Nothing she had endured, no weak moment or bad day, had imperiled her very life.

"Are your affairs in order?" she asked as the coach clattered down the lane.

"I beg your pardon?"

Ash seemed distracted, as if he perhaps regretted taking Della into his confidence.

"Are your affairs in order?" Della said. "You know, 'To my brother Sycamore, I leave my horse. To my brother Oak, I leave my cat.' That sort of thing."

"I haven't any pets."

Never a good sign. "You have family. Are your *affairs in order*, Ash Dorning?"

He took off his hat and set it on the opposite bench, so Della did likewise with her bonnet. The sun had gone behind a cloud, and outside the coach, a brisk breeze was tossing yet more leaves from their branches.

"I haven't had any affairs to put in order," Ash said, "not until lately. Taking over management of The Coventry Club has put some coin in my pocket, true, but what little wealth I'd leave behind, my family would sort out."

The Coventry was making money hand over fist, to hear George tell it. "Why did you kiss me?" Della asked.

Ash was gazing out the window at the wooded hedgerows and harvested fields beyond. "I told you. I thought I was doing better. You are lovely. I gave in to misplaced optimism and behaved badly. I am sorry. I should have explained the whole situation to you long ago."

You are lovely. Della stored away that somewhat annoyed admission to examine later. "I meant just now. You kissed my cheek where half of London might have caught you at it."

He spared her a disgruntled glance. "You are still lovely. I suppose that can't be helped, but you are also... What is the point of your inquiry?"

To reassure herself that melancholia would not deliver him a fatal blow. Ash Dorning would see to his final arrangements before he let that happen, and he would not go around kissing women in public.

"When you are well," she went on, "can you function as a husband functions?"

His expression went from disgruntled to puzzled. "I perform my

duties at the Coventry. I earn coin. I show up at my brothers'
weddings. I box. I hack out in the park on fine mornings. I fence at
Angelo's and maintain my correspondence. Is that what you mean?"

The coach hit a rut, and Della was bounced against Ash's side.
"You are being deliberately obtuse. I mean can you...?" She waved a
hand. "As men do with their wives, mistresses, the occasional frisky
footman, and passing dairymaids of a generous and lusty nature."

His gaze returned to the landscape beyond the window. "I do
believe the temperature is dropping."

"Winter approaches," Della said. "The temperature will drop.
You are avoiding the question."

"The question is exceedingly personal and not very polite."

Della had long ago learned patience with the missishness of
grown men. She waited as the horses trotted along and a bank of
pewter clouds rolled up from the south.

"To answer your question," Ash said, "when I am in good spirits,
I enjoy every blessing of physical health to which the typical Dorning
male is heir. Fortunately, Dorning males are thick on the ground, and
nobody will look to me to secure the succession."

Of Dorning brothers, there was an abundance—seven—but none
had as yet fathered a male child. Society kept track of those details, as
the Dornings undoubtedly did too.

"Why do you ask?" Ash's question could not have been more
diffident.

"I am trying to make sense of your decision to forgo marriage."
Della pulled her cloak more closely around her, for the day was
growing chilly. "You apparently enjoy good physical health, a normal
complement of animal spirits, an interesting occupation, and every
other indication of success for much of the year. For a few months or
weeks at a time, you are out of sorts. That requires that you give up
any aspirations toward a wife and family. Do I have this right?"

"When the beast is upon me, I am not merely out of sorts, Della."

"You are melancholic, then, and the melancholia invariably lifts.
You did say that."

He sighed the weary, bedeviled sigh of men the world over when confronted with inconvenient logic. "And if the melancholia doesn't lift, Della? When it's bad, I am of no use to Sycamore at the club. I am of no use to my family. I am of no use to anybody."

Della recognized that she was upset on Ash's behalf, but the upset had an angry edge. She was not angry *at* him, but she was angry nonetheless.

"What use am I, Ash Dorning? Does the world truly need my excellent needlepoint? My unreliable contralto? My impressive aim with a bow and arrow? Will the short men of Mayfair go into a collective decline when I am no longer on hand to waltz with?"

He caught her hand and kissed her gloved knuckles. "I would go into a decline if you were no longer on hand to waltz with. I realize I have burdened you with an uncomfortable confidence, but there's nothing to be done, Della. I will manage, and you will understand why I must manage alone."

"The pigheadedness of the average adult male defies every superlative," Della said, tucking closer. "Does a wounded soldier expect no help from the surgeon? Does a woman in her confinement apologize for being ungainly? Does an auntie of venerable years feel ashamed of her slow gait? I could smack you, Ash Dorning, and you will not prevaricate yet again. Why did you kiss me on the cheek in full view of the Dickson's guests?"

"Nobody was looking."

"Somebody is always looking."

Ash wrapped an arm around her shoulders. "Budge up, before you start shivering. I kissed you because..."

Della laid her head on his shoulder and threaded an arm around his waist. Ash was warm, if a bit on the lean side, and the day had grown not merely brisk, but nippy.

"I kissed you because Lady Caldicott needed to see that at least one man doesn't care two figs about your little escapade with Chastain."

Never had Della encountered a greater example of masculine

stubbornness. "That was a kiss for show, then? A display for the crowd?"

Another sigh, quite huffy. "Della..."

She draped the folds of her cloak across his legs—lest he take a chill, of course.

"I kissed you because friends are affectionate with each other on appropriate occasions."

So grumpy. So grumpy and alone. "In broad daylight," she mused. "Gossips lurking behind every bush. Very appropriate."

"Have mercy."

"I like it when you kiss me," Della said. "If having Lady Caldicott skulking about inspires you to such friendliness, I will recruit her to accompany me on all of my outings."

Ash caught her in a one-armed hug. "You are awful, that's why I kissed you. You are a virago, a termagant, and a shrew. Such women are regularly at risk of being kissed by the men whom they befriend."

He made no sense, and he made perfect sense. "I am forewarned." Della subsided against him, savoring his embrace, and hoping that in some small way, he was also savoring hers.

～

ASH HAD UNDERESTIMATED DELLA HADDONFIELD. She was undismayed by a serious case of recurring melancholia, and she was devilishly affectionate. She could not know what a balm to Ash's soul—and what a torment—her hugs, pats to the arm, and simple animal warmth were.

When Ash had handed Della down from the coach upon their return from yesterday's Venetian breakfast, he'd dared to kiss her on the cheek again. He had been making a point, about taking no offense at Della's inquisitiveness, or not needing Lady Caldicott on hand to inspire his friendly gestures.

She had kissed him back, a quick smack on the lips, and whatever point she'd been making, Ash had been too dumbstruck to fathom it.

"I'm for Angelo's," Sycamore said, gaze on the rain pelting the windows. "If I don't break a good sweat, I will break somebody's head at the club tonight. Join me?"

Sycamore loved anything sharp—knives, swords, darts, bayonets, broadaxes, razors. Even the coulter or chisel of a plow assembly could catch his eye. On the wall of his bedroom, he'd arranged a series of daggers in a fan of lethal steel.

Ash forbade him from cluttering up the rest of their apartment with his little hobby.

"Angelo's it is," Ash replied. "The books are in order, the inventories up to date, the bills paid. I might as well attend to my fraternal duty and put you in your place."

Sycamore tossed Ash a cloak. "You are still preparing to leave Town, I take it?"

"We're walking? In this downpour?"

"I need to move," Sycamore said, buttoning his greatcoat and turning up the collar. "Bloody rain deprived me of my morning hack."

Ash shrugged into his cloak and resigned himself to soaking his second-best pair of boots. "We could go to Jackson's."

"My unborn children cry out in horror at the notion," Sycamore replied. "Only a fool steps into the ring with you at this time of year, darling brother. Jackson himself won't oblige you."

He had once, and Ash had nearly put out the famed pugilist's lights. Not the done thing and more than a little disappointing.

"Jackson is getting on in years," Ash said. "You're bothering with an umbrella? We're traveling a mere half-dozen streets."

Sycamore touched some hidden button or handle, and a blade snicked out from the end of the unopened umbrella.

"I carry a fashionable accessory, the better to protect my doddering elders. Shall we be off?"

The day was dreary, but Ash's reluctance to face the elements was only the normal variety of gloom on a rainy autumn day. When the beast stalked him in truth, reluctance became dread, and a half-dozen streets might as well have been the length and breadth of England.

"I hear you kissed Lady Della at the Dickson's do," Sycamore said as they struck off in a mizzly rain. "Are you trying to ruin what's left of her reputation?"

"How the hell—? Do you pay Lady Caldicott to bear tales?"

Sycamore set a brisk pace. "I partnered her at whist last night. She misses nothing, and we won two shillings. Her ladyship fears that you disrespected Della and that nobody will hold you accountable."

Women liked Sycamore. Old women, young women, girls in leading strings. Governesses and duchesses were equally keen to enjoy his company, while Ash... He didn't leave London to get away from Sycamore, exactly, but Cam's particular version of fraternal loyalty could be taxing.

Sycamore doubtless felt the same exasperated affection for his older brothers too.

"I merely bussed Lady Della's cheek," Ash said, "in a friendly sort of way."

Sycamore shoved him. "I will merely buss your arse with my boot if you trifle with her ladyship, Ash. She's on the thinnest of thin ice, and you can't play spillikins with her good name. One clumsy move, and she won't be able to show her face in London for the next five years."

"I suspect Della would find that fate quite agreeable."

Sycamore yanked him back from the curb as a passing coach hit a puddle and splashed water in all directions.

"What is that supposed to mean?" Sycamore demanded. "London is the throbbing epicenter of culture, politics, and all the most interesting vices. The countryside is fine for recovering from a bout of excess or hiding from creditors, but nobody seeks banishment from the capital."

"You thrive here," Ash said, stepping into the intersection as the coach went on its way. "Not everybody does."

"Which brings me to my original question. Are you still heading for Dorset in another fortnight?"

"Why wouldn't I?" The weather had been unusually mild for so late in the year, which meant the club still saw a fair amount of traffic. The instant the weather caught up with the calendar, business would drop off.

"Has it occurred to you, brother darling, that your low spirits might be made worse by leaving Town?" Sycamore asked. "There's nothing in Dorset that we can't arrange for you to have here."

"I've tried spending winters in Town, Cam. It didn't work."

"You tried it once, and you tried it all on your lonesome. I won't neglect you as you allowed Casriel and Willow to do. I can hire quacks to bleed you, pretty young nurses to bathe you, or a cheerful mistress to suck some life into—"

Ash served him a quick backhand to the gut, which slowed Sycamore down not at all. "None of that helps."

Sycamore strolled along, swinging his closed umbrella like a walking stick. "I really must get back to Dorset more often, if Dorning Hall now boasts ladies of easy virtue to cheer a fellow past his low moods. I'm sure morale among the male staff has improved noticeably if that's the case."

"I'll continue on to Angelo's," Ash said, though he'd probably instead detour to Jackson's. "You need to spend some time with Monique." Sycamore had many lady friends, the latest of whom was a baronet's widow ten years his senior.

"Mone tossed me over," he said, twirling his umbrella like a baton. "Said I was great good fun for a fling, but too intense to have underfoot regularly. I doubtless wore her out. She's off at some house party in Cow-turd-shire."

"Sorry, old boy. I know you liked her."

"I like them all. I *love* a good, hard fuck. Settles me down for at least a day."

Ash was reminded of his discussion with Lady Della, about how a fight *settled him down.* "Your attempts to shock with bad language would impress, were you still in the nursery. You doubtless bored Monique with your constant importuning. Do you ever think about settling down in truth?"

Sycamore tucked his umbrella under his arm, a cavalry officer striding along with his riding crop. "I think about it all the time," he said. "To delight in a lusty romp is simply how the Creator made us, and may heaven be thanked for His generosity both to us as a species and to me in my particulars. But to share life with somebody who loves *me*... That would be... One can hardly fathom the joy."

"One can hardly fathom the fortitude such a lady would possess." Ash refrained from harsher teasing, because Sycamore sounded so wistful. "Tell me, Sycamore, do you fancy Della Haddonfield?" The question was mostly idle. Mostly.

Sycamore's fist plowed into Ash's arm. Layers of thick wool blunted the blow, though it stung pleasantly nonetheless.

"Do not think to procure a husband for her," Sycamore said, "as her family has been trying to procure for her. I understand why you are playing the devoted swain, but the better question is why you don't marry her yourself."

Ash had toyed with that question in a theoretical, had-he-over-looked-something sort of way. "I won't marry, and you know why. Lady Della accepts my reasoning."

"I suspect she would accept your occasional fit of the dismals too."

"It's more than a fit of the dismals. You've seen me."

"No, actually, I haven't. When you are overcome by your malady, you disappear to your room, like a bear in winter. Nobody sees you. Trays go up, trays come down barely touched. Thrash me for saying so, but you seem to just give in to it, as we all give in to cold weather. Nasty and inconvenient, but it passes eventually. That's the extent to which you combat your malady."

Ash would have slammed his brother to the walkway, but Sycamore's lecture came from frustrated worry rather than judgment.

"What would you have me do, Cam?"

"Spend the damned winter in Egypt for a change. Try closeting yourself with those pretty nursemaids I could hire. Employ a madam to thrash you with fresh nettles once a week if that's what it takes, but don't just... Don't lie in a ditch like a fallen soldier hoping the invading army passes before anybody notices he's still breathing."

"Waiting for the enemy to march on by has saved many a man from a bullet."

Sycamore paused on the steps of Angelo's establishment. "Two years ago, you would have been long since returned to Dorset, the drawbridge up, the portcullis lowered. Last year, you made it through September, and this year, you're doing at least that well. Why the hell won't you be encouraged by the obvious? Why the hell must you hoard your misery as if it's your only valuable possession?"

Sycamore trotted up the steps before continuing. "Della Haddon-field is fierce and smart. She might bring something to the fight you lack, and she would never desert you. Maybe you've been going about this all wrong, Ash, and it's loving company you need rather than a badger's lair to hide in."

Ash would have followed him up the steps, but Sycamore stopped him with the tip of the umbrella pressed to his chest.

"Not today," he said. "I'll slice you to ribbons if we fence today. Provoke one of Jackson's Corinthians into pummeling you, but please recall you're escorting Della to a musicale tomorrow. It won't do to appear in public with two black eyes, Ash."

Ash nudged the umbrella sword aside with a single finger. "I will fence with somebody else if you're truly in the grip of an ungovernable temper, but you've pinked me before, and I'm none the worse for your bumbling." Far from it.

"I feel guilty when I pink you," Sycamore said. "And you know it, so you always let me draw first blood. If you used one-tenth the guile outwitting your melancholia that you use twitting me, you'd be the happiest of men."

Among Sycamore's older brothers, it was holy writ that Cam was brave to the point of recklessness. Ash knew Sycamore better than their older siblings did, and thus he knew that Cam was rarely reckless. He was, however, shrewd to the point of genius.

"If you must cut me," Ash said, keeping his voice casual, "try not to scar my face. As noted, I am to appear at Lady Della's side tomorrow evening. One wants to look presentable."

One wanted a good deal more than that, alas. Though Ash had begun to wonder if maybe Sycamore didn't have the right of it: Melancholia was an ailment, not God's judgment. If Ash couldn't beat it entirely, could he maybe do a better job of fighting it?

CHAPTER SIX

"You're sure you want to attend the musicale?" Nicholas asked, propping a shoulder against the doorjamb to the family sitting room.

Since Della's misadventure with Chastain, she'd been less comfortable in any confined space, and Nicholas effectively blocked her only means of egress from the parlor. He was the dearest, sweetest, most tenderhearted older brother a woman ever had, but he was still enormous and impossible to move unless he chose to move.

She set aside her embroidery hoop. "I will be branded a coward or worse if I fail to appear at tonight's musicale, Nicholas."

He ambled into the room. "I could go with you. George is still underfoot. He loves music and would be happy to take you."

There was time—barely—for either Nick or George to dress in their evening finery without making Della *too* late.

"If you come with me," she said, "I will be seen as hiding behind my family's consequence. Ash Dorning will serve for the present. The Haddonfields and Dornings are connected, and he's merely a younger son. He's exactly the sort of escort nobody will remark."

Nick settled beside her, which did nothing to quell her sense of being hemmed in. He would expire of mortification before laying a hand on a woman in anger. That wasn't remotely what bothered Della. She still took the opportunity to shift several inches away when she tucked her stitchery into her workbasket.

"Ash Dorning escorted you to that ridotto, or rout or whatever it was," Nick said. "Perhaps young Sycamore should be pressed into service."

Della liked Sycamore Dorning. He was as kind as he was blunt. But he was also randy, self-important, occasionally calculating, and evasive in a way that was hard to describe.

"Sycamore is the more visible face of The Coventry Club's management," Della said. "He generally chooses to move in different circles than his siblings do." Though Sycamore was certainly received, and the matchmakers took notice when he attended a gathering.

Nick rested an arm along the back of the sofa. "You mean Sycamore Dorning is still chasing the merry widows. A wife would inspire him to give up that game."

Della rose with what she hoped was casual grace. "What do you have against Ash Dorning, Nicholas? His prospects march with Sycamore's. He's not the mighty swordsman with the ladies that Sycamore is, and Ash has been a loyal ally when lesser men are trying to pretend they've never danced with me."

Nick remained seated, which might be rude in the eyes of a high stickler, but Della would rather have him off his feet than looming over her. He probably knew that too.

"You kissed Ash Dorning, Della mine. When he handed you down from the coach, I saw exactly what transpired between you. He took liberties, and you raised the bet. What the hell was that about?"

Della settled into a wing chair at the end of the sofa. "You waited two days to ambush me with this question? Waited until Ash is expected at any moment?"

"Servants talk, Della," Nick said. "Even our servants, and they hear talk. Our coachman and grooms know I retrieved you from

Alconbury. Our butler watched your little exchange with Dorning, as did any number of parlor maids gawking out the windows."

"As you gawked out the window?"

"I care about you, but it might surprise you to know I am also somewhat concerned for Dorning."

Had Nick raised his voice, had he lectured or even sermonized, Della could have ignored him, but his tone was reasonable, and—much worse—he was making a valid point.

"Ash and I are friends," Della said. "Friends are occasionally affectionate."

"Had you not eloped with Chastain, I would not remark that affection, but, Della, matters have reached a delicate pass, and I don't think you grasp all the particulars."

"I am dangling over a pit of ruin, Nicholas, I know that. I cannot afford to test Society's tolerance any more than I already have."

Nick scrubbed a hand over his face. "To blazes with Society, baby sister. I saw Dorning's face when you kissed him. I know not what Banbury tale he spins for you, but that man is smitten. He's arse over ears for you, and you toy with him at peril to his well-being and your reputation."

At peril to his well-being? "Is his melancholia common knowledge?"

Nick picked up a little music box made of blond wood and inlaid with cherry and other darker colors. The pattern formed a pair of doves, singing on a branch of pale blossoms and made for a pretty ornament on the low table before the sofa.

"Dorning told you of his affliction?" Nick asked, winding the mechanism.

"He has. He describes it as a profound misery, but not life-threatening. It passes. Did you know of it, Nicholas?"

A tinny little hornpipe chirped forth from the music box. "Not until recently. Susannah and Leah correspond, and Willow Dorning has mentioned his brother's malady to our sister. The family doesn't bruit it about."

"No," Della said, once again getting to her feet. "Nor do they question Ash's management of his malaise. They let him disappear for weeks at a time, hiding in his room, neglecting his well-being. He's determined not to marry because he's prone to this illness."

"Then you must respect his decision," Nick said, holding the music box to his ear, "and refrain from tempting the man with what he cannot have. Teasing him is unkind, Della, and also imprudent."

Voices in the foyer below suggested Ash had arrived. "And if he teased me first?"

Nick set the music box on the table. "Like that, is it?"

"Would you object if he offered for me, Nick?" From what untapped well of fanciful longing had that question come?

Nick rose. "I would have concerns. I would not object. The Dornings are in the same posture we are—climbing out of decades of indifferent finances. Any settlements would have to ensure that you will be cared for even should your husband's health prove unreliable. Dorning Hall has no dower property anymore, and Ash's sole income, from what I've heard, is a gambling establishment trading as a supper club."

This time, Della's mind took off in two directions at once. Firstly, Nicholas had considered the possibility that Della and Ash might marry, considered it to the extent that he'd done some research. The union would have his blessing, assuming his normal fraternal questions about the bride's security could be addressed.

Secondly, even knowing that Ash Dorning's mental health was unreliable, *Della* would not object if he offered marriage. Far from it.

Though, of course, he wouldn't offer. Would he?

～

THE WHITFIELD MUSICALE was well attended, as the relatively few autumn entertainments tended to be.

For Della's sake, Ash was pleased. After showing the colors at several more such gatherings, she'd start next spring's Season on firm footing. Whispers were inevitable, but if Chastain kept his idiot mouth shut, outright ruin could be avoided.

"The cellist was the best of the lot," Della said at the interval. "The rest of the program is mostly sopranos or flutists. Shall we have a look at the buffet?"

So far, they'd received a few friendly greetings, some terse nods, and one attempted cut from a young lady familiar with Chastain's émigré fiancée. As neither Ash nor Della had ever been introduced to the young lady and Della had refused to meet her gaze, the gesture hadn't quite come off, and nobody appeared to have noticed.

"You are fretting," Ash said as he escorted Della to the gallery. "You are asking yourself how you could have handled the twit in the yellow muslin more effectively."

Though Della was smiling politely at nothing in particular, she looked to Ash like a woman developing a megrim. Sycamore suffered megrims. His pain was evident in a pinched quality around his eyes, though he hated when Ash implied that he was in less than roaring good health.

"I am asking myself if I'd like lemonade or punch," Della said, passing Ash two plates. She had the plates filled a few minutes later and led him to the punchbowl. "Your preference, Mr. Dorning?"

To see you smile, to share a quiet coach ride cuddled up next to you, to trade harmless kisses with you... The longer Ash pondered his last outing with Della, the more his resolve to be nothing more than her friendly escort faltered.

"Let's have one glass each of punch and lemonade," he said. "We can share."

"Meaning you will decide which you prefer and leave me the other. I have brothers, Mr. Dorning. Not as many as you, but enough."

He leaned closer. "Meaning I will have an opportunity to put my lips to the rim of the glass in the same place your own lips have recently been."

That was sheer buffoonery, the next thing to a jest, but Della wasn't smiling. "Let's find someplace quiet to eat. I prefer not to shout at a supper companion."

Ash followed her from the gallery down the corridor to the guest parlor, which was even louder than the gallery had been.

"A loud room has advantages," he observed. "Let's try the library, which is around that corner and about halfway down."

"A loud room is generally a crowded room," she said, following his directions, "and I do not deal well with crowds."

He'd noticed that about her. In the proverbial Mayfair crush, Della could usually be found in the cardroom, or among the sparse company of the wallflowers. She would spend time on torch-lit terraces or wandering a gallery, rather than mill about on the crowded edges of the dance floor.

"A loud room," Ash said as she poked her head into the library and immediately stepped back, "is a room where a couple in conversation must sit very close together to hear each other. Let's try the green room."

"Good thought, but where is it?"

"Up one floor and immediately above the gallery."

She took a sip from the glass of lemonade. "How do you know this?"

"I have a good sense of direction, and I have been a guest here once before."

The parlor reserved for musicians to use for warming up was deserted. Ash arranged chairs around a small table and seated Della with her back to a cheery fire.

"The quiet is lovely," she said, taking another sip of lemonade, "and I am actually hungry."

"Do you object more to the noise or the crowding?" Ash asked some minutes later. Della had demolished two apple tarts and was making inroads on her cheddar slices.

"Both. I am short—"

"Petite, my lady. Diminutive, dainty."

"Short, and I cannot see over crowds. I have two memories of my family losing me as a child. Once at a May Day celebration, once at market. I refused to go on any such outings again until I was nearly out of the schoolroom."

"They *lost* you?"

She nibbled her cheese placidly. "They did not realize I was unaccounted for until they'd returned home at the end of the day. Quite lowering, to be so easily misplaced."

"Lowering? I hope your governess was sacked."

"My governess was not to blame. I was in the care of my older siblings, who thought it a great lark."

On Ash's worst, most dismal day, he could not imagine losing track of his younger sister, Daisy, no matter how crowded the village green, no matter how many other siblings were assigned to supervise her.

"How did this happen?"

Della made a face. "They each thought I was with the other. The footmen sent to look for me found me on the church steps as darkness fell. The second time it happened, I knew to simply go to the church and wait. This is why I will always have a shawl with me, and I will always have a flask in my reticule. Tea or lemonade usually, though I bring brandy if the evening might run long."

"How old were you?"

She considered the last of her cheese. "Four the first time, five the second, maybe five and six? Nobody is quite certain."

That her entire family had failed to remark the dates of these mishaps bothered Ash almost as much as the idea that Della still carried a flask against the day when she would again be *misplaced*.

"Well, I am glad to have you all to myself," Ash said, though as the words left his lips, he realized that having Della all to himself was imprudent. They had time to finish eating, but a return to the general company was in order before their absence was remarked.

"I have been thinking of our last conversation," Della said.

As had Ash, and of the way they'd parted. And of the sweet contentment of rolling along in a coach with Della tucked against his side. She was a desirable woman, but more significantly, she was *dear.* Fierce, outspoken, vigorous of mind, and energetic of body. Her company was a tonic, and Ash would miss her more than ever when he quit Town.

"What about that discussion has merited your consideration?" Ask asked, setting his empty plate aside.

"Have you decided not to marry because you think no woman would have you, or because you simply aren't interested in having a wife on hand, with all the loss of privacy and tedium that entails?"

"Not *interested?" Tedium?* She thought wedded bliss would be *tedium?*

Della rose and faced the fire, meaning Ash was free to admire the graceful lines of her back and the way her hair curled over one shoulder.

"My brothers are faithful to their wives," Della said. "Once they marry, they don't stray. Before they marry, they are free with their favors, but when they find the right person... I suspect your brother Sycamore is the same sort. He will cut a very wide swath until he gives his heart. Then he will be a pattern card of domestic devotion."

Ash rose, collected Della's shawl from the back of her chair, and joined her at the hearth. "Are you asking if I'm *cutting a wide swath,* Della? If I'm wallowing in London's many vices between my bouts of low spirits and simply enjoying myself too much to consider taking a wife?"

The firelight found all manner of highlights in her hair, even as it cast her features half in shadow. He draped her shawl over her shoulders, stealing a caress across her nape as he did.

"Something like that," she said. "Because if your hesitation to marry is because of the other reason, you're wrong."

"What other reason?"

"If you think no woman would have you, you are much mistaken, Ash Dorning."

He did not know what to think, because it appeared, unless his ears deceived him and his heart was equally misguided, that Lady Della Haddonfield was considering proposing to him.

He turned her by the shoulders. "If I were to marry anybody, any lady in the whole of God's creation, I would account myself most fortunate and blessed to find myself married to you. But I cannot in good conscience ask that of you."

"What if I am asking it of *you?*" She slipped her arms around his waist and leaned against him. "What if I am inviting you to try a life with me, Ash Dorning? If we don't suit, you can set me aside, and we'll live apart, enjoying cordial relations on necessary occasions. Many couples don't remain together for most of the year."

She was willing to be misplaced *again*, for his sake, and that broke his heart.

"You deserve better," he said, never more certain of anything in his life. "You deserve to speak your vows with a man who can offer the whole bit, Della, until death, not until he's overcome once again by the mulligrubs."

She peered up at him. "And what do you deserve?"

Before he could answer her, she kissed him. This was no friendly peck on the lips. This was every forbidden kiss Ash had ever dreamed of, every sweet, slow taking of his mouth, every plundering of his wits and testing of his self-control.

His self-control quit the field at a dead gallop as Della opened her mouth and pressed close. While she was petite, she was also womanly, and she knew what she was about. Her palm glanced over Ash's falls, and—he was the King of Idiots—he grabbed her fingers and repeated the gesture, pressing her hand firmly to his privities.

The problem was not that he'd gone too long without sharing intimacies—though he'd gone months—the problem was that he was mad for Della Haddonfield and had been for ages.

And by the heavenly powers, she knew how to *handle* a man, how to proclaim without saying a word that he was desperately desired and wearing too many clothes. The unabashed press of her breasts to his chest confirmed the same happy news, as did the enthusiasm with which she welcomed his tongue into her mouth.

Ash's body *woke up*, woke up from a hibernation he hadn't realized he'd been enduring. He had formed the thought that the sofa would accommodate a couple comfortably, followed by the notion that Della might like to have her breasts freed from her décolletage, when a soft click had Della going still in his arms.

A click, then a gasp.

"Mr. Dorning," Lady Caldicott snapped. "What on earth are you about?"

Ash gathered Della close, perhaps in a vain hope that her face would remain shielded, perhaps because he couldn't bear to let her go.

"Lady Caldicott," Ash said, nodding rather than bowing, "and Miss...?" Yellow Muslin stood at her ladyship's side, looking equal parts horrified and fascinated.

"Penelope," Lady Caldicott said, "leave us, and keep your mouth shut, my girl." The young lady slipped out the door, doubtless intent on keeping her mouth anything but shut.

"I know we can trust your ladyship's discretion," Ash said, still not turning loose of Della, who had burrowed into him as if he was the only source of heat in the entire shire. "A mere kiss does not merit anybody's ruin."

"Della Haddonfield," Lady Caldicott said, "turn loose of yonder swain. You either tell me you're marrying Mr. Dorning, or I will personally petition every hostess in Mayfair to see you hounded from polite society."

"We're not—" Della began, easing away from Ash.

"We are engaged," Ash said, keeping hold of Della's hand. "Lady Della has just agreed to make me the happiest man in the realm and to become my wife. You will please allow us some time to inform our families." The words came out oddly confident, with just the right amount of arrogance.

Della shook her head. "You don't have to do this."

"He does too," Lady Caldicott said. "You are a menace to the unsuspecting bachelors of good society, Lady Della. No better than you should be, and I am sad to say, your mother was the same. I will expect to hear news of your engagement within the week. I mean this as the greatest kindness when I say most people will be curious to know whether your firstborn takes after Mr. Dorning or some other fellow."

Della weathered that salvo with a perfectly calm expression.

"We are sorry to have upset you," Ash said, "but I will not tolerate insults to my intended."

"One week," Lady Caldicott retorted. "I will hold my peace for one week. No more." She left without closing the door.

Della sank onto the sofa, her face as pale as snowdrops by moonlight.

Ash came down beside her. "I am sorry for that, my lady."

"I'll leave," Della said, drawing her shawl tightly about her. "Leave London, leave England." Her breathing hitched as if she'd just finished a hard bout of tears. "I am sorry too, Ash. I should not have accosted you."

He shoulder-bumped her gently. "We accosted each other. Rather spectacularly." He'd known he desired her, but hadn't allowed himself to contemplate what having that desire reciprocated would feel like.

Della smacked his arm. "This is serious. I should have known I could not keep my hands off you."

"The fault is mine, Della. I'll not have your reputation martyred to my unruly desire." That desire still hummed through him, but so did Della's proposition. A trial marriage, one that could become a more distant partnership if necessary.

The terms felt fair to the lady—as Della had noted, many romantic unions ended up in the same posture five years later—but such a marriage also felt... inadequate.

Dishonest on Ash's part, because he was certain he'd disappoint her—or almost certain.

"What would you have us do?" Della asked, rising to gather up her evening gloves from the table.

"What would *you* have us do?" Ash countered, getting to his feet. "If we marry, you are stuck with me. If we don't marry, you are ruined. I cannot recommend either choice, but should we wed, I will try to be the very best husband to you I can." That promise scared him witless, but she deserved at least his best efforts.

Della pulled on her gloves and smoothed them up her arms. That unselfconscious little gesture, even in this outlandish situation, hit Ash with an erotic edge. In at least one regard, he could ensure their marriage got off on very sound footing.

"You leave this up to me," Della said, "and I am too upset at the moment to think straight. Let's endure the flutists and sopranos and take the week Lady Caldicott has given us. Your choices are really not any better than mine, do you but know it."

On that cryptic remark, she quit the parlor, leaving Ash to follow her from the room.

◈

THE TALK that had been dying down roared back to life. Nobody said anything to Della directly, of course, but as she rode down the bridle path, George at her side, the behavior of the other equestrians spoke volumes.

"They know," she said as her mare pinned her ears at George's gelding. "Lady Caldicott didn't give us even a day."

George had been reading in the family parlor when Della had returned from last night's musicale. He'd apparently sensed from her expression that the evening hadn't gone well, and Della had sketched the general situation for him.

George's gelding sidled closer to the verge. "Her ladyship likely didn't give you ten minutes, or Miss Penelope Hammond didn't. When a woman who has overstepped turns around and oversteps again barely a fortnight later, tongues will wag, Della."

Wagging tongues were to be expected. What troubled Della more were the men she'd considered cordial acquaintances looking at her as if she'd been put on the kill list for their local hunts. She had become, overnight, not simply *soiled goods*, but *fair game*, a creature to be pursued and used.

Her morning hack had been instructive.

"Lady Della." Sycamore Dorning sat atop a blood bay gelding. In the slanting sunbeams, Cam Dorning was the picture of masculine pulchritude, from his tastefully understated cravat pin to his gleaming field boots. He tipped his hat to her, then nodded to George. "Always a pleasure when the rain moves off and we can start the day with a good gallop, isn't it?"

He turned his horse to fall in step with Della's mare.

"Dorning, greetings. How fares the club?" George asked.

"Splendidly. How fares marital bliss?"

"More splendidly than you can imagine, young Sycamore." George waggled his eyebrows, though he might have been five entire years Cam's senior. "Might I impose on you to escort Della down the path? I see the Pickering twins, and they will talk the leg off a chair, but they are good fellows, and I ought to acknowledge them while I'm in Town."

Meaning they would cut Della, but had no reason to cut George on his own.

"I will gladly escort Lady Della," Sycamore replied, "if she has no objection?"

"None at all," Della said. "I'll see you at home, George."

George trotted off, his gelding whisking his tail at Della's mare.

"So I ask myself," Sycamore said, "why a lovely and unattached female would send me a late-night note asking me to meet her for an early hack. But then, my charm is abundant, my good looks are the envy of Bond Street, and among the ladies, my legendary talents as a passionate—"

"Braggart," Della interjected, "are without peer. Ash didn't say anything?"

"Ash never says anything," Sycamore retorted. "He is the soul of self-sufficiency, the pattern card of discretion. Then he nips off to Jackson's and nearly gets himself killed because he's seething over some customer's slight to a dealer."

"That's not why he boxes," Della said, though Sycamore's perspective was interesting. "Ash didn't say anything about the musicale?"

"Not a word. The gossip at the club last night was that you were all but tearing Ash's clothes off, and he was not objecting. Ash neither confirmed nor denied the rumors, but rather, went about his usual late evening duties at the club with his usual pleasant and damnably self-possessed air."

While Della had tossed and turned all night. "The gossip isn't wrong."

"I'd rather hoped that was the case." Sycamore tipped his hat to a passing matron perched on a sturdy cob. She offered Della no acknowledgment whatsoever.

"You wish to see me ruined?" Della asked.

"No, love. I wish to see you and my brother happy. You are mad for each other, and that you can inspire Ash into making torrid advances suggests you are also *made* for each other."

"I don't want to force Ash into marriage," Della said, "but if I refuse him, he'll think it's because of his blue devils, not because I am trying to put his welfare first."

"So you care for each other too much to try for shared happiness? Spare me from such backward devotion."

Sycamore, blast him, had a point. "How bad are Ash's blue devils?"

"Why do you want to know?"

"So I can be a better wife to him. He will try to protect me from the worst, and that's pointless chivalry."

Sycamore held back a branch for her. "To be honest, my lady, Ash's bad spells are awful. The names we give them—the mulligrubs, blue devils, low spirits, doldrums, dismals—are nearly whimsical compared to the reality. Ash becomes a different person, the antithesis of the urbane, polite fellow who cuts such a fine figure on the dance floor. He becomes a creature of darkness and mourning, though for what I cannot say."

"He keeps to himself?"

"He remains in his room for days at a time. Casriel made him agree that the door would not be locked, but the concession Ash demanded was that nobody would open that door without Ash's permission. He will go for three days without eating, a week without shaving. He refuses the physicians, but in fairness to him, he has tried all of their suggested remedies to no avail. He is truly afflicted."

This recitation, so free of Sycamore's usual drollery, made Della's heart ache. "What remedies has he tried?"

"What remedies hasn't he tried? A bland diet, morphia, cold plunges, a beef-tea diet, frequent bleedings, inversion—"

"Inversion?"

"Being hung upside down by his heels. Fasting, temperance, abstinence—from the ladies, which would part me from my every reason to live—abstinence from strong spirits, patent remedies, memorization of sermons or Bible verses, quiet... He has tried them all to no avail. If you marry him, Della, you will be marrying a man who is periodically quite out of sorts."

"How long does this go on?"

"Months sometimes. Weeks otherwise. Winters are the worst, but Ash can hit a rough patch any time of year. Occasionally, I will think he's drifting into the doldrums, but he'll rouse himself. Other times, I'm rollicking along, my brother his usual self at breakfast, but that same afternoon, he retreats to his room, and I don't see him for the better part of a week."

Della drew her mare to a halt on the verge and let her have a loose rein. "Then this illness is both a misery and unpredictable. How long has he had it?"

Sycamore's gelding stopped as well. "You should be asking Ash these questions, my lady."

"And would he answer them honestly?"

"For you, if you caught him in the right mood, he might bare his soul, if he hasn't already. May I be blunt?"

That Sycamore would ask was alarming. "Of course."

"The physicians generally contend that marriage and procreation are helpful to the melancholic."

"They do?"

"In that order, while I contend—never mind. In any case, there's reason to believe, reason grounded in medical science, that the right wife might bring some ease to Ash's situation."

Della certainly hoped as much. "But?"

"But to fail at marriage would wreck Ash's soul," Sycamore said gently. "To disappoint the people who love him eats at him as badly as the sadness itself. You take a great risk if you marry Ash, for yourself, also for him."

Della considered that advice, which was meant as kindly as Sycamore Dorning meant anything. "And what is the risk if I, who involved Ash in my troubles, turn away from him?"

"Don't marry him out of guilt, Della."

She gathered up her reins. "He was determined to *not* marry me out of guilt."

Sycamore nudged his gelding forward. "And people wonder why my amours are so plentiful and superficial. Have a frank discussion with Ash, a frank, private discussion. Tell him why you're marrying him and leave pity out of it. He neither wants nor deserves your pity."

Nor did Della want his. What a coil. "Will you see me home?" she asked.

"Of course, and unless I miss my guess, you can expect a call from Ash this afternoon. Make him get down on bended knee, Della. A little begging works a treat on a man's hubris."

"As if you'd know about begging a woman for anything."

CHAPTER SEVEN

Ash's spirits were unaccountably good as he waited for Della to join him in the Haddonfield family parlor.

"Mr. Dorning." Della looked pale and composed, also quite fetching in a blue afternoon gown and cream silk shawl. "Shall I ring for tea?"

"I was hoping you'd allow me a turn in the garden," he said. "The day is mild, and we should enjoy the pleasant weather while it lasts." And also remain out of earshot of well-intended, meddlesome siblings.

"Let me fetch a second shawl," she said. "I could use some fresh air."

Ash could not read her mood, but she had received him, which suggested her brothers weren't planning to call him out, and she wasn't planning to dodge off to the family seat.

"Take your time," he said. "My afternoon is otherwise free."

Her smile took on a hint of mischief. "As is mine."

She returned a moment later, a crocheted shawl atop the cream silk. "I crossed paths with Sycamore in the park this morning."

"He did mention that. I have wondered if he hacks out so regularly for the exercise or to flirt."

"Likely both. Also to gossip."

Della led Ash through a pair of French doors and into the walled back garden. Leaves carpeted most of the walkways, though a few chrysanthemums were still showing some color, and pots of pansies added cheer to the terrace.

"This way," she said. "The conservatory has a terrace that's mostly private, and I would like to have you to myself for a time."

That was very promising. "You don't sound particularly ruined, Della Haddonfield, but I have to tell you, the club was rife with talk last night. Lady Caldicott didn't waste a moment."

"I received both the cut direct and nasty looks in the park this morning," Della said. "I have truly put myself beyond the pale."

"You did not put yourself there." On that point, Ash was very firm. He'd spent much of the night in thought and gone for a long walk at dawn. Honor demanded that he offer Della marriage, and pure selfishness prayed she'd accept. She had all but proposed to him —he hoped—but Ash's all-but-proposal might have been so much more of Della's frank discussion in the aftermath of Lady Caldicott's meddling.

Ash had avoided Della for months, with the best of intentions. Last night, he had kissed her behind a closed door, fully aware of the risks that behavior entailed. That he'd taken those risks suggested to him that he wanted an *excuse* to offer for Della, which suggested to him that... Well, he wasn't sure what that suggested.

"You are determined to be gallant," Della said, linking arms with him. "I am determined to be honest. I asked Sycamore to meet me in the park because I wanted his description of your melancholia."

That too, was encouraging. "Did he oblige?"

"He really hadn't much to say. You have tried some accepted remedies, which have failed you. Your malady prompts you to isolate yourself, and while it's worse in winter, you are never entirely safe from it."

They ambled down a path that in summer was likely shady, but now was carpeted in dead leaves. "Your description is prosaic, as if I suffer megrims instead of weeks of irrational despair."

"I think we are making too much of your melancholia, Ash Dorning. The whole business of marriage is specifically set forth on for-better-or-for-worse terms, suggesting every couple deals with challenges. Perhaps the wife can't carry a child to term, perhaps the husband is prone to drinking excessively. Maybe she becomes consumptive, or he loses his sight. We are frail creatures."

"I want to argue with your logic, to claim that my particular frailty is the worst to ever befall mortal man, but that would be arrogant. Are you frail, Della?"

She seemed to him the picture of glowing good health, despite her petite stature. Della cut through life like a sloop running close to the wind. She harnessed the gale for her own ends, and the waves presented no obstacle.

"I am frail," she said, "but I am also much enamored of you, Ash Dorning."

That was *very* encouraging. "Why me, Della? I am not particularly wealthy, I am not entirely sound. When the current scandal fades, you will still be the daughter of an earl, comely, and wonderfully well connected. You could do better than to settle for a semi-addled younger son."

Having embarked on a course of blunt truths with Della, Ash wanted to keep to that path, much to his surprise.

She dropped his arm to open a side door to the conservatory. "In here," she said, extending her hand. "We have more to say to each other."

The air inside was warm, and because cold weather approached, the space had the quality of a leafy bower. The tender plants had all been arranged along the glass walls, and lemon and orange trees created an overhead canopy of green.

She closed the door and gave the lock a twist. "I have made lists in my head," she said, preceding Ash down a winding gravel walk, "why we would suit, why we would not. I excel at making lists. We are of appropriate stations, we dance wonderfully together, our families are already connected and of equal rank. Our siblings get on cordially, and our family seats aren't that distant."

She paused before the door that connected the conservatory to the main Haddonfield residence. "My lists were lengthy, and yet, they did not convince me that marriage is the right course for us." She gave this lock a twist as well. "The gardeners are on half day. We will not be disturbed."

An engaged couple was permitted some privacy, but then, Ash and Della weren't quite engaged.

"You haven't told me why you will consider marrying me, Della, as opposed to marrying any old younger son with a few groats and decent manners."

She took him by the hand and towed him along another path. "You are kind," she said. "Even when you tried to keep your distance from me, you did so because you were trying to spare me from an attraction that you believed had no future. When I was so despondent over Jonathan's unwillingness to acknowledge me, you were kind. Even your kisses are kind."

"Kind?" Ash had behaved as a gentleman toward Della—for the most part—but kind kisses did not comport with what they'd exchanged the previous night. "You'd marry me because I'm a nice fellow?"

"You are a very nice fellow," she said, "also kind, and that is more attractive to me than all the strutting peacockery or witty banter in Mayfair. Sycamore probably tells himself that he took on the Coventry in a bold exercise of business acumen and financial derring-do. That his keen judgment and superior cunning have taken Jonathan's idea and burnished its glory to an unprecedented shine."

"That might be Cam's humble version of events," Ash said. "The usual version includes saving London's entire economy, defeating the French, and teaching the cherubim how to wield their harps."

"Precisely, but the fact is, without you to talk him out of his more fanciful flights, to tend to the books, to keep the staff from quitting en masse when Sycamore is in a biting mood, the club would have closed its doors in a week flat."

She had led Ash to a corner of the conservatory outfitted as some sort of reading nook or hideaway. A well-cushioned sofa long enough to accommodate a reclining Haddonfield male sat before a trio of wide hassocks. Pillows adorned the sofa corners, and a pair of worn quilts had been folded over the back. The glass walls let in hazy light, while the plants along the walls ensured privacy.

"What has the Coventry to do with your reasons for marrying me?" Ash asked. "And why are we here?"

"I'll get to that," Della said, occupying the middle of the sofa, "but the point of my digression is that you quietly allow your younger brother to strut and carry on, the great entrepreneur, such a keen young business talent—and he desperately needs to be regarded as such—while you are the unacknowledged net that allows him to occupy his trapeze so successfully.

"That is *kind*, Ash Dorning," she went on. "Sycamore loves that damned club, but he'd make a hash of it without your hand on the ribbons. You could fritter away your days in the country, but you do what you can for Sycamore, when the rest of your family simply wishes he'd do his impersonation of a cockerel someplace else."

Ash took the place beside her when she patted the cushion. "You mustn't call Cam a cockerel to his face, no matter how apt the description. For all his posturing, he's tenderhearted."

"And that is precisely what I mean. You could easily characterize your brother as an obnoxious mushroom, yet you defend him. That is the behavior of a wise, kind man."

Ash was losing the thread of the argument—the discussion. Della had brought him to a secluded location, behind two locked doors, on the gardeners' half day.

"Della, what are we doing here?"

"I made my lists, but the reason we should marry did not lend itself to a tidy description." She rose, then settled herself astride Ash's lap. "I thought to convince you of our compatibility by having my way with you."

~

"THIS IS OUR FAULT," George said, gazing down into the back garden, where a moment before, Della had led Ash Dorning down the path.

Literally and perhaps figuratively.

Nick remained behind his desk, an absurdly delicate French piece with exquisite inlay. "How is Della's *tendresse* for one of the less prepossessing Dornings our fault? We've escorted her through Season after Season, introduced her to everybody from ducal heirs to American explorers. She has been gracious to all and smitten with none. Then *he* shows up."

George did not know Nicholas all that well. Nick was the oldest legitimate sibling; George was an "extra spare." They had different mothers. Their stations were different, and the roads they'd traveled had been very different. Nick had known from a scandalously young age that his intimate interest lay with the female of the species. George had never enjoyed the clarity of an exclusive preference in either direction.

Nick had been the Bellefonte earldom's heir, his path in life affected at every turn by that reality. George had been far down the birth order in a very large family, an indifferent scholar and somewhat given to reckless associations.

But Della vexed them both equally. Perhaps it was time she vexed a husband instead.

"We should never have referred to Della as our changeling," George said. "She has darker hair than the rest of us, and she's not as tall as her sisters. She's still a perfectly normal exponent of the species."

Nick rose and picked up the cat who'd been lounging on the

windowsill. "Children have nicknames, and as it turns out, she is a changeling."

"Your nickname was *Viscount Reston*. Not quite the same thing, Nicholas."

The cat, a massive orange tom named Inigo, began to purr as Nick scratched his neck. "What are you getting at?"

"Can you imagine being called the family changeling and then learning you are, in fact, a legitimate bastard? We don't know when Della found those love letters, but she had to conclude we knew her secret before she did. Then every dowager and maiden auntie in Mayfair referred to her as the Haddonfield changeling."

Nick held the cat away from his chest. "This damned beast is shedding as winter approaches. He's doing it on purpose."

The condensation covering the walls of the conservatory ensured the couple within had privacy. Nobody would think to look for Della and her swain there, particularly not on the gardeners' half day. Della, as always, had pondered details and possibilities, and woven her own path to her own objectives.

While Nick, the head of the family, complained about cat hair.

"Are you aware that Ash Dorning typically leaves Town every winter?" George asked.

"I am. Susannah has confirmed that Dorning becomes melancholic."

The cat yawned and batted at Nick's chin.

"Doesn't that worry you?" George asked. "Della is involving herself with a man of unreliable temperament."

"Of course it worries me, but every lad who ever went to university, every midshipman in the Royal Navy, is afflicted with melancholia. Poets wear it like a badge of honor, and spinsters turn to it as a fashionable accessory. I told Della I would not object to Dorning as a suitor. Given the current situation..."

"You know she and Dorning were found cavorting at last night's musicale?"

"Leah had lunch with a gaggle of hens and became apprised of the gossip. That my own brother hasn't seen fit to share with me news that affects our sister disappoints me."

Nicholas was a complete failure as an authority figure. His attempts to scold never came off as anything more intimidating than a grumble.

"Leah simply beat me to it," George said. "The melancholia worries me, Nick. It's not an affectation that can be put on and taken off like a favorite morning coat."

Nick turned away from the window and put the cat on the sofa. "What would you know of such a malady? You are my ever-cheerful, gallant Squire Jollychops. Children swarm you in the churchyard and songbirds light on your shoulders."

"Jealous?"

Nick cuffed him on the arm. "You try being the earl. The House of Lords is a lot of bleating old men squabbling over how to divide the spoils of Britain. If the French hadn't tossed over their own lot of gilded parasites, my titled colleagues would re-institute forty days' service and serfdom."

"While they begrudge the peasants bread. We can discuss politics another day. It's Dorning I'm concerned about now."

Nick took a seat on the sofa, and the cat marched into his lap. "So am I. He seems a decent sort, and the Dornings are good folk, but... why him? Why has Della decided she must have him?"

Still, the couple tarried in the conservatory. George wished them the joy of their botanical adventure and joined Nick on the sofa.

"Della not only decided she must have him, when he left Town without a word to her, she did not give up her choice. When he refused to answer her letters, she remained convinced of his value. When she needed a champion following the fiasco with Chastain, she turned to Dorning."

"Or he to her. What aren't you telling me, George?" The cat curled up into a marmalade feline comma on Nick's thighs. "These are my favorite breeches, you wretched pestilence."

"You call me Squire Jollychops," George said, "but I wasn't always such a happy fellow."

"You have a temper," Nick said. "You've always had a temper, even as a little fellow. You'd come after your elders, fists swinging over some slight, and we'd laugh at you. Then you'd make us wish we hadn't."

George had learned to make the first blow count and then run like hell. "You said every university boy becomes melancholy. I was no exception."

"You were no scholar either," Nick said, "but everybody loved George Haddonfield. Probably a greater accomplishment, to leave Oxford with a wide circle of friends instead of perfect Latin."

"Nick, I was miserable. Everybody else was swiving the tavern maids, lodging at the merry widows' boardinghouses, and exchanging notes with the tutors' daughters. I was lusting after my classmates." *And* after the tavern maids, merry widows, and tutors' daughters.

"Must we air this ancient history?" Nick asked gently.

"I did not know who or what I was, I made no sense to myself, and I could discuss the problem with no one." Least of all with his great, strapping, swaggering brothers.

Nick passed him the cat. "And, Haddonfield that you are, you couldn't keep it in your breeches either. What has this to do with Della and Ash Dorning?"

George did not allow the ruddy beast to touch his breeches, but instead put the cat on the carpet. "When melancholia is severe, life is at risk."

Nick rose and went to the window, the cat strutting in his wake. "You think Della will soon be a widow if she marries Dorning?"

"It's possible. Very possible, if Dorning's malady is chronic." George had had occasion to read the medical literature regarding disorders of mood.

"How bad was it, George?" Nick asked as the cat stropped his boots.

"Must we air this ancient history?"

Nick speared him with a look. "You had nobody with whom you could discuss your situation, and you're refusing to discuss it when I invite you to?"

George was happily, wonderfully married. The present Mrs. Haddonfield knew her husband's past, knew the breadth of his preferences, accepted them, and had his undying devotion—and fidelity—as a result. But arriving to that happy situation had been a long and tormented road.

"I would have killed myself," George said. "I had made arrangements to dispose of what little I possessed. I had the gun, and I had planned to end my days by the millpond at Belle Maison. I would be found by a tenant that way rather than a family member, and I wouldn't spatter Mama's carpets with my life's blood. I planned to shoot myself in the heart so nobody would have to deal with patching up my skull for a viewing."

Nick was looking at him as if he'd sprouted snakes for hair. "You would have... You *planned* to kill yourself?"

"Society felt that men such as I deserved to die by the executioner's hand, Nicholas, surrounded by a jeering crowd while I wet myself twitching on the end of a rope. My own family wanted me to go away or be somebody different. I could not imagine a woman would want me for a husband, not with my past, and the men... When intimacy is a hanging felony, much desperation and risk attends the whole business."

"You planned... You *planned* to take your own life?" Nick sounded near tears.

"Della found me drafting a farewell note." Cleaning his gun, actually. The note had been drying on the blotter. "She begged me to reconsider. She said she'd always felt that at least one other Haddonfield didn't fit the merry Viking mold. If I abandoned her, she would be left alone among loving strangers. She doubtless already knew of her illegitimacy by then."

More than that, George would not say. Della had kept his confidences, and he would keep hers.

"I am sorry," Nick said. "I am abjectly, damnably sorry, and I am just as sincerely glad Della talked sense into you."

"She did not let me out of her sight for weeks." And nobody, not Nick, not Nita—the family healer—neither relentlessly brisk Kirsten nor observant Beckman, had noticed Della's vigilance.

Or knew what it had meant to George.

"Does she truly regard us as loving strangers?" Nick asked, a particularly insightful question.

"You were off to public school before she was taking breakfast with the family, Nick. Ethan was gone even sooner. Beckman left immediately after you. The older sisters regarded Della as a sort of mascot. If Della is attracted to a man who is regarded as different by his own family, I can understand her choice."

Nick picked up the cat again. "You're saying Della and Dorning are kindred spirits?"

"Something like that."

"Loving strangers... Bloody, bollocking hell." He cradled the cat against his chest, doubtless getting cat hair all over his morning coat. "They haven't come out of the conservatory."

"If Dorning has an ounce of gentlemanly consideration, they won't for at least another hour."

Nick muttered more profanities as he stood by the window, petting the cat.

∼

DELLA DID NOT GIVE Ash a chance to respond to her declaration before she took a taste of his mouth. She sank onto his thighs and prepared to besiege him.

Ash grasped her gently by the arms, as if he thought to lift her off his lap. "Della, we need to talk, to think this through."

"Talk later, love now." Inside her head, arguments and misgivings were as noisy as a group of musicians all intent on practicing a different etude at the same time. "I will think myself into a taking, but when I kiss you..."

He cupped her elbows. "When you kiss me?"

She rested her forehead against his. "Everything is lovely when I kiss you, and lovelier when you kiss me back."

He smoothed her hair off her brow and obliged her, his lips lazy and sweet against her mouth, on her eyelids, on her forehead. The cacophonous debate in her head gradually grew quieter. The anxious roiling in her belly eased.

She took Ash's hand and pressed it over her breast. That he didn't jerk away, rise, and leave at a dead run encouraged her.

Though he did shift his hand to her back, urging her against him. "Della, you haven't said you'll marry me. I will not take that which can be given only once."

"You can't take it," Della said, cuddling close. "I gave it to Freddy Throckmorton."

"Who?"

"Some cousin or other of our neighbors in Kent. Freddy was very dashing. I was an idiot, and the cherry cordial was much stronger than it tasted. Freddy was forever offering me cherry cordial that summer. When Freddy went back to university, I was honestly relieved."

"You didn't miss your first love?" Ash sounded more amused than dismayed.

"He wasn't my love. He was a rake-in-training who might have turned me into a sot. I had a narrow escape. Might you resume kissing me, please?"

Ash stroked her back in slow, smooth caresses. "I'm deciding whether I should invite Freddy Throckmorton into the ring with me at Jackson's."

"You can't. He married some American and left England before my come out." *Why won't you kiss me?* Della would normally have put the question to Ash directly, but the soothing movement of his hands on her back suggested she was—as usual—fretting over nothing.

"My first was my Greek tutor's housekeeper," Ash said. "Lovely woman, probably ten years my senior, and while I don't recall much Greek, I have very fond memories of the instruction I received from her."

"You won't let me ravish you, will you?"

"You sound gratifyingly disappointed."

Della was actually quite comfortable, bundled into Ash's embrace, drowsing on his shoulder while he rubbed her back.

"I have it in my head," Della said, "that you will think up some noble reason why we must not marry, but if I can compromise you, then you won't abandon me again."

His hand stilled, then resumed stroking her. "I am sorry, Della, for not explaining to you at the time why I left Town. I was fine one day—better than fine—and the next, the beast had me in its grip. Sycamore put me in the coach with instructions to the coachy to deliver me to Dorning Hall in one piece. I don't recall much of the journey."

"No apology needed. May I ravish you now?"

He anchored his hand at her nape and shook her gently. "We must talk first."

Della sat up, the better to read his expression. "About?"

His gaze was serious, his grip on her neck gentle. "I would rather avoid the near occasion of fatherhood for the present."

Della traced his lips with her index finger. "You don't want a seven-months firstborn? I suppose there will be talk, between my elopement with Chastain and being found behind a closed door with you."

He shook his head. "That has nothing to do with it. My concern is that I am not fit to raise children. You are an adult, and should I become incapacitated, you can turn to others for support. A child ought to have a father he or she can rely on."

In all of her worrying and what-if-ing, Della hadn't foreseen this difficulty. "You don't *want* children?"

"That's not what I said, Della. I said I would not be a reliable parent. I don't want to be a father unless I can be a good father. At present, I cannot make that promise."

Could a man have too much honor? "I never thought to have a white marriage, Ash Dorning, but if those are your terms, then I can live with them."

"You would marry me without any hope of intimacy?"

She smiled. "There's always hope. Intimacy and conception are very different matters."

His expression turned severe. "If we marry, we will take precautions to avoid conception. Perhaps in time, my situation will improve, but that's as much hope as I can offer. Will you wed me, Della? Knowing what you do about me, will you still marry me?"

She did not have to think, did not have to sort through maybes or on-the-other-hands. "Yes, I will marry you. By special license would suit if you're determined to be so proper—and even if you aren't."

He kissed her, a press of lips almost solemn in its tenderness. "Then we shall be wed, and I will do my damnedest to be a good husband to you."

Della's relief was immense, like the relief she'd felt when the first footman had found her on the church steps, wrapped her in his cloak, and carried her home in his arms. She returned Ash's kiss, nothing solemn about it, but drew back to ask an important question.

"When do we tell our families?"

"Today. When we're finished here." He'd not hesitated for an instant before answering.

"You'll let me ravish you now?"

He rose with Della straddling his waist, turned, and laid her supine upon the cushions. "We will not anticipate our vows, Della, not quite."

She was so full of frustrated longing she nearly pulled him down on top of her. "What does 'not quite' mean?"

Ash shifted the hassocks around so he sat near her hip. "I'll show you. Close your eyes and think of our wedding night."

$\sim$

ASH FELT like one of those street urchins who juggled oranges for tuppence, though he was no sort of juggler. His body enthusiastically anticipated intimacies with Della, a woman he'd desired from the moment he'd seen her.

His heart wrestled with the notion that he'd just become engaged to that same woman, against all sense and probability to the contrary.

His intellect, the part of him that kept peace at the Coventry, minded the books, and managed the staff, started listing all the ways in which marriage would necessitate changes. He was calculating probabilities and discards, based on the few cards he held in his hand. He and Della could not, for example, live with Sycamore. They would need their own dwelling, their own staff. Rooms above a shop would not do for an earl's daughter...

And tackling those issues now was simply beyond him. Della lay on her back on the sofa, looking disgruntled and delectable. She had brought Ash to this conservatory, prepared to make love with him, and by God, she would not leave entirely unsatisfied.

Why she had been so desperate to sample his charms, he did not know, and that was part of a niggling sense that something about the whole situation required further study. Later—later when his intended wasn't regarding him as if he'd threatened to take holy vows instead of wedding vows.

"Did you enjoy the encounters you had with Freddy Throck-muddle?" he asked.

"Throckmorton. Not at first, but Freddy's advances improved with practice."

"Or with more cherry cordial." Ash stole a kiss. "If I ever do meet this scoundrel, I will thrash him, not for sharing intimacies freely offered, but for plying you with drink. My lady, tell me you are not wearing a corset."

"I am not wearing a corset. Two chemises, and my..."

She watched while Ash undid the bow at the center of her décolletage. "You were saying, my lady?"

"I'm not wearing drawers either."

Della had been very determined on this seduction, and Ash was very determined that she not be disappointed.

"Commendably foresighted of you," he said, loosening both the bodice of her dress and the two lacy confections beneath that. He left her treasures shielded, though only just. "How about we remove your slippers?"

He slid them off her feet, and set them aside. "Here is how this works, Della. I will dust off a few of my Greek lessons, and you will inform me if they meet with your approval. You will be honest with me. You will not endure unwanted attentions and wash down your objections with cherry cordial."

"Greek lessons? Ash Dorning, you are comporting yourself in a most—"

He slid her skirts up to within three inches of her knee. "Not exactly Greek lessons. Lessons from a Greek tutor's housekeeper. In her way, she was erudite and generous with her knowledge."

Beneath Della's skirts, Ash shaped her muscular calf through the silk of her stocking. When she made no objection, he slid his hand higher, past her lacy garter, learning the contours of her bare knee.

"Enlighten me," Della said, some of the starch wilting from her tone.

"I'd rather kiss you." Ash started slowly, alternating between glancing touches to her breasts and further boldness beneath her skirts. By the time he had eased her dress and chemises aside, her skirts were rucked up past her knees.

He paused, because he *needed* a pause, and because he wanted to imprint the image of Della on his memory.

"You cannot stop," she said, gaze on the glass ceiling. "If you stop now, I will throttle you."

She didn't even try to cover herself, but lay in a wanton sprawl, one bare breast peeking from layers of cream lace, a pale knee thrust up from her skirts and petticoats.

"I am not stopping," Ash said. *I am falling in love, all over again.*

Della turned her head to regard him, some confusion in her gaze. "I would rather—"

He silenced her with a kiss, and with forays north of her knee that ended in a delicate exploration of her most intimate flesh. He asked questions tactilely—*May I?* and *Like this?*—and Della answered with sighs and subtle movements of her hips. By the time he had two fingers hilted in her heat, she had set up a slow, demanding rhythm.

There being a shortage of hands in such a situation, Ash used his mouth on her breasts, counterpointing her undulations and ignoring his own rising desire. Amid the sheer loveliness of being intimate with Della came the thought: *At least I'm good for this.*

He shoved it aside like the serpent in paradise that it was.

Della unraveled on a soft, happy groan, her body clutching at his fingers as she held him in a fierce embrace. She did not ease her grip on him until long moments later, when she lay back, her chest rosy, her skirts rucked to her thighs.

"Gracious days, Ash Dorning." Her smile was dreamy and sweet. "If you applied yourself to Greek as you did to the housekeeper's lessons, you would have taken a first, I'm sure."

He removed a handkerchief from his pocket. "This next part isn't something the housekeeper had to teach me."

Della watched while he unbuttoned his falls and brought himself off in a few quick strokes. That she was observing, half naked and replete, made Ash's pleasure that much more intense. When Ash had tidied himself up and stood to rebutton his falls, Della propped herself on her side and stroked a finger down the length of his softening cock.

"You have surprised me, Ash Dorning."

That she would be so bold surprised him—and delighted him. "Pleasantly, I hope."

"Wonderfully. That thing you did with your thumb..." She rolled to her back and rested her forearm across her forehead, as if she'd had too much cherry cordial. "I have become the greatest admirer of your right hand in all of Britain. I am quite fond of your mouth too."

Ash finished buttoning himself up, and in defense of his best intentions, he drew Della's skirts down over her knees. He used a watering can to rinse off his fingers and returned to the sofa to find Della sitting up, her bodice once again modestly tucked and tied.

"That was not what I had planned," she said as Ash took the place beside her.

"I'm sorry to disappoint you. On our wedding night—" He'd withdraw, and use sheaths, and generally ensure no baby resulted. The thought was a trifle lowering, but then, he'd *have* a wedding night with Della, and that was not lowering at all.

Della interrupted him by taking his hand. "That was *better* than what I had planned. I hadn't realized... Well, suffice it to say my Greek education will benefit from further association with you."

"You'd like to nap for a bit, wouldn't you?"

She shifted to curl up on the sofa with her head in his lap. "I would like to tear the clothes from your body and swive you witless. Had planned on it, in fact."

Ash stroked her hair, not quite sure what to make of her plans for him. The sense of vague unease returned, along with a worry that Della was inordinately eager to consummate their engagement. Perhaps Chastain had shaken her confidence. Perhaps she was simply that most delightful of women, a lusty lady.

They were to be married, and at that moment, Ash was content to stroke Della's hair and plan his interview with her brother.

CHAPTER EIGHT

"Now see here, William." Torvald Chastain drew himself up to his full height—five inches less than William's own six feet—and rocked back on his heels. "Your mother and I don't mind a bit of high spirits. Wild oats, drunken tomfoolery, that sort of thing. But tearing off to Gretna Green with the Haddonfield girl exceeded the bounds. I could not keep the general contours of the situation from your mother, and she will be some time getting over the shock."

Papa's lecture hadn't changed in the fortnight since he'd interrupted the best fun William had had since the fourth time he'd been sent down from university. Papa had broken the unspoken rules by allowing Mama to learn of William's excursion with *the Haddonfield girl*—though Lady Della was quite long in the tooth as *girls* went—and Mama had been merciless in retaliation.

"Clarice don't want to marry me," William said for the thousandth time as he propped an elbow on the mantel. "She never has."

Papa laced his hands behind his back. "Did she say that?"

"She don't have to say it. She don't like me, and I ain't too keen on her either." Clarice pretended to be shy, but William knew her type. She would hoard her marital favors and make him beg and wheedle until he lost patience with her games. Then she would sulk and pout and try to make him feel guilty. Breaking off the engagement was the only gentlemanly thing to do, and if Clarice had a brain in her Frenchie head, she'd admit it.

But she didn't have a brain in her head. She had an abacus where her heart should be and parents who knew damned good and well she wouldn't do any better than a baronet's son.

"Her charms will grow on you once you're married, believe me, lad." Papa opened the humidor on his desk and withdrew a pair of cheroots. "Your mother and I were nearly strangers until the wedding night. We found our way forward nonetheless."

So why am I an only child? William had never asked that of either of his parents. They weren't an affectionate pair, but they were allies. Witness, they'd ganged up on William regarding this marriage, and now Papa had broken male ranks to help load Mama's scolding-cannon with heavy shot.

William accepted a slim Havana from his father, held a spill to the hearth fire, and lit his cheroot. "Clarice won't let me smoke," he said. "She don't even let me kiss her." Not quite the whole truth. Upon the occasion of their engagement a month or so ago, Clarice had allowed William under her skirts.

But only the once, and she'd refused to permit him even a peek at her bubbies. She had turned her face from him and endured his love-making with a martyred air.

Hell of a way for a fellow to plight his damned troth, with the lady acting as if he was late to choir practice and wearing dung on his boots.

"Clarice is playing hard to get," Papa replied, propping a hip on his desk. "Your mother was the same way, but she wanted her own household and her own pin money. I daresay she wanted a child. She reconciled herself to her situation with eventual good grace. Clarice will too."

"I won't reconcile myself," William said, blowing a smoke ring and watching it waft across Papa's study. "You can drag me to the altar, and I'll stand beside Clarice as mute as a marble statue. I'm already in disgrace for that bit with Lady Della. Backing out of the wedding won't cause any more scandal." The scheme with Lady Della had almost worked, damn the luck. Another quarter hour, and even Papa would have agreed that William had to marry the earl's curvy little daughter rather than la-di-da émigré Clarice.

Della Haddonfield didn't put on airs. She was a fetching little heifer, too, not a dried-up Frenchie nun, and Della, whatever her faults were, had a temper. William adored gaining the upper hand with a woman who had a temper. Della had bigger bubbies than Clarice, too, and William had a fondness for a bouncy pair of bubbies.

"You will marry Clarice, William, and you will do it Monday next. I have the special license."

William pitched his cheroot into the fire, though he'd taken only a few puffs, and good cheroots were dearly bought.

"I don't care if you have a bloody decree from the king, Papa. You can't make me shackle myself to a cold, Frenchie bitch."

That was a little harsh—Clarice was practical, and her parents were calling the tune—but William's parents responded to hyperbole. He'd learned that before he'd been breeched.

"Language, son. Language. A married man learns to choose his words. You will wed Clarice, and you will do so happily. Her father has offered to modify the settlements."

"Her father can sod himself."

Papa winced. "Truly, your mother's fears that I have let you fall in with low company have some basis in fact. If you marry Clarice, you'll be a wealthy man, William. Clarice's parents understand that you're a nervous groom—"

William snorted and helped himself to another cheroot.

"—and they would like to reassure you with an additional sum, to be used to establish your own household."

"I won't have to live with you and Mama here at Tidemarsh?" William liked the sound of that very much. Tidemarsh—which Papa referred to as the family seat, though he'd purchased it only twenty-five years ago—was a rambling old manor in Exactly Nowhere, Surrey. William hated the place and hated even more the idea that his marriage would unfold under his mother's judgmental eye.

"You can set up housekeeping in Town, or find a little property of your own. A landed gentleman knows a life of ease and independence, William. Have a look at what Clarice's papa is willing to do to sweeten the pot."

A landed gentleman. To not have to wait for Papa to stick his spoon in the wall, to know that Mama wouldn't be poking her nose into William's married business, to have a place to stash Clarice when a fellow wanted to spend some time in Town...

"Show me." William blew another cloud, while Papa produced some folded pages covered with tidy script. William scanned the words, mining a lot of Frenchie blather for the specific figures. The sum proposed was beyond William's wildest imaginings.

"You don't suppose Clarice is breeding, do you?" A pleasing thought, to consider he could have got her with child on the first go. She would be breeding soon enough in any case, for if William had to marry, he'd take full advantage of his rights once the vows had been spoken.

Perhaps he could provoke Clarice into slapping him next time. That would take matters in a very interesting direction, and breeding women were known to be randy.

"Clarice is a good girl," Papa said, "but, my boy, I believe we are up against an example of female determination. Your mother and Clarice's mama conceived of this match, and it's a fine match. The ladies will not be denied the satisfaction of seeing you two youngsters wed."

William had put aside youngster-dom at the age of fourteen, when he'd caught a willing maid alone in the dairy. He'd been indulging in an adult male's diversions ever since and did not look forward to the nuisance of explaining his little indulgences to a wife.

Though, as Papa had said, a landed man enjoyed independence.

He could go up to Town whenever he pleased, lodge at his clubs, and leave the wife stitching samplers and tending her brats back in the shires.

William passed the epistle back to his father. "Tell Papa-in-law to add another thousand pounds, and I will marry the woman. I'll want a traveling coach and some teams to haul it, and those don't come cheap." Funds were always a problem, though for an enterprising fellow like William, a modest sort of solution was never that difficult to devise. He was tired of modest solutions and pinchpenny trades-men, though. If he was to get leg-shackled, he'd at least get leg-shackled in style.

William expected his capitulation to inspire hearty good cheer from his father, but Papa remained perched on the corner of the desk, exuding nothing heartier than long-suffering.

"William, do you understand why Clarice is willing to marry you?"

William blew the next cloud straight up. "Because I am devilishly good-looking, charming when I want to be, and received everywhere. I am an excellent whip, I have scads of chums, I cut a handsome figure on the dance floor, and I am a dead shot. Besides, I am heir to a tidy sum and a handsome estate. Why wouldn't any woman short of a duke's daughter marry me?"

"Ladies aren't as impressed by those attributes as you might think. They want cosseting, doting, and flattery. Your mother is never so pleased with me as when I ask her opinion on mercantile matters, and her advice is usually sound."

Papa was trying to be subtle, and he wasn't very good at it. He was also holding himself out as an expert on ladies, when he was himself a rather short, dull-witted, portly, aging cheese nabob whose uncle had distinguished himself in some war or other. Papa had lucked into his father's cheese fortune and his uncle's little title, then lucked into Mama's generous settlements. That made the old boy no expert on anything except being lucky.

And tattling to Mama at the worst possible time. "I'll give Clarice babies," William said. "I'm good at that too."

Papa's smile was pained. "Part of what you will give Clarice is connections, William. She's the daughter of émigrés, desperate for acceptance. Your lineage can be traced back to the Conqueror on your mother's side, and Clarice craves that evidence of English respectability."

William nearly told his father, *Then you marry her*, except Mama would take a dim view of bigamy. Besides, a brand-new traveling coach was delightful to contemplate. The fancy ones had benches that folded out into sleeping arrangements, and the possibilities *that* presented to an enterprising and charming fellow were marvelous.

"I've said I'll marry her." William stubbed out his cheroot on the sole of his boot. "I would rather have married Della Haddonfield."

"From the looks of things when I came upon you in Alconbury, her ladyship was having second thoughts."

"I love it when the ladies have second thoughts," William said, flicking the stub of his cigar into the fire. "Convincing them to see things my way is great fun for all concerned."

"I'm glad you're willing to put some effort into charming Clarice," Papa said, pushing away from the desk. "Perhaps you will be glad to show off your pretty new wife at your godmother's house party."

"A house party?" William liked house parties. The food and drink were free, the opportunities for romping plentiful. He also enjoyed the evening card games, where a whole flock of pigeons who seldom frequented London gaming hells were available for plucking. "Godmama's estate is ever so pretty this time of year. I could do some shooting."

"Think of it as a wedding journey," Papa said, tucking away the settlement proposal. "Clarice will be introduced to our circle of friends, and you can get to know each other better in pleasant surrounds."

"Tell Godmama the happy couple must have separate bedrooms.

A connecting door will do, but Clarice will need her rest." William would make sure of that. *Begin as you intend to go on,* Mama always said. For once, her advice was worth following.

"I'm sure Lady Wentwhistle will be happy to oblige. I will send our acceptance to Clarice's papa by special courier."

"You do that," William said, sauntering for the door. "I will contemplate my good fortune over a pint at the inn. Make my farewells to the tavern maids, so to speak."

"Just be sober Monday morning," Papa said. "Your mother will never let you hear the end of it otherwise."

William bowed and withdrew, but Papa, of course, was wrong. If William was tipsy when he spoke his vows—and he would be somewhere between tipsy and roaring drunk—*Papa* would never hear the end of it. William would be too busy getting to know his wife better.

~

"SO YOU INTEND to marry Ash Dorning?" Jonathan's question was casually put, along the lines of, *So I hear you've taken up the viola.*

"I do," Della said. "The solicitors are already at work on the settlements."

Jonathan wandered from one piece of cutwork to another, from a childhood sketch to dried flowers in a frame. This parlor had belonged to Della's mother, though Della considered it hers now.

"And nobody thought to consult me regarding the settlements?" Jonathan pretended to study a poem an eight-year-old Della had written for her mama, something about a cat and a butterfly. Mama had asked Nick to make the frame, and thus a child's verse had been preserved for all to gawk at.

"I would not expect Nick to consult you," Della said. "He is the head of my family and regards me as his responsibility."

"Well, I expect *Nick* to consult me. Not only because I have more means than Nick and Casriel put together many times over, but also because I am your brother and well acquainted with Ash Dorning. What are you reading?"

"A medical treatise." On disorders of the mind. Della shoved it into her workbasket. "If you are here to talk me out of the wedding, don't waste your breath."

"I would not dream of attempting to dissuade the most determined female in the realm from an objective she fixed upon months ago. Will Ash Dorning make you happy, Della?"

Della had seen Jonathan in a rage, bewildered, courting, and at cards. His commercial acumen bordered on genius, and his knowledge of politics was frankly astonishing. She had never seen him quite this diplomatic.

"A husband and wife can only love each other," she said. "Happiness is not within Ash's power to give me, but if I can give it to him, I will."

Jonathan tossed a bouquet of fading chrysanthemums into the dustbin, opened a window, and dumped the water into the garden.

"Ash Dorning is a good man," he said, closing the window and setting the empty vase on the hearth. "An honorable, hardworking, all-around-decent fellow. He's of suitable station, and he will do his utmost to be a good husband to you."

"If you append a *but* to that very accurate list, I will disown you."

Jonathan grinned, because he and Della did not publicly acknowledge their connection. Disowning him was an idle threat, and he knew it.

"The only *but* I would add is," he said, smile fading, "but he comes with a damned lot of siblings, and one of them is Sycamore."

"I like Sycamore." Mostly. "A considerate brother wouldn't disparage my in-laws."

"I am a caring brother," he said, approaching Della. "That is a different article. I want your marriage to prosper, regardless of how many in-laws you acquire."

Had Jonathan blustered and paced and battered her with advice —he was happily married and thus an expert on countless topics—

Della could have listened patiently, poured him two cups of tea, then shown him the door.

But he refused to accommodate her with typical fraternal bluster, so she let herself admit a smidgen of the truth.

"I am worried that Ash will be disappointed in his choice of wife. He solves a problem for me by offering for me."

Jonathan, a notably reserved and dignified man, wrapped her in a hug. "That you approach the marriage with some humility is good, Della. When I offered for Theo, I was the most humble, hopeful, tormented bachelor ever to present a lady his heart on a platter. She had no reason to trust me, no reason to see the good in me, but she did. I awaken every day, thanking God above and my lovely wife for my blessings."

Della stayed in his arms for the space of two breaths, then eased away and offered her brother a smile. "Shouldn't you be lecturing me about something?"

"Theodosia forbade me to lecture either you or Dorning. I'm also not allowed to issue threats. I hardly know how to go on." He looked genuinely bewildered.

"You're going on quite well. Will you stand up with me when I speak my vows?"

Della had clearly surprised him, and surprised herself, with that request, for ladies usually chose another lady to witness the ceremony.

"Me and Theo?"

"Of course Theo is welcome at the ceremony, but I'm asking you, Jonathan. You could have kept me at a distance. You could have refused to acknowledge me. Once you realized I wasn't attempting any blackmail schemes, you became my brother in truth. I would like you to stand up with me at the wedding."

"Of course I will stand up with you. Will that offend any Haddonfields?"

Della was weary of considering what might offend, vex, worry, annoy, disappoint, embarrass, or discommode any Haddonfields.

"I will put it to them that I chose you so as not to have to choose among my Haddonfield siblings. They can make of that what they will." Della would doubt her decision a thousand times between now and the ceremony, but it was still the right decision.

Jonathan wandered off to inspect her little poem again. "Does Ash know you are reluctant to have children?"

"What on earth are you going on about?"

He took out his handkerchief, plucked the poem from the wall, and dusted the glass and frame. "When Willow and Susannah, or Nick and Leah—I forget exactly who—last added to the nursery brigade, you told me you could not see yourself ever bringing a child into the world."

"I ought not to have said any such thing." Ought not to have admitted it, not to Jonathan.

He rehung the poem and tucked his handkerchief away. "Theo says small women often deliver babies easily, and it's the Amazons who have the most difficulty. Has to do with the hips or something."

That Jonathan discussed such matters with his wife was a revelation to ponder another day. "Nobody delivers a baby easily, Jonathan. I thank you for your concern, but Ash and I have discussed the situation and resolved it to our mutual satisfaction."

That Ash would simply state his reservations, acknowledge his fears, and put the welfare of a child ahead of his own masculine pride had stunned Della. Men generally wanted children. Therefore, women either married and bore children or became that most pathetic and vulnerable of creatures, the poor relation.

A wretchedly stupid system.

"A matter is resolved to the mutual satisfaction of the parties in a business negotiation," Jonathan said, peering down at her. "For a woman on the brink of holy matrimony, you aren't exactly radiating joy, Della. Is there anything I can do?"

He hadn't mentioned Ash's bouts of melancholia, hadn't ranted about the settlements, hadn't spouted eternal verities according to Jonathan Tresham.

"If I think of something," Della said, "I will ask you."

"You never do," Jonathan replied. "You are the most self-suffi-cient, self-contained female I know. You never ask anybody for anything. If Ash Dorning has won your esteem, then I conclude he's a more formidable fellow than I had thought."

"He's very formidable."

Jonathan sent her a curious look. "Are you blushing, Della? I believe you are. My, my."

"Out," Della said, grinning as she pointed to the door. "You are about to lapse into your odious-brother mode, and here you were doing so well. Leave now, and I will see you at the ceremony."

Jonathan did not merely bow, but instead wrapped her in another astounding hug. Only then did he kiss her cheek and make his farewells, leaving Della to marvel that he'd called at all.

Sooner or later, Jonathan's logical, precise mind would light upon the other explanation for why a match between Della and Ash Dorning made sense. Ash was more formidable than most people assumed him to be, and Della was less formidable.

Much less formidable.

~

"SYCAMORE'S GIFT to us is his absence," Ash said, twisting the key in the lock. "He will remove to the apartment at the Coventry, and this space will be ours to use as long as we please."

Viewed through the eyes of an engaged man, Ash's dwelling did not impress. The carpets needed a good beating, mud being pervasive in autumn. The windows were opaque with London grime, and the foyer was bereft of any beauty.

Not a vase of flowers, not a pretty landscape, nothing but a gilt mirror hanging over a serviceable sideboard. Sycamore was nothing if not vain.

The foyer did not smell particularly enticing either, having an air of damp wool and coal smoke.

"This will be a temporary dwelling," Ash said, unbuttoning his coat. "A place to get our bearings. Cam and I own several rental properties as well, and I could buy or trade him out of one of those, if you like. They make us a fair bit of coin during the Season, and two of them are empty right now."

Della peered about in silence, making no move to take off her cloak or bonnet.

"Della, please say something."

She crossed into the guest parlor. "That's the Coventry, across the street?"

"This building is connected to the Coventry by tunnels. We've never been raided, but should the authorities make an unscheduled call, the guests need means of egress besides the obvious. The wine cellar actually runs the length of the street, and there are two other exits. One by way of a mews. Another opens into a carriage house."

Since becoming betrothed three days ago, Ash's life had been busy. Negotiating settlements with Nicholas Haddonfield had entailed much discussion, until Ash had deduced Haddonfield's agenda. His lordship wanted to maintain control of Della's portion, which struck Ash as sensible. Once that obstacle had been dealt with, the details had been simple to sort out.

That had still left much correspondence to draft to various siblings—Casriel in particular was owed a report as head of the family and a party to the settlements. A frank discussion with Sycamore regarding Ash's future at the club had also been required, and the fraught matter of shopping for a morning gift yet remained.

And throughout all of this busyness, Ash had wondered if his behavior in the conservatory had been ill-advised. Should he have obliged Della's passion more fully? Should he have limited their affection to kisses and embraces?

"Della, you are notably reticent on the occasion of setting foot in our first marital home. Is something amiss?"

Della remained by the window, gaze on the traffic below. "I am delighted to be marrying you," she said.

Ash braced himself for a *but*.

"And I realize that our engagement has been precipitous, which is entirely my fault."

"I will forgo arguing that point."

"But the reality of becoming a married woman is still a surprise. That should not be possible, when for the entirety of my life, marriage has been held up as the great goal toward which every lady of gentle birth must aspire. Marriage is the consummation devoutly to be wished for, literally and figuratively, and here it is, but I'm..."

She looked small and bewildered by the grimy window. Also remote.

"Della, may I ask you something?"

She nodded.

"Why did you run off with Chastain?"

She crossed the room and took a seat on the sofa. This being the guest parlor, and seeing little use, the sofa was a lumpy castoff that looked more comfortable than it was.

"Not here," Ash said, extending a hand to her. "The family parlor, to use a euphemism, is more commodious."

He escorted Della down the corridor and sent up a silent prayer that Sycamore had put away his naughty prints.

"A bachelor lair," she said, picking up one of Sycamore's prints. "And this passes for art in such an establishment."

"Sycamore collects satirical prints, but his tastes tend to the pruriently satirical. He'll take that with him when he leaves." Or Ash would burn the damned thing.

The family parlor was warm, the furniture comfortable, and the carpet slightly worn. Ash had spent many an hour in here tending to ledgers, budgets, and invoices.

"Sycamore and I have our best rows here," Ash said, poking some air into the fire as Della untied her bonnet ribbons. "We agree that arguments in front of the staff are ill-advised, so this has become the arena where we verbally spar. Might I take your cloak?"

Della made no move to take it off, so Ash undid the frogs.

"Will we have rows, Ash?"

"Very likely. You will scold me, I will grumble at you. The Coventry or Sycamore will annoy me, and you will have a megrim exactly when I most try your patience." He drew her cloak from her shoulders and draped it over the chair behind the desk. "Then we will make up, as newlyweds do, and all will be well again. Tell me about Chastain."

With a flick of her wrist, she sent her bonnet twirling in the direction of a coat rack in the corner, such that the bonnet landed precisely on the only empty hook.

"Good aim, my lady."

"An easy target." She smiled wanly. "I am ashamed of my behavior with Chastain. I behaved impulsively, and when I behave impulsively, the result is usually disastrous."

Was she marrying impulsively? "Let's sit, and if you are hungry, I can put together a tray. We have a warming pantry arrangement on this floor, and a full kitchen is downstairs, though we often eat at the club." That would have to change once Della became the lady of Ash's house.

She took a seat in a corner of the sofa. "I am not hungry. I like this room."

She did not invite Ash to take the place beside her, but they were to be married, and at some point, courtesies could become absurdities.

"About Chastain, Della?" he asked, joining her on the sofa. "Were you truly eloping with him?"

She shook her head. "I am the last unmarried Haddonfield, and this is such an abomination against the natural order that all of my siblings—there are eight, counting Ethan, not to mention their well-intended spouses—have conspired to bring the universe back into harmony. They fling bachelors at me as if they were sowing seeds in a biblical parable. Did you know that half the City is earnestly attempting to marry their sons to women from titled families?"

"I was aware of that trend." Ash rested an arm along the back of the sofa. "And half the peerage is trying to marry their sons to the daughters of wealthy cits."

Della hunched forward. "Much desperation results."

"Were you desperate?"

"I missed you desperately."

Nice try. "I missed you too. About Chastain."

"Town has emptied out. The shooting is well under way, opening hunts around the corner, the house parties have begun, and still here I am, stuck in London. I was at some card party or other, partnered by a strutting twit who could not keep his hand off my skirts beneath the table. I excused myself from play and determined then and there that I was finished.

"No more smiling while my person is disrespected, no more standing up with men who hope to waltz away with my settlements, no more bad jokes about pocket Venuses and small packages."

Ash mentally eliminated two phrases from his vocabulary. "You were angry."

"I was desperate. I think I was born desperate."

While Ash's burden had been to be born despairing. "You took desperate measures?"

"I thought I was being practical, clever even. Chastain wanted out from under his betrothal, I wanted to be sent home having narrowly escaped disgrace. My plan went awry. Chastain's father took much longer to catch up with us than he should have. Chastain became quite inebriated, and instead of having a cleverly engineered, narrow escape quietly hushed up, I am all but ruined."

Ash drew her back against his side. "You are all but married. A very different prospect, I hope."

"Can we let the business with Chastain drop, Ash? I was foolish, and he was a cad, but the whole matter is behind me, and there's little point in revisiting it again."

Ash would let the matter drop, though Della's explanation rang hollow to him. Not false, but not entirely true. She was leaving out pertinent details, the sort of details that could get Chastain called out, no doubt.

Ash wrapped an arm around Della's shoulders, wanting nothing so much as to ease the tension she still carried. "Chastain's father has procured a special license. Young William will soon be the lawfully wedded husband of Mademoiselle Clarice Fontaine."

"How do you know that?"

"When I arranged for our special license, I made a few discreet inquiries."

Della relaxed against him. "Thank you. I wish Miss Fontaine only the best of luck. She will need it, if she's to manage William."

Ash wanted to ask Della more questions: Why should William's impending nuptials be a source of relief to Della? Why should they be of any interest at all to her? If Della wished Miss Fontaine only the best of luck, why steal away with the woman's intended?

But then, desperation had its own logic, as Ash well knew.

"I've missed you," Della said, cuddling closer. "It's a happier sort of missing you than what I've endured previously, but it's still missing you."

"Odd, isn't it, how that works? I've been a human whirlwind these past three days, sending letters in all directions, haggling with your brother—I still haven't found you a morning gift—but the missing-you part is always there. The longing for you. Should I have made love with you in the conservatory, Della?"

She skated a hand over his falls, where nascent arousal was—as usual, when he was close to Della—clearly in evidence.

"Why didn't you?" she asked, casually stroking him through his clothes. "Why did you deny yourself what was on offer?"

He could not be entirely honest. He'd been wary of her eagerness, sensing in it something of contrivance. He'd been unwilling to risk conception when no settlements were agreed to. He'd been emotionally unprepared for that degree of intimacy, which, with Della, would have been more binding than any proposal.

But he did not have to lie. "I still think I will wake up and find myself at my desk across the street, the sound of laughter and conversation a dull roar beyond the office door. I think—I fear—that our engagement will be snatched away and that this will have been a fever dream or a form of derangement. You are my heart's true delight, Della. That I am to have you for my own boggles my mind."

She arranged herself straddling his lap, a position she seemed to like and Ash loved. "I have the same fear. My Ash will be snatched from me, and I will be thrust again into the arms of any half-sober fortune hunter or bachelor uncle. I could not bear to lose you."

Had that been what had driven her boldness? "You won't lose me, Della. By this time Monday, we will be man and wife."

She curled down to rest her head on his shoulder. "I am indisposed, or I would drag you by the hair to your bedroom and finish what we started in the conservatory, Ash Dorning."

How casually she confided the intimate details of her biology. "Are you uncomfortable?"

"Not a bit. I am inconvenienced. You needn't buy me a morning gift."

Wrong. "What sort of gift would you advise?"

They fell to teasing then, while Ash enjoyed the torment of frustrated arousal, along with a sense that he and Della were growing closer. They hadn't quite cleared the air where Chastain was concerned, but they'd put the matter to rest.

"What have you found to occupy yourself," he asked, "while I have scrutinized every shop on Ludgate Hill?"

"Tidying up my social calendar," Della said, "sending regrets to events I've been invited to. I don't want to be an object of talk, no matter how eagerly the hostesses would welcome me."

"We need to put in an appearance at a few gatherings," Ash said, stroking her hair. "Show the flag, weather the gossip, be publicly besotted."

Della kissed him. "I am besotted."

"As am I."

She regarded him, as if considering where to kiss him next. "I was invited to a house party at Lady Wentwhistle's estate. I haven't sent regrets yet. That will be a relatively quiet affair."

"Her property is in Sussex? No, Surrey, and from there I could take you to Dorning Hall. My mother was a crony of hers. She ought to be something of an ally."

Having been kissed, Ash was now hungry for more kisses. Appeasing that hunger was foolish, because it aroused him further. Before he was once again pleasuring himself while Della looked on—though, would that really be so bad?—he made a decision.

"Accept Lady Wentwhistle's invitation," he said. "Tell her you will bring along your new husband. We will make our debut as a couple in congenial surrounds, and by next spring, we will be old news."

Della curled into his embrace. "My besotted and inventive new husband. I have dreamed of you, Ash Dorning."

The feel of her nestled against him was sublime torment. "I have dreamed of you too, Della. How much longer will you be indisposed?"

"Until Tuesday, probably. Bad timing, I know."

"Anticipation will double our joy." And likely wear out Ash's right hand too. His frustration was a passing aggravation compared to the delight of holding Della and anticipating more intimate pleasures with her.

A thought stole through Ash's joy, like an eddy of cold air in a cozy parlor. *This can't last. This joy cannot last.* He was resigned to the normal cooling of infatuation that befell every couple as love matured. He was terrified, though, of his personal beast, which could steal not only the present joy, but any hope of future joy as well.

He closed his mind to that fear, kissed his intended, and resumed teasing her about morning gifts, bridal nerves, and how a newlywed groom would comport himself at a house party.

CHAPTER NINE

"I love weddings the same way I adore children," Sycamore said, accepting a flute of champagne from a passing waiter and taking a glass for Tresham too. "As long as I am neither groom nor papa, the whole business is delightful."

He'd stood up with Ash for the ceremony, there being no other Dornings within hailing distance, while Tresham had stood up with Della. Sycamore handed over the second flute and touched his glass to Tresham's.

"To happily married siblings." Who were at the moment standing by the hearth, beaming at each other and accepting good wishes with the slightly dazed good cheer of the very recently wed.

Tresham saluted with his glass and sipped. "I was not included in the settlements negotiations."

The champagne was lovely, light, a bit sweet, and bubbly enough to tingle the nose. "Why should you be?"

"Because I am Della's brother." Tresham stated this fact as if it equated to being a royal duke.

"Until a few years ago, you were nothing to her."

"Then I returned to London, she confronted me, and now we get on splendidly."

Della had not only confronted Jonathan Tresham, the wealthy heir to a dukedom, she'd inspired him into behaving as a long-lost brother ought to—discreetly, of course.

"She's your only sibling, and you're losing her," Sycamore said. "Makes a man think."

Tresham scowled at him. "I'm not losing her, you are not losing Ash, and besides, he's not your only sibling. Far from it."

Sycamore downed half his drink, for inebriation loomed as a worthy pursuit. "He might as well be my only sibling. You have no idea the injustices the youngest of seven brothers faces. How he must exert himself simply to be noticed in a forest of older, larger, worthier, more competent fellows."

Tresham pretended to admire a painting of some old Haddonfield patriarch from the days of William and Mary.

"Should I get out my violin, Sycamore? Does your 'Ode to Self-Pity' require accompaniment?"

Tresham had been raised as an only child, his education mostly under the direction of a fairly doting, titled uncle. He'd had his tribulations, of course, but Sycamore's compassion on this joyous day was limited to himself.

With perhaps a bit left over for Ash and Della, who were not embarking on the marital journey from the usual port of call.

"When my brothers were ready to mount up and tear across Dorsetshire on their ponies," Sycamore said, "Ash would wait for me. I needed to stand on a box to groom my pony. My brothers delighted in hiding the box."

"Is this an explanation for your singularly contrary nature?" Tresham asked, peering at the signature on the painting.

"In part. In a heap of siblings that large and that male, one must be contrary or starve." Not for food, but for notice, for consequence. "Ash was decent to me just often enough to prevent me from turning into the barbarian my brothers so often accused me of being. Witness, he was dispatched to ensure I did not fall on my arse with the Coventry, and he took on the challenge without complaint."

Ash had also taught Sycamore how to smoke a cheroot—without inhaling—how to calculate odds playing vingt-et-un, and how to drink without getting drunk. Though as to that, Sycamore was already a bit tipsy. He finished the rest of his drink and set down the empty glass.

"What will you do about the settlements?"

"How is one brother decent to another?" Tresham countered.

The litany grew longer the more Sycamore contemplated the topic. "Ash explained things to me. How to deal with women, how to not follow in Casriel's footsteps and become a father at too young an age. How to handle drink and avoid a wager I could not afford. How to wager shrewdly, though I cannot figure odds the way he can. What to expect at university. Why my mother didn't like me."

"Your mother didn't like you? A woman of discernment, apparently."

"She didn't like anybody but her cronies," Sycamore replied. "I needed Ash to point that out to me, and the poor woman did not like herself or her lot in life either." How could she, when she'd been a widow without means whose dunderheaded sons rode roughshod over her sensibilities? "I thought I was smaller than my older brothers. Ash explained that I was exactly the same size he'd been at a younger age. I wasn't smaller, I was simply younger, but to a boy of seven..."

Ash had shown him the doorjamb, whereupon Papa had pencil-marked the heights of several of the older brothers as they'd aged. Somewhere around son number four or five turning ten, the ritual had faded from family practice.

Tresham passed Sycamore his mostly full glass. "Does this lament have a point?"

Sycamore thought for a moment, the champagne having obscured that point. "Ash is my brother. He's also my friend."

Tresham's gaze went to the happy couple. Della said something, and Ash bent nearer to hear her over the hum of conversation in the parlor. The doors had been folded back to open the space so it flowed into the music room, and a Haddonfield female was adding harp music to the general din.

Casriel had tried playing the harp to cheer Ash up over the course of a very long, dreary winter. It hadn't worked.

The angle of Ash's body as he leaned closer to his new wife, the utter focus he gave her words, while pretending to attend to the room full of guests, made Sycamore want to smash his champagne glass against the hearthstones.

You cannot have him. He belongs to me.

"One is not entirely comfortable with the admission," Tresham murmured, "but I regard Della as a friend as well. She is fearless with me and loyal. But for Theo, I'm not sure I can say as much about any other living person."

"Exactly," Sycamore said. "Fearless and loyal. If she breaks his heart, I will... I don't know what I will do."

"And if he breaks her heart... the same. The question thus becomes, what can we do to ensure nobody's heart is shattered unnecessarily?"

That was a backhanded invitation to conspire and the best news Sycamore had heard all day. "The newlyweds are off to a house party, and I have been invited to the same gathering."

Tresham's dark brows rose. "Have you?"

Invited was something of a fabrication. "Lady Wentwhistle was friends with my sainted mother. I am unwed, an earl's son, gorgeous, charming, witty, an excellent dancer, kind to animals, fond of children, and—because all that doesn't matter—notoriously randy and increasingly well to do. She allowed as how I would make a handsome addition to her gathering."

"She feels sorry for you, or she has a goddaughter who hasn't taken."

"She has more godchildren than Napoleon had mistresses. Did your sister just kiss my brother?"

"And he kissed her back. Such is the nature of the institution, Dorning. Gratuitous affection, liking, babies. You mustn't be jealous. Perhaps Lady Wentwhistle can fix you up with one of her goddaughters."

"I am willing to take that risk, which tells you how worried I am for my brother." And for Della. Not even the champagne could pry that admission from him.

Tresham took another pair of flutes from another passing waiter. "Ash has married an agreeable and intelligent female, Sycamore. He hasn't bought his colors to join a regiment in India. Della appears smitten, and all should—"

Sycamore took the second glass of champagne and waited for Tresham's brain to catch up with his bloviating mouth.

"You're worried about the melancholia," Tresham said, peering at his drink. "I am too."

Tresham, as silent partner and former sole proprietor of the Coventry, still had the run of the premises. He'd seen Ash's bad days as few others outside of family had.

"Ash is doing better this year," Sycamore said, "and marriage ought to have a salubrious effect on any fellow's humors,"—marriage to Della Haddonfield, anyway—"but Della hasn't seen him at his worst."

"If he's violent..." Tresham's gaze promised that Sycamore, having allowed this union, would pay as high a price as Ash should Della come to harm at her husband's hands.

"He's not violent, not like that. He loves a good boxing match—a little too much—but when the sadness is upon him, it's as if all spark, all energy has departed. You could beat him to flinders, and he'd barely notice."

"You've tried?"

"I tried slapping some sense into him once. The lack of reaction from a man who prides himself on the use of his fists was eerie." Terrifying, in fact, as if Ash were already dead, and his body couldn't be troubled to climb into a coffin.

"What's to be done?" Tresham asked.

"I will attend Lady Wentwhistle's house party," Cam said. "You will keep an eye on the Coventry for me."

Tresham's posture radiated offense. "I promised Theodosia I wouldn't..."

Sycamore held up a hand. Mrs. Tresham took a very, very dim view of gambling, having seen how that activity could pass from recreation to obsession. Tresham's decision to sell the Coventry was entirely the result of Mrs. Tresham's opinion on the matter.

"You need not be visible," Sycamore said. "We have good managers, and I won't be gone more than a fortnight. I want to tell the staff that they can consult you should something untoward arise. You are still an owner, and you know the business intimately."

"I must ask Theo." Tresham did not appear ashamed to be asking his wife's permission, not in the least.

"I already did," Sycamore said, swilling the whole glass of champagne at one go. "Your lady wife made no objection. She understands that I am concerned for my brother and you are concerned for your sister. Now hand over that glass. I have yet to congratulate the happy couple, and the task requires fortitude."

Tresham passed over his champagne. "Tell me something, Sycamore. Were you in love with Della, perhaps a bit inconveniently smitten?"

Sycamore held the glass. He did not drink from it. "With Lady Della? Don't be ridiculous. I am in love with myself, or so the family lore goes." He saluted with his champagne and sauntered off in the direction of the newlyweds.

~

DELLA HAD SPOKEN her vows confidently, but as Ash had recited his, her chest had gone tight. He was promising to forsake all others and cleave only unto her, for better or for worse. The magnitude of his oath, offered with such a gravely affectionate smile, had threatened her composure sorely.

"How quickly do you suppose we can leave?" Ash murmured when they had a break from the well-wishers.

He had a way of bending near, of almost nuzzling Della's ear while whispering to her, that made her knees go unreliable.

"Not for another thirty minutes," she said. "Some guests are still at the buffet."

Sycamore approached, holding a champagne glass like a royal orb. "Ready to flee out the nearest window?" he asked.

"Yes," Ash replied, just as Della said, "Don't be silly."

"With me," Sycamore said, "you will soon learn to be honest, my lady." He took a deep drink of his champagne, while gazing at her over the rim of his glass. The gesture came off more accusing than flirtatious. "I am known in the Dorning family as the sibling who ferrets out all secrets."

"You are known in the Dorning family," Ash retorted, "as the pest who can't mind his own business. That's champagne, baby brother, not the last of the summer ale."

"And excellent champagne it is too. Why don't you fetch a glass for your bride?"

Della did not want Ash to leave her side. "I'm not—"

"Shoo," Sycamore said, waving his free hand. "If any dragons should happen by, I am more than competent to protect the damsel in your absence."

Ash kissed her cheek. "I'm sorry. The family tree boasts a half-dozen more much like him, but we need only deal with them on holidays."

He wove away through the milling guests, leaving Della to smile at her new brother-in-law. "This is the part where you tell me I'm looking radiant, and you would envy your brother terribly, but for the fact that you are now blessed to count me among your family connections."

"You were among my family connections before this wedding," Sycamore said, "and you look a bit knackered, to be honest."

Sycamore offered that observation in a less than kindly tone, which made the tight feeling return to Della's chest. She studied her hands rather than meet Sycamore's gaze.

Her left hand sported a sparkly gold ring, which Ash had somehow purchased and had sized to fit her finger. She'd taken off her gloves to make a pass through the buffet, then set her plate aside, untouched.

Perhaps that accounted for a vague heaviness of spirit, much like an impending crying spell.

"I am tired," she said. "Preparing for a wedding on short notice was taxing. If you have something to say, Sycamore, say it."

He nodded. "Better. Here is what I have to say. Don't hide the truth from me, Della Dorning. I'll eventually figure it out anyway, and you are family now. We are supposed to trust one another."

An awful weight settled in the pit of Della's belly. William Chastain had frequented the Coventry. He'd bragged of his wagering to her, laughing about losses that would have sent many a man off to the country to hide from creditors.

What else had he bragged about and to whom? "What do you think you know, Sycamore?"He took another speculative sip of his drink. "I know my brother has frailties and that you are a new bride who has not enjoyed a long engagement. If Ash should run into difficulties, you won't try to manage on your own, agreed? His siblings know him, we love him, and we won't let any harm come to him. If he falters, you will call for reinforcements. Your word on that, please."

His tone was imperious, almost threatening, and Della wondered why anybody would ever describe Sycamore Dorning as frivolous or hotheaded. He had a coldness in him that surprised and intimidated.

"You'd take my husband away from me?" The heaviness in Della's belly turned acidic and anxious. She liked Sycamore, she'd even to some extent trusted him, but that self-possessed, flirtatious, casually confident version of him was nowhere in evidence.

Sycamore looked like he'd say more, but Ash returned, bearing a flute of champagne.

"Stop annoying my bride," Ash said, passing Della the drink. "Be a good brother and tell whoever is playing the harp that it's time to enjoy the buffet. I am ready to pitch that instrument through the nearest window."

Sycamore passed Ash his glass of champagne. "Feel free to leave," he said. "I'll make your excuses to the assembled gawkers." He leaned over and kissed Della's cheek. "I meant what I said."

He strode away, his charming smile once more in place.

"He means well," Ash said, putting Sycamore's glass on the mantel. "What was he haranguing you about?"

"I'm not sure." Della set aside her glass, untasted, as well. "Might we depart?"

Ash looked at her—truly inspected her person—and took her hand. "Slipping away quietly is not the done thing, but then, we'd best begin as we intend to go on, and that will mean disregarding convention from time to time."

He led her from the room, and while that provoked a few indulgent smiles from the guests, nobody started a fuss.

"Just keep walking," Ash said, "as if we're nipping out to the garden to enjoy some fresh air."

The afternoon had turned unseasonably warm, almost balmy, and a few guests had taken their plates out to the terrace.

Ash strode on, pausing only long enough to pass a shawl and bonnet to Della in the foyer and drape a cloak over her shoulders. He tapped his hat onto his head, collected his walking stick, and ushered her out into the afternoon sunshine.

The Dorning town coach stood at the foot of the steps, matched grays in the traces. "My carriage is not magical," Ash said, escorting her down the steps, "but magical things can happen inside of it."

"Things like peace, quiet, and privacy?"

"Those too. In you go." He took the place beside her on the forward-facing seat, an aberration Della rather liked.

"I never realized what an ordeal a wedding day is," she said. "How the hours drag and how ritual weights the whole business." How people felt entitled to stare and how every smile hid questions.

Exactly how ruined was the bride? Did the groom care? Had he been bought? Had he sampled her wares before making his decision? Was the bride's figure perhaps a trifle fuller than it had been in spring?

Della had seen those questions, smiled, and clung to Ash's side through them all.

Ash thumped his fist against the roof. "You are my wife now. I like that part of this day rather a lot. I do not like my brother trying to play nursemaid on my wedding day."

Was that all Sycamore had been about? "He worries for you, but I suspect he also worries about how he'll go if you should decide to leave the club."

Ash doffed his hat and set about untying the ribbons to Della's bonnet. "He does worry, and he keeps it all very much to himself. Cam is the proudest man I know, which, considering Worth Kettering is among my in-laws, is saying a great deal." He loosened the ribbons and lifted the bonnet from Della's hair, careful not to disturb her coiffure. "Come here, Mrs. Dorning. I have been mad to put my arms around you."

She went into his embrace gratefully as the horses clopped along at a walk. "Do you think about leaving the Coventry?"

"I hadn't. I make a handsome living there, the revenue allows me to invest in other properties, and Sycamore can't handle it on his own. He could hire a bookkeeper, manager, or second-in-command, but he needs a minder. Don't tell him I said that."

"I suspect he already knows."

Minutes passed in blessed, peaceful quiet, while Della rested against her husband—her *husband*—and counted backward from one hundred in French. She was only a little anxious, not recite-the-alphabet-backward anxious.

"Sycamore was warning you about my melancholia, wasn't he?"

Ash sounded very unlike a happy bridegroom. "I don't know whether to pummel him or thank him."

"He reassured me that if your spirits sink, your family is still available to care for you. I wasn't sure whether to pummel him or thank him either."

"My spirits likely will sink," Ash said, pulling the shades, "but not today. How about a kiss for your doting husband?"

They kissed and cuddled and held hands the rest of the way back to Ash's apartment—their apartment—and Della was able to relax more as they journeyed closer to their new home. They would not have a wedding night with all the trimmings—she was still indisposed —but she and Ash were married.

What God had joined, no man could put asunder, at least not without expensive lawsuits and an act of parliament. The finality of being married comforted Della as little else could.

She hoped it comforted Ash as well.

∼

FOR A TIME IN HIS YOUTH, Ash had been fascinated with his cock. The pleasure it yielded was amazing, a secret delight that—he suspected this was typical of the young male—struck him as a wonder of nature intended solely for his discovery. He'd pleasured himself frequently, and making the intimate acquaintance of the female of the species had only enlarged his circle of wonder.

He might scoff at Sycamore's declarations about loving a good romp, but he also understood the sentiment, at least when he was well. When he was unwell, an absence of sexual desire was among the most alarming manifestations of his illness.

He not only felt no desire, he felt undesirable.

And thus, his lack of dismay at being unable to enjoy a typical wedding night with Della troubled him somewhat, but then, he knew the vows would soon be consummated, and he most assuredly did desire his bride.

Ash had had the apartment thoroughly cleaned and aired, making the place altogether brighter and fresher. Della's trunks sat in the middle of the formal parlor, irrefutable evidence that life was changing. They would be loaded into the traveling coach tomorrow, along with Ash's effects, and a sort of wedding journey/come out would ensue for Ash as a husband.

"You're quiet," Della said, passing him her cloak. She kept the shawl about her shoulders as she tossed her bonnet onto the peg usually reserved for Ash's top hat. She truly did have extraordinarily good aim, at least where millinery was concerned.

"I am relieved," Ash said, putting his hat on the peg Sycamore typically used. "The wedding, lovely as it was, still had some qualities of an ordeal. Come here."

She went into his arms as if they'd been married for years instead of hours. "I forgot to eat, or I was too nervous to eat."

"Nervous? I would never have guessed. Excited, perhaps. Eager to be alone with your handsome husband. Should I have carried you over the threshold?"

She kissed his cheek, then eased away. "We're not *that sort* of couple."

Whatever did she mean? "We should find a tray of sandwiches and some lemonade in the family parlor. I didn't eat much myself."

They did justice to the tray companionably, and by the time their plates were empty—Ash had been hungry, too, come to find out—Della was yawning. Ash made it a point to carry her over the threshold of the bedroom—he was *that sort* of husband—which provoked much laughter from his bride.

She undressed him as efficiently as any valet, and he served as her lady's maid. When they climbed into bed and cuddled up, spoon-fashion, Ash's desire was a barely noticeable current, a mere ember buried beneath fatigue and maybe a little sadness.

He brushed Della's hair away from his mouth and wrapped a companionable arm around her waist. She sighed, wiggled, and went silent, her breathing easing into a slow rhythm, while Ash pondered the day's developments.

Was he sad? Well, yes, perhaps.

His bachelorhood had died as he'd spoken his vows, not that bachelorhood deserved a wake. His freedom had died as well, for every decision—whether to eat at the club or dine at home, to attend divine services or catch up on sleep, to pleasure himself or make love with his wife—now involved another precious soul, and that was a profound change indeed.

If his loneliness had also expired upon the occasion of marriage, then the bargain was well met. Except, lying in bed with his arms around his wife, Ash's loneliness had not died—not yet—and neither, he suspected, had Della's.

He drifted off, reassuring himself that becoming a couple took time, and he would doubtless feel differently after a few weeks of marriage.

~

"YOU ARE among the first to arrive," Lady Wentwhistle said, wrapping Ash in a polite hug. "Your mama would be pleased, Ash Dorning. Quite pleased indeed." She let him go and turned a less effusive smile on Della. "You have made quite a catch, my lady. Quite a catch. The circumstances of your nuptials will doubtless cause some talk, but what house party doesn't benefit from some salacious gossip?"

Della was too tired to do more than smile politely at that blatant insult.

"Mrs. Terry will show you to your room," Lady Wentwhistle said. "We're having an informal buffet tonight and tomorrow night. Once all of the guests have arrived, the more formal entertainments will begin. I hope you won't mind that you're sharing a room?"

"We're newly wed," Ash replied, beaming at Della. "Why waste a second bedroom that won't see any use?"

"You Dorning men take after your father," Lady Wentwhistle

said, gesturing to the housekeeper. "Which suggests you, too, might have a large family. Until this evening."

Della managed another curtsey and followed the housekeeper up a set of steps that seemed to have no end. The day had been long and fraught, with a horse going lame, muddy roads, a near accident occasioned by a trunk coming unmoored, and an odd lack of conversation with Ash.

Perhaps facing the gossip Lady Wentwhistle so clearly relished left him nervous too.

"You aren't in the guest wing," the housekeeper said. "This is the unused part of the family wing, and I think you'll find it quieter. The views are lovely, and you're not far from the footmen's stairs if the gentleman would like to nip down to the terrace for an evening smoke."

She pushed open a door carved with leaves and vines and led the way into a little parlor done up in oak wainscoting and burgundy upholstery. The drapes were burgundy velvet, the desk an ancient literary fortress in dark oak, and the marble of the fireplace shaded brown.

A thoroughly masculine space—also nearly gloomy.

"The bedroom is through that door," Mrs. Terry said. "We'll send up a footman to light the lamps no later than seven of the clock, but sconces in the corridor are kept lit throughout the day. A maid will be along with a tea tray in the next quarter hour or so. If you need anything else, please use the bell-pull."

She curtseyed and would have withdrawn, but Della stopped her.

"Would a bath be possible?" she asked. Her wedding night approached, or as good as, and she was both stiff and travel-stained.

"Of course, my lady. We'll have the tub up here in less than an hour." She popped another curtsey and withdrew, closing the door behind her.

"Not exactly a cheerful room, is it?" Ash asked, going to the window. "At least our portmanteau has arrived."

The little trunk sat before the cold hearth. No telling when the rest of the trunks would appear. "Perhaps we should light the fire," Della said. "The sun is out for now, but evening approaches."

Ash came away from the window. "Would you like to change into a dressing gown?"

Della had eschewed the services of a lady's maid—she was a new bride, for pity's sake—and appreciated Ash's solicitude.

"Let's wait for the tray to arrive, then I'll change."

"I'd forgotten this place has a maze," he said. "As boys, my brothers and I played there by the hour. Every large family should have a maze."

Della suppressed a shudder. "We have a maze at Belle Maison. Susannah fell asleep reading there one summer afternoon, and Mama nearly had an apoplexy when Suze didn't show up for supper. After that, the earl gave orders to have the hedges cut to waist height."

"You don't refer to him as your father?"

They had so much to learn about each other. "When his lordship was alive, I called him Papa. He was in every way an affectionate and doting parent. I think he worried that I would not feel loved once Mama died. Nick says that Papa felt guilty, that the old earl concluded Mama would not have strayed had her spouse been more devoted. Their marriage was a product of an earlier era, so who knows how they went on?"

Ash took a spill from the jar on the mantel. "Here is how we will go on. I will be faithful to you, and I expect faithfulness from you in return. We will be *that sort* of couple." He kissed her on the mouth, a now-see-here kiss, then disappeared into the corridor, returning a moment later with the spill lit.

He used the flame to start a fire laid on the parlor's andirons, then used another lit spill to start the fire in the bedroom hearth. This was probably a typical husbandly consideration, though Della had no way to know for sure.

"The heat feels lovely," she said. "A declaration of fidelity is also nice to hear. I will not play you false, Ash."

"My mother strayed too," he said. "Had an affair with one of my paternal uncles, or so we surmise. Whatever went on, my parents patched it up. My father was no Don Juan, but he was devoted to his damned botany and often left Mama at Dorning Hall for months at a time, awash in children, often with another baby on the way. I don't intend to be like him."

The tray arrived, the somewhat awkward mood did not dissipate, but the food helped fortify Della's spirits. She sat beside Ash on the sofa, passing him the salt cellar and the butter dish and realizing that he must have been famished.

"Will you assist me at my bath?" she asked when a platoon of maids had filled the tub.

Ash eyed the steaming tub, then dusted his hands over his empty plate. "If I assist you at your bath, there will be water everywhere. The tub is not big enough for both of us, though that would hardly dissuade me from my enthusiasm for your naked form."

"For my—?"

Ash passed her a glass of lemonade. "I could devour you, Della Dorning. All day in the coach, I was aware that the benches fold out into a surprisingly comfortable bed. You were indisposed yesterday, soon you won't be, and we are married."

"I'm not," she said, feeling an odd lightness of heart. "Indisposed."

Ash rose rather abruptly. "Enjoy your bath. I'm off to reacquaint myself with the maze. You might consider taking a nap after your bath, for I doubt you'll get much sleep tonight."

Another kiss, this one involving his tongue and his hand pressed to her breast, then he groaned and all but dashed out the door.

CHAPTER TEN

Della was a frequent bather, especially in winter, when the bath was one of few places she was genuinely warm. She eased into the tub Lady Wentwhistle's staff had provided and felt the day's worries drain from her mind.

She denied herself the pleasure of a leisurely soak and set about her ablutions. To leave London had been lovely, a relief without compare. True, she had also left her family, and any house party had its share of gossip and intrigue, but she was with her husband, and tonight they would consummate their vows.

The worries tried to crowd back, even past the anticipatory glee of a delayed wedding night, so Della busied herself washing her hair. By the time the tub had been taken away, and she was sitting before the hearth on a footstool, the worries were again nibbling at her peace.

Where was Ash? Did he already regret this marriage? Would Lady Wentwhistle stir the pot of gossip, or—for Ash's sake—make an attempt to shield Della from the worst of it? Would Ash think it very forward of his new wife if she awaited him naked in the bed itself?

Before the blazing hearth, her hair grew dry enough to braid, but she left it down. Weren't brides supposed to wear their hair down? How did one manage all those flowing tresses in bed? She rummaged in the portmanteau and found a thick pair of men's wool stockings to put on her feet, though they bunched at her ankles.

As darkness fell, she did not climb into the bed, there to await her husband, but instead unpacked the portmanteau, putting the clothes in a lavender-scented wardrobe and verbena-scented clothes press.

Where was Ash? Had he come to harm? Been called back to London? Was he putting off consummation of the vows, and if so, why?

She was about to pour herself a cup of cold tea from the remains of the tray when Ash returned.

"Sorry to be so long," he said, tugging at his cravat. "I ran into an old chum from school in the stable, and he wanted to discuss the Coventry and..." He left off trying to undo his neckcloth. "Your hair is gorgeous."

"I didn't know whether to braid it."

"I'll braid it." He prowled closer, bringing with him the scent of hay and scythed grass. "I missed this privilege last night. Do you know how arousing I find the sight of my stockings on your dainty feet?"

"I was cold. I should have asked."

He bent close enough to whisper. "As long as I am the fellow taking the stockings off of you, you need never ask to borrow them."

A pleasant shiver passed over Della. "Let me help you out of your clothing, husband. I've missed you."

She got no further than divesting him of his cravat when a sharp rap on the door heralded the porters lugging in a pair of large trunks.

"I suppose I should find something to wear down to dinner," Ash said, passing the older porter a coin. "I can hardly show up in all my dirt."

Della waited until the porters had left, then locked the door behind them. "Ash Dorning, you will undress now. Wash if you want to, and I will lay out a set of clean clothes for you. You are married."

He rested his forearms on her shoulders, his hands gathering her hair. "I wandered the maze, trying to wrap my mind about my great good fortune, but all I could think about was getting you naked in that bed."

Della leaned against him. "I soaked in the tub, trying to wrap my mind around my great good fortune. All I could think about was getting you naked in that bed. I think we will suit very well, Ash." She'd thought about more than that, but intimacy with her husband had dominated her imagination.

Della had Ash's waistcoat half undone and his shirt unbuttoned when a loud triple-clang sounded from somewhere below.

He pulled the trailing end of the bow of her chemise. "That is the bedamned first dinner bell."

"We can miss supper."

He stepped back, and Della barely suppressed a growl of protest.

"I would rather we didn't, Della."

The first bell meant guests would assemble in the parlor in thirty minutes, when the second bell would be rung. The third bell would signal that the party was to proceed to the buffet or the table.

"We can be late, then," Della said, "and go down after the second bell."

Ash caught Della's hands in his own. "When I first make love with my new and delectable wife, I will need more than thirty minutes to do justice to the occasion. If we miss the meal, we will become objects of greater speculation than we already are."

"I want to stamp my foot and tear your clothes from your body, Ash. I have longed for you since the moment I first kissed you, and now I am to be thwarted by a supper buffet?"

"We are both to be thwarted, but I promise you, my lady, a delay now will only inspire me to greater passion later."

Della wanted both—the now *and* the later—and she did not want to face the whispers and sly looks at supper.

"Must we?" she asked, closing her eyes. "This house party seemed like a lovely way to start married life, with idle diversions, no family hovering, none of London's stink and bustle, but now... I want privacy with my husband, and there's none to be found."

Ash wrapped her in his arms. "I want privacy with you too, madam, but we must face the other guests sooner or later. We can plead fatigue and retire early."

"And to think I've often admired your practicality."

He patted her bum. "Let me braid your hair. We will be the picture of decorum as we go down to supper, and only we will know that the true dessert course will be served in our bedroom while the other guests gather around the tables for a hand of piquet."

Della made herself step back. "You promise we will retire early?"

"No matter when we withdraw, the other guests will remark our leave-taking. We will retire as early as decently possible."

Marriage meant compromise. Della had seen that with her siblings, over and over. In-laws, children, daily life... They all wore on a marriage, either forging it into a union or fraying its edges. In this case, Ash was right, and Della was being peevish for no reason.

"We will be married for decades, I hope," she said, smoothing Ash's lapel. "I can wait a few more hours to share a bed with you, but they will be long hours, Ash Dorning. Long, slow hours."

"Then be assured I will make long, slow love with you, Mrs. Dorning."

Dressing, by contrast, was accomplished with disappointing dispatch. Braiding Della's hair was the work of a moment for Ash, and by the time Della was ready for him to do up her laces, he'd seen to his ablutions and donned his evening finery.

"I'm a bit wrinkled," he said, passing Della's corset strings forward for her to tie off in front. "I suppose we'll all be a bit wrinkled this evening. You do have the most delicious fragrance, my lady. All honeysuckle and sunshine."

"I bring my soaps and sachets with me when I travel. May I ask a favor of you, Ash?" She was being ridiculous, but this first supper had taken on the proportions of an ordeal.

He remained behind her, a large dark presence reflected in the cheval mirror. "Anything."

"Don't let me out of your sight tonight. Don't wander off to smoke a cheroot with the fellows, don't disappear to the men's retiring room without telling me." If the meal was a buffet, the men would not remain at the table to enjoy their port, and Della would not be consigned to gossip and catlap with the ladies.

Ash met Della's gaze in their reflection. "You think the tabbies will pounce?"

"I know they will, and I'm prepared for their claws, but I'd rather not face them just yet." That wasn't the whole of Della's concern, but it was close enough.

"I don't blame you. We will be in each other's pockets all evening, then, and you will keep the curious and rude away from me too."

Della tied off her corset strings, donned her petticoats, and slipped her evening dress over her head. The gown was modest to a fault, the neckline worthy of an elderly spinster, the fabric an unre-markable brown velvet. Ash did up her hooks without being asked, and then the moment had arrived to go down to supper.

Ash offered his arm, and they were halfway down the main stair-case before Della felt the first wave of dread crash over her.

Not on the steps. Do not faint on the steps. Do not collapse on a stairway. She'd done that once at age eleven and given herself a fero-cious shiner. She had learned to take stairs quickly or not at all.

"Don't be nervous," Ash said, patting her arm as they reached the landing. "We will smile fatuously at each other all evening long and send each other melting glances. I will have only inanities to add to any conversation, and... Della, are you well?"

She hated that question. Hated it, but just then, she was not well. She was battling the sensation of a horse sitting on her chest and the certainty that the world was about to end.

"I'm fine. A bit tired."

They started down the second flight of steps. "As am I. I have little enough positive to say about the French army, but French roads are far superior to ours. Would you like to jaunt over to Paris in the spring?"

Breathe in. Pause. Breathe out. Pause. Breathe in... "Perhaps. I am anxious to see Dorning Hall."

Della was not merely anxious, she was in an immediate, irrational welter of panic. The problem had befallen her frequently enough that part of her mind could watch the situation and know it would pass, but the rest of her—the vast majority of her awareness—was caught up in the maelstrom.

Breathe in. Pause. Breathe out. Pause.

"You look a bit pale," Ash said as they made it to the bottom of the steps. "Are you chilly?"

"I forgot my shawl." In her current state, that oversight loomed as the mistake that would presage the destruction of the world. "I'll fetch it and be right back down." The dread became a crushing force in her mind, even as she told herself to just keep breathing.

"No need," Ash said. "I will happily retrieve it for you." He patted her hand again and trotted up the steps, leaving Della alone, barely able to speak, and certain that eternal damnation was at hand.

～

ASH HAD SOUGHT the stables in search of enough privacy that he could pleasure himself, though it wouldn't have been pleasure. It would have been taking the edge off in hopes of acquitting himself competently with his new wife.

Della was nervous, of that much he was certain. She'd been quiet all day in the coach. A thousand times, Ash had almost asked her if Chastain's pawing had truly fallen short of rape. To preserve Ash from dueling, she might lie about even that.

That Della had gained some experience with the Throckmorton bounder was no consolation. She'd been *relieved* to send her first lover packing, but a husband couldn't be as easily dispatched.

Ash fetched her shawl from the back of her vanity stool and

headed back down the corridor at an indecorous jog. Della had asked him not to leave her alone, and she waited until he rejoined her to go into the parlor.

The second bell sounded just as Ash nearly ran over some fool idling about in the middle of the corridor.

"Sycamore?"

"Ash." Sycamore bowed. "Have you taken to wearing a shawl in your dotage?"

"What in seven putrid purgatories are you doing here?" Though Ash had a suspicion, one that made him want to pummel his baby brother.

"I am preparing to comport myself graciously to all and sundry and to most especially charm any friendly widows. That was the second bell, if I'm not mistaken. Shall we go down, or would you like to put your shawl away first?"

"Damn you, I do not need a bear leader on my wedding journey."

"Perhaps wedded bliss has addled your wits," Sycamore said, turning to saunter toward the main steps. "This is a house party, a party which transpires at a house. This is not a wedding journey. Lady Wentwhistle was short a few handsome, debonair bachelors, and I allowed myself to come to her aid. If you and Della are underfoot while I'm having a bit of a frolic, that is nothing to me."

Sycamore was usually a better liar. "Who is managing the club?"

"Tresham is keeping an eye on things. It's not like we're off to darkest Peru, old boy, and the time of year is hardly our busiest. Why, if that isn't my darling sister-in-law at the foot of the staircase."

"Wait." Ash grabbed Sycamore by the arm when he would have descended the steps. "You will leave Della alone. You will leave me alone. You will not hover, you will not lurk. You will not try to be helpful or protective or any other polite term for your damned meddling."

"I never meddle. Marriage has made you crabbed and contrarious, Ash."

"Your arrival did that. Promise you will keep your distance."

At the bottom of the steps, Della stood unusually still, and Ash thought she'd edged closer to the giant potted ferns spaced around the Wentwhistle foyer.

"You promise me you won't interfere with my diversions," Sycamore said, jerking his arm from Ash's grip. "I'm told the Marchioness of Tavistock is among the guests."

Sycamore made that disclosure with just enough self-consciousness that Ash was supposed to think the pretty marchioness had inspired Cam's sudden interest in making up the numbers at a rural house party.

"Do not meddle," Ash said, starting down the steps. "I will pummel you to flinders if you are in any way bothersome, and I do mean pummel, and I do mean to flinders."

If Della had overheard this disagreement, she was politely ignoring it. Ash came around the landing, Sycamore at his heels.

"Della, look who I've found," Ash said, trying for a light tone. "Sycamore has inserted himself into the guest list in hopes of furthering his amatory interests."

Still, Della did not turn to greet them. She stood still as a garden statue, gaze fixed on nothing in particular Ash could discern. He reached her side and took her hand.

"Sycamore, make your bow to my lady wife."

"My lady." Sycamore bowed without attempting to take her hand. "A pleasure."

"Sycamore." Della nodded as Ash draped her shawl around her shoulders. "This is a surprise."

She clutched the shawl as if chilled, though the foyer wasn't all that cold.

"Ash must have neglected to mention my plans to you," Sycamore said. "Shall we repair to the guest parlor?"

"You never mentioned your damned plans to me," Ash said, "and you will take yourself off to the guest parlor like the unattached bachelor you are. My regards to the marchioness."

Sycamore must have sensed that he'd crossed a line. He for once heeded the dictates of the self-preservation instinct and took himself off.

"You are not glad to see him," Della said. "I don't suppose I am either."

"The degree to which I am 'not glad' to see my brother begs to be expressed in language unfit for a lady's ears. I'm sorry, Della. Sycamore is trying to be helpful, but I've told him to keep his distance lest I thrash him."

Della had apparently found a reserve of calm in the short time Ash had been away from her. Her features were serene, her composure vast. She wore her crocheted cream shawl like a celestial robe, and her posture radiated dignity.

"He meant well," she said, starting off at a sedate stroll toward the guest parlor.

"That will be Sycamore's epitaph." Though if heaven were merciful, Cam wouldn't need an epitaph anytime soon.

Della sauntered across the marble foyer at Ash's side, the hum of conversation growing louder as they approached the door to the guest parlor.

"Do you know what I'm looking forward to right now, Ash Dorning?"

Ash bent close enough to steal a whiff of her honeysuckle scent. "Taking me upstairs and having your way with me?"

"That too. I am looking forward to walking into that guest parlor on your arm and seeing the envious looks from all the ladies. Perhaps that's why we find Sycamore so near at hand. Now that you are no longer among the eligibles, he has a better chance of being noticed."

"You would have me pity the blighter." Though Della's reasoning had a ring of credibility. Sycamore's exaggerated sense of *amour propre* meant he might enjoy holding himself out as the last unmarried Dorning.

Della rearranged her shawl and took Ash's arm. They entered the guest parlor to find a crowd already assembled and Lady Wentwhistle making introductions. She did not acknowledge them specifically as they paused by the door, which suggested she was tossing Della to the tabbies.

A liveried footman came by bearing glasses of champagne. Ash took two.

"Whom do we know?" he asked quietly. "And would you like some canapés?"

Della pulled off her gloves and stashed them in a pocket, then accepted one of the glasses of champagne. "A little something to eat wouldn't go amiss, and we know half the room."

And yet, nobody approached them. Conversations went on, glances came their way, but nobody came near, almost as if this were a stage play, and the chorus awaited a specific cue.

"Why, if it isn't Lady Della," said a hearty male voice to Ash's right. "What a pleasure to see you... *again*. And Mr. Ash Dorning. Lady Della, do please introduce me to your new husband. I'm sure he and I have *much* in common."

William Chastain smiled at Ash. Della took Ash's hand as if she feared he would plant Chastain a facer or call him out.

"Chastain," Ash said, bowing. "How could you possibly forget? You and I have met on numerous occasions when luck has run against you at the Coventry's tables. Please do make your bow to my lady wife."

Chastain managed an adequate bow. "Felicitations on your nuptials, my lady." He sent an insolent glance at Della's décolletage and then lower. "And, Dorning, I'll cheerfully see you over a hand of cards, if you think to test my luck."

That was an oblique threat to call Ash out. Della's grip had grown desperately tight, and Sycamore was watching from across the room.

"You will excuse me if I decline that offer," Ash said. "I am newly wed and have better things to do than play piquet." He turned without bowing and led Della across to the sideboard where the canapés were on offer.

They hadn't quite reached their destination, and conversations had barely resumed, when the Marchioness of Tavistock curtseyed before Della.

"Felicitations on your nuptials, my lady, Mr. Dorning. I wish you every happiness." She was a willowy woman, auburn-haired, with strong features. Her age could not be much more than twenty-five, but her self-possession was that of a dowager. As a widowed marchioness, she was also very likely the ranking guest at the party, and her gesture all but compelled the other guests to follow suit.

Della stood hand in hand with Ash, graciously accepting good wishes for the next fifteen minutes, and her calm good cheer never faltered.

All the while, Ash was aware of two things. First, Chastain watched this little performance from a corner of the parlor, his expression hovering between snide and calculating.

Second, Della's hand was colder than a January night wind.

～

"I HAVE TO WONDER," William Chastain mused. "Did dear Mama know that Lady Della and her toady would be on the guest list? I believe she must have."

"Dorning is an earl's son," Francis Portly replied. Portly, whose build was actually on the lanky side, was a jovial sort who paid his debts graciously, though they were always the modest sums resulting from cautious play. "As toadies go, he outranks you, Chastain."

William arranged his cards. In any combination, they weren't much of a hand. "He's an earl's younger son, all but in trade, and he married used goods to keep her from ruin."

He tossed out a five of clubs, then realized that had been a poor choice.

Portly laid a ten on top of the five and moved his peg two points. "Dorning is an earl's increasingly wealthy son, and he married an earl's daughter, not some émigré's *little nun*, as you so ungallantly

refer to the new Mrs. Chastain. Besides, you are accounted responsible for Lady Della's ruin. Not well done of you, sir."

They had chosen to play this friendly game of cribbage in the
library rather than the cardroom, the better to make frequent use of
the decanter.

William had referred to his bride as a *little nun* often in Portly's
hearing. Clarice wasn't quite a nun—she hadn't insisted on having all
the candles out on their wedding night, for example—but she
certainly wasn't a siren. She was *modest* and *agreeable*, vexing qualities in a wife.

Lady Della, by contrast, had some fight in her.

William laid another five on Portly's ten. Portly finished the
pointing with a jack and moved his peg another hole.

"Portly, you wound me. I attempted to rescue a spinster from her
lonely fate, spare the fair Clarice a husband she didn't want, and you
paint me the villain."

"Count up your hand."

"A pair of fives." Fives were particularly valuable cribbage cards.
That a pair of them had yielded only two points was also annoying.

"Fifteen-two, fifteen-four, fifteen-six, and a double run for fourteen." Portly moved his peg about halfway up the board. "The settlements wounded you. I thought you'd never stop bellowing."

Portly had served as William's witness at the wedding and had
thus heard William's outrage as Papa had explained the details of the
arrangements. Even Clarice had seemed displeased that most of the
money remained under the collective control of the parents. William
was sure that provision had been added after he'd seen Fontaine's last
offer.

Clarice would doubtless attempt to bankrupt William with her
fripperies, but he'd teach her the folly of trying to manipulate her
husband. He was looking forward to it, in fact.

"I have never been reliant upon my parents' largesse," William
said, refilling his brandy glass. "Marriage won't change that."

Portly found another six points in his crib. "Marriage should change that. You are begging for a bullet between the eyes, Chastain, and the Dornings know their way around firearms. Your father's title will die out with you, and the fair Clarice will become a wealthy widow. Is that what you want?"

What William wanted was to see Lady Della and her devoted Dorning brought low. Della had broken her word. She had promised to tell Papa that the elopement was her idea and that she earnestly longed to marry William. Instead, she'd been yodeling to the rafters about *how dare you* and *this is not what we discussed.*

Her *volte-face* meant William was doomed to marriage with a woman who was about as interesting between the sheets as an old pillow. Clarice's complete lack of amatory enthusiasm added insult to indignity, and once William got her away from this infernal house party, he'd explain to her the welcome he expected to find in her bed.

"I'll ruin Dorning," William said, accepting the deck of cards from Chastain. "He's the gentlemanly sort. He'll be easy to ruin." William shuffled and managed to get the five of clubs from his sleeve back into his hand while Portly poured himself another drink.

"Have you seen Ash Dorning at Jackson's?"

"Bah. I can defend myself. Pugilism is a sport for men who have no good looks to risk. Dorning thought he'd be the knight in shining armor and make me look like the villain. I don't appreciate that. Tried to provoke me before supper too."

"You delude yourself," Portly said, picking up his drink and leaving his cards facedown. "I saw you slip the five of clubs up your sleeve, Chastain. If you think to cheat your way into a small fortune at this house party, you will have to do better than that."

William grinned. "Just keeping you on your toes, old boy, and you are right. I am only a passable cheat. I am a much better bully. Suppose I'd best be about it. The Marchioness of Tavistock is quite pretty for an older female, and she's wealthy enough to regularly gamble. I know a few things about her darling step-son."

Portly sipped his drink. "You will come to a bad end, and I will read your eulogy. I will comfort Clarice—and her inheritance—in her hour of need, and we will name our firstborn in honor of your sainted memory."

"A man after my own heart," William said, though he wished Portly the joy of Clarice's limited charms. "Seriously, I need to get my hands on some blunt if I'm to comport myself in the style to which a man of my station is accustomed. Keep your ears open, Portly. You never know when a bit of gossip will turn into more than a bit of coin."

"Pass me the cards," Portly said. "I was at the Coventry a few nights ago and heard the staff talking. Seems Ash Dorning was due to repair to the family seat again for the winter, and only Lady Della's situation changed his plans."

"What's so unusual about that?"

"He suffers melancholia so severe he must be removed from society for months on end."

William was not a superstitious man, but he did believe in his own good instincts. Those instincts warned him with a pleasant tingly feeling in the region of his cock when portentous news had been imparted. Beneath the table, he arranged himself behind his falls.

"Do go on, and don't spare the details."

"You'll let me have a turn with your curricle?"

The curricle had been payment for a debt of silence incurred by a beer baron's randy young son. "Of course, but you will not wreck my conveyance lest I emasculate you."

Portly dealt another hand—wouldn't do to appear to be merely gossiping and getting drunk should any busybodies poke their noses in the door—and began to recount what he'd seen and heard of Ash Dorning's little problem. Given what William already knew about Lady Della's little problem, the possibilities for lucrative mischief were endless.

～

THE EVENING HAD BEEN ENDLESS, but Della was at long last behind a locked door with her husband.

"You want to leave, don't you?" she asked Ash as she undid his cravat. "Want to be gone by morning." Della certainly did.

"Lady Wentwhistle was a friend of my mother's," Ash said, staring over Della's left shoulder. "She has clearly heard the gossip about you and Chastain, and she didn't see fit to whisper to you or to me that the bounder was among the guests. Perhaps Sycamore got wind of it, in which case why didn't he say anything to us?"

Della was almost glad that Chastain had shown up. She'd been all but overcome with panic simply standing at the foot of the steps. Had Chastain's ambush in the guest parlor not distracted her from that near disaster, she might have succumbed to her nerves before she and Ash had consummated their vows.

Instead, she'd spent the evening smiling until her cheeks ached and clinging to Ash's hand. Her nerves had held up, and the gossip-mongers had been thwarted.

This time. She undid the buttons of Ash's waistcoat and then those of his shirt. "We failed to provide the grand scene Lady Went-whistle was hoping for. Perhaps now the house party can settle into the usual semi-discreet debauches house parties are known for."

She turned and swept her hair off her nape. Ash made short work of her hooks.

"You are so calm," he said, slipping his arms around her waist. "So serene in the face of provocation. Is this the result of having so many older siblings? Sycamore takes a different approach to being the youngest."

"I am not calm. Inside, I am a pathetic mess, but pride prevents me from collapsing into a fit of the vapors." *Usually.* With Ash's arms around her, Della was tempted to say more. *Sometimes, I can hardly breathe. I have been known to faint from sheer terror when nothing terrifying is about. I am not entirely sane.*

William Chastain had used the words *hysterical* and *daft,* and he hadn't been wrong.

"You," Ash said, kissing her shoulder, "are the steadiest person I know, Della Dorning. If your abundant womanly charms, quick wit, and unstoppable determination didn't steal my heart, your sheer good sense would. I'll give you first crack at the privacy screen, while I warm the sheets."

He patted her bum affectionately, and some of the evening's misery fell away. At long, long last, Della—she was Della *Dorning* now—was to be intimate with her beloved, and what did a serious bout of nerves matter in the face of that great joy?

She moved behind the privacy screen and finished undressing. "I will meet William's bride," she said when she'd put the toothpowder to good use. "I'm not looking forward to that."

"And Mrs. Chastain is probably dreading the sight of you," Ash said. "But being ladies, and sensible, you will doubtless once again disappoint the gossips. We will be the dullest couple ever to partner each other at piquet."

"I'll avoid the tables if you don't mind," Della said, emerging from the privacy screen as she belted her night-robe. "Chastain is likely to spend most evenings at cards, and he is not to be trusted."

Ash was in a dressing gown as well, a purple silk banyan that picked up the color of his eyes. "I will happily pass on the cards as well, then. Chastain doesn't cheat that I've seen. He's at the Coventry often enough that we'd notice if he mishandled the cards."

A cheat was very bad for business. A gaming hell was technically an illegal establishment to begin with, and a crooked gaming hell was a doomed business. The Coventry Club was a supper club, to appearances. The authorities either knew it to have too many discreet exits to be productively raided, or they feared to find too many of Society's most powerful families ranged around the tables. King George happened by on occasion, as did his numerous brothers and their mistresses.

"Maybe Chastain doesn't cheat," Della said, taking the seat at the vanity, "but he doesn't play well either. It has been my misfortune to partner him, and my observation is, he makes the impulsive play that a moment's reflection would reveal to be the inferior choice."

Ash came to stand behind her. "Allow me." He withdrew her pins one by one, then undid her braid, putting the ribbon into the pocket of his night-robe. He brushed out Della's hair more patiently than any lady's maid ever had and took his time braiding it up again.

His touch was soothing and light, and by the time he'd tied another ribbon around the end of Della's braid, she was pleasantly drowsy. He dipped a hand into her night-robe to cup her breast, and the lassitude acquired an edge of desire.

"I like that," Della said, leaning back against his thigh.

"Mrs. Dorning." Ash bent low to whisper in her ear. "You appear to have misplaced your nightgown."

His hand on her bare breast was warm. His fingers brushing across her nipple created heat in the pit of Della's belly.

"I am about to misplace my dressing gown too," she said, "and I live in hope that you will do likewise."

He added a second hand so both breasts were gently palmed and stroked, while against Della's back, Ash's cock provided evidence of burgeoning arousal.

"I'll bank the fire," he said, withdrawing his hands. "You douse the candles."

Della would rather have feasted her gaze on her husband's candlelit nudity, but that would give him an opportunity to feast his gaze on her unclad form. Now that the moment was upon her, she was simply not that bold. She blew out the candles, draped her dressing gown over the foot of the bed, and climbed under the covers.

Ash stood for a moment by the hearth, his back to her. What was he thinking, and were his thoughts happy?

He banked the coals, pushing them to the back of the andirons so the room was cast in deep shadow. Della nonetheless noted a sheath soaking in a glass of water on the bedside table.

"I won't conceive," she said, "not this close to my menses. We need not use the sheath tonight."

Ash ambled over to the bed, draped his dressing gown atop Della's, and paused. "You're sure?"

"I'm as sure as a midwife's wisdom can be. Sheaths aren't foolproof either, you know." And good God, her husband was a magnificent specimen.

Della had enough light to know that Ash was aroused, well endowed, and happy to let her see that. He put a knee on the mattress and situated himself on all fours over her.

"You are not to be stalwart and composed with me in this bed, Della. You will tell me when I'm blundering, or when I could pleasure you better by slowing down, speeding up, or going about matters differently."

He hung over her, out of kissing range, and the covers came between them. "And will you be as forthcoming, Ash? Will you tell me what you like and how to go on as your lover?"

He laced his arms behind her neck. "God, yes. Kiss me."

Della obliged, her hands skating over Ash's chest and arms, until she was concocting vile curses aimed at the bedcovers.

"Damn you and your noble self-restraint," she panted. "Please get under the covers with me."

Ash sat back on his heels. "The covers are the only reason I *have* restraint, you daft woman. If you knew where I want to put my hands, my mouth, my cock..."

You daft woman. Even as a near endearment, the term stung. "And what about where I *want* your hands, your mouth, and your cock? What about my hands and my mouth?"

Ash flipped the covers off of her. "And your honeypot?" He stroked the curls between her legs, and the humor left his gaze. "Are you sure, Della?"

He brushed his thumb over a part of Della's body that Freddy Throckmorton had had a dozen names for, and no clue how to touch. Quim, muff, cunny...

"Do that again, please." Not that he'd stopped.

The mood shifted from playful to focused, with Della intimately exposed to her husband and racked by more desire than she'd thought possible. This was different from the interlude in the conservatory, because they were naked, on a bed, with all the time in the world.

And because this was merely a prelude to greater intimacies.

"You are so lovely," Ash said, applying a bit more pressure. "I could look at you all night." He used his free hand to caress her breasts, until Della caught him by the wrist.

"I want you inside me, Ash."

"Then you shall have me." He braced himself over her on his forearms and knees, but rather than join their bodies, he resumed leisurely kisses and slow caresses to Della's breasts.

"You are driving me mad," she whispered. "I vow I will seek revenge."

"Hence the term marital bliss. I want this to be perfect for you, Della." He raised up enough to peer down at her by the last of the fire's embers. "I have this idea, which I know to be foolish, that if I can get this right, then our marriage will be safe."

She brushed his hair back from his forehead. "I have the same idea. If I can get this right, our marriage will be safe. Maybe that means our marriage is already safe."

Ash kissed her again, nothing leisurely about it. As his tongue teased at her mouth, he teased at her sex with his cock, until by slow degrees, he thrust, she rocked, and they joined their bodies.

"You are delicious," Della said, locking her ankles at the small of his back. "Scrumptious and..."

He shifted up over her, changing the angle from scrumptious to whatever transcended scrumptious.

"You were saying?"

"Harder," Della said, gripping him with her legs. "Harder, please."

He laughed and, without speeding up, obliged her. Della felt as if he'd lit a Catherine wheel inside her, each thrust adding to the fire until every star in the night sky illuminated her from within.

When she would have screamed, Ash covered her mouth with his own. She lashed her arms around his neck and clung as the pleasure washed through her like a scouring storm. When the gale ebbed, she clung even more tightly.

Ash eased up enough that she could breathe and limited his movements to lazy, shallow thrusts. "Say something," he murmured. "I am in torments of uncertainty. Did you find satis—?"

"I found you." Della hugged him. "If I were any more satisfied, I'd have expired from an excess of pleasure." *How I love you.*

But to say that might make Ash think what she valued was his lovemaking. She did value his lovemaking, but also... *him.* The considerate, patient, attentive, passionate, luscious man she'd married.

The tenor of his movements shifted, becoming more sinuous. "Pleased to hear it. One wants to make a good first impression."

"Yes, one does, and I'm failing miserably. You will think me the most selfish of wives." She knew he hadn't let himself find completion, and that created an island of worry in a lake of contentment.

"I think you passionate," Ash replied. "And delectable, and my God... Della. I understand now why my married siblings are forever taking naps."

She laced her hands with his. "Yours too?"

They laughed, which caused interesting sensations in interesting places, and then Ash was driving her up again. Her fuse was short, and the resulting explosion was all the more spectacular. When Ash withdrew and spent on her belly, Della was too replete to remonstrate with him—and also too grateful.

CHAPTER ELEVEN

Della slept on beside Ash, her breath breezing across his shoulder. She had loved him witless not only before they'd fallen asleep, but also in the middle of the night, no sound save her gasps of pleasure and the soft creaking of the bed ropes. Della liked to hold his hands when she made love, lacing her fingers with Ash's and gripping him tightly.

He loved that. Loved that she sought every connection with him she could make.

He'd managed to withdraw both times, but it had been a near thing indeed. He'd have to work on his self-restraint, and what a fraught, delightful undertaking that would be.

Weak morning sun suggested the hour was upon them to rise, though Ash dreaded leaving the bed. This house party, which should have been an easy first outing as man and wife, was off on a decidedly troubling foot.

"So I did not dream last night happened," Della said, rolling to her back. "You are a revelation, Ash Dorning. Rather than make sentimental declarations, allow me to state that Freddy Throck-morton knew nothing. Less than nothing."

Ash would have liked to have heard her sentimental declarations. "I'm sorry. You trusted him, and he wasn't worthy of that honor. Do I ring for a tray, or shall we run the breakfast gauntlet?"

Della lay naked, one pale breast peeking from beneath the covers. "Must we?"

Ash touched a fingertip to her nipple and watched her flesh ruche from that simple caress. "Today, we must. You and Mrs. Chastain need to greet each other civilly, and I must ignore William."

Della traced Ash's nipple with the tip of her third finger. "I still don't want to let you out of my sight."

"If you keep that up, we will be late for luncheon, much less breakfast. I would not bet on supper either." And how he loved that she would make free with his person, no hesitation or missishness about her.

"The next time we get married, we are going on a true wedding journey, Ash. One where we can stay in bed for days, nobody knows us, and we recover from our bedsport with solitary picnics from which we return with leaves in our hair and grass stains on the knees of your breeches."

Rather than tempt fate, Ash left the bed. "We can make a leisurely journey over to Dorning Hall when we leave here, take our time and *all the pleasures prove*." He stirred the ashes on the hearth, then added half a scoop of coal to the embers. The chill in the air helped dissuade his cock from untoward ideas, though a surprising, naughty part of him liked parading about in the altogether for his wife's delectation.

"You will think me ridiculous," Della said, sitting up, "but I honestly do not want to be among these people without you at my side, Ash."

He considered his tousled, lovely wife as she piled pillows against the headboard.

"Staying close to you will be no imposition, Della, but please assure me that Chastain did not in fact force himself on you."

She gave the pillow a particularly hard smack. "He tried to force himself on me. I told you that. He and I had an agreement. We would essentially feign an elopement so that he could elude parson's mouse-trap, and I could retire to Kent in peace. We sent an anonymous note to his Papa, alerting him to our departure, but Papa Chastain was remiss in his duties, by a good eight hours."

Ash set about laying fresh clothing on the bed. "Do you suspect that William delayed delivery of the note?"

"I do now that I've had some time to think about it. He's sly like that, and mean."

"He frightens you." Ash took the place on the bed at Della's hip. "He can't hurt you now, not without getting past me first. Whatever he threatened, whatever he implied, you are safe from him."

Big words from a man who might in a week's time be unwilling to leave his room, but Ash meant those words nonetheless. Somehow, for Della, he'd make the effort no matter megrims, mulligrubs, or melancholia.

"What is that?" Della asked, shifting to peer at Ash's thigh.

"That is my mighty pizzle. You and he got fairly well acquainted last night." As the words left his lips, Ash realized exactly what *that* Della had referred to.

God damn the morning sun, anyway, though Della was bound to notice sooner or later.

"You are scarred," she said, brushing her thumb over the scored flesh on Ash's thigh. "How did this happen?"

He could joke, lie, prevaricate... He had with the occasional casual lover. But this was Della. Chastain had apparently lied to her, and that alone meant Ash would be truthful.

"I cut myself," he said. "Sycamore and I took to fencing with each other when it became clear that sparring in the boxing ring was ill-advised. He is quite good with a foil, better than I am, and he frequently pinked me."

Della's brows drew down. "*Pinked* you? I thought the blades were to have tips on them so nobody got hurt."

"For beginners, yes, but untipped foils make the whole business more interesting. Sycamore likes the mental advantage of drawing first blood, and I found those small wounds beneficial." Soothing, pleasant, luscious. Ash had all manner of shocking affection for small wounds.

Della reached behind him to retrieve her dressing gown, then extricated herself from the covers to sit beside him on the edge of the bed.

"This has to do with the melancholia, doesn't it?" She regarded the parallel scars on his thighs balefully. The wounds were small, about an inch across, a dozen on the inner side of each thigh.

How to explain the temptation to trade one pain for another? "If I cut myself, my mood improves. I suspect the resulting lift to the spirits rather than blood loss is why some physicians recommend bleeding for melancholia. The cut itself, that burning, stinging pain, can result in a soothing of depressed humors."

Della passed him his dressing gown. "I am at a loss for words. The scars don't look fresh."

Ash shrugged into his robe, and Della straightened his collar, adding a little pat to his chest. That she would touch him so casually was inordinately comforting.

"I stopped the cutting when I realized two things. First, the effects were increasingly temporary. I might feel a bit steadier for only a few hours, and for that I was risking infection."

Della took his hand and leaned against his arm. "Second?"

"Second, the knife was becoming more problem than solution. I cut myself on my legs so my brothers would not notice scarring on my arms or torso if ever I removed my shirt. King George indulges in regular recreational bloodletting for nonexistent fevers, while I became furtive about a few little nicks. I was making a ritual out of the cutting itself, looking forward to it, fretting over it, and hiding away my knife and bandages. I cannot control the melancholia, but I can stop myself from becoming partial to peculiar behaviors. Besides, the boxing is more effective."

Della knelt up on the bed and hugged him. "No wonder William

Chastain can't cow you. He's a mere whiny schoolboy compared to the foes you've faced."

She held Ash close, and a tension he had been carrying for a long time eased. "I would understand if you were appalled, Della. I'm appalled myself."

"I could never be appalled at your battle scars, Ash Dorning, nor should you be."

He wrestled her into his lap and hugged her tightly. She was wrong, of course. A grown man playing silly little games with a knife ought to appall anybody, but Della didn't see it like that.

Thank the merciful powers, Della didn't see it like that at all.

～

BREAKFAST BEGAN UNEVENTFULLY, with Della receiving only a few cool stares or curious glances as she and Ash availed themselves of Lady Wentwhistle's buffet. The breakfast parlor wasn't large enough to accommodate two dozen guests, so the gallery had been set up as a sort of mess hall.

"Not the corner," Della said as she and Ash paused just inside the gallery doors. "We don't want to look like we're hiding."

"There." He gestured with his chin toward a small unoccupied table in the more sparsely populated half of the room.

"That suits," Della said, preceding him between empty tables.

He seated her and went off to find them a pot of tea, while Della draped her shawl over the back of the chair and watched him go.

What a marvelous person she'd married. Ash was a passionate, inventive, tender, and sweet lover, and a formidable man. To manage the demons that drove him, while appearing calm and self-possessed, impressed her to no end.

She needed that same ability, to tame a dragon while looking as if she were petting a house cat.

"May I sit with you, Madame Dorning?"

The question was slightly accented and the speaker a lady whom Della had dreaded to meet.

"Mrs. Chastain, good morning. We have not been introduced." Inane thing to say, and Mrs. Chastain's smile suggested she agreed with that assessment.

She was of average height—meaning taller than Della—and attractive looks. She had dark hair and large dark eyes, a faintly olive complexion, and an ever-so-slightly strong nose. Her air, though, was one of good humor, and she was exquisitely kitted out in a blue velvet morning dress.

Clarice Chastain had that indefinable quality of *presence*, which eclipsed any defect Society might find with the size of her nose or the nature of her accent.

"We have not been introduced," she said, setting her plate on the table, "and yet, we have much in common. We must give the gossips something to whisper about, yes? William is lazy, he sleeps half the day away, and I am without company."

She seated herself, while across the gallery, Ash had been waylaid by Lord Wentwhistle.

"Please do join me," Della murmured. "My husband has gone in search of a teapot, but I hold out faint hope his mission will be successful."

Clarice folded her table napkin across her lap. "Your husband is better-looking than mine, but you must not tell William I said so. William suffers vanity upon vanity, worse than an aging rogue watching his handsome looks fade."

Della put her table napkin on her lap—ye gods, this woman was self-possessed—and fumbled for something to say.

"I'm sorry about the elopement. We weren't supposed to get farther than St. Albans."

Clarice split open one of two croissants on her plate. "You did me a favor. William knows he was ungentlemanly, and I will make him pay for that when the time is right. My papa added a bit to the settle-ments to tempt William back to good behavior, and I will make

William pay for that too. He has much to learn, so Papa made sure William's purse will be well managed by our parents. Don't you put butter on your toast, Mrs. Dorning?"

Lady Della. She was still Lady Della, but Della suspected Clarice was making a shrewd point by using the form of address that emphasized Della's recent nuptials.

She took a pat of butter from the butter dish and scraped it across cold toast. "Will you be happy with William?"

"I am happy enough. And you? Does Mr. Dorning make you happy?"

"Very. Our families were connected previously. I have long admired him." *And I admire him even more since becoming his wife.* Della thought of the scars on his thighs, the pugilism, the long winters in Dorset. She had married a warrior, though Ash would find that description baffling.

Clarice studied her over the jam pot. "You seem to be most genuinely enamored of your spouse. He is quite handsome. His eyes are wise."

Ash's eyes were beautiful too. "I really am sorry for the elopement."

Clarice set the jam pot by Della's plate. "I know why William ran off. He did not want to marry a dull stick. He is not ready to put away his toys, but then, few men do so willingly when they have been as indulged as he has. I do not understand why you would take your chances with a man of William's character. He is not always nice, and you are a diminutive female."

For a *dull stick,* Clarice was both perceptive and forthright. Della might admit to liking her were the circumstances different.

"I grew tired of being paraded before the eligibles Season after Season. All of my siblings are happily married, and they could not stop pairing me off with this spotty boy or that presuming heir. A failed elopement was to earn me retirement to the family seat in Kent."

"An understandable goal," Clarice opined, making a little moue while holding a piece of croissant before her mouth. "You did better than planned, eh? You are not banished to Kent. You are instead married to the fellow who is bringing us our teapot."

Ash approached the table, a tray in his hands bearing a teapot, cups, saucers, milk, and sugar.

"Good morning, ladies." He set down the tray and bowed to Clarice. "I don't believe we've been introduced."

Della appropriated the teapot. "Mrs. William Chastain, may I make known to you my husband, Mr. Ash Dorning. Ash, Mrs. Chastain. Please do join us."

Clarice waved her bit of croissant. "We are frustrating the gossips, Mr. Dorning. They would like to see us hissing and spitting like a pair of cats, but we refuse to oblige them. Lady Della grew weary of waiting for you to offer for her, so she took matters into her own hands, *et voilà tout*, you propose the marriage, and all is well. Lady Della is very clever."

The notion that Della had eloped as a stunt to get Ash's attention sounded just outlandish enough to appeal to the gossips.

"My wife is an exceedingly resourceful lady," Ash said, "and I am endlessly grateful that we are wed. Tell me of your family, Mrs. Chastain. Do your parents bide here in England?"

Ash likely knew exactly where her parents bided, how many acres they owned, where their wealth came from, and what they were worth. Running the Coventry meant knowing to whom credit should be extended, for whom a hansom cab should be called before the third bottle of port, and which straying wife was sleeping with which straying husband.

Ash and Clarice prattled on, about mutual acquaintances of mutual acquaintances, while Della ate toast and eggs.

"Perhaps you will fetch us a fresh pot, Mr. Dorning," Clarice said, turning big brown eyes on Ash. "Making new friends is thirsty business, but a lovely way to start the day."

Ash had little choice but to once again go in search of a full teapot.

"He loves you," Clarice pronounced when Ash was out of earshot. "That can be difficult, to start with love. Messy."

"I suspect starting without it can be difficult too. Lonely."

Clarice's air of friendly sophistication faltered. "What you say is true. William will be a challenge, particularly early in our marriage. I wanted to warn you, Mrs. Dorning. William bears grudges. He's furious with my papa right now, but he's also unhappy with you. That you and Mr. Dorning are well suited is an insult to William. I would not turn my back on him if I were you or Mr. Dorning."

"Are you threatening me, Mrs. Chastain?"

"*Mon Dieu, la fierté des Anglais... Non*, Mrs. Dorning. I do not threaten. The last thing I want is for William to becloud the early days of our marriage with more foolishness. I am asking for your assistance."

And she accused the English of having pride? And yet, Della understood the burning desire to be just another couple, just another new bride.

"I will do nothing to provoke William, and Mr. Dorning will also make every attempt to avoid further drama."

"My thanks, and here is Mr. Dorning with our fresh pot. You will excuse me, though, for I must consult with my maid regarding the attire in which a lady flies a kite. I did not foresee such a challenge when I packed for this house party. Mr. Dorning, good day."

She rose, curtseyed, and departed, leaving on her plate a croissant slathered in butter and jam.

"What?" Ash said, picking up the croissant and biting off an end.

"I do not know if she's very devious, very sweet, or both. She asked that we not provoke William."

"Which tells you," Ash said, pouring cups of strong, hot tea, "William hasn't been honest with her about the whole elopement. She doesn't know how badly he behaved toward you."

Della added sugar and milk to her tea. "She said William is angry with me, and I believe her."

"If Chastain misbehaves again, we will deal with him discreetly,"

Ash said, taking another bite of the croissant and getting crumbs everywhere. "Don't fret, Della."

If there were two words Della did not appreciate hearing in that calm, breezy tone, those words were *don't fret*. The new Mrs. Chastain had gone out of her way to warn Della not to provoke William, William knew things about Della that could ruin her despite her marriage to Ash, and all Ash had to offer was *don't fret*.

Della sipped her tea—and fretted.

～

"DID the ladies compare wedding nights over their breakfast tea?" Sycamore posed the question casually as Ash walked the path circling the exterior of the maze.

"Go flirt with the chambermaids, Cam. I haven't the patience to deal with you at present."

Sycamore fell in step at Ash's elbow. "As hard as they work, the chambermaids deserve a bit of flirtation, but alas, they are all nervous of house party bachelors. Where's Della?"

"None of your goddamned business."

Sycamore stopped to pluck a trio of Michaelmas daisies and arrange them as a boutonniere. The lavender color was only a few shades lighter than his eyes.

"The marchioness asked me to tell you that she is available to partner you or Della at whist should the need arise."

"My thanks, Sycamore, but please do not discuss my situation with your paramours." *And go the hell away.* Except Sycamore was like a wasp. Swat at him, and he hovered all the nearer.

"Her ladyship is not my paramour, but hope springs eternal in the human breast, or somewhere south of the breast. I do think she likes me. Widows grow lonely for want of affection, and I'm the friendly sort."

Ash came to a halt on the north side of the maze, where the tall

privet hedges shielded him and Sycamore from anybody peering out
of windows along the back of the house.

"You are the pestilential sort. Be off with you. Della has asked that I
remain by her side for the early days of this house party, and you are oblit-
erating what little solitude I have." That Ash should seek solitude troubled him, but then, no couple could thrive living exclusively in each
other's pockets, and a considerate new husband let his wife get some rest.

"You bungled the damned wedding night," Sycamore said, "and
you are testy and out of sorts as a result. How many times have I told
you the ladies like tenderness and laughter? They want cuddling and
sweet nothings, gentle kisses and adoring words. Not a lot of blighted
swordsmanship followed by sweaty snoring."

Ash resumed walking when he wanted to pelt off at a dead run.
"Why are you tempting me to draw your cork?"

Sycamore stuck to Ash's elbow like a nanny with her charge.
"Don't be daunted by a few fumbled overtures on the wedding night.
You have decades to improve your performance, and Della strikes me
as a lady who will let a fellow know where his work needs
improvement."

"Shut your mouth, Sycamore."

"Della is well?" he asked. "The fair Clarice didn't slip poison into
her tea?"

Della is none of your business. Ash refrained—barely—from
saying that and backing the warning up with a swift fist to Sycamore's
gut. He was stopped by many memories, of Sycamore struggling to
keep up with brothers who had longer legs, brothers who were twice
Sycamore's age, brothers who thought using words Sycamore didn't
understand was a clever sort of code.

"Della is quite in the pink. She's having a lie-down. There's not
enough breeze to fly kites anyway."

The weather was unsettled, like Ash's mood. Though the sun
filtered through a hazy overcast, the air was still and heavy, as if a
summer afternoon had been misplaced amid autumn's falling leaves.

"The point of flying kites is not to fly kites," Sycamore remarked. "Will you participate in the tournament?"

They'd reached the back entrance to the maze, and Ash longed to dodge between the tall hedges and lose himself in wandering. Except, he knew this maze, knew exactly how to reach the little Cupid statue at the center, and knew Sycamore would simply follow him through every turn.

"What tournament?"

"When the weather refused to oblige the ladies' kites, somebody suggested we get up a tournament of games. Every day will offer an afternoon session and an evening session, save for Sunday. Teams of two, double elimination play. The games will rotate among whist, piquet, and cribbage, possibly billiards, I'm not sure what else. Archery perhaps. It's a clever idea, and if it works, we should try it out at the Coventry."

Ash kept walking past the opening to the maze. "Did Chastain make this suggestion?"

"I believe Francis Portly came up with it, or perhaps I might have mentioned the notion, and Portly took it up."

The idea of a multiple-game tournament over a period of days was actually interesting. "Is this why you've invited yourself to this gathering, because you wanted to try out a novel idea before testing it at the club?"

Sycamore jammed his hands into his pockets. "Of course not. I am here to pleasure the willing and stand up with the shy. A friend to womankind at large, as usual. Some obliging brother might mention to the marchioness what a capital fellow I am."

Ash rounded the corner and started back in the direction of the house. "You concocted this tournament so you can partner Lady Tavistock over a period of days. Assist her to aim her shots at the billiards table, discuss strategy with her between hands of cards. She will take you into profound dislike before the house party is half over."

"She will appreciate how effectively I keep the vultures from pestering her. She's quite well-off and a damned fine-looking female. Some men have no restraint."

And the marchioness was a very astute gambler. She won consistently, always considered the odds, bet prudently, and was never afraid to walk away from a losing streak. Ash considered reminding Sycamore of that last characteristic, but discarded the notion.

"I have wondered about something," Ash said, steps slowing, "regarding Chastain."

"He's not to be underestimated, Ash. I pity his new wife."

"She warned Della at breakfast that Chastain is carrying a grudge. Della was also surprised to learn that William will be kept on a tight rein financially because Clarice's papa took that little jaunt to Alconbury amiss."

Sycamore wrinkled his nose. "Chastain will hate being forced to live on an allowance. Odd, that. We expect the ladies to budget their pin money without complaint, but many grown men can tolerate no fetters on their spending."

"And that raises a question," Ash said, keeping his voice down as they strolled along the maze's long side. "If Chastain has been on such a miserly budget since coming down from university, how has he managed to consistently and in a timely manner pay his many debts of honor?"

Sycamore halted. "That is a troubling question. Accepting the proceeds of stolen goods would implicate the club in criminal activity, wouldn't it?"

"Yes," Ash said, stopping as well, "and worse yet, gambling hells are often used to transfer funds to legitimate purses from the other kind. Nearly any sudden windfall can be explained as a run of good luck at the tables."

Sycamore resumed walking, his pace brisk. "Our tables are scrupulously clean. We are fanatical about that. Our dealers are honest, and we pay them enough to ensure their loyalty."

"My question is all but idle," Ash said, falling in step beside him. "One of those little thoughts that floats by on a passing breeze." And yet, like ledgers that wouldn't tally, the thought wanted further study. Ash ambled along in silence, until he and Sycamore had nearly returned to the foot of the garden.

A giggle emanated from the gazebo several yards off. The little structure was hung with multiple layers of netting, so the occupants were shielded from view.

"Is that the sole allure of house parties?" Ash muttered. "Frolicking, strumming, and getting a leg over somebody else's spouse?"

"Asks the man whose wife is off napping *sans mari*."

Ash jabbed an elbow into Sycamore's breadbasket, hard—harder than he should have. The blow wasn't planned, and that only added to Ash's unsettled mood.

"Jesus, Ash," Sycamore wheezed, hands braced on his thighs. "Jesus and all the little angels. Have you been working on that move? You'd drop the average footpad where he stood."

Though Ash had hardly slowed his brother down. "You impugn Della's loyalty at your peril."

Sycamore straightened. "I was impugning your common sense, you lackwit, for leaving your new wife to nap all on her lonesome not three days after speaking your vows."

A groan came from the direction of the gazebo, and Ash wanted to deliver a few more blows to the unsuspecting.

"Della needed to catch up on her sleep."

Sycamore sauntered toward the back terrace. "Well, that's all right, then. The honor of the House of Dorning has been upheld, and the lady needs her rest. I meant what I said about the marchioness."

Ash struggled to recall Sycamore saying anything of merit. "When you said what?"

"About putting in a good word for me. She can have her pick of the fellows, and my only advantage is faultless charm."

"And bottomless hubris, not to mention an absurd fascination with wielding your microscopic poker and a compensatory obsession with knives."

When Sycamore should have retorted with equal parts hubris

and humor, he instead winced. "You're in a rotten mood for a newly wed Dorning."

And that was the damned truth. "Sorry." Sycamore's pizzle was in proportion to the rest of him, hence the jest was permitted between brothers when private, but Ash's remark was still... a bit much, particularly following an unreciprocated blow. "I am out of sorts, and I do apologize."

"Are you managing, Ash?"

"I am tired, and Chastain's wife accosting Della at breakfast was the outside of too much. Mrs. Chastain was pleasant, but Della was upset by the encounter. I thought to leave my wife some solitude to gather her wits. Perhaps I'm in need of a nap myself."

Sycamore gave him the sort of up-and-down perusal that made Ash want to howl.

"It can start like this," Sycamore said. "You get irritable and nasty, and then the melancholia descends."

A thousand irritable and nasty retorts sprang to mind, which only underscored Sycamore's point.

"I know," Ash said. "Damned if I have a clue what to do about it." Particularly with Della begging him not to let her out of his sight, Chastain circling like a hungry boar hog, and two more weeks of Lady Wentwhistle's dubious hospitality to endure.

$\sim$

"NOT THE SHAWL," Della said, retrieving it from the maid's grasp. "I keep that with me." Moreover, washing a crocheted shawl when that article was clean made no sense.

The maid, a rosy-cheeked, blond young lady by the name of Trask, curtseyed for the fifteenth time.

"Sorry, my lady. I do beg your pardon. I'm not really a lady's maid. I'm barely a chambermaid, but Lady W needed the extra hands, and here I am."

"I am very pleased to have your assistance," Della said, though she would have been more pleased to finish her nap. "I'm sure Lady Wentwhistle has faith in your potential, or she would not have relied upon you to take up these duties."

Trask gazed at Della as if she'd spoken in Finnish.

"She trusts you," Della said, "and to be honest, my needs are few. Sponge off a few frocks, iron a few others. Mend the occasional tear, and mind my linen doesn't get lost in the laundry."

Trask's shoulders dropped two inches. "I can do that, ma'am. I mean, my lady. I'm a laundry maid, truth be told. I'll see to your clothes and make a proper job of that. You don't need me to tend to your hair?"

"I will manage that myself."

Trask smiled, revealing perfect teeth. "I'm that relieved. I have no idea what to do with a lady's hair. Never used a pair of curling tongs except once when my sister was trying to catch Whit Sylvester's eye. That did not go well, though she's Mrs. Sylvester now, with two little ones underfoot. Names are Jenny and Jake. I can mend and wash and iron with the best of them, but I'm not the fancy sort."

Trask was not the quiet sort either. She chattered as she gathered up Della's carriage dress and riding habit. She chattered as she tidied up the clothes in the wardrobe. She fell silent only as she wrestled with the window sash, which had refused to close the last inch.

"I'll run a bar of hard soap along the sides," she said. "Works a treat. It's this weather. Too dampish for me, makes the wood swell. My mother always said..."

Her prattling ceased as she peered down at the terrace.

Della joined her at the window. Ash could very likely get the damned window shut without anybody using any expensive soap. Della had watched him circling the maze, though now he stood talking with Sycamore near the foot of the garden.

"If I might ask, who is that gent by the steps, my lady?"

Oh, him. "The blond fellow?"

"He's been in and out of the gazebo since luncheon."

"His name is William Chastain. He and his new wife are among Lady Wentwhistle's guests."

Trask's fair brows drew down. "He has a *new wife?*"

William and Ash would not be able to see each other, given the height of the privet hedges. Della did not like knowing they were in the same county, much less the same garden.

"He does, a pleasant lady of French extraction." About whom Della had myriad reservations, though at least the dreaded confrontation had been dealt with.

"Oh, the Quality," Trask muttered, moving away from the window. "I'll have your clothes back to you by tomorrow, my lady. You're sure I can't brush off that shawl for you? I'll be ever so careful."

"No, thank you."

Though it took three more curtseys, Trask eventually went bustling on her way. Della considered returning to the bed, where she'd been all but asleep when Trask had interrupted her. To have been roused from near slumber left Della more tired than if she hadn't tried to nap at all.

Rather than doze off while waiting for Ash to return, Della wrapped herself in her mother's shawl and took out her needlepoint. A wife's privileges included providing her husband with monogrammed handkerchiefs, and stitchery was a more productive pastime than speculating about why Trask had inquired specifically after William Chastain.

CHAPTER TWELVE

Ash could have walked for another three hours, but he was mindful that Della awaited him in their rooms.

How long was a midafternoon nap?

Should he have joined her for her respite?

Was a nap a means of inviting a husband to enjoy marital pleasures in the middle of the day? Ash thought not, because Della wouldn't be that coy.

Or would she?

Perhaps a nap was an invitation merely to cuddle and exchange those sweet nothings Sycamore seemed to think no woman should be without, though what did Sycamore know about anything?

Ash was lost in his mental peregrinations as he passed William Chastain at the foot of the terrace steps. Chastain's cravat was slightly askew, and his hair looked windblown on a day without much breeze. His afternoon activities had included either overimbibing or swiving—or both—and Ash doubted the elegant Mrs. Chastain would have let her husband rise from a frolic in such an untidy state.

Ash nodded at Chastain and kept walking rather than indulge in verbal fisticuffs in his present mood. He slowed his steps as he approached the entrance to the house.

An older woman sat alone at a wrought-iron table. She looked slightly familiar and more than slightly upset. Her eyes were sheened with tears, and she clutched a handkerchief in one pale hand.

"Lady Fairchild?"

She looked up, her gaze more worried than friendly. "Sir?"

"Ash Dorning, at your service. May I join you?" He did not want to join her, but she was clearly in distress. They had doubtless been introduced at some point, though he knew he hadn't met her at the Coventry.

"You have the Dorning eyes," she said, gesturing to the only other chair at the table. "You are here with your new bride?"

"I have that honor. Would you like to take a turn in the garden?"

"No, thank you." She sent Chastain a withering glance, then seemed to collect herself. "I was well acquainted with your father, Mr. Dorning. I've been introduced to Lady Jacaranda, and I'm sure I've crossed paths with your oldest brother—he's Casriel now. So strange to think your papa has gone to his reward."

"My youngest brother, Sycamore, is among the guests too."

Lady Fairchild folded her handkerchief and tucked it into a pocket. "Mr. Sycamore Dorning is a scamp by reputation. I don't move much in Society, but I've heard about his club. Does he have the same gorgeous eyes as the rest of you?"

"We don't dare put it like that lest his head swell beyond the proportions necessary to fit through the average parlor door."

She studied Ash, and he realized she was a very attractive woman.

"Your father had that same humor, an ability to poke gentle fun. It's a lovely quality in a man. Were you walking off the dismals?"

If she'd burst into a Monteverdi aria, Ash could not have been more surprised. "I beg your pardon?"

"Your dear papa used to walk off the dismals. He'd roam endlessly over hill and dale and take extended walking tours in every little corner of the realm. I wandered many an hour in his company, and he used to say the fresh air was a tonic. He was between wives when I knew him best, and he grieved for his first countess sorely."

"I was under the impression Papa's walking tours were in the interest of collecting botanical specimens."

"He always had a specimen bag over his shoulder, and I do believe he was interested in botany, but when I knew him—this would have been quite a long time ago—he was somewhat at loose ends. Lord Fairchild was in Vienna at a diplomatic posting, and I appreciated your father's companionship so very much."

So Sycamore came by his scapegrace flirtatiousness honestly? Ash had never considered that theory. "What else do you recall about my father?"

She smiled at her hands. "He was a terrible flirt. Men newly grieving can be that way, as can women, I'm told. He was a good listener, he didn't need to be the center of attention, and he loved his children to distraction."

That comported with what Ash recalled of his father. Papa had been quiet, studious even, and yet he'd been able to charm Mama from the worst of her tempers and vexations.

"And you say he was prone to the dismals?"

"He was a new widower, Mr. Dorning. Women are all but compelled to make a great, endless display of their grief. Men are expected to carry on. Your father had a title weighing him down, motherless children to care for, and various siblings and cousins all looking to him for support and influence. He had much to be dismal about."

For a moment, Ash had felt a glimmer of hope that his malaise was not entirely random. Perhaps he'd inherited a propensity for overabundant black bile from his father, but no. Melancholia and grief were separate varieties of despondency.

The one had an obvious cause, the other was simply a failing of the animal spirits.

"I'm glad Papa found good company," Ash said. "Did you also know my mother?"

Lady Fairchild's smile became slightly ironic. "I did, nowhere near as well as I knew your father. My husband had come home from his posting by the time your father remarried, and you younger children came along at a great rate. I assume the union was happy."

"It was, though not without the occasional rough patch." Mama and Papa had had spectacular rows that had often ended with the couple retiring to their apartment and emerging an hour later much more in charity with each other.

"When my husband took a posting to Canada, I nearly murdered him, but we weathered that challenge. Married life isn't always easy, but in the end, the joys outweigh the sorrows. I knew Lady Della's parents, too, and my gracious, her papa cut quite a swath. Society was different back then. We were less afflicted with propriety, and that wasn't always a good thing."

The discussion had done what tromping around the garden had not—distracted Ash from a grouchy mood.

"I have much enjoyed chatting with you, Lady Fairchild, but my wife awaits me inside, and a new husband treads lightly. May I escort you to the library or the conservatory?"

"The conservatory is a fine idea. My daughter is likely to be lurking among the ferns with a book. Catherine says all those plants crowded together make for salubrious air. I think they make for a better place to hide with a dubious novel, but you mustn't tell her I said that."

"My wife and your daughter would doubtless get on well. We must make it a point to introduce them if they haven't already met."

Ash left her ladyship in the humid warmth of the conservatory and found Della awake and stitching at her embroidery when he returned to their rooms.

"Shall I open that window the rest of the way?" he asked, crossing the bedroom to shove at the sticky sash. "Old houses and changeable weather are a bad combination. I thought you were stealing a nap."

He kissed her cheek, just because he could, and was rewarded with a shy smile.

"Lady Wentwhistle has assigned a laundry maid to look after me. What Trask lacks in other skills, she makes up for in an ability to chatter."

Della was perched in a wing chair by the window, taking advantage of the natural light. She made a pretty, domestic picture, swaddled in her shawl, plying her needle. The sight of her caused Ash an ache, not entirely sexual, and a hope that decades hence, he would still be admiring her as she stitched away an afternoon.

He took the second wing chair and pulled off his boots. "I had an interesting discussion with Lady Fairchild. I gather she's here with her daughter Catherine."

"The bluestocking?"

"You know her?"

Della let her hoop fall to her lap. "Not well, but I like her. She is not a slave to convention, and like me, she has not taken."

Ash undid his cravat next. "I was fascinated to learn that Lady Fairchild and my father were quite well acquainted when he was, as she put it, between wives."

"Do you suppose they had a liaison?"

Ash thought back over the conversation and recalled Lady Fairchild's smiles. "Yes. When she speaks of him, she recalls him with a special fondness. Her air was wistful with remembrance, as if he was dear to her in the way of a lover."

Della put aside her hoop, rose, and settled into Ash's lap. "That is very interesting. When you meet Lady Fairchild's daughter, take special notice of her eyes."

"I would rather take special notice of my wife, situated so cozily in my lap."

"You started to undress. Your wife has taken notice of you too, and she has not had her nap."

Ash rose with Della in his arms and deposited her on the bed.

"You are not to move. I have a sudden compulsion to get my mouth on your quim."

"Your mouth on my—?"

"And yes, to answer the question I see lurking in your eyes, your mouth on my cock wouldn't go amiss either. Tell me about Miss Catherine's eyes."

Della instead lay back and drew her dressing gown up, up, up, past her knees, past her thighs, and to her waist.

Ash shrugged out of his coat and got his waistcoat and shirt off in two seconds flat. "Mrs. Dorning, you are my heart's true delight and the answer to my dearest dreams." To say nothing of the endless esteem in which he held her generous and lusty nature.

Della undid the belt of her dressing gown and untied her chemise. "All very lovely, Ash, but right now, I would also like to be your wife."

"And I, your husband."

He spent a good long while worshipping at the altar of Venus and reveling in Della's attentions to his dandilolly and tallywags. Not until she was a sweet, sleepy weight on his chest, and Ash was drifting toward the bliss of slumber himself, did he recall their earlier discussion.

"Della?"

"Hmm?"

"What will I notice about Miss Catherine's eyes?"

Della yawned, slid off him, and cuddled up at his side. "They are the same color as yours."

⁓

DELLA ROSE and left Ash slumbering amid the pillows. She privately suspected that lack of good sleep contributed to any mental burden, for she certainly fared worse when tired, and Ash could use the rest.

She also wanted to test herself with a short, unescorted foray from their rooms. To literally cling to Ash's hand was unbecoming, and sooner or later, he'd resent her for it. Her objective was modest—the library—and required nothing more than confirming directions with a footman and traversing a flight of stairs, the main foyer, and a carpeted corridor.

That so small an accomplishment as finding the library should cheer her was pathetic, except she'd also smiled and nodded to a half-dozen house party guests, greeting four of them by name. Tomorrow, after the last guest had arrived, Lady Wentwhistle would take a more formal hand in the introductions.

Della decided that her successful sortie merited a reward in the form of some witty words, so she set another objective: Find *Gulliver's Travels*. Dean Swift's political satire was as imaginative as it was insightful as it was droll.

The butler kindly steered her to the library shelves farthest from the door, where comedy, plays, and satire were stored. She was lost in perusing monographs and bound volumes in both French and English when she heard a footstep behind her.

"Well, if it isn't my erstwhile partner in amatory adventures." William Chastain stood six paces away, effectively blocking Della's exit. The rows of shelves were about four feet apart, and sidling by him would mean passing within grabbing distance.

Assaulting distance.

"Mr. Chastain." Della curtseyed, hugging *Gulliver* to her chest. Her gesture was courteous and controlled, but inside, she was buffeted by a riot of self-reproach.

Stupid, stupid, stupid, to think William would continue his disporting in the gazebo. He'd enjoyed its privacy with two different women while Della had observed from her window, and his cravat was tied off-center.

"*Mrs.* Dorning." He bowed, giving the honorific ironic emphasis. "I suspected you were breeding when you agreed to run off with me. Was it Dorning's brat you would have stuck me with?"

He sauntered two steps closer, and Della's heart began to pound.

"If you will recall, sir, our elopement was never to have resulted in marriage. I did you the favor of attempting to free you from a union you sought to avoid. I am sorry for it now and have apologized to your wife for my behavior."

Blond brows rose in apparent consternation. Della seized her moment to dash past him.

"You accosted Clarice?" William asked, stalking after her. "You had the gall to impose yourself on my wife?"

"Clarice accosted me," Della retorted, refusing to give William the pleasure of chasing her about the room. She stopped by one of the floor-to-ceiling windows, where anybody on the terrace could see her.

"Clarice would never be so forward," William retorted. "She's as retiring as a Puritan spinster. You are lying."

"Mrs. Chastain and I shared a table at breakfast, and it was she who asked to join me. Ask anybody. Ask my husband, for he took his meal with us."

"I will inform my wife that in future, she is to avoid your company, or I will apply appropriate discipline. Stay away from her."

God help Clarice Chastain. "We are at a *house party*, Mr. Chastain. Your wife understands that nobody's interests are furthered by fueling gossip. Would that you had as much sense."

The words were more foolishness tossed at a man who had no honor, but Della needed Chastain to go away, and an insult might chase him off.

"You think you are so clever, tossing me over for an earl's son," Chastain said, coming closer on a whiff of brandy fumes. "Do you want me telling Dorning the real reason I could make off with you? Does he know he's married to the next thing to a bedlamite?"

Della gazed out at the terrace, where eight or ten people sat in small groups, and a knot of young men lounged along the balustrade.

"Your wife," she said calmly, "has suggested I staged a failed elopement to get Mr. Dorning's attention. Her version of events will scotch gossip, but in fact, you know full well that all I wanted was to be left in peace at my family seat. Come one step nearer to me, and I will scream, and a dozen people will see you menacing me through this window."

Della went on, though the tingling had started in her hands and arms. "Your cravat is askew, and you've been seen frequenting the gazebo with both an unmarried young lady and Mrs. Tremont. You are getting off on a very bad foot, Chastain, and my husband would be unlikely to believe your dishonorable maunderings anyway."

Except... Ash would have to believe them eventually, because Chastain's accusations would be true.

"Why I ever tried to come to your aid," he spat, "I do not know, and if you run off with a man, you should expect him to exact a little in-kind payment, Della Dorning, even from a scrawny little thing like you. Thanks to my attempt to aid you, Clarice's settlements are all but lost to me, and I am not only leg-shackled to a nun, I now have her expenses as well as my own to manage on a miserly allowance. For that, I will have revenge."

"You never sought to aid me," Della retorted. "You took advantage of me, threatened me, and all but kidnapped me."

He tugged his cravat to the right, though it still hung off-center. "Who will believe you? Who will believe that an aging spinster had to be coerced into running off with one of London's most eligible bachelors? I'll tell you who. Nobody. Your conjectures approach fantasy, my lady, another symptom of a diseased mind. Your husband is a confirmed melancholic, and your antecedents are rumored to be less than legitimate. Ruining you, him, his silly little club, and the Dorning family's pathetic mercantile initiative will be the work of a moment for a person of my resourcefulness."

Della was chilled, despite the library's stuffy air. "Why do this? Why be so cruel? Your plans with me went awry, but that is not my fault."

"Cruel?" William stomped away. "Cruel is putting a young man's finances on a leash so tight that he can barely hold his head up, despite his family having more blunt than you can imagine. Cruel is marrying me off to a woman who likely hides rosary beads under her pillow. Cruel is expecting me to banish myself to goddamned Surrey for the rest of my life, pretending the stink of the yeomanry is my favorite perfume. This marriage has *buried* me, Della Dorning, and you were my last prayer of resurrection."

He sent her a final scathing glance and took himself from the library.

Della sank into the nearest chair—not in view of the window—and endured the shaking hands and pounding heart that inevitably came with a nervous spell. From the welter of dread seething in her mind, three thoughts emerged.

First, William had been absolutely intent on raping her back in Alconbury. He hadn't ended up in her bed as a function of drunken confusion. He'd been determined to violate her, and that all but confirmed that he'd delayed sending any note to his father.

A consummated elopement—even were the consummation rape rather than lovemaking— would have resulted in the Chastain family accepting a marriage between Della and William.

Second, Della would have been tempted to allow the match.

He'd come upon her in the middle of a full-blown attack of nerves at Lady Winterthur's autumn ridotto. She'd been curled in a little ball behind a row of potted ferns, shaking, crying, barely able to breathe, and Chastain had seen all of that.

By marrying him, Della would gamble that his unwillingness to tell Society of his wife's mental infirmities outweighed his desire to ruin her. Sleeping with the enemy was a survival strategy as old as the Romans. To protect her own family, Della would have allowed William to affix the marital ball and chain to her ankle.

Third, William was right: Not even Ash would believe Della's version of events, and now Della's subterfuges had put Ash, his family, and his businesses at risk of harm.

Her conclusions were rational, but she could hardly study them—much less figure out what to do about them—when thoughts swarmed like ants, and her body felt too weak to rise. She instead focused on her breathing, on the sure knowledge that every spell passed eventually, and on the details in the room around her.

A figure of the Apollo Belvedere in white porcelain on the mantel. The musty smell of old leather-bound books. The faint chatter from the terrace. The feel of *Gulliver* clutched so tightly in her lap. The dry thirst parching her mouth.

When Sycamore ambled into the library ten minutes later, Della had almost succeeded in calming her body, while her mind remained in riot.

He tossed himself into the wing chair paired with Della's, all lanky grace and daytime elegance. "They're choosing up partners for the games tournament," he said. "As a professional in the gaming business, I thought I'd best recuse myself. What's your excuse?"

Why do I need an excuse? "To the extent archery figures in the proceedings, I have my mother's keen eye for accuracy. I would beat all the men and cause talk. I'd rather spend the time with my husband anyway."

Sycamore appeared to accept that assertion reply at face value, and well he should, for it was the absolute truth.

~

ASH LAY BESIDE HIS WIFE, wishing she were asleep, knowing she was not. They'd been married on Monday, today had been the longest Friday of Ash's life, but already he knew the difference between the waking and sleeping rhythm of Della's breathing.

He knew that the shawl she treasured had been among the last articles her mother had crocheted, he knew that loud noises unnerved her, and today's shooting exhibition had strained her composure to the utmost, though she had accurately critiqued the form of every man who'd taken up a pistol and predicted the inaccuracies of his aim to the inch.

Ash knew he loved her and that something troubled her, something more than the usual annoyances common to any prolonged social gathering. He suspected marriage to him numbered among her woes, but would not irritate her seeking confirmation of his fears.

"I'll rub your back," Della said, curling over onto her side.

They hadn't made love last night. Della had accepted Ash's suggestion to *have a cuddle* when she'd straddled his lap and begun kissing him. She was apparently waiting for him to make the next intimate overture, and he wanted to, but in his present mood, he did not trust himself to do justice to the occasion.

"You can't sleep either?" Ash replied, threading an arm under her neck and drawing her against his side.

"It's the weather. It can't make up its mind, and thus we get the humidity of summer, a touch of autumn's chill, and the weak sun of winter. Lady Wentwhistle has a talent for scheduling the exact wrong activity for the weather."

Today would have been a lovely day to fly kites, but instead, her ladyship had scheduled shooting.

"You chose not to participate in the games tournament," Ash said. "May I ask why?"

"In the first place, my skill with a gun would honestly shame any of the fellows trying to look so competent and dashing. I can't help it. I hit what I aim at, unless I purposely miss. In the second, Chastain was participating, and I want nothing to do with anything he touches."

Ash had hoped that tensions in that regard were easing for Della. Perhaps Chastain had annoyed her, a thought both logical and unacceptable.

"I can still thrash him for you, Della." A sound mutual pummeling might actually help Ash's unsettled mood, though he doubted Chastain could give a good account of himself.

Della stroked Ash's chest, tracing patterns of muscle and bone. "Promise me you won't provoke him, Ash. He won't play fair, and you will come out the worse for it."

If anybody had told Ash that Della was the sort of wife to cling to her husband's hand on even a short garden stroll, that she'd attempt to extract promises from him regarding a matter of honor, that she literally didn't want her husband out of her sight, Ash would have laughed.

Less than a week into his marriage, he wasn't laughing. He loved her touch, loved how affectionate she was, but did not love that she was so frequently anxious.

"I have already promised you as much, Della. We can leave if being around him bothers you so greatly."

She was quiet for a time. Beyond the window, the wind whipped moonlit trees, sending leaves cascading into the garden, and a gust of laughter drifted up from some late-night revelers on the terrace.

"When I am around William Chastain," Della said, "I feel as if I am in the presence of a rabid animal, and though I want to run as far and as fast as my legs can carry me, the last thing I ought to do is turn my back on him."

The same stark metaphor applied to melancholia. Ash dared not ignore it, dared not turn his back on the lurking possibility of its return.

"Your thinking has merit," he said. "If we face down Chastain at this gathering, then we've put paid to his mischief. If this house party engenders more drama where he's concerned, we'll have to start all over again next spring. Would you like a nightcap?"

Ash did not crave a tot of brandy so much as he wanted to get up and move.

"No, thank you, but go find a drink if you want one. I saw decanters in the library and more in the gallery."

The evening round of cards took place in the gallery, meaning Chastain would be there. "I'll forage in the library. Get some sleep."

He kissed her, and she let him go without another word. Perhaps Della was relieved to have the bed to herself, though, not by word, deed, glance, or silence had she expressed anything but delight to be in Ash's presence.

He dressed hastily, not bothering with a cravat, and slipped into the chilly corridor. The library was all but deserted, only

Sycamore lounged by the fire, keeping company with some book of verse.

"You look adorably tumbled," Sycamore said, setting the book aside. "What could possibly send you prowling in such a state and at such an hour?"

"Traveling put me at sixes and sevens," Ash said. "I made the mistake of taking a long nap on Wednesday, and now I'm more discombobulated than ever."

Sycamore let that remark pass, though they both knew a hallmark of Ash's melancholia was a tendency to reverse his days and nights.

"Care for a nightcap?" Ash asked, crossing to the decanters.

"Why not? Lady Wentwhistle is still putting out decent libation. By this time next week, we will doubtless be offered lesser vintages."

Ash poured them each two scant fingers. "I thought you'd be observing the tournament play." And one red-haired player in particular.

"I looked in earlier, but keeping an eye on a lot of gamblers is how I make my living. To do so here would hardly be a diversion. Besides, play is progressing in the usual fashion. Mrs. Tremont and the marchioness are a formidable pair, Chastain loses because he's reckless, and much groping under the table is happening on all sides."

"What's Portly doing?"

"Partnering Mrs. Chastain, who is also an astute, if conservative, player."

"Who has the thankless task of partnering Chastain?"

"Lady Tavistock's step-son, and Lord Tavistock, unfortunately, is young enough and green enough to follow Chastain's lead. They are careless of their losses, but I can see the marchioness's temper silently flaring."

Ash took the wing chair nearest the fire. "Do you ever tire of the nonsense that inevitably accompanies wagering?"

Sycamore considered his drink. "Yes, but then I consider that Grey needs us to make a go of our venture, Tresham is counting on us to do right by a thriving business we essentially lucked into, and if I ever aspire to something more than managing a gaming hell, I'd best look after the biddies in my coop now."

That was the most mature, sensible sentiment Ash could recall hearing Sycamore express. "The Coventry is thriving, Cam, and that's largely because you know whom to charm and whom to chide. If you want to sell up in a few years, I won't object."

"Marriage is working its wiles on you."

Not marriage, but the knowledge that Della did not enjoy Town life, and neither, to be honest, did Ash.

"We have few friends in Town," Ash said, "because everybody is a potential customer, and we keep a polite distance from them lest we end up being their creditors. When the dismals come over me, I face a hundred-twenty-mile journey back to Dorning Hall, and as to that, I'm married now. A property of my own closer to Della's family in Kent makes much more sense."

Sycamore finished his drink and wandered to the sideboard. "You want a property of your own?"

"Yes. I'm no Town dandy. The melancholia grew worse when I moved to London. It wasn't so bad up in Oxford, nor at home."

Sycamore poured himself another finger and held up the decanter. Ash shook his head. "But, Ash, you go back to Dorning Hall, and the condition doesn't improve for weeks or months. Perhaps if you dwelled in the shires all year round, you'd be in worse shape. How's Della managing?"

This conversation was extraordinary for its lack of fraternal posturing—on anybody's part. Ash set aside for later consideration the notion that Sycamore behaved like a brat only because his brothers goaded him into it.

"She hates being in proximity to Chastain, but she's coping."

"She and he had some sort of confrontation here on"—Sycamore held his drink up to the candelabrum on the mantel—"Wednesday, I think it was. I was on the terrace and saw them through the window. Della was not happy, and Chastain looked positively thunderous."

And Della hadn't said a word about this—the confrontation she dreaded most—to her own husband.

"They were angry with each other?"

"Della gets this remote, prim look when she's trying not to display a temper. She reminds me of the marchioness in that regard. Lady Tavistock is ready to plant her darling step-son a facer, but she never speaks a cross word to him."

"Tavistock is seventeen. Cross words would only injure his fragile manly pride. Did Della say anything to you about her argument with Chastain?"

"She did not. I waited until Chastain left the library, then loitered in the corridor, admiring busts—of philosophers, not the other kind—and peering at paintings. When she remained in the library for a good ten minutes, I joined her."

"Had she been crying?"

"Not that I could discern, but she was as pale as a goose's arse. If you and I partnered at whist, we could ruin Chastain in three days' time. I've been studying him, and you long ago discerned every weakness in his play."

Ash sipped his drink, trying to sort out whether he was upset with Chastain, Della, himself, or all three. "Thank you for that kind and shrewd offer, Sycamore. I might take you up on it."

"Or, I could ruin Mrs. Chastain," Sycamore said, resuming his seat, "but she is blameless, pleasant, and already condemned to marriage with William. I like her laugh. I could cuckold Chastain, but again, the lady might suffer for having sought pleasure in my arms."

"And Chastain might blow out your brains, leaving me to manage the Coventry when I haven't your wit or gracious charm."

"There is that. You're managing, Ash?"

The late hour, the tenor of the discussion, and sheer fatigue of the spirit had Ash answering honestly.

"I am managing, but no more than managing. Marriage is an adjustment, and this house party was a bad idea, though I couldn't know that when I suggested to Della that we come here. I'm restless and out of sorts, and that does not bode well for the days ahead."

He didn't need to be more specific, but he realized that he and Della must have a frank talk about many things, including what she should expect when the melancholia descended again, for it would.

It inevitably would. If anything signaled an approaching bout, it was a lack of interest in sexual intimacy, and Ash had never desired a woman as unrelentingly as he had desired Della. He could make all the excuses in the world—the weather, travel, the strain of too much company—but he had declined not twenty minutes ago to make love with his darling and lusty new bride.

Sycamore tossed back the last of his brandy, gathered up his book, and rose. "In the days ahead, please recall you have a brother who, in addition to his charm, graciousness, wit, and savoir faire, is also devoted to your welfare. If I thought it would help, I would kill Chastain for you, but I know Della would not approve."

He wrapped an arm around Ash's head, kissed his crown, and took his leave.

Ash remained behind, sipping brandy he did not taste and framing a discussion with Della that would be neither easy nor pleasant.

CHAPTER THIRTEEN

"Damn thirsty business," William said, leading the way into the library, "fleecing the lambs." He made straight for the sideboard, found three clean glasses, poured two of them half full, and filled the third nearly to the brim.

The half-full glasses he passed to Portly and to Trevor, Marquess of Tavistock.

"To fleecing the lambs," William said, raising the third glass a few inches and then tossing back half its contents.

Tavistock, who had probably never stayed awake past midnight in his lordly little life, took the barest sip.

"Excuse me for pointing out the obvious, Chastain," Tavistock said, "but when do we get to the actual fleecing part?"

"Got you there," Portly murmured, subsiding into a wing chair. "Tavistock, be a love and add some coal to this dreary fire."

Portly hadn't a mean bone in his body, but his family was merely gentry, and he wasn't above putting a marquess to a footman's job for the deviltry of it. Tavistock complied, the stupid git, then took a wing chair for himself.

"If we're gambling to win," Tavistock said, "then it seems to me that the idea is to have the coins coming to our side of the table. We've been at this for three days and nights, Chastain, and my entire quarterly allowance has disappeared into pockets other than my own."

William perched on the arm of Portly's chair. "Patience, dear boy. We're lulling the opposition into a false sense of confidence. The tide will turn, and we will take them all unawares."

"That's the theory," Portly muttered.

William smacked him on the back of the head. "Partnering Clarice has put you out of sorts. Perhaps you ought to develop a sprained hand and drop out of the tournament."

"I'll partner Mrs. Chastain," Tavistock said. "She's won a damn sight more with Portly than I have with you, Chastain. If Portly wants to switch, I'm willing."

The arrogant little puppy.

"Portly," said the man himself, "is not about to change partners. That would be ungallant. Besides, Chastain won't have me. Your lordship has much more cachet than a mere commoner like myself."

Tavistock was too wet behind the ears to know when he'd been insulted.

He took another parsimonious sip of his drink. "Step-mama will confine me to the family seat until I'm twenty-one if I continue to lose."

"No," William said, "she won't. If I were you, I'd show her bloody ladyship what's what. She ain't your guardian, and she's dependent on you for her blunt."

Tavistock peered at William over his drink. "You have met my step-mother? She's the redhead who eats *testicules frits de chasseur de fortune* for breakfast and drinks the blood of encroaching mushrooms for a restorative tonic. Her funds are her own, and they are ample."

"Apply the back of your hand to her ladyship's disrespectful mouth," William said, "and she'll decamp for a dower property. What you spend is between you and your guardians. They know you'll come into your money soon enough, so they won't gainsay you."

"Fried balls of fortune hunter," Portly translated, "or something like that. Quite colorful."

"You propose that I raise a hand to my step-mother?" Tavistock asked.

"The sooner, the better," William said. "Put her in her place, and she'll be much happier for it. Women respect a man who exercises his authority with confidence."

"He's been married a week," Portly said, winking at the boy. "Renowned expert on the happy female, that's Chastain."

Tavistock looked from Portly to Chastain. "A gentleman does not raise his hand to the fairer sex. I know bugger all about cards, but I know that much." He made this pronouncement with the touching dignity of the very young male.

"We will leave management of your step-mother to you," William said, "but you must trust me that our strategy with the cards cannot fail. You will have your quarterly allowance back twice over, but you must find the nerve to stay the course, Tavistock."

Tavistock was six feet tall if he was an inch, but he'd yet to fill out. He was all elbows and knees, blushes and curious silences. A lamb waiting to be fleeced, in other words.

"I should ask Sycamore Dorning for some pointers," Tavistock said.

William burst out laughing, despite the idea having significant merit. "Sycamore Dorning? He is so hesitant to pick up a hand of cards he wouldn't even participate in a tournament that includes dowagers and beldames. Portly, have you ever heard such nonsense?"

Portly, who had admittedly spent the past three evenings partnering Clarice, was a bit slow with his lines.

"Dorning might know something about cards," Portly said, "*might*, but he knows more about how to manipulate customers into leaving their money at his tables."

"Precisely," Tavistock said, striking his palm on the arm of the chair. "And I need to stop leaving my money at Lady Wentwhistle's tables, so who better to ask—?"

William held up a hand. "Have you ever been to that nasty little establishment Dorning owns?"

"Not yet, but the fellows say the Coventry is all the crack. Even better than when Tresham owned it."

"Tresham won't turn it over to the Dornings," William said, lowering his voice. "Word is, he don't trust 'em. They're jumped-up farmers who happened to bumble into a title a few centuries back. They're peddling soaps and sachets now, probably to keep the Coventry afloat."

That was an inspired bit of conjecture, if William did say so himself.

"The Dornings have an earldom," Tavistock countered. "If they are jumped-up farmers, what does that make you, Chastain?"

So the pup had teeth? "I know better than to trade on centuries-old trappings, Tavistock. The Coventry passes around free champagne from the stroke of midnight. Consider that the patrons have already spent several hours swilling wine at their fancy suppers, washing down their club dinners with port, or imbibing for the duration of a performance at Drury Lane. How carefully do you think those customers are watching their cards by the time they sit down at the Coventry tables?"

Tavistock's fair features showed equal parts fascination and horror. "You're saying The Coventry is dirty?"

"I would never speculate in such a direction except in strictest confidence to my closest friends," William replied. "Let it suffice in present company to say I have frequented the Coventry less and less as I see more and more there that disappoints me."

"Step-mama gambles there," Tavistock said, rising on a yawn. "She promised to take me if I comported myself well during this house party."

"My dear boy," William said, collecting Tavistock's abandoned drink, "I will take you there when next you're in Town, if you truly want to go. I can't think why you would, though."

"Run along to bed," Portly said, gesturing with his drink. "You must be sharp for tomorrow's play."

Tavistock bowed his good-night like the proper young dunce he was, and William took the chair the marquess had vacated.

"Poor little angel," William said, smirking at his brandy. "What would he think of those fine establishments that let a man apply his firm hand, the birch rod, or a riding crop to the bare posterior of a cheerfully willing female?"

Portly crossed his legs at the ankle and slouched down in his chair. "He'd think the silly reasons for which a man will give up his coin are without limit. Telling him to slap his step-mother was vile, Chastain."

"That was inspired. The woman don't know her place by half. He won't do it. He'll dream of it, though. I might dream of it. Redheads tend to need firm guidance."

"You are drunk. Tavistock is right to be worried."

William brought the decanter over from the sideboard. "Now, now. Don't be nasty, though partnering Clarice would put any man out of sorts. I do appreciate your sacrifice, Portly, and of course Tavistock is worried. I want him worried. The ones who worry are the easiest to pluck. Look at Lady Della. Quaking in her slippers, she was, and she damned near got me out of parson's mousetrap."

Portly held up his glass. "To Lady Della's slippers, then. What have you got on Tavistock?"

"This one is easy. Mrs. Tremont's brother is a backdoor usher, if you get my drift. Likes to sail the windward passage with handsome young lads. I'll tell him Tavistock is of the same persuasion, and when he accosts Tavistock for a little backgammon, I'll come upon them in flagrante delicate."

"Delicto."

"I'll have evidence against them both."

Portly was quiet for so long, William thought he might have the rest of the decanter for himself. "Chastain, you are the wicked brother I never had, and I say this with all good will: You are losing a necessary sense of caution. It's one thing to cadge a few coppers from a dowager who has been indiscreet in her pleasures."

Portly scrubbed a hand over his face before continuing. "Sodomy, on the other hand, is a hanging felony, and Tavistock, despite his tender years, is a marquess. The Dornings run the most popular gaming establishment London has ever seen, and they are related by marriage to the earls of both Bellefonte and Grampion, the Kettering fortune, and the Pepper mercantile empire."

William toed off his boots. "Should I be singing a hymn, Portly, for surely you are sermonizing?"

"Be careful," Portly said, pushing to his feet. "If you must bring down the Coventry, be very, very careful, and spare me the details. I will squire Clarice around more faithfully than a new footman just up from the country waits on a tipsy duchess, but I want no part of your latest scheme."

William poured himself another drink. "I am always careful, darling. You know I am. I'll catch the young marquess in the middle of a friendly kiss, one the wrong sort of person might misinterpret. Then I will do him the very great favor of explaining to his she-dragon step-mother exactly what the price of my silence will be. I get my blunt, Tavistock gets a valuable lesson in deportment."

Portly paused, hand on the door latch. "And the Coventry?"

"The Coventry will be the subject of unfortunate talk, rather a lot of it. My objective is to take from Della Dorning that which she values most—her husband's peace of mind and thus hers as well. It's truly an elegant little scheme."

"It's a doomed scheme. I bid you good night."

Portly closed the door with a soft click, leaving William to enjoy the rest of the decanter by himself.

◞

DELLA HAD LEARNED to keep track of her siblings because they could not be trusted to keep track of her. They meant to, of course, just as they meant to listen to her remarks at supper or answer her questions at the breakfast table. The older Haddonfield siblings were easily distracted from their good intentions, however, and thus Della had learned to pay attention.

She kept a close watch on her family and on her surroundings. As it had become apparent that she would not outgrow her nervous spells, she had also learned to notice the easiest path out of any room or building. She noticed where a lady might withdraw discreetly to gather her wits when her thinking mind was convinced that the world was soon to end.

She took particular care with stairways.

She learned to use the attributes of invisibility—her youth, lack of height, and femaleness—to her advantage. When in company, she dressed on the plain side of good taste, she wore a simple honeysuckle fragrance, she laughed softly if at all.

And yet, the instant Ash stepped out onto the terrace, he strode right for the small table she occupied in the shade of the overhanging balcony.

"Hiding in plain sight," he said, bending to kiss her cheek. "I hope breakfast was uneventful?"

For all he wore riding attire like it was made to show off his physique, Ash looked weary. Della had fallen asleep alone in their bed and awoken to a note that Ash and Sycamore had gone for a morning hack.

"I broke my fast with Lady Tavistock and her step-son," Della said, setting aside her book. "His lordship is painfully young, and her ladyship tries hard to treat him as an adult, but he's a bit tiresome."

Ash sank into the chair beside her so they both had a view of the terrace. "Seventeen is a difficult age. A fellow's majority is still several years off, but a year or two at university has already worked its dubious magic on his sense of adult male entitlement. What are you reading?"

"Mrs. Wollstonecraft. I was surprised to find her in Lady Wentwhistle's collection, though the volume does not appear to be much read."

Ash regarded the guests enjoying the morning air, some seated elsewhere on the terrace, some drifting down into the garden. His air was distracted as he watched Lady Fairchild's daughter Catherine descend into the garden on William Chastain's arm.

"Chastain did not attempt to approach you at breakfast?"

"He did not come down to breakfast, as far as I know, though young Lord Tavistock pronounced Chastain a capital fellow. His step-mama nearly choked on her eggs at that observation. How was your ride?"

Ash stripped off his riding gloves and laid them on the table as he continued to regard the other guests. "A new mount is always a little more work, and the gelding I took out was high-strung and overly fresh. I told Sycamore about Lady Catherine's eyes, and he confirmed that Papa had a dalliance with Lady Fairchild."

"How could he know such a thing?" And why was Chastain showing Miss Catherine his favor?

"Sycamore has read all of Papa's journals and diaries, and for the better part of a year, Lady Fairchild was the earl's frequent companion. They met *by agreeable happenstance* at least twice at a distance from London. Once in the Lakes, once in the New Forest."

"Does this upset you?"

Ash bent to remove his spurs. "Yes, if I'm to be honest. One should know these things. What if I'd taken a notion to court the woman when Sycamore was off gaining his disgust of Oxford?"

What a horrid thought. "Jonathan thought I wanted to blackmail him at first. Thought I would demand money for the return of his father's letters."

Ash set one spur on the table and leaned forward to remove the other. They were little blunt silver nubs, more decoration than anything else. A high-strung horse would notice them, though, and demand a very quiet leg from the rider lest the rider be unseated.

"How old were you when you learned your mother had strayed, Della?"

"Quite young, too young. Mama had not been gone long, and it was like losing her all over again. We expect our parents to be first and foremost our parents, but they were and are people separate and apart from their roles in our lives."

"Lady Fairchild said Papa started taking his walking tours to deal with his grief."

Miss Catherine passed out of sight into the maze, Chastain at her side. "But your father was still going on those walking tours long after he remarried. Perhaps he found the habit salubrious generally. I wish Miss Catherine had not allowed Chastain to lure her into the maze."

"You truly loathe the man," Ash said, regarding her. "Are you afraid of him?"

What did Ash know or suspect? What would Ash think if Della told him the truth? "Yes, Ash, I am afraid of him. He is not honorable. He took a bad decision on my part and turned it into a disaster. Mrs. Chastain has warned me against him, and when William came upon me in the library earlier this week..."

Ash was watching her closely, both spurs now gripped in his hand. "You met him in the library?"

"I did not *meet* him. I sought to venture forth without bothering you for an escort, merely to find a book. I was between two sets of shelves when Chastain came upon me. He blames me for the fact that his parents and in-laws have put him on a tight financial leash and further blames me for the fact that he and Clarice are married at all."

"And you did not think to tell me of this encounter?" Ash sounded annoyed, possibly angry.

"I am telling you now. I see no benefit to heated confrontations, more talk, or more scandal. All I wanted was to quietly retire to Kent, and now all I want is to quietly travel with you to Dorning Hall."

A shiver of dread passed from Della's nape down her arms. That she could have a spell while sitting on a sunny terrace and talking with her husband was unthinkable. She began counting her breaths, purposely slowing her exhalations, and mentally reciting the alphabet backward.

"This bedamned house party," Ash muttered. "I wish we had not come here."

Z, Y, X, W... "As do I. Shall we leave?"

"We can't leave. Chastain will say we quarreled, or that I caught you flirting with him, or he found me making advances to his wife. He'll say you were unwell and imply your indisposition was the result of carrying his child."

V, U, T, S... The shiver came again. "I can envision France rebuilding her fleet in secret and invading English shores. I can imagine plague laying half of London low and the air becoming unbreathable, a coal mine collapsing on my head... But for a man to *lie* in such a fashion, to invent malicious falsehoods... What sort of heart indulges in such meanness?"

Mrs. Tremont's brother, a charming fellow with a sly wit, ambled onto the terrace with the young Marquess of Tavistock. Their heads were bent close as his lordship gestured in the direction of the stables.

The older fellow snapped off a yellow chrysanthemum and tucked it into Tavistock's lapel. Tavistock grinned, which made him look about eleven years old, and they disappeared onto the path that led to the paddocks.

For some, this house party was merely a house party. For Della, it was becoming a circle of hell.

"Chastain is losing at the cards tournament," Ash said, "and he's pulling Tavistock into debt with him."

R, Q, P, O... "Perhaps Chastain will leave early." Though Della knew better than to hope for that miracle.

"We have little more than a week yet to endure. We'll manage." Ash spoke as if fortifying himself rather than reassuring Della.

"Are the blue devils becoming troublesome, Ash?"

He spared her a glance, haunted, fleeting, irritated. "They

inevitably will reclaim me, Della, but that is hardly a problem. You simply leave me in peace, and I will eventually come right."

"Should we try a walking tour?" She'd surprised him, and herself, with that suggestion. "You haven't tried a walking tour previously, have you? What have we to lose?"

Ash tucked his spurs into a pocket and somehow withdrew into himself at the same time. His gaze became glacial, and between the letters N and M, Della felt herself shrinking, becoming less visible, less substantial.

"I have tried everything," Ash muttered. "Nothing works but tenacity."

Though Della's heart was now thumping to the rhythm of bottomless dread, she nonetheless answered calmly. "If your efforts to date have been unsuccessful, Ash Dorning, you'd be lying beside your parents in the family plot. What you have done so far *has* worked. You are walking proof of success. I am merely suggesting we investigate other measures that might work even better."

She wanted to take his hand and never let him go, wanted to bury herself in his embrace and wrap him in her own. He sat two feet and an entire continent of injured male dignity away, so Della instead wrapped her shawl more closely around herself.

"I am sorry," Ash said, his posture easing. "I did not sleep well, and I, too, wish we could leave. I sense another bout of the blue devils approaching, and when that happens, you must not be offended. Ignore me, pretend I am laid low with a head cold or something. Ten days from now, we can climb into our coach and put this damned house party behind us, but, Della, I fear it will be a long ten days."

K, J, I, H... "We will weather these days together, Ash." She reached for his hand just as he stuffed his gloves into his pocket.

William Chastain emerged from the maze at Miss Catherine's side. The lady was smilingly shyly, and Chastain gazed straight at Della, his expression smug. He'd seen Della reach for her husband and seen Ash either avoid her gesture or fail to notice it.

"Perhaps we need a late morning nap," Della suggested.

"No more naps," Ash retorted. "I nap, then I can't sleep at night, then I'm out of sorts." He rose, and Della felt as if she was being abandoned once again on the village green. People all around her, oblivious to her little world coming to an end, while everybody she knew and loved simply went bustling off into the crowd.

G, F, E, D... "I wasn't suggesting we sleep, Ash." *Just hold me, please hold me.*

He bent down to kiss the top of her head. "You would wear me out, and then I would sleep through luncheon. Enjoy your reading." He patted her shoulder and strolled away, gaining more than a few admiring glances from the ladies on the terrace.

Della smiled at his retreating form for the benefit of those ladies, then took up her book and stared at it as she blinked back tears.

C, B, A.

Backward, all backward, and wrong. This was not how the day, the house party, or the marriage was supposed to go. Something had to change, but Della's reserves of determination were exhausted as she sat wrapped in her mother's shawl and pretending to read the words of an unhappy female who'd been ridiculed sorely for arguing that women were every bit as dear to the Creator as men.

~

ASH HAD FORGOTTEN his riding crop, and because it had been a gift from an uncle, he considered it worth retrieving from the stable. Then too, he would need it to beat himself with if he couldn't figure out a path forward with Della.

He'd been afraid of disappointing her in bed.

Afraid she'd not confide in him about Chastain's attempt at bullying her in the library.

Afraid she'd pack him off to Dorning Hall without her if he admitted his mood was deteriorating.

He was disgusted with his own cowardice, and Della was likely disgusted with him too—exactly the response he never wanted to provoke from her.

Francis Portly sauntered out of the stable, though he wasn't attired for riding. "Mr. Dorning, good day. Out for a hack?"

"My brother and I have already enjoyed the morning air on horseback." Ash stepped to the left, and Portly moved in the same direction.

"Sorry," Portly said, smiling sheepishly. "Have you closed up the Coventry while you and your brother enjoy the countryside?"

"We have not. Tresham minds the club in our absence, and Sycamore will soon return to Town, while my wife and I continue to the family seat in Dorset."

"I notice you aren't participating in the tournament."

Portly was one of those perpetually invite-able bachelors who had a competence from some auntie, but not enough blunt to raise a family. He was not bad-looking, and his air was usually friendly and good-humored. Ash had seen him at the Coventry only in Chastain's company, though, which was no sort of recommendation.

"I spend most of my nights in Town among gamblers," Ash said. "I have more interesting activities available to me now." *Forgive me, Della.*

"Your lovely wife," Portly said, his gaze going past Ash's shoulder up the path toward the house. "Felicitations, by the way. I don't know the lady well, but she's certainly pretty."

Stay away from my wife. The anger behind that sentiment was entirely irrational, also welcome.

"Lady Della is in every way worthy of esteem," Ash said. "If you'll excuse me, I need to retrieve something from the saddle room." He had to dodge around Portly, who was apparently intent on detaining him in the stable yard.

Ash half expected to find a lady adjusting her décolletage in the saddle room, or maybe Chastain hiking a lady's skirts, but the only people on hand were the Marquess of Tavistock and Mrs. Tremont's brother, one Barrymore Golding. The saddle room door was open, and Tavistock had a saddle over his arm.

"Dorning, good day." Tavistock beamed great good cheer at Ash as he set the saddle on a rack in the aisle. "Golding and I are for a hard gallop. Shall you join us?"

Such youthful high spirits were hard to look upon, almost as if Tavistock was relieved to see even a near stranger, provided that stranger was a man-about-town. Tavistock could still shave every other day, and nobody would notice the days he missed except his step-mama and his valet.

"No, thank you," Ash said. "Take the gray in the corner stall if you want a challenge. He's very light to the aids and still needs to work out the fidgets, even after a hack to the village and back. You won't need spurs."

Golding came out of the saddle room, Ash's riding crop in his hand. He was blond, tallish, a natty dresser, and bore an air of perpetual amusement. Ash suspected Golding lived off his sister and his wits, but he was not a patron of the Coventry, so his means were of no particular interest.

"Dorning. How's married life?"

Considering that Ash barely knew Golding, the question sat awkwardly. "Married life is delightful, and that is my riding crop you have."

Golding passed it over. "Married life already calls for the use of a riding crop? Delightful indeed."

Tavistock winced. "I say, Golding. You don't insult a man's new wife with such casual vulgarities."

Golding smirked. "My apologies, and Tavistock, perhaps we'll ride out another time." He used one finger to nudge at the little yellow flower in Tavistock's lapel, then sauntered off down the barn aisle.

Tavistock watched him go, then pulled the flower from his jacket and tossed it into the nearest empty stall.

"Thank you," Ash said. "I was about to pummel him, and that would have caused talk."

Tavistock leaned his back flat against the barn wall, the picture of daunted youth. "He sat next to me at breakfast, full of gossip and naughty jokes. His hand brushed my thigh more than once, but in that casual way hands sometimes do. I daresay I've caught his eye, but I didn't realize the problem until we were in the saddle room, and he accidently put his hand on my bum—twice."

I hate house parties. "That is awkward."

"It's bloody awful. Portly said Golding is a capital fellow, but then, Portly thinks Chastain is a capital fellow, and you will think me a complete simpleton if I don't stop babbling. It's just that Chastain can't play cards worth shite, and my entire allowance is already bobbing about in the River Tick, and it was Portly who told me Chastain knows what he's about at cards. Step-mama is ready to wash her hands of me, and that is not a good feeling, Mr. Dorning. Not a good feeling at all."

Ash detected a pattern lurking in this lament. Something to do with Portly, Chastain, cards, and betrayed trust. He also saw a boy who lacked that most valuable of blessings—and curses—abundant, meddling, well-intended family.

Ash hung his riding crop on a nail and peeled out of his jacket. "Put your hand on my bum."

"I beg your pardon?"

"Put your hand on my bum. I'll show you how to put a stop to it once and for all." Ash turned his back to Tavistock and, after a moment's pause, felt a tentative pat to his arse. In one motion, Ash turned, grabbed the offending wrist, and brought his knee up just shy of Tavistock's tallywags.

"You're fast," Tavistock said as Ash turned loose of his wrist. "Damned fast."

"And if you touched me by accident, I'd simply say my reflexes got the better of me—blame it on schoolyard fisticuffs—and I meant nothing by it. But if you did not touch me by accident, you'd be writhing on the floor, praying for the lives of your unborn children."

"Can you show me how to do that?" Tavistock said.

Ash spent about five minutes teaching Tavistock how to put Golding on the floor, how to follow up with a combination of blows Golding was unlikely to anticipate, and how to keep his guard up.

"You have reach over most men by virtue of your height," Ash said, shrugging back into his jacket and retrieving his crop. "Use that. The speed will come with practice, and strength can be built over time." Ash felt marginally better for having broken a sweat, though he was still unsettled over his conversation with Della.

"Thank you, sir," Tavistock said, donning his own jacket. "I was thinking of asking Mr. Sycamore Dorning to show me a few pointers regarding the cards. Chastain is truly an abominable player. It's like he's trying to impress people with how casually he loses."

Or take some sort of revenge on the father who was likely covering all those losses? "I have noticed Chastain's lack of skill. If you can change partners, you should."

"But a gentleman wouldn't, would he?" Tavistock asked, coloring about the cheeks as he and Ash ambled down the barn aisle.

Tavistock had not blushed to admit Golding had fondled his arse —he'd been rightly angry about that—but the idea of disappointing Chastain mortified him.

"You have doubtless heard that Chastain attempted to elope with Lady Della," Ash said.

Tavistock nodded, gaze on the nearest horse. "One doesn't bandy a lady's name about, but Portly gave me the general idea."

"Portly doesn't have the whole tale, but I can tell you, my lord, not to trust Chastain with your coin or your good name. He's not honorable."

Tavistock sighed such as only the aggrieved adolescent male can sigh. "Step-mama said as much, and I was determined to ignore her advice. She doesn't know what it's like to be a perishing marquess, everybody toadying, nobody telling you what's what. Portly and

Chastain weren't toadies, so it never occurred to me they might be worse than toadies." Tavistock stopped outside the gray's stall. "Chastain doesn't like your club. That should have told me something right there. Step-mama would never sit down at your tables if you weren't running an honest hell."

"We run a very honest hell."

The horse stuck his head over the half door and whuffled. To Ash, the gelding had an anxious eye, for all he had good conformation and smooth gaits.

"No confidence," Ash said, stroking the horse's ears. "I suspect he's not had the best training."

"He and I should get on famously," Tavistock said, fishing a lump of carrot from his pocket and feeding it to the horse. "You're a handsome lad, though, aren't you?" He pet the horse for a moment, giving him a good scratch under the chin. "What am I to do, Mr. Dorning? I will be pockets to let until my majority at the rate Chastain is bankrupting me."

Ash could tell Tavistock what every English gentleman was advised to do in the face of every adversity: carry on and bear the consequences without complaining. Nobody ever told the gentleman why he was to be so stoic or why he wasn't to complain about blatant injustices.

"Your step-mother doesn't want to see you used and exploited by the likes of Chastain," Ash said, "but she needs to know you've learned something from your mistakes. I suggest you apologize to her, explain your situation, and ask for her advice. This time, listen to her."

"She will ring such a peal over my head." Tavistock smiled slightly. "Step-mama can do more damage with her tongue than any headmaster ever did with the birch rod. I admire her tremendously, and the solicitors are terrified of her."

While Sycamore was half in love with the woman. "Let her have her say, and if she tells you that pressing business calls you back to the family seat at dawn tomorrow, off you go."

"I'm seventeen, Dorning. I haven't any pressing business."

"You might point that out to her. Tell her you'd like to manage a small property close to home, get your feet wet so to speak. My brother wasn't all that much older than you when he took over managing the whole earldom from our father. My father would step in occasionally, but mostly he let Casriel learn by trial and error."

"I have the error part well in hand." Tavistock gave the horse a final pat. "Wish me luck."

"You don't need luck. Your step-mother loves you and has probably been praying that you'd seek her help before Chastain put you truly in dun territory. I also suspect Sycamore would be happy to sit down with you over a few friendly hands of cards. What he doesn't know about reading other gamblers isn't worth knowing, and once you begin to think in terms of probabilities, your luck will improve significantly."

"Thank you," Tavistock said, offering his hand. "We are barely acquainted, Mr. Dorning, but I hope at some point I can be of as much service to you as you have been to me."

Ash shook hands, oddly touched at Tavistock's earnestness. "Glad to be of use, your lordship."

Tavistock was off down the path, his stride the loose-limbed gait of youth. Ash remained at the stable until the first luncheon bell rang, trying to sort out why the exchange with Tavistock had made him so uneasy.

Tavistock was a decent young fellow who'd known enough to ask for help when he was in over his head, but he was already in debt because of Chastain, which meant Chastain was in debt too.

In debt, and apparently not at all concerned about it, despite having told Della that marriage had not improved his finances at all.

CHAPTER FOURTEEN

Della savored the sense of security and peace that came from waking with Ash snuggled along her back. She remained still lest she rouse him and mentally fortified herself for another day of house party purgatory. The tedium of socializing with two dozen acquaintances was bearable, even William Chastain's smirking presence was endurable, but the growing sense of distance with Ash was breaking her heart.

She'd draped herself over him when he'd come to bed late the previous evening, and he'd tolerated her kisses. As it had become clear to Della that he was humoring her, he'd petted her shoulder and suggested they get some sleep. He'd been not the least bit *stirred* by her overtures. When Della had climbed off of him, he'd rolled to his side and wished her pleasant dreams.

She'd spooned herself around him, and when she'd wrapped an arm about his waist, he'd taken her hand and kept her gently but firmly from exploring below his waist.

How could two people occupy the same bed and have such a vast silence between them? How could they have started the week so passionately and already have this aching awkwardness wedging its way into their marriage?

"You're awake?" Ash asked.

"Not quite asleep." She laced her fingers through his. "I like cuddling with you."

Without moving, without even changing his breathing, Ash retreated in some intangible way. "I'm sorry, Della. I know you were in an amorous mood last night, but sometimes cuddling is all I can offer."

"Do you know how dearly I treasure your cuddling? I feel safe when you hold me, and cherished and real. I can breathe when your arms are around me."

"You can breathe?"

She had almost said too much. "You keep me wonderfully warm. I like knowing you are sharing a bed with me."

"Even when I'm restless?"

What was he asking? "You are no more restless than I am. Does something in particular keep you awake?"

Ash rolled to his back, and when Della rearranged herself along his side, he wrapped an arm around her shoulders.

"Why do you suppose Lady Fairchild's daughter is allowing Chastain to play the gallant with her?" he asked.

This was not pillow talk, but it was something. "You noticed that too. Chastain is not at all bookish, and Miss Catherine lives for her poetry and essays. Every day, I see her on his arm at some point, and I do not like how Chastain regards her."

"She is my half-sister," Ash said. "As closely related to me as three of my legitimate siblings. Perhaps my misgivings are laughable, but I feel a duty to warn her away from him."

"As do I, but whatever mischief Chastain is up to, I also fear to provoke him by saying anything to her that he might get wind of, but somebody ought to say something." A concerned half-brother, perhaps.

Ash began a slow pattern of caresses to Della's arm and shoulder.

"I don't know what to make of Mr. Portly," Della said. "He's agreeable and occasionally witty, but never cutting. He's partnering Clarice Chastain in the tournament with every appearance of good cheer, but he keeps company with William. Either William has a hold over him, or Mr. Portly lacks discernment in his choice of friends."

"Portly wasn't dressed for riding," Ash murmured. "And no other guests were on hand, save Tavistock and Golding. I had the sense Portly was serving as lookout for a tryst, but Tavistock had no interest in trysting."

"And," Della said, "Tavistock is William's partner at cards. Something is afoot that bodes ill for somebody, and William is behind it. He has also spent time in the gazebo with Mrs. Tremont on more than one occasion. I will keep my distance from Clarice, but I do not envy her the spouse her parents chose for her."

A spouse Della herself might have been stuck with, but for Ash's gallantry.

"The next time I suggest we accept a house party invitation, smack me," he said. "I will hand you my very own riding crop, and you can serve me a few good stripes to bring me back to my senses."

"Would it help with the melancholia if I took the crop to you?" Della asked. "This topic has come up before, but I'm asking in all seriousness now." The idea appalled her, though schoolboys were regularly birched for any number of transgressions.

Ash rolled away from her and climbed out of the bed. "I will not ask my wife to beat me. Don't be ridiculous." He was beautifully naked, also angry. "That would be the request of a lunatic."

Della retrieved her robe from the foot of the bed and shrugged into it. "But if the cutting and boxing help, why not a riding crop? Entire brothels exist to gratify the whims of those who enjoy that sort of thing."

He stalked behind the privacy screen. "Cutting and boxing don't help. They are temporary reprieves and not very good ones. I've explained that to you."

Della bounced off the bed and stood just beyond the privacy screen. "Would beating *me* help?"

An instant of silence followed that question, that act of desperation. Ash came around the privacy screen, his expression aghast.

"I would never, under any circumstances, consider such a thing or even... Della? Why would you...?" He wrapped his arms around her. "No. No, you daft creature, whacking at you with a crop could never do anything but horrify me. Don't be an idiot, and please never make such an offer again."

A measure of Della's worry eased. "I like when you hold me like this, so tightly."

He gave her another three breaths of that lovely, snug embrace before returning to the privacy screen. "I hope we have exhausted the topic of melancholia and riding crops for the duration of this marriage, Mrs. Dorning. Find something to wear, and I'll do up your hooks."

Irritability meant low spirits stalked him. Della found a brown morning gown in the wardrobe, along with a chemise, stays, and stockings. Ash donned riding attire and made a brisk business of assisting Della to dress.

"You will avoid Chastain?" he asked, sitting on the chest at the foot of the bed to pull on a tall boot.

"I will make every effort to avoid him, and I will try never to be alone if I must leave this room."

Ash tugged on his second boot, and he looked so damned luscious, Della nearly howled.

"I will ask Sycamore to keep an eye on Chastain," he said, "because I agree with you. Chastain is up to something untoward, and I'd rather we not become once more entangled in his schemes."

Della had become entangled in his schemes. More fool her. "I understand. Have a pleasant ride."

Ash collected his gloves, spurs, and crop, but paused by the bedroom door. "Della, would you rather we had separate bedrooms? I'm sure Lady Wentwhistle can find me a chamber under the eaves, or I can sleep in Sycamore's dressing closet for the next week."

If Ash had raised his hand to her, Della could not have felt the blow more keenly. "Is that what you want?"

He pulled on his gloves, and she loved watching him do even so mundane a thing as that. "I make the offer out of a concern for your peace of mind. Newlyweds who ask to have separate bedrooms halfway through a house party will cause talk, but I will cheerfully weather the talk to spare you unhappiness."

He hadn't said he wanted separate beds, he hadn't said he didn't. "Let's not be hasty, then, but I appreciate the offer." About as much as he'd appreciated the offer to birch him out of his blue devils.

Ash would have left on that bewildering exchange, but Della caught him around the waist in a hug. "Please be patient with me, Ash. I am new to being a wife, and I want very much to do well at it."

She could feel the desire to leave throbbing through him, feel his distaste for her desperate display. He gave her a swift hug.

"We'll muddle through," he said, "but this house party cannot end soon enough." He kissed her cheek and was out the door in the next instant.

❧

"NOT THE PATH BY THE GAZEBO," Sycamore said, taking Ash by the arm. "I saw Mrs. Tremont stealing off in that direction barely ten minutes ago."

Ash was abnormally annoyed to think of others casually trysting when he'd left Della unsatisfied. "You'd think she'd exercise some discretion."

"Mrs. Tremont is swiving Chastain," Cam said as casually as he'd observe that a wood thrush was making all that racket from the direction of the maze. "She said enduring his attentions was an unavoidable necessity, while a round with me would be pleasure. I was not flattered."

"I hate house parties." Why would Mrs. Tremont feel obliged to entertain Chastain?

"I'm not so keen on this house party, but it's nearly half over, and I haven't called anybody out. We must take encouragement where we find it."

"No duels, Cam. No challenges, no taking offense at drunken maunderings. I refuse to serve as your second." *Ever again.* Sycamore had participated in two duels, and on both occasions, Ash had kept the matter from the notice of their family and served as Cam's second. In each instance, the other party had fired first and poorly, and Sycamore had mercifully deloped.

"If somebody insults me," he said, "or my friends, or my business enterprise, I will take as much offense as I jolly well please."

Sycamore sounded as if he relished a dawn meeting, just a little outing to liven up an otherwise dull autumn morning. The weariness his posturing engendered blended with the awful start to Ash's day to result in an unintended confidence.

"I could not make love with my wife."

"Della's angry with you? Impressive bungling, Ash. She's put you on the cot in the dressing closet already?"

"No, Cam. Della is not angry with me. She was willing, and I was willing, but I couldn't... I didn't. Bloody hell."

"You *could not* make love with your wife." Cam sounded puzzled to contemplate such a possibility.

"I just said as much. It's this house party, Chastain lurking on the stairwell, Clarice accosting us at breakfast." *You underfoot and threatening to stir up mischief for the hell of it.* "I offered to sleep elsewhere, and she was dismayed."

Della had been hurt, and worse, Ash had the sense she had been *panicked.* She'd not refused the suggestion outright, though, and that tore at his heart. The ashamed part of him knew he deserved to be banished, the rest of him hated any more distance between him and Della.

"Well, don't expect me to oblige her," Sycamore said. "I have a few scruples left, though I misplace them on occasion for a good cause. Besides, Della would gut me if I so much as flirted with her."

"A reassuring thought." Too reassuring.

Sycamore came to a halt on the path. "Ash, mind you don't insult your dearest brother. I would cheerfully die to keep Della safe, but she is *your wife.*"

They resumed tromping along, the grass showing hoarfrost at the foot of the hill below the stable. The morning was beautiful, as only a crisp autumn morning could be, with sharp, bright sunbeams turning the fading leaves to gold and russet. The scent of woodsmoke put a tang in the air, and the frisky yearlings in the nearest pasture were well on the way to wearing winter coats.

Ash nonetheless battled the urge to continue to the carriage house, where he'd order the traveling coach readied. He could collect Della and their portmanteau and be away from this place before breakfast.

Which would start talk, solve nothing, and closet him alone in the vehicle with Della for the next two days. Then they'd be at Dorning Hall, with well-intended family nosing about and expecting them to make calls on half the blasted, smiling, rubbishing shire.

"Tresham reports that all goes well at the Coventry," Ash said, not that he gave a hearty goddamn for the Coventry at the moment. What must Della think of him, going limp as week-old celery even as she sought her pleasure? Even as he'd *invited* her to seek her pleasure?

Sycamore's steps slowed. "He does?"

"I asked him to keep an eye on the place in my absence before you added your request to mine. He generally provides that service when I leave Town, and I don't see why this year should be any different."

"Ash, I keep an eye on things. I *run* things, in fact, and do so well enough without Tresh serving as my nanny."

Ash would normally agree, just to keep the peace, but his failure to perform a husband's most pleasurable office had left him vastly out of sorts. He suspected he would not come right until Della was once again sighing with contentment in his arms.

"You manage things," Ash muttered, "which is why I come back to London in the New Year and find half the bills unpaid, the ledgers weeks out of date, the staff feuding, and the inventories in disarray."

Sycamore twirled his riding crop through his fingers. "The customers are happy, the bank accounts are happy, and I am happy. Besides, you like putting everything to order and scolding me for my lapses when you return."

"I would *like* to pummel the living shite out of you for your laziness and self-absorption, but Lady Tavistock might take exception to your own brother marring the perfection of your features." The Earl of Casriel might frown on his brothers scrapping in the stable yard, too, to say nothing of what the Countess of Casriel would think of her in-laws for such behavior.

And what would Della think, knowing that Ash turned to pugilism to improve his mood?

Sycamore must have sensed that Ash spoke more in earnest than in jest, because Cam for once kept silent.

"I'll show you Tresham's figures when I'm done reviewing them," Ash said. "Della asked if beating her would help my melancholia. She wasn't being naughty or daring, Cam. She was simply desperate to help me. I was nearly sick. In my worst imaginings, in my worst nightmares, I could not conceive of such a thing."

That admission, terrible as it was, served as a partial apology for a vile mood.

"Then your imagination grows as lethargic as the rest of your mind," Sycamore said, his tone merely curious. "I'm not suggesting you take her up on that offer, for I would have to kill you if you did, but I am suggesting that Della is looking for solutions to your melancholia, while you merely look for a place to hide."

I hate this day. "What the hell are you talking about?" They'd reached the stable yard, and a groom approached. "I'll take the gray."

"The frisky chestnut mare for me," Sycamore said. "But don't tighten the girth too snugly. She wants a gentle hand with that part." The groom trotted off, and Sycamore fixed an uncharacteristically serious eye on Ash. "You should listen to your wife, Ash. She's willing to fight for your happiness."

"By making bizarre suggestions?"

"By using her imagination. You and I both know people who enjoy inflicting pain on others. For some, it's an interesting and strictly consensual sexual diversion. For others, it's a bully's small-minded nastiness. Chastain strikes me as the latter sort. At university, you were more willing to wrestle with your blue devils. You rowed, you developed your penchant for boxing there. You tried a few pipes of opium, and you took up with the Greek goddess housekeeper. Since then, it's as if you've turned elderly, never venturing far from the fire for fear your rheumatism will act up."

"I am not elderly."

Sycamore patted Ash's cravat, a gesture that should have earned him a black eye. "You are not happy. I make allowances as a result, but now you are married. Della is an ally, and all you can think to do is sleep in the dressing closet at the first awkward moment. I despair of you, Ash. I truly do."

He sauntered off, likely never knowing how close he'd come to a sound thrashing.

Ash found the gray gelding's nervous energy a good fit with his mood. The morning hack became a steeple chase, with Sycamore falling farther and farther behind on his winded chestnut. Riding like a demented Cossack resulted in an improvement in Ash's perspective, such that by the time he swung off the gray, he was determined to sort a few things out with Della.

Sycamore ambled into the stable yard a few moments later, looking as windblown as his horse.

"Did it help?" he asked, climbing from the saddle and stroking the mare's sweaty neck.

"I'd still like to pummel you."

"Let's have some breakfast before I oblige you. Old fellows like you need to keep up their strength."

The taunt held no heat, and as they strolled back to the house, Ash had the satisfaction of knowing he'd outridden his dashing younger brother.

"My virgin eyes," Sycamore murmured as he and Ash rounded a bend in the trees. "That is Chastain's new wife and his best friend, and I do not believe their embrace qualifies as platonic."

Clarice Chastain was plastered against Francis Portly in a manner suggestive of intimacies either recently granted or soon to be shared. Portly's demeanor had much of protectiveness about it, for all that it was far too familiar.

"I suppose the gazebo was taken," Ash said, half of his good mood dissipating. "I did not take Mrs. Chastain for a fool, but provoking her spouse will only redound to the misery of all. Please make my excuses at breakfast."

"This is a house party, Ash," Sycamore replied, resuming their progress. "Since when did you become a Puritan?"

"More of a Quaker, Cam. I want peace, calm, and quiet solitude. Instead, we have a rural bacchanal, when I should be on my wedding journey." Though the house party would conclude in a week. Ash clung to that singularly fortifying thought. "I am bothered by something, though."

"You are bothered by everything of late."

"This is something you can investigate. Why would Mrs. Tremont allow Chastain under her skirts? She's a widow, she has means, she can dispense or withhold her favors as she pleases. She does not care for Chastain, and yet, she apparently accommodates his demands. Not only is Chastain newly married, he's courting the favor of Lady Fairchild's daughter and doubtless bothering the maids too. Why does Mrs. Tremont feel she must humor his demands?"

"That is a puzzle, isn't it?" Sycamore murmured as they emerged onto the tall hedge forming the back side of the maze. "Particularly when a half-dozen randy young swains would eagerly accommodate her. I will get you an answer."

"Be discreet, Cam."

He waved his riding crop and sauntered on. "Discretion is my middle name."

His full name was Sycamore Erasmus Momus Dorning, Momus being the god who'd instigated the Trojan War before being banished from Olympus.

~

"I WISH I hadn't watched the card play last night," Della said, rolling a stocking up over her calf. "Poor Lord Tavistock looked bilious by the time the games concluded."

Ash's nose was buried in some letter from Jonathan Tresham that had arrived a day or two earlier. He was not watching Della dress— she'd purposely eschewed the privacy screen for that activity—and had barely spoken since they'd risen a half hour earlier.

"How much did Chastain cost Tavistock?" he asked.

Della named a figure. "And that was only last night's damage. People are talking."

Ash set aside his correspondence. "That is appalling. One has nearly to cheat to drop that much in one informal night of play."

Her bare leg hadn't earned his notice, but gambling, which he saw night after night, had. Della tied off her garter and took her foot off the vanity stool.

"Chastain treated it all as a lark. He's costing Tavistock an enormous sum, and I get the sense Chastain truly enjoys making the young marquess miserable. Have you seen my...?"

Ash leaned forward so Della could retrieve her shawl from the back of his reading chair.

"Lady Wentwhistle ought to intervene," Ash said.

"*Lord* Wentwhistle ought to intervene," Della countered. "The hand of God ought to smite William Chastain, but I suspect a jealous husband is the closest we'll come to that brand of justice. Aren't you attending services?"

Ash rose and took her shawl from her, folding it over his arm. "Sycamore will happily escort you. All five of us in the coach would be a bit crowded."

"Five?"

"The marchioness and Tavistock, you, me, Sycamore. Cam fancies her ladyship. I'm not sure what she's about with him. You will enjoy the outing to the church, and I will finish reading Tresham's figures."

Ash, who could absorb a ledger the way a conductor read an open score, had been perusing Tresham's figures for two days.

"Jonathan sent me something as well, Ash. I've been debating whether to show it to you." And dreading the discussion Jonathan's generosity would provoke.

"That sounds serious."

Della opened her reticule, fished beneath her flask of tea, and produced a folded piece of paper. "My darling brother was peevish because nobody consulted him on the settlements. Jonathan will use this sum to establish a trust for me if I ask it of him, and he will manage the trust according to my directions."

She passed Ash the bank draft, but he glanced at the figure without taking hold of the paper.

"You are a wealthy woman." No inflection, no emotion. Nothing. Not gratitude, relief, insulted pride, glee—not any sentiment Della could detect. But then, Della herself did not know how to feel about Jonathan's gesture.

"We can simply deposit the bank draft, Ash, which would make *us* wealthy."

"*We* are quite solvent, my lady. More solvent by the week." He sauntered off, looking splendid in breeches, shirt, and waistcoat. He'd not shaved, and to Della that hint of rakishness made his looks all the more appealing.

"What would you have me do with this?" Della asked.

"What do you want to do with it?"

"Tear it up?" Della stuffed the offending paper back in her reticule lest she do just that. "The money makes me anxious, if you must know. Everything makes me anxious. I want to be left in peace to be a good wife to you and sort out how our marriage should go on, and I feel as if I can't catch my breath. I look up, and there's Chastain watching me. I take a book to the terrace, and Lady Wentwhistle's coven falls silent when I walk by. I sometimes think I should do as Susannah did that day long ago and take a book into the maze and fall asleep."

She was babbling, so she jerked her reticule closed and willed herself to silence. Now was not the time to tell Ash he'd married a fretful ninnyhammer who shook like a leaf for no reason, occasionally fainted from worry that had no basis in fact, and dreaded the end of the world every fortnight or so.

Ash set aside her shawl and, to her great relief and surprise, took the reticule from her and wrapped her in his arms.

"If you disappeared into the maze, I would find you. A week from tomorrow, we will get into our coach—just the two of us—and gallop off to Dorning Hall. Young Lord Tavistock will leave tomorrow, called to the side of his supposedly ailing tutor. With the marchioness's permission, and his lordship's consent, I arranged to have a letter ostensibly from Tavistock Hall delivered first thing tomorrow morning. Chastain will be left without a partner for next week's games. Tavistock's debts will be paid as they stand upon his departure tomorrow."

That Ash had the matter of the young marquess in hand was an enormous relief.

And his arms around Della very nearly made all come right. She and Ash had slept as strangers last night, and Della had awoken to see Ash dressed and already reading by the window—or staring at Jonathan's tallies.

"Thank you," she said, closing her eyes, the better to hug her husband. "I felt as if I was watching a runaway team head for a steep curve. Chastain sank that poor young man more and more deeply into debt, and nobody intervened."

"Sycamore had a word with Lady Tavistock." Ash's hold on Della loosened. "I will say something to Lady Fairchild when our paths cross again. Can you think of any reason Mrs. Tremont would tolerate Chastain's attentions?"

Don't leave me, don't go away. Hold me, please. "Because Chastain will spread talk about her brother otherwise. Mr. Golding is known to have left-handed tendencies. George once told me as much. You'd be surprised the things George knows and who he knows them about. Will you come to services with me?"

She ought not to have asked. Ash stepped back, wearing his politely charming smile. "I'll decline that honor for today. I might go for a hack instead, but don't tell anybody I'm enjoying myself on the Sabbath."

He'd returned from yesterday's hack looking like he'd ridden through a Channel storm. "Tomorrow, I'll ride out with you."

"I'd like that." He passed Della her shawl, and she knew that he would not waken her to join him for tomorrow's ride. He'd make up some taradiddle about letting her rest, and one more activity they might have shared would be denied her.

"Enjoy your hack," she said, retrieving a bonnet from the wardrobe. She was halfway to the door before Ash's voice stopped her.

"Della?"

She faced him, and dread welled at his solemn expression. He was preparing to remove to another room, preparing to politely set her aside. Perhaps he planned to leave her at the family seat while he returned to Town. Perhaps he would send her to Kent rather than Dorning Hall.

He'd grown increasingly remote, and she had no idea what to do about it.

"I want you to be happy," he said. "That is how I want our marriage to go on, in whatever manner will make you happy. I appreciate your brother's generosity, but any decision regarding that money must rest with you."

"I hardly know what to do with it."

Ash remained two yards away when Della longed for his embrace. "Why don't we get through the next week, and when we are free of this durance vile, you can consider the question at your leisure."

She went to him and gave him a swift hug, retreating before he could stiffen or pull away. "I like that idea." She kissed his cheek and moved toward the door. "I like that idea exceedingly, and thank you again for thwarting Chastain's plans for Lord Tavistock. We cannot leave this place soon enough to suit me."

"Agreed."

There seemed to be nothing more to say, an increasingly frequent occurrence between Della and her husband, so she left Ash alone in their rooms and steeled herself for the weekly penance known as divine services.

CHAPTER FIFTEEN

"Tavistock leaving is all to the good," William Chastain said around a mouthful of eggs. Lady Wentwhistle believed in that tribulation of the body and spirit known as keeping country hours, at least regarding breakfast. Because a man needed adequate sleep to recover from his day, William's eggs were thus cold, and the only toast remaining on the sideboard was overdone.

When he and Clarice had their own home, the toast would be cooked to perfection, or William would chastise his wife accordingly.

Though Clarice was proving a bit of a challenge. She sniffed, and blinked, and never actually cried, while giving William wounded looks that promised his mother would hear about his lapses in husbandly consideration.

Clarice either didn't care or didn't notice that William had enjoyed the charms of three other guests, but she took vast exception if he came to bed without washing thoroughly and using his tooth-powder. So he washed and used his toothpowder and spared himself Clarice's dramatics. He figured another few days of that, and she'd let him get back to the frolicking and fondling marriage was supposed to entail.

Maybe she'd even let him touch her bubbies.

"Tavistock will pay up before he rides off," Portly replied, "or his step-mama will, and you'll be left holding your half of the markers."

"The marchioness will make good on my vowels and then some. All I need do is mention to her that Golding was seen in a compromising embrace with the marquess, and her purse will be mine to raid at will." The scheme was so simple and elegant, William chided himself for not thinking of it sooner. And Martha Tremont would hoist her skirts for Beelzebub to keep her brother safe, though she doubtless enjoyed manufacturing her little pretense of reluctance.

Portly tipped his tea cup and peered at the dregs. "I didn't actually see them, Chastain. I told you that."

"They were alone in the saddle room, and Golding did not keep his hands to himself. He'd bugger a sheep on a bet and probably has."

"Tavistock is not a sheep, and nobody has buggered anybody."

"You don't know that. Besides, the fair Miss Catherine has confided in me—by indirection and innuendo—the irregularity of her antecedents, and thus Lady Fairchild's jewels are all but in my grasp. If all else fails, Mrs. Tremont will part with a few baubles to keep her brother's name from my lips. Pass the butter."

Portly obliged, though somebody had got crumbs on the three pats remaining in the dish.

"When did you become mean, Chastain? You've always been a bit sly and had a nasty streak to your humor, but these people never did you any harm. You cannot expect to offend a marquess, two well-born widows, and God knows who else in the course of a single house party and not find yourself the object of talk."

William scraped cold, crumb-y butter over cold, half-burnt toast and promised himself he'd have a good, hard go at his wife before noon. Damned woman needed to know her place, and what was the point of having a wife with bouncy tits if a husband couldn't play with them?

"You have become tiresome, Portly. Perhaps it's you who enjoyed groping young Tavistock. Wouldn't that make an interesting rumor?"

Portly set down his tea cup. "I am known to be your best friend, Chastain—your only friend, come to that. If you call my proclivities into question, how long do you think your own will remain above suspicion?"

"Forever," Chastain replied languidly. "My ability to please the ladies is beyond doubt. In fact, I think I might allow Lady Della Haddonfield a chance to partner me now that Tavistock has tucked tail."

"Dorning won't permit you to bother her," Portly said, sitting back.

"Who said anything about bothering? She can be my tournament partner, or meet me in the gazebo of her own free will. She and I have unfinished and very pleasurable business. I can't imagine Dorning has done justice to his marital obligations. Damned man hasn't left his room since Saturday."

"He escorted Lady Della to dinner last night."

"And left when the ladies went to swill their scandal broth. Lady Della is looking neglected, and I know just how to cheer her up."

"Chastain, if you cannot leave well enough alone on your own account, then limit your mischief for Clarice's sake."

William had had as much bad food as he could tolerate and more bad company than any man should have to endure.

"You ask why I'm being a bit exuberant about my usual pleasures at this house party," he said. "When did I turn mean, you ask. I'll tell you when. I became mean when a spinster who by rights should have thanked me for running off with her, instead bollixed up an ingenious plan that met both of our needs."

William gestured with his toast and got crumbs on his cravat. "I became meaner when my parents forced me to wed a prim little Frenchie bitch who now lays claim to half my allowance, but refuses to allow me to pet her diddies. Because of her, I cannot afford new boots, much less a mistress, and I refuse to bear those insults quietly."

"Then set your wife aside," Portly said, an uncharacteristic gravity to his tone. "Clarice was forced into the marriage too. Don't take out your tantrum on her, Mrs. Fairchild, Mrs. Tremont, the marchioness, and Lady Della."

"You make it sound as if I pick on women. Stop being ridiculous."

"You do pick on women. You've taken to bullying them and committing the next thing to rape. I'd wash my hands of you, Chastain, but somebody will have to serve as your second when the inevitable occurs, and I feel I owe Clarice that much."

William took out the flask he'd filled in Lady Wentwhistle's library and tipped half the contents into his tea cup.

"So noble of you, Portly. I vow I'm touched. I'll name you as guardian of my firstborn." Already had, in fact, because Papa had insisted on wills and trusts and whatnot to go with the marriage settlements. Before William had put away his flask, Lady Tavistock came into the gallery in company with Lady Fairchild. "I wonder if the marchioness's muff is the same flaming red as her hair. One way to find out, I suppose."

"Sycamore Dorning would kill you for even thinking that, and I'm not sure I would mourn your passing, Chastain." Portly rose, bowed, and stalked off, leaving William to salute his retreating form with a half tea cup of decent brandy.

House parties were such fun, and this one was about to become more enjoyable still.

William had spotted Lady Della reading on the terrace, which seemed to be her favorite pastime. The time had come to liven up her morning and maybe even provoke her into another one of those vastly amusing bouts of hysteria.

❧

DELLA ADOPTED the strategy of reading on the terrace because it allowed her to keep an eye on her husband. Ash sat before the window of their bedroom, two floors and a universe of low spirits away. Should anybody glance up, they would think that fellow in the window was taking advantage of the light to read.

Della knew Ash had sat in that chair for most of the previous afternoon, slowly flipping through a deck of cards and losing hand after hand of solitaire. He claimed to be calculating probabilities, and she'd left him to it, rather than pester him when he so clearly needed to be left in peace. His words, about watching the children in the garden at Dorning Hall, had come to her, so she'd chosen a place on the terrace where he could watch her and she could watch him.

Sycamore seemed to realize what was afoot, for he'd not interrupted her, not plagued her with teasing and prattling, as he was inclined to do. She almost wished he would—almost.

A shadow fell across her copy of Sir Walter Scott's *Marmion*.

"My lady, good day." William Chastain loomed above her, doubtless enjoying the view of her décolletage.

Even from a distance of several feet, Della could smell the brandy on his breath—well before midday—and the scent unnerved her.

"Mr. Chastain, good morning." She turned a page of her book, even knowing such a blatant hint would do nothing to deter him.

He took the chair next to hers, spreading his legs and lounging back in his seat. "Lord Tavistock is doing a bunk. He's spun a tarradiddle about an old tutor falling ill, but he's simply dodging out on me. Can't take a few losing hands. Typical of the Quality."

That was petty sniping, suggesting worse was on the way. "Lord Tavistock received a letter by special courier this morning. Everybody taking breakfast at the time saw the letter put into his hands. His old tutor has fallen gravely ill."

"Anybody can arrange for a handy epistle to show up in the right location. I can send letters to the London papers, for example, and on occasion, I have. Might have to warn the general public that his lordship is a molly boy in marquess's clothing, for example."

A shiver of dread passed down Della's arms and settled in her middle. "Lord Tavistock is no such thing, and you know it. How is Mrs. Chastain?"

"A bit too haughty for her own good, but I'll bring her around once we're done with this fool's errand. Tavistock's departure leaves me in want of a tournament partner, Lady Della. I thought you might like to take his lordship's place."

Della said the first thing that came to mind. "My husband would not allow me to partner you."

Chastain smiled, and the unease in Della's belly became outright nausea.

"The professional gambler forbids his wife to participate in a few friendly hands, and like the biddable little twit that you are, you humbly obey him. Where is he, by the way? A proper gentleman escorts his lady to services and joins her at meals."

Della closed her book while she still had control over her extremities. "If you'll excuse me, I need to return this volume to the library."

Chastain clamped a hand around her wrist, and Della's vision dimmed. She shrank back into her chair and tried to focus on simply breathing. Dread rose up inside her like an incoming tide, though she knew that reaction was out of all proportion to the situation.

She was in public, and Chastain could not carry her off before an entire house party. Then too, Ash might be watching from his aerie, and Chastain would not risk Ash Dorning's ire.

"You must not abandon me, my lady," Chastain said, his grip becoming painful. "I am a reasonable man and newly wed myself. If you don't want to partner me at cards, then partner me in the gazebo. The cushions are wonderfully soft, and I love going about my pleasure while other guests stroll mere yards away. The risk that my lover might cry out in pleasure adds to the fun, don't you think?"

"Let go of me."

"What's it to be?" Chastain asked, rubbing his thumb over Della's wrist. "A few days of letting me bankrupt the new Mrs. Ash Dorning, or a few turns on the pillows in the gazebo? Perhaps you'd like to oblige me with both? I'm quite skilled between the sheets, my lady, though I can get a bit enthusiastic. Dresses get torn, coiffures are disarranged. That sort of thing."

"Unhand me."

He tugged on her wrist so she had no choice but to lean closer to him.

"I can offer you a third choice," Chastain went on, his tone thoughtful. "The best option, in my opinion. Leave Ash Dorning. He only married you to stop the gossip, and he's not much of a bargain, if the talk is to be believed. He's mentally unstable, and the last thing you want, my lady, is to risk visiting upon a child the weaknesses in both the sire and dam lines. The poor thing would likely be born an idiot. Just pack your things and leave. Dorning will figure out the rest and probably thank you for it."

For an instant, Della was tempted to consent to that plan. The difference between separate bedrooms and separate lives was one of degree.

But that was not a decision for William Chastain to make on her behalf, and that Chastain would vilify Ash so casually added a current of ire to Della's panic.

She opened her mouth to berate Chastain, but all that came out was a harsh little wheeze. The sound of her constricted breathing added to her anger and her determination. Chastain had come upon her once before in the middle of a bad bout. She'd not give him the satisfaction a second time.

"Or," Chastain went on, "I could simply tell Mr. Ash Dorning that he's married to a woman who turns into a gibbering lunatic for no apparent reason. She hides in alcoves and loses her powers of speech between one set of dances and the next. She moans like one possessed and rocks like an imbecile under a Beltane moon. Most distressing to come upon such a sight."

"Go to hell." Della could barely enunciate her words, and she could not get her breath, but she could twist her wrist, as George had taught her to do years ago. She shot to her feet, though her legs were shaky and her vision had narrowed such that all she could see was the steps leading down to the garden.

She dodged blindly into the maze while Chastain's laughter stole the last of her wits, and dread choked the air from her lungs.

∼

AN OSTINATO of guilt occupied Ash's thoughts, try though he might to deflect his misery with make-believe card games and complex probabilities.

He should rise from the chair and offer Della a turn in the garden.

But no. Strolling placidly amid the flowers was a Sunday activity, when more rigorous entertainments were frowned upon.

Ash had missed services yesterday, which meant today was Monday. Today, he'd missed his morning hack, which was bad of him, because it set the stage to miss breakfast, and why not lunch and dinner too?

He'd hated Della's look of defeat when he'd sent her down to dine without him, but he was truly miserable company, fit only for staring at clouds and calculating how many minutes until the house party ended—9,800, give or take, depending on how early he and Della departed on Monday next.

Or, given a queen, deuce, and an ace showing on the hands of opposing players in a game of vingt-et-un—and a seven on the dealer's hand—should he stand or hit when holding seventeen dealt from a new deck? How did the odds change when holding sixteen?

He should shave, but he'd shaved yesterday right before dinner. This early in the day, he would not yet resemble a barbarian. Besides, he'd probably not leave his room until it was time to go down to dinner again, if he went down.

He should...

His gaze was no longer on the clouds or an imaginary card table, but rather, on the terrace below. Something wasn't right, though his sluggish mind took some time to solve the puzzle.

Della's shawl was draped over the back of an empty chair, and William Chastain occupied the next seat over. Della would never have left her shawl sitting about like that, much less where Chastain could touch it, or worse, rend it or make off with it.

Ash waited for Della to emerge from the house to retrieve her shawl, but as best he recalled, which wasn't well at all, she'd not gone into the house. She'd been reading, and a book bound in red leather lay facedown on the flagstones at Chastain's feet.

Della would not disrespect a book like that.

She would not willingly sit beside William Chastain.

She would not approach Chastain even to retrieve her shawl.

The insidious voice of inaction whispered to Ash that Della was likely strolling the gardens with Sycamore. She would send a footman to fetch her shawl at any moment. Perhaps she had delivered Chastain a good set-down and would return for her shawl.

Except, Chastain sat there, legs splayed in a posture of utter unconcern. No pink handprint marred his handsome cheek, and neither did he pick up the book at his feet.

The voice of inaction contrived more arguments in favor of remaining in the chair. Della would not appreciate a husband who sent her down for breakfast alone, then demanded to know her whereabouts two hours later.

Chastain was apparently spoiling for a confrontation, and if Ash marched onto the terrace making accusations and asking questions, Chastain would doubtless become difficult.

And still, Della was nowhere in sight.

"Bloody hell." Ash rose, his joints protesting even that much movement. He stalked from the room, equally resenting the exertion and his own gumption, knowing himself to be a fool. But he was a *married* fool, and the situation on the terrace made him uneasy on behalf of his wife.

He snatched up Della's shawl with barely a nod to Chastain.

"She's in the maze," Chastain called as Ash headed for the garden.

Ash stopped at the top of the steps. "I beg your pardon?"

"Lady Della took a fit of some sort and went pelting off into the maze. She was quite out of sorts. I don't think she likes being married to you, Dorning, nor is she entirely in her right mind."

"Or perhaps she found the company here on the terrace unsuit-able." Rather than bicker with Chastain, Ash descended the steps and entered the maze. "Della?"

He did not recall seeing anybody in the maze from his window perch, but that hardly signified. He'd been watching cards dealt in a fictitious game, then clouds moving across the sky. By the hour, he'd watched the autumn breeze steal dying leaves from tree branches as sadness stole the will to move from his mind.

Goddamn stupid melancholia. "Della, where are you?" Ash did not call loudly, lest he create a scene, but he moved up and down the rows of privet systematically, working his way from one dead end to another, then taking the path that advanced toward the center of the maze.

Della did not like mazes, and that Chastain was watching for her to emerge from this one meant she might be waiting in the middle.

"Della?"

Ash reached the clearing around which the maze had been configured, finding the space deserted. The statue of Cupid, arrows clutched in a chubby fist, remained on a pedestal in the middle of a rectangle of grass, and two benches were arranged along the hedges to Cupid's left and right.

No, Della, so where the hell could she—?

A blur of brown velvet hurtled against Ash's side.

"Della?"

She clung to Ash as if every demon ever to escape the pit pursued her. "Hold…" The word was rasped, and Della sounded as if she'd run the entire distance from London. "Hold… *me.*"

She made a terrible noise, which Ash realized was an inhalation, but drawn as if her lungs were constricted by some paroxysm.

He took her in his arms, draping her shawl around her shoulders. "I'm here, Della. Can you tell me what's amiss?"

"Don't… go."

He would not have recognized that desperate, hoarse voice as hers had he not heard the words himself. "I won't leave you. Shall we sit? I can hold you while we sit for a moment."

"Hate this. *Hate it.*" She took another of those noisy, anguished breaths. "Chastain said..."

Chastain was a dead man. "We can discuss that later, I promise." Ash gathered her in his arms and sat with her on the bench, and that was apparently a bright idea, because as Della sat on his lap, the tension she carried eased. Her arms around Ash's neck became less desperate, though she kept her cheek pressed to his shoulder.

"You have married a crazy woman."

"No, I have not. I suspect at present my wife is upset."

"I wanted to give you your privacy."

Her hands were scratched, though the skin wasn't broken. She had apparently thrashed about in the maze until she'd found Cupid by blind chance. Having melancholia felt like that—a lot of blind thrashing around to end up exhausted and nowhere of any import.

"I need for you to be well and happy, Della, much more than I need any sort of privacy from you. That is not merely gentlemanly manners talking either. I saw your shawl on the empty chair next to Chastain and knew something was seriously wrong."

"He's still out there?"

Ash hated the dread in Della's voice and hated Chastain for putting it there. "He will likely be underfoot for the next week, but if you want to leave here, Della, we can be in the coach within the hour. I can stare out of one window as well as another. We're blasted newlyweds. We can take up our wedding journey whenever we please."

Except that leaving halfway through the house party would be most unusual, and Chastain would put the worst possible complexion on the whole business. Sycamore would take exception to Chastain's gossip, and another duel would likely result.

"I should have told you," Della said, climbing off Ash's lap and taking the place beside him. "I'm sorry, and now it's too late."

He tucked an arm around her shoulders, not to comfort her,

though he hoped his touch did comfort her, but because he needed the contact. "Told me what?"

"You'll send me away." She drew her feet up and curled into him. "You need a wife who can be of use to you, who can make your situation better, not worse."

"Della, I would never send you away, though I can imagine circumstances where you will find my company tiresome. We can face almost anything if we face it together." A tired platitude, and a soul-deep conviction of recent provenance. Ash had contemplated separate bedrooms for Della's sake, but his own selfish preferences lay in a different direction.

"You face your melancholia alone," Della said.

And just look how well that's going. "Tell me about what upset you."

"I worry," Della said, twiddling the fringe of her shawl. "To put it that way is like saying that your melancholia makes you a trifle distracted. I am so good at worrying, I should be appointed to a government post that oversees all worrisome matters specifically to ensure that those matters are the subject of endless fretting."

"But you never seem anxious."

"Do you seem sad?"

"Sometimes." Though likely not. To his family, he simply appeared lazy, unmotivated, and directionless—and to himself too, of course. "I'm often not sad so much as I simply lack the will to do the tasks before me." Eat, dress, wash, those sorts of tasks. Basic adult functions.

"I cannot seem to stop worrying, once I get started," Della said. "I have worried over everything from a French invasion to Nicholas's premature death to my own demise from influenza to the King of Rome growing up to plunge the entire European continent back into war."

The King of Rome was Napoleon's legitimate son, a mere child very likely still concerned with ponies, kites, and Latin grammars.

"You have a vivid imagination."

"For bad things, and sometimes, my imagination grows hysterical. My thoughts explode into foreboding, into unshakable certainty that all of creation is about to end and the fiend has been loosed upon my loved ones. I am overcome with panic that has no basis in reality. I babble and stammer, I can't catch my breath, my balance goes awry. On occasion, I faint when overcome with these feelings. I'm sorry. I am a hysterical ninnyhammer of the first water, and now you are stuck with me."

She was still shaking subtly, still unnaturally warm, as if she'd been crying.

"I married you," Ash said, giving her a one-armed hug. "Being stuck with each other was rather the point." Or he hoped it was. His reassurances had Della regarding him so solemnly that the dread she'd described began to creep over Ash's heart. "What did Chastain say, Della? Tell me exactly what he said."

She straightened beneath Ash's arm and untucked her feet to sit primly beside him. "He said I should leave you, and I am tempted to agree with him."

Had the stone Cupid toppled onto Ash's head, he could not have felt a greater sense of fate dealing him a blow. He'd sat for hours yesterday afternoon, watching nothing in particular, while Della had read on the terrace below him. Today, she'd taken up guard duty once again, while Ash had drifted among the clouds, too bloody melancholic to leave his bloody chair.

"I've left you alone in the market day crowd," he said, removing his arm from Della's shoulders. That he should emotionally abandon his new wife made him sick with sorrow and rage, but no matter.He could make it right, or at least make it less wrong. "I'm sorry for that. Damned sorry. I am the one person upon whom you should be able to rely, and a week into our marriage, I've turned my back on you. If you want to leave me, I will understand, Della."

She did not immediately answer, and Ash realized that a fate worse than melancholia might yet be his.

~

"THANK YOU." The Marchioness of Tavistock offered the words grudgingly.

Sycamore accepted them with equal bad grace. "You may tell Lord Tavistock he is welcome. I could have tended to the markers on his behalf. You should not have had to do it."

Her ladyship was not a cameo-pretty woman. Her jaw was angular, her russet brows too heavy, and her nose too strong. Cam loved simply looking at her, for no emotion or thought was allowed to mar her serene countenance, unless she allowed it. Her eyes alone gave her away, a startling jade green that could flash with ire or radiate mirth, and her mouth...

A mouth like that on a woman was reason for mortal man to give thanks to the Creator. On the rare occasions when her ladyship displayed anger, that mouth was a flat slash of disdain. When she smiled, especially when she smiled at him, Cam's mind went happy-stupid, and his blood pooled behind his falls.

She had smiled at Sycamore exactly twice in all the months he'd known her, and she wasn't smiling now.

"I wanted to know specifically to whom Trevor had become indebted," her ladyship said. "I did not want Mr. Golding accosting me two house parties hence and mentioning an overdue debt of honor my step-son had overlooked."

She sat at an elegant little escritoire inlaid with all sorts of fancy work in patterns of flowers and leaves. The piece was all wrong for her. By rights, her ladyship should be looking over battle maps spread out in a field tent and ordering generals about.

Sycamore did not dare risk propping a hip on the corner of the escritoire, so he instead ambled to the window, while silently lecturing the riot in his breeches into submission.

"If Mr. Golding makes a nuisance of himself, you will apply to me, your ladyship, and I will sort him out."

"You will confront him in public, make a great drama over a few pounds, perhaps even meet him on the field of honor, and expect my undying gratitude."

Sycamore rested his hips against the windowsill and considered the woman at the desk. "If I want to call anybody out, it's your late spouse. Tavistock must have soured you on all men forever."

Had Sycamore not been visually worshipping the magic of sunlight on her hair, he would have missed the haunted look that passed across her features.

"One mustn't speak ill of the dead, Mr. Dorning."

"Why not, if the dead comported themselves like ruddy blighters? One should be honest."

"One should be kind, discreet, and grateful for one's blessings."

He wanted to argue with her for the pure joy of watching her temper rise, but her morning had been trying enough. With the coin Sycamore had provided, she'd paid off all of her step-son's gambling losses, and the sum had been outrageous. Sycamore had sent to London for the funds midweek, anticipating the direction Lord Tavistock's tournament play would take.

"Whoever made up that rule about not arguing with a lady does not have my gratitude," Sycamore said, turning to regard the back gardens and the terrace below. "Arguing with ladies is some of the best fun to be had and making up after the argument more enjoyable still. I see Chastain lurking on the terrace. Is he expecting Mrs. Tremont to come wafting by on her way to the gazebo?"

The marchioness rose and joined him at the window. "Don't judge her. Chastain would see her brother arrested on a whim. If she didn't accommodate Chastain's rutting, he'd extort more blunt from her than even she can afford. She doesn't mind putting a stiff prick to its best use, though Chastain's finesse as a lover apparently ranks somewhere below the rutting-schoolboy category."

The words *stiff prick* coming from her ladyship were wildly exciting, though her tone of abject disgust was rather lowering.

"You don't care for stiff pricks?"

"Don't be vulgar."

But I like being vulgar. "Not an answer, my lady."

She sighed mightily. "If you expect me to spread my legs for you because you made me a short-term loan, you are doomed to disappointment. You will have the money within a fortnight."

"I am disappointed that you would think so ill of me. You are a widow exerting herself to protect a family member, and I am a gentleman happy to aid you."

She slanted him a considering look. "You can be a gentleman. One also hears you acquit yourself with considerably more skill than a rutting schoolboy and more frequently than any schoolboy ever dreamed of indulging himself."

Exactly where and from whom had one heard that? Had one perhaps *solicited* such information?

"I like to share pleasure with willing ladies. The rumors regarding my skill are understated and those regarding the frequency of my liaisons overstated. I am also discreet, your ladyship, and while I can be protective, I am not possessive. If you'd like to inspect my equipment, I'm cheerfully amenable to that exercise behind a locked door. You may look but not touch, until we've reached the usual agreements regarding temporary exclusivity and the desirability of avoiding conception."

She smiled ruefully—smile number three. "I deserved that. The problem is, I do like you."

Sycamore's four favorite words had been *take me to bed*. He flung them aside in favor of *I do like you*. "So many find my company agreeable," he murmured, "despite my best efforts to be dashing and knavish."

"I suspect when you don't get your way, you can be very knavish. You have my thanks for playing banker. Tavistock had a narrow escape, and how Chastain will pay his half of the markers puzzles me. Mrs. Tremont can pass him a pair of earbobs, Lady Fairchild might part with a necklace, but after another week of losses, trifles like that won't suffice."

"Why would Lady Fairchild part with a necklace?"

"Because her daughter has the famous Dorning eyes, but not the famous Dorning last name?"

"These things happen."

"And these things interfere with decent settlements and an adequate match, when a shy, plain woman gets to be a certain age and has had no offers."

Sycamore's flirtatious impulse was checked by a nasty thought. "Do you suppose Chastain has been forcing himself on Lady Fairchild?" Mrs. Tremont was an apparently merry young widow, but Lady Fairchild was the mother of Cam's half-sister and did not strike him as amenable to romping.

"Chastain has a new wife, and he's dallying with Mrs. Tremont. He's a pestilence to the servants, though Lady Wentwhistle knows to assign only the experienced maids and footmen to the guest wing, and they usually work in pairs. I doubt Chastain has the stamina to also inflict himself on Lady Fairchild."

"I am hardly reassured that a lack of stamina might be all that stands between Chastain and felonious conduct toward the ladies." Sycamore declined to mention that his own stamina defied womanly comprehension when he was truly inspired. What did an ability to last in bed matter if a fellow was an oaf?

Lady Tavistock patted his cravat. "You want an excuse to blow his brains out. This is part of why I like you."

"What are the other parts?"

"You can whistle up a small fortune in coin of the realm in less than a week, and you are discreet."

Such ringing endorsements as those would have Sycamore joining the clergy. He peered down at the back garden rather than take her ladyship's hand and press kisses to her wrist. William Chastain lolled in a chair on the shady side of the terrace, his posture suggesting he'd like to be stroking his crotch—or he'd like for somebody else to stroke his crotch.

I'm not like him. I'm not. "I am a gentleman, my lady, and I will thank you to—I see my brother and his new wife cuddled up at the center of the maze."

"They have been there for the past ten minutes. I'm glad Mr. Dorning is spending time with Lady Della. Chastain might limit himself to extorting baubles from Lady Fairchild and commandeering trysts with Mrs. Tremont, but I don't like how he's been looking at Lady Della."

Neither did Sycamore. "How has he been looking at Lady Della?"

"As if he'd enjoy hurting her."

Sycamore did catch Lady Tavistock's hand and bowed over it most correctly. "I fear you are right, and I should have a pointed discussion with my brother."

"Not this instant, Mr. Dorning. Your brother is attending to pressing marital business."

"Right, not this instant, but the moment he toddles out of the maze." Looking dazed and replete, Sycamore hoped. Another nasty thought occurred to him. "My lady, how come you to know the look of a man who'd enjoy hurting women?"

She moved closer, her hand still joined with his, and kissed his cheek. "A gentleman would not ask, but I'm touched that you did." She led him to the door, and when he stood before her wanting to say something, do something, *think* something, she gave him a gentle shove and closed the door behind him.

CHAPTER SIXTEEN

If you want to leave me, I will understand...

Sitting next to her husband, Della could calm herself enough to speak and even to think. Ash was offering to set her aside—and to *be* set aside.

A yellowed oak leaf went twirling by to land at Cupid's feet. "Chastain would love for us to separate."

"To blazes with Chastain. What do you want?"

Who asked her that, save Ash? "I want peace and safety. I want to have my bouts of hysteria where nobody will remark them."

"That is easily arranged. You have the means to purchase your own property, though I'd ask that you not establish a household too far from Town. I would rather that I provided you such a home, and I will happily do so, but the dwelling will be more modest. I would like to visit you from time to time, when I'm well, but I will understand if you'd prefer less of my company."

Della had heard Ash speak like this on other occasions. When explaining his illness to her, for example. All rational discourse and articulate speech. Not a sentiment in sight. He sat in his mental window, detached from the workings of the heart...

Except Ash wasn't detached. He was caring, conscientious, honorable, and dear. "What do you want, Ash?"

He shook his head. "That doesn't signify."

She took his hand in both of hers. "It signifies to me."

"Then I must admonish you to look to your own interests, Della. You need a husband who can make a safe place for you, who can help you weather the vagaries of a temperament prone to worry—a problem I had no idea you struggled with. Of all men, I am clearly not that useful fellow. Chastain accosted you in plain view, while I..." He looked up as if importuning the heavens for absolution. "While I calculated gaming odds and contemplated clouds."

As a little girl left to watch the sunset on the church steps, Della had watched the clouds. Close on the heels of that memory came some combination of thought and instinct that settled the last of her nerves.

Ash might have occupied a reading chair by the window for much of the morning, but he, too, had been abandoned on the village green.

"I am afraid of Chastain, but I love you. The love is bigger than the fear, Ash. Much bigger. You took my part when my family would have made the situation worse with bloodshed. You tried to protect me from scandal when I had made a hash of my life. Of course I love you. Besides, Chastain is a bully, and he's preying on others. You saw what he did to Lord Tavistock, and Tavistock is a boy who means nobody any harm."

Ash looked at their joined hands. "You don't need to say these things."

"Actually, I do. I am a fretful hysteric who will doubtless make a spectacle of myself at somebody's card party or at home, and I am also honest. I worry terribly in bad moments, but my heart is in working order, and that heart belongs to you." She snuggled closer. "Always will too."

He took out a handkerchief embroidered with a coat of arms on one corner. Della thought he'd pass it to her, though she was actually in quite good spirits considering the panic she'd been in a quarter hour ago.

"You love me." His voice shook slightly. "You say that, knowing I am afflicted with the stupidest ailment ever to trouble the human mind and body."

"You are afflicted, I am afflicted, but that's not the entirety of who we are." Della worked out that truth as she said it, and the words felt right. "I am also your wife, sibling to a horde of Vikings, a passable violinist, Tresham's pesky half-sister, and maybe someday I will be somebody's mother. You are more than a periodic case of melancholia, Ash Dorning."

He pressed the handkerchief to his eyes for a long moment, while more leaves drifted down, and the lunch bell sounded in the distance.

"I have to..." He took a breath, then let it out. "I must hold you. Please, Della."

She rose and plucked the handkerchief from him, then straddled his lap and wrapped him in her arms. Ash embraced her as well, the fit and snugness so purely perfect Della felt something inside shift and bloom.

She might have cried a little, perhaps Ash did too, but then somebody started kissing somebody else, and the mood became if not playful, then lighter.

"We can be seen from the windows," Della said, wiggling, the better to enjoy Ash's nascent arousal, "and we will be late for lunch."

"You have a leaf..." He gently brushed a leaf from her bodice. "I am unwilling to provide an erotic spectacle for Lady Wentwhistle's guests, but lunch fails to interest me at the moment. Tell me why you are afraid of Chastain."

Della would have moved to sit beside him, but Ash held her fast. The tale came pouring out as she rested against his shoulder, from the moment Chastain had come upon her curled up and incoherent behind a bank of ferns, to the moment he'd tried to rape her.

"He's seen me at my worst, Ash, and he will tell all of Society you married a madwoman. Bad blood, mental instability, and the irony is,

I'm not even a true Haddonfield, but they would all bear the burden of gossip on my behalf. I cannot have that on my conscience."

Ash stroked her back, and as far as Della was concerned, winter could come in all its fury, and she and Ash would remain cozy and content in the center of the maze, so light and warm was her heart.

"I've seen you at your best," Ash said, "and if you are willing to take on the challenge, I believe we can cast William Chastain into permanent disgrace."

"That sounds dire—also lovely."

Ash kissed her nose. "Disgrace sufficient that he won't bother either of us ever again. Do you know what I'd like at this moment?"

"To leave the house party?"

"No, actually. I would like to nap with my wife and have everybody at the luncheon table remark our absence and be jealous of us."

"I'd like that too." Della didn't have a chance to get to her feet, because Ash shifted her so she was cradled in his arms.

He carried her out of the maze without a single wrong turn, past a dozen smiling guests, and straight up to their room, where they did indeed nap.

Eventually.

⁓

ASH REGARDED his recumbent wife and envied his brother Oak the ability to draw. Della lay curled on the mattress, the covers thrown back. She was clad in only her white crocheted shawl, the weave loose enough to hint at the pale glory of her haunch, the tassels lying against her thigh.

If Ash yielded to the temptation to brush aside those tassels, he'd be in this bed for another hour, and what a pleasant hour it would be. His arousal had been more of the slow-burn variety, gaining momentum gradually as he and Della had talked, cuddled, and talked some more. That stealthy approach to lovemaking was new for him and had yielded surprisingly intense pleasure.

Or perhaps, a man who could not rely on his body to rise to the occasion was more likely to savor the instances of pleasure that came his way.

Della had poured out the burden of managing an imagination given to wild flights. Her earliest memories were of adults telling her how sickly and fragile she was, even though she didn't *feel* sickly or fragile. Then her mother had fallen ill, her oldest siblings had been abruptly sent off to school or worse, and—she recounted the stories so calmly—there was that business about her family occasionally losing her, followed by the revelation that her father was not her father.

Laid end to end, the litany was enough to make anybody distrustful of life.

"You are looking at me," she said, rolling over to her back. "I love waking up next to you, and I love the look in your eyes right now."

Love. She had seized on that word and fired it at him now with the accuracy of a sharpshooter. Well, nothing for it, then. Such courage merited a reciprocal display of valor.

"I love you. I love that you entrust your worries to me. I dearly love that you are my wife."

He also loved how the tassels draped themselves over the thatch of curls between her legs. The image was all Della and arousing as hell. Why did his damned mind focus on clouds instead of memories of Della and her tassels? When next he was compelled to stare out of windows, he'd put that question to himself.

"I am not very steady, Ash," Della said. "Chastain could make little trouble for you if I were less prone to the collywobbles in my mental pandenoodles."

Ash could not reassure Della out of a lifetime's habit of worrying any more than she could tease him out of chronic and profound blue devils. But he could and did love her, and maybe over time, that might make her worrying—and his blue devils—less devilish.

"Chastain has threatened you, Della, but unless I miss my guess, he will soon threaten the Coventry as well. He will intimate that our tables are crooked, our wine drugged, our staff little better than pickpockets. He will offer to shut his mouth in exchange for an endless procession of cash and bother, and I am not inclined to accommodate him."

Ash reclined against the bed's headboard. Della snuggled up to his thigh and rested her knee against his leg.

"Chastain did threaten the club," she said. "My choices were to partner him at cards for the rest of the week, or leave you here among these Philistines with only Sycamore to take up for you."

Ash brushed Della's braid back over her shoulder. "Chastain did not offer you the option of a turn in the gazebo?"

Della drew her shawl up over her face and bundled closer. "I hate him, Ash. I hate him so much it frightens me. He's everybody who ever mocked me for being upset and unequal to life. He's a canker on the arse of society, the well-born dandy who refuses to toss the starving crossing sweeper a coin and thinks that's hilarious. I know why Sycamore is sometimes reckless, for if I were a man, I might be reckless as well."

Sycamore. Ye gods, Cam would have to be managed, but then, managing Sycamore had been Ash's life's work—and that needed to change too.

"What you do have," Ash said, "is a fat bank draft from your doting brother and a devoted husband who knows his way around a deck of cards. If you're sure, Della, then I will deploy those resources to rout our enemy."

She emerged from her shawl to work enough mischief on Ash's privy parts that desire stirred, and the topic under discussion fled Ash's mind.

"We've already missed lunch," Della said, giving him a slow, wet lick, "and yet, we are having a feast. I am making a point."

"If your point is that I am the most blessed of all husbands, your argument has won the day."

"Earlier, when we tried to make love and you lost your starch,"—another lick—"we didn't talk about it. We did not trust each other enough to muddle through. I could have done *this*." She *did* all manner of things, and lost starch became an incomprehensible impossibility. "But you didn't ask, I didn't offer, and the moment set us apart from each other."

"Della, sometimes your best efforts won't stir me to this state."

She shifted up to straddle his lap, her shawl forgotten among the blankets. As if they'd been married years instead of days, she took him in her hand and positioned him for a sweet, lazy joining.

"Your state, or lack thereof, is not the point," she said, moving on him languidly. "The point is that we must have the courage to trust each other. You will find me someday, cowering in my wardrobe, convinced Hessian mercenaries are about to invade Hyde Park."

A naked Della was an irresistible Della, but then, so was a clothed Della. Ash palmed her breasts, thinking them the most perfect breasts ever created by God. Size, weight, shape, the delicious pucker of her nipples at the slightest touch. Perfection twice over.

"You will find me," Ash said, "staring off at nothing, unable to gather the will to shave."

"I will shave you, if you like, and you will lift me from the wardrobe and help me tidy my hair. But, Ash?"

He was losing the ability to follow her logic. "My love?"

"I liked how your beard..."

He rubbed his bristly cheek lightly across her breast. "That?"

"There and elsewhere. I adore being married to you."

As pleasure welled, adoration did too. Adoration for Della, for physical joys that could be snatched from even a bad day. With Ash's happiness, hope also welled. The lows would come again, but if he could appreciate his joys fiercely enough and hold the lows loosely enough, a good life was possible.

A life for which he would be profoundly grateful.

He put all of that—the adoration, hope, and gratitude—into his loving and felt the same miraculous benedictions from Della. They did not simply steal pleasure from a trying day, or enjoy marital privileges with one another.

They *made love*, created it with their bodies and hearts, and gave it into each other's keeping to treasure for all time, come what may.

～

A SLIGHTLY DISREPUTABLE-LOOKING Ash Dorning approached William on the back terrace. Dorning had carried Lady Della from the maze, and then neither party had shown up for lunch. The ladies speculated that Lady Della might be in the family way, as many new brides were, while Chastain had suggested Lady Della's delicate nerves were not up to the challenges of marriage to the Doleful Dorning.

Portly had not yet taken up the refrain on cue—*Doleful Dorning* was quite clever—but then, Portly was growing a bit doleful himself.

"Chastain." Dorning came to a halt several feet away. He did not smell inebriated, but he'd neglected to shave, and his cravat hadn't been properly starched since dawn's early light.

"Dorning. One is moved to inquire regarding her ladyship's health after that curious display before lunch. Will she be quitting the house party? Perhaps seeking the consolation of the Haddonfield family seat?"

William hoped not. He'd like a turn under her skirts—was practically owed that much—and he'd also love to watch her husband stand helplessly by while William sank Dorning's wife into a disgraceful degree of debt. Dorning would pay off the debts for all concerned rather than be publicly labeled a cuckold.

A lovely plan. One of William's better ones, because it left for another day the delightful business of ruining the Coventry with gossip and rumor.

"My lady wife enjoys quite good health," Dorning replied. "She did point out to me that with Tavistock gone, you are lacking a partner for the remainder of the week's tournament."

William could put the puzzle pieces together easily enough. Dorning had either seen or been told that Della and William had been in close conversation before lunch. Della had had no choice but to divulge a version of the conversation to her spouse and perhaps throw in a little histrionic swoon, as high-strung females were wont to do.

"I offered the post of partner to Lady Della," William said. "She suggested you would exert your husbandly authority to forbid her even that much diversion. You own a gambling hell, such as it is, and you deny your wife a few games among friends. Word of advice: People remark that sort of behavior, Dorning. It suggests you already don't trust your wife to behave sensibly, or you can't afford to drop a few pounds at the tables."

Those remarks were, in William's humble estimation, well-placed shots. Sycamore Dorning lounged on the shady side of the terrace in conversation with Mr. Golding. Miss Catherine Fairchild—nose in a book, as ever—sat not far from them.

Dorning would behave himself in front of such witnesses, alas for all concerned.

"Thank you for that advice, Chastain," Dorning said. "Regarding the card tournament, I would not want a fellow guest to miss out on the remaining play, and thus I offer myself as your partner. My role managing the Coventry means I don't often have the opportunity to engage in friendly games, and my wife is not inclined to accommodate you. She needs her rest, being newly married. Late nights at the tables don't appeal to her."

Dorning for a partner? That was not part of William's plan. "You're newly married too."

"And that happy circumstance *frequently* renews my energies. I'm sure you grasp the notion, having so recently spoken your own vows. What say you, Chastain? A few friendly hands over the next several days, my skill combined with yours, and devil take the hindmost? Tavistock's slate has already been wiped clean, and yet, you have substantial losses to recoup."

Lord Tavistock—or rather, the marchioness—was supposed to cover William's losses to date. She was proving hard to catch alone, though, and Golding had been less useful at manufacturing fodder for threats.

Golding, in fact, had completely bungled the business with young Tavistock, according to Portly. But then, William had played his hand with Golding subtly, lest the fellow realize he'd been manipulated.

A shrewd man knew when to change tactics, and recouping losses rather than increasing them was always a better strategy. Lady Fairchild's baubles might well be paste—who brought their finest jewels to a rural house party, after all?—and Mrs. Tremont was inclined to hoist her skirts rather than pay for William's discretion in actual coin.

Which took a lot of the fun out of the whole endeavor.

Besides, if William continued losing, he'd just threaten to expose Lady Della's mental instability, and Dorning would pay off the debts willingly enough.

"Dorning, I accept your offer, and devil take the hindmost."

Dorning bowed and ambled off, while William congratulated himself on knowing when to bend circumstances to his advantage. If he won, so much the better. If he lost, Dorning would pay and pay and pay.

A delightful plan indeed.

~

"CHASTAIN WILL RUIN YOU," Sycamore said, pacing the length of the gallery. "He will ruin you—my business partner and brother—and Della, or finish ruining her. You cannot best him, Ash, not with the cards you hold now. If you sink him into substantial debt, he takes you down with him. If you earn him buckets of money, he'll be encouraged to try the same scheme again and make you repeat the performance."

Sycamore was prone to dramatics, but Ash had to concede these fears were sensible. The gallery had been set up for the afternoon's play—piquet—while at the sideboard, servants laid out sandwiches, canapés, and two different blends of punch.

The session would begin in twenty minutes, and this was as close to privacy as Ash was likely to have with his brother.

"What would you have me do, Sycamore? Chastain threatened Della with rape—again. He's menacing every female, from the maids to Lady Fairchild. He's threatened to ruin Mrs. Tremont and her brother, and he's already driven Tavistock off and cost his lordship dearly. Somebody has to stop him."

Sycamore waited until the footman at the sideboard had departed. "Why is that someone you, Ash? You've already had a bad day, dodging out of Sunday services, lurking in the window. You missed breakfast and luncheon today, and you are freshly shaved at midafternoon. I know the signs of impending doom, and without putting too fine a point on matters, you are not at your best."

"True, but Chastain will underestimate me as a result. I suspect I have underestimated myself." Ash had come to this conclusion while swaddled in Della's shawl, his cheek pillowed on her breast. A good place to think, that, sprawled over his wife's luscious, drowsing, sated form.

Sycamore helped himself to a sandwich. "How can you underestimate yourself?"

"Della trusts me to see this through. I trust Della to support me in the endeavor. She has been struggling with her own demons, and Chastain has been preying on her insecurities. If I don't stop him, he will simply continue his bad behavior and very likely make an attempt to wreck the Coventry's reputation too."

Sycamore paused, the remains of the sandwich halfway to his mouth. "He'd go after *the Coventry*? That is the bleeding outside of bloody too much, Ash. Tresham is still a partner in the club, and Tresham won't take kindly to a baby baronet spreading schoolyard rumors."

Ash ladled a tot from the men's punchbowl and passed the glass to Sycamore. "I tell you Chastain has twice threatened Della with rape, and you urge me to caution. I mention the Coventry, and you are up in arms. You disappoint me, Sycamore." Not a sentiment Ash had often voiced, though he'd frequently experienced it.

Sycamore sniffed at the glass and set it aside. "I am upset, and I beg your pardon. Chastain of course deserves to be called out on Della's behalf, or soundly thrashed at least, but you won't allow me that pleasure, nor indulge in it yourself. This ordeal by cards will go on for nerve-racking days. Why not simply lure Chastain to the stables and sort him out with your fists?"

"I might do that as well, if Della permits it, but Chastain's come-uppance must be public and by using the weapons he himself has chosen. I can handle myself at the tables, Cam, but you are not to create any unnecessary drama."

Sycamore resumed demolishing his sandwich. "I never create unnecessary drama."

"Two duels that I know of. Sent down from university twice in the same term, which cost Casriel dearly in academic donations. Horse races without number. A rotation of upset ladies in and out of your bed, some of whom air their grievances at the club. Rows with everybody from our sommelier to our dessert chef to the second coachman. I could go on."

"Not rows, pointed discussions, and no aggrieved ladies have aired their disappointments at the club for months. Avoid the men's punch, by the by. Lady Wentwhistle is trying to mask inferior spirits with an abundance of treacly cordial. Tell me about Della's inse-curities."

Ash and Della had discussed what exactly should be said to family regarding her infirmity. Della had been reluctant to disclose her ailment, but Ash had pointed out that his whole family knew of his difficulties and had only tried to help.

As much as he'd *allowed* them to help.

"Della is prone to fits of intense dread, to anxieties that she knows are out of proportion to any rational fear, though they overtake her mind nonetheless. In the grip of her panic, she feels shaky, she has difficulty breathing, her imagination comes untethered from logic and sense."

"And," Sycamore said, ambling over to the ladies' punchbowl, "she never knows when this ailment will strike. She can be fine for weeks, then from nowhere, her thoughts race, and the dread wells from some mental oubliette. Perhaps this affliction is common to those stuck at the bottom of a huge pile of siblings, though I know Daisy is free of it."

A quarter hour remained until the tournament resumed, and people would doubtless start taking their seats any minute. Ash took his brother by the arm and steered him through balcony doors that had been opened to admit fresh autumn air.

"Sycamore, explain yourself."

Sycamore gave him a mulish look appropriate to an intransigent six-year-old. "You taught me how to shave."

"You had nearly cut your throat, and while one didn't want to offend your delicate pride, somebody had to show you how to go on."

Sycamore tossed the last of his sandwich into the garden below and gazed out over the front drive, which the double row of lime trees had carpeted in golden leaves.

"There are books that will show a fellow how to tie his cravat, recipes he can follow for boot polish, but shaving must be demonstrated."

Sycamore chose the worst possible time to try for subtlety—of course. "I am scheduled to begin figuratively pummeling the local bully in fifteen minutes, and now you recite ancient history?" Though Ash had the sense that whatever point Sycamore was dancing up to mattered.

"Casriel was there one day, he was off to school the next. We still had tutors and nannies on every hand, but Casriel—the best of us—got sent away. He reappeared a few months later, but he wasn't the same. He had chums besides us. He spoke of things I could not understand. Rugger and lights out and tossing boys in a blanket. I felt like somebody had stolen my best brother."

I am your best brother. "I missed him too."

"But you grasped that he'd be back. Nobody told me he was ever coming back. I thought I'd lost him for good."

And being Sycamore, he'd kept that horrible fear all to himself.

"Mama left the room if I happened to blunder into her parlor," Sycamore said. "Papa took off for his blighted walking tours and was gone for weeks. He kept threatening to go to South America, and all I knew as a small boy was that South America was full of crocodiles and jungles. I was barely breeched, and my papa would rather wrestle crocodiles than read me a story."

"He didn't go." Not a helpful observation, but Ash hardly knew what to say.

"Nobody told me it was all just idle talk, Ash. Then Will went off to school, Mama began her dramas in earnest, Jacaranda staged her revolt, Papa died, and I know exactly why Lady Della sometimes feels as if she dwells in the middle of a never-ending maelstrom nobody else can see."

Ash had not explained that aspect of Della's situation to Sycamore, but Cam had divined it for himself.

Sycamore spoke calmly, while a tear trickled down his cheek. "I am not wild, my family is wild. I just do the best I can, and then my only sensible brother, the only real brother I have, the fellow who notices that some things need explaining, goes off to read law. I'm not smart like you, Ash. I cannot read law by the hour and comprehend any of it. I tried university because you expected it of me, but I failed at that too. It's as if, having been raised on a steady diet of mayhem, I cannot abide any routine. I sound daft."

Ash took the place beside Sycamore at the balcony, when he wanted to tackle his brother and start a rousing and completely pointless round of fisticuffs. Gentle fisticuffs, if such a thing existed.

"You are actually making sense for the first time in years, Cam, which ought to be grounds to raise the general alarum. Allow me to hazard a theory, and please do not pitch me into the rosebushes for stating my conjectures."

"Della would pummel me for raising my hand to you."

"You long for a good pummeling from a pretty lady. My theory goes as follows: You are outrageous in an effort to ensure I will not lose sight of you. If this is the case, I commend your strategy, because it has worked." And why had Ash never seen such an obvious connection before?

Sycamore produced a little gold cloisonné box with a dove enameled on the lid, opened it with an elegant flick of his fingers, and offered Ash a mint. "To clear the taste of that punch from your mouth."

Ash took the mint because Sycamore was buying himself time to regain his composure.

"I don't set out to be outrageous," he said. "I am simply myself, and the results are outrageous."

"A fine dodge, Sycamore, but not fine enough. Horses do not decide to race each other. The riders declare the challenge and decide the course."

Sycamore put away his pretty little box, which, if Ash guessed correctly, had once belonged to their mother.

"I have wondered," Sycamore said ever so casually, "if you don't suffer the mulligrubs simply because you need to get away from me."

And there it was, the signature Cam Dorning punch to the gut, delivered without warning and carrying an ungodly sting.

"I have little control over my melancholia, Cam. If I had wanted to get away from you, I'd simply have taken an apartment at the Albany, assigned managers to handle my jobs at the Coventry, and reserved my encounters with you for Hyde Park's bridle paths."

"But that would be obvious," Sycamore said, "and you are a subtle sort of fellow."

Too subtle, apparently. "Melancholia is a disease that trades in dishonesty, Cam. When the beast has me in its grip, it whispers lies to me. It says nobody needs a dreary fellow like me, and I am tempted to agree. The beast tells me that my family would be better off without me, and again, the words sound so true."

"They are not true," Sycamore said, rounding on him. "The truth is..." He blinked, stared at the denuded limes, blinked again.

"I know the beast lies, Cam, because I can say to it, 'Cam needs me. Cam would be sad to lose me. Cam would miss me and be properly angry that I yielded to such mendacity.' Those are truths no beast can wrest from my grasp. The rest of our siblings have spouses and children and lives, but you see an Ash Dorning beyond this rotten disease, and you would grieve the loss of him. 'If that is true of Cam,' I say to the mendacious beast, 'it's doubtless true of my whole family,' and thus, the wretched affliction loses another round."

Della also saw and valued her husband—another uncorruptible truth—and from that foundation, a brother and a wife, Ash could thwart the beast's false words and false world. He knew that now and let the truth of it fortify him against all devils, whether blue or wearing gentleman's finery.

"I hate your melancholia," Sycamore said. "I want to call it out and shoot it dead, then slice off its balls and feed them to rabid dogs."

I love you too. Ash whacked Sycamore on the back, hard enough to convey affection, not hard enough to send him stumbling against the railing.

"Let's geld Chastain figuratively instead, shall we? Della and I will manage the melancholia, assisted by you and anybody else who cares to join the affray, but Chastain remains to be dealt with."

"And Della's panics?" Sycamore said. "Is family allowed to join in that melee as well?"

"Could I stop you?"

"No, and why would you want to, when I make such a staunch and clever ally?"

"Idiot." Ash turned to pass through the French doors and take his place at the tables, but Sycamore caught him by the arm and dragged him into a ferocious embrace. Ash's first impulse was to simply endure the moment, another fleeting display of Sycamore's drama, but Della's words, about courage and love, stayed that reaction.

Ash wrapped his brother in a good, tight hug and did not step back until Cam let him go.

"You will sink Chastain's prospects past any hope of redemption, Ash, one hand of cards at a time," Sycamore said, "and I will discreetly buy up his markers from the other guests. By the time you are through with William Chastain, not a hostess in England will permit him into her drawing room for at least five years."

"Let's go for ten," Ash said, straightening Sycamore's cravat. "And toss in Paris for good measure."

CHAPTER SEVENTEEN

Della did not want to watch the tournament, but she also refused to leave Ash alone on the battlefield. She compromised by choosing a place in the gallery where she could see Ash, while Chastain, sitting across from Ash, could not see her.

Sycamore had appointed himself her bodyguard, and Della was glad for his company.

"You are for once not chattering," she said as the cards session moved into the second hour. "Your silence is nearly unnerving." She and Sycamore were playing a wager-less game of cribbage, though her mind was not at all on her cards.

"I'm keeping an eye on matters across the room," Sycamore said, "and Ash told me all about your hysterical nerves. Does your mouth go dry? I always carry a flask in part because the damned panics leave me parched."

If Sycamore had dealt Della the perfect hand she could not have been more astonished.

"I beg your pardon?"

"Ash is being cautious," Sycamore said, shuffling deftly. "He's losing modestly for most hands, but winning enough to make a small net gain even in the face of Chastain's ineptitude." Sycamore dealt them each six cards. "And yes, Ash told me that you and I have more in common than a protective attitude toward my brother. My mouth goes dry when I am taken captive by worry. I get the shakes, I wheeze. I fret that I will wet myself, but so far, that hasn't happened."

Sycamore met her gaze across the table, his expression perfectly bland, though his gaze was watchful.

Oh, Sycamore. Della picked up her cards and saw only pips swimming in her gaze. "I bleat," she said. "I sound exactly like a sheep when I try to breathe. A gurgling wheeze when I draw in a breath. Sometimes, I faint."

"I haven't fainted yet," Sycamore said, tossing two cards face down on the table. "One more thing to worry about. I keep hoping I'll outgrow it, but no luck. Can you see Lady Tavistock?"

"She and Mrs. Tremont are by the windows. They are playing Portly and Mrs. Chastain. The game looks quite friendly."

Della discarded the first two cards her fingers grasped. "Did you tell Ash about your panics?"

Sycamore cut the deck, and Della turned over the new top card. "Had to. He thinks his damned doldrums make him some sort of freak. I wasn't out of the nursery when I... Well, I thought he had a right to know. I trust Ash."

Three words, and yet, Sycamore had probably never uttered them about any other family member.

"I trust him too, Sycamore, and I trust you. The marchioness is really quite striking, isn't she?"

Sycamore's smile was purely sweet, none of his usual naughtiness. "She *likes* me. I don't think she liked her husband very much, but she likes me."

"I like you too," Della said, "though admitting as much will doubtless swell your head to the proportions of a small asteroid."

"Everybody likes me," Sycamore said. "The predictability of my appeal approaches tiresome monotony. This evening, Golding will keep you company."

Della was trying to make sense of her cards—how could Ash concentrate with all the tumult of the day?—when Sycamore's words sorted themselves in her mind.

"I beg your pardon?"

"Golding. Chastain lied to him, told him Tavistock was—my signature delicacy fails me—yearning for a left-handed tryst with a man of experience. Golding is mortified that he was so easily and dangerously manipulated. Golding, among others, will ensure that you are never alone for Chastain to accost."

Della had formed no particular opinion about Mrs. Tremont's brother, but avoiding more threats from Chastain was imperative.

"Ash had you arrange this?"

"He did. Mrs. Tremont, Lady Fairchild, Miss Catherine, the marchioness, myself... a few others, and the staff too are charged with keeping you company when Ash cannot. Chastain does not know how to play fair, and when Ash wrecks him, Chastain will try to threaten you."

"Let him try. I am not the cowering ninnyhammer he forced into a sham elopement."

"I dearly wish the marchioness would force me into an elopement. She could grab me by my darling little *ear* and drag me anywhere. I would go willingly to my fate."

Sycamore kept up that outrageous banter for the next hour, while Della lost one game after another. She was too preoccupied watching Ash and Chastain, trying to read the course of their play from what she could observe.

Ash smiled occasionally, Chastain drank at a great rate, and Della told herself not to panic. The week would be long and expensive, but the battle was worth winning, and she and Ash—and now Sycamore and apparently half the other guests—were determined to win it.

∼

"YOU'RE TOYING WITH CHASTAIN," Sycamore said, appropriating a purple and yellow viola blossom from the bouquet on the library's sideboard and tucking it into his lapel. "Playing out the line. He won't know what hits him when you haul him flopping and gasping onto the riverbank tonight."

Ash had spent his week doing exactly as Sycamore said. Winning some, losing a little more. Winning more than that, losing yet still more. The oscillations in his fortunes—and Chastain's—were increasing so gradually, that Chastain did not appear to have noticed that play had become quite deep.

Not deep enough.

The tournament was now down to a single table. Ash and Chastain would play the marchioness and Mrs. Tremont. Both women had lost to Ash and Chastain earlier in the week, and Ash intended to see them, among many others, made whole and then some.

"You look very jubilant for a man who's about to spring a trap," Sycamore observed taking a nip from his flask, then holding it out to Ash.

Ash shook his head. "The trap isn't sprung yet. Chastain's usual recklessness has been held in check by the notion that he could win a fortune if our luck holds. He's not accustomed to winning, and ineptitude could make him more unpredictable than arrogance usually does." Ash had spent his week managing the cards, calculating odds in his head, keeping track of what had been played and what had not, and also managing Chastain.

With humor, with liquor, with strategic asides, and well-timed breaks. The whole business was tedious as hell, but then, Ash had become deucedly skilled at managing tedium. Melancholia had done that for him, given him the discipline to carry on despite a lack of enthusiasm, to maintain a quiet vigil a short mental distance from his own mind.

Della came into the library, looking lovely in a dinner gown of raspberry velvet. She kissed Ash's cheek and graced him with a whiff of honeysuckle.

"Win or lose, Ash Dorning, I love you madly."

He kissed her back smack on the lips. "Win or lose, Lady Della Dorning, I love you madly. Where is your shawl?"

"Already packed. I know travel on the Sabbath is frowned upon, but I don't see any reason we shouldn't leave after services tomorrow."

Sycamore lurked at the sideboard, taking the stopper from each decanter and sniffing the contents by turns.

"Sycamore," Ash said, "you'll follow us to Dorning Hall?"

The last stopper settled back into the bottle with a light *clink*. "I beg your pardon?"

"You're coming to Dorning Hall," Della said, making it a statement. "Ash and I want to celebrate our nuptials with the whole Dorning family, so we've asked Oak to jaunt down from Hampshire and Jacaranda to bring her brood from Trysting. Willow's puppies are safely born, so he and Susannah can join us too. Casriel was amenable, and if you can bear to give up the blandishments of London for another fortnight, you will make the family gathering complete."

Sycamore for once looked at a loss for words. Ash etched the image on his memory and thanked Della for it. When he'd discussed Sycamore's situation with her, she'd proposed a Dorning family reunion—an annual event if the first one went well—and Ash had been so pleased with the notion, he'd kissed her, and well... the discussion had paused while other matters had taken temporary precedence.

"I wouldn't mind popping over to Dorset," Sycamore said, "but the Coventry doesn't run itself."

Nice try. "I sent Tresham a note," Ash said, "and he's happy to keep an eye on the club for the duration. Play is slowing now that hunt season is in full cry."

Sycamore ran a hand through his hair, stared at the carpet, took out his flask again, then seemed to recall that he'd just imbibed.

"Dorset it is, I suppose. The whole noisy lot of us, with children and in-laws, and Willow's dogs, and all of it. One finds the prospect somewhat daunting."

"Good," Della said. "A periodic challenge will give you something to dwell on besides your boundless charm, devastating good looks, and complete lack of humility. Shall we up to the mezzanine?"

She took Sycamore by the arm, and he, looking somewhat dazed and bashful, went without a peep. Surely the sky would soon fill with winged pigs.

For the final match, the session had been moved to the library, which allowed spectators to gather on the mezzanine above, or to play casual games at the several tables set up for that purpose. Guests filed in chatting and laughing, for the libation at supper had been ample and good quality.

Mrs. Tremont and Lady Tavistock took their places at the table, while Ash waited.

Chastain eventually sauntered in, Portly on one side, Mrs. Chastain on the other.

"Luck to all," Portly said, bowing to the ladies. To Ash, he offered a nod that might have held something of a warning.

"Dorning," Chastain said, "a word."

Ash joined Chastain near the fireplace. "Are you drunk?"

"Of course not, but good wine should not go to waste. You?"

Absolutely sober. "I'm prepared to enjoy myself this evening. I've moderated my drinking in anticipation of a celebration at the end of the night's play." A celebration with Della. And the wonderful part was, it didn't matter if that celebration included sexual intimacy, good wine, or any other traditional pleasure.

It probably would, it might not. The celebration would be joyous and intimate nonetheless, provided Chastain received the drubbing he deserved.

"I do enjoy celebrations, and these women need to be taught a lesson. The marchioness in particular is too proud by half. I might let her work off some of her debt to me, if you get my drift."

If Chastain had rubbed his crotch, his drift could not have been more obvious. "You settle your markers, I'll settle mine," Ash said. "But be warned: My strategy for the evening is to lull the ladies into a false sense of confidence. I want them to think our luck has turned for the worse."

Chastain regarded the two women across the room. "I fancy that notion. Set them up for a hard fall. The Tremont bitch mocked me. Said things to my face no woman should say when a man's at his pleasures. Not sporting of her."

Not sporting, to mock a man who used extortion to gain sexual favors? Perhaps Chastain was the truly addled party at the gathering.

"Then I hope justice is on the side of fair play tonight," Ash said, "but you must not flinch when we pile up initial losses. I mean to be daring, Chastain. I want this house party talked about for months."

Chastain patted Ash's shoulder. "Count on me, Dorning. We've made a surprisingly good team, despite my little adventure with your wife. You're welcome to her, by the way. I never did fancy her."

Sycamore's words, about feeding body parts to rabid dogs, came to mind. "Fortunately, her ladyship does fancy me. Shall we to the table?"

Ash took the seat that let him keep Della in his peripheral vision, for he needed the reassurance her presence provided. Sycamore looked bored sitting beside her, and that was reassuring too.

The evening went as Ash had planned, as if for once the fate that had dealt him such low cards in some regards had decided to pay off her IOUs. The ladies won steadily throughout the first hour, then lost just as steadily. The whole time, Chastain affected his typical blasé indifference, though he became increasingly fidgety as the sums owed by the ladies climbed.

He grew still as the second hour progressed, and then he began to drink in earnest. He peered at the cards as if he'd no notion of their significance. The hands on the clock advanced, and the library grew silent, save for the shuffling of the deck and the placing of bets. Play had ceased at all the other tables, and Ash was reminded of the sparring ring at Jackson's. When a good match got under way, it became a spectator event.

"Final hand," Lord Wentwhistle pronounced. "Gentlemen, you are quite well to go, and the first bet is yours."

Ash looked up to find Della faintly smiling down at him. She blew him a kiss.

Win or lose, he had her love. Mulligrubs, blue devils, the bumptious baby baronet... They could all be dealt with when Della beamed such calm regard at him.

"Chastain, let's make it interesting, shall we?" Ash said. "Let's bet the lot of it."

Chastain scooted about in his chair, ran a finger around the inside of his cravat, and stared hard at Ash. "Every penny?"

"Takes courage, I know," Ash said. "If we lose, the ladies will own us, but we haven't been losing for the last hour, have we? We've put our opponents quite handily in their places. Let's finish this."

The marchioness was pale and composed, but her eyes flashed green fire. Mrs. Tremont's expression was carefully blank. They had played well, but Ash had played better, and luck had—up to that point—been with him.

"Right you are, Dorning," Chastain said, thumping the table with a fist. "Luck is with us, our skill is superior, and the damned females oughtn't to get above themselves."

"Chastain," Lord Wentwhistle chided, "mind your tongue."

"I'll mind my tongue. Dorning, deal the cards, and, ladies, may the best *men* win."

Nobody smiled at that remark. Mrs. Chastain was looking bilious, and at her side, Portly for once appeared grim.

The ladies conferred for a moment before agreeing to meet Ash's proposed bet. The amount in play was far beyond what ought to change hands at a typical house party. If Ash could manage to lose, the marchioness would recoup her step-son's losses many times over, and Mrs. Tremont would be well fixed for some time to come.

Ash shuffled deftly and was passing the cards to the various players when he caught a shift in Della's expression. He cocked his head, slightly enough for her to perceive the gesture, and she tugged at the cuff of her sleeve.

What was she trying to tell him?

Sycamore did the same thing, casually tugging at his right sleeve with his left hand while staring intently at Chastain.

Between the card passed to Mrs. Tremont and the card passed to Lady Tavistock, Ash's brain connected the hints from Della and Sycamore with the peculiar angle of the lace at Chastain's wrist. Chastain had a bloody card up his sleeve. The game was vingt-et-un, and he had doubtless stashed an ace out of sight. He'd hidden his perfidy behind a steady procession of wineglasses, one of which— recently refilled—sat before him.

Chastain intended to cheat his way to victory. Why in the hell hadn't Ash foreseen that? Chastain thrived on cheating, bullying, and lying, and he wasn't about to give up those habits at this hour.

"Don't you intend to deal any cards for yourself, Mr. Dorning?" Lady Tavistock asked.

"Sorry," Ash said, smiling blandly as he considered the available options. Ruining the ladies was not among them, and yet, he had only one possible option, one ally who could see Chastain's cheating thwarted.

"I'm a bit fatigued," he said, "also parched. Could somebody pour me a glass of brandy? Better still, Della, my darling, might you toss me down my flask?"

That a wife would carry her husband's flask in her reticule ought not to surprise anybody married for more than a fortnight. That Della had grasped Ash's plan was a secret known only to him and conveyed by the way she cocked her head for a moment, the slightest tilt to one side.

She rummaged in her reticule, simpered at Ash, and let fly with her flask.

TIME BECAME a progression of detached moments while Della watched her flask arc through the air. No sound penetrated her mind as silver flashed in candlelight, and the projectile connected squarely with William Chastain's full glass of claret.

Wine went everywhere, including all over Chastain's hand, cuff, sleeve, and lap. Ash was on his feet in the next instant, offering Chastain a clean handkerchief and gathering up the wine-spattered cards.

"My apologies, Chastain," Ash said, while the ladies looked on, nonplussed. "My profound apologies. Shall we take a short break before finishing our play? You will want to tidy up, I'm sure."

Through this litany, Chastain spluttered, pulled at his sleeves and falls, and glowered up at Della. He muttered something about clumsy damned females and accursed wine stains, while Della breathed freely for the first time in more than an hour.

"Well met," Sycamore whispered. "Damned well met." He squeezed Della's hand, and his expression as he smiled at her had something of amazement in it.

Francis Portly was looking at her similarly, while Mrs. Chastain looked merely calm. "Mr. Portly," she said, "would you be so good as to fetch me a glass of punch? Lady Della, let us take a turn in the corridor while matters are sorted out at the table. The air here is quite close, don't you agree?"

"I'd rather not miss the final play, madam."

"William will change his shirt before play resumes. Of this, I am certain."

She'd sent Portly off on a pretext, and the mezzanine had grown warm. Della passed Sycamore her reticule and moved into the corridor with Clarice.

"Mr. Dorning will ruin William," Clarice said. "You must convey to your husband my profound thanks. A lesser man would have ruined me."

Della did not entirely trust Clarice Chastain, though the woman seemed in complete earnest. "Why exactly shall I thank my husband on your behalf?"

"Because if Mr. Dorning's objective was revenge, he would do as William did to you—dragged your name through the mud, subjected you to ridicule, made you an object of scorn. A lady's good name is her dearest and most fragile possession, and William attempted to destroy yours."

The image of the shattered wineglass came to mind. "William tried to effect that plan. Mr. Dorning thwarted him. I am a happily married woman." And wasn't that the best revenge of all?

"I am not a happily married woman," Mrs. Chastain said, glancing about the deserted corridor. "But I am content. I conceived Francis Portly's child about two months ago, and it became necessary to acquire a spouse with means and standing sufficient to appease my parents. Mama had been in discussion with William's mother for some time, and so." She lifted one shoulder, not quite a shrug. "My darling Francis is, unfortunately, without prospects."

All Della could think was, *The poor child, to be born into such circumstances.*

"You will say I was foolish," Clarice went on, "and you would be correct, though William will not suspect the truth. I made sure of that."

"I am sorry." For Clarice, for Portly, for the child, and even a little bit for William, pathetic oaf that he was.

Clarice waved a hand in a gesture of dismissal. "For the passing inconvenience William causes me, I have a bit of *éclat* among the lesser hostesses as the wife of a baronet's heir. I have security, I am free of my parents' meddling, and I will have Francis's frequent company. One must be practical, *non*? I did honestly fear you and Mr. Dorning would make trouble for me, but you instead do me a great service."

"By bankrupting your spouse?"

"By removing William from polite society. William is reckless and spoiled, and outgrowing those faults will take time. Perhaps you have given him that time."

"And perhaps nothing will inspire him to grow up."

Clarice used a nearby pier glass to inspect her appearance, which was flawless. "I will dutifully retire to the country with my husband. His loyal best friend will visit us frequently. For me, this is a solution to many problems."

That Clarice would explain this to Della was a curious relief. "I wish you all the best," Della said, "though I suspect William will be a difficult husband."

Clarice smiled. "No, he will not. He wants a firm hand, craves it, I suspect, and I can be very firm. I will reward his good behavior and punish him when he disappoints me. He has done nothing but disappoint me so far."

Della shuddered at the images those words brought to mind. "Might we return to the library? I really do want to see the final hand played."

"Of course. That bit with the flask was brilliant, my lady. Mr. Dorning could easily have exposed William as a cheat, but instead only William's foolishness will be exposed. I do not expect such gallantry from the English."

"From Mr. Dorning," Della said, hand on the door latch, "you can always expect gallantry. I certainly do."

Clarice resumed her place on the mezzanine beside Portly, accepting a glass of punch from him. She smiled and leaned in as if to listen more closely amid the chatter of a dozen conversations. Portly bent nearer to her as well, and though he was smiling, Della detected the pain of resignation in his eyes.

Portly's firstborn would call another man father—albeit a man with a minor title. Another man would avail himself intimately of the woman Portly loved. Portly would not wake up morning after morning cuddling his darling close. He would not confide in her his worst fears with any hope that she would be at his side to best those fears.

"How can you possibly look so sad," Sycamore muttered, "when you are about to see your nemesis foiled?"

"Clarice, William, and Portly are entangled in a sad situation, and William probably suspects as much on some instinctive level—or he will soon—and there's nothing he can do about it."

"You pity him?"

"I do, and I cannot convey to you adequately what a pleasure it is, what a relief, to pity that man. In another quarter hour, I will pity him yet more. I want everybody to be happy, but some of us wouldn't know happiness if it bit us on the arse."

Sycamore passed Della her reticule. "Put in a good word for me with the marchioness, if you're determined to see everybody happy. Her esteem would make me very happy indeed."

"Earn her esteem, Sycamore, and she will be happy too."

Sycamore regarded the marchioness, who was taking her seat at a card table topped with fresh linen on the main library floor below. "If I knew how to do that, I would be partnering her ladyship at yonder table, and a few other places as well."

"She typically bides in Town over the winter," Della said, "and now you will hush so that I might watch my husband mete out justice to a knave long overdue for punishment."

A thought popped into Della's head—*where is my shawl?*—but she knew where her shawl was, folded neatly between Ash's waistcoats and Della's spare night-robe in a trunk in her dressing closet. Besides, she did not need to be dragging a shawl with her everywhere when she had Ash's smiles to keep her warm.

∼

ASH HAD SAVED the hands of vingt-et-un for the final night's play, because Chastain, being fundamentally reckless, would predictably ask for another card when any fool knew to stand on a count of seventeen or better.

And Ash, having a bevy of brothers and a surfeit of experience with tired, arrogant, half-drunk gamblers, trusted himself to turn Chastain's recklessness into ruin.

"Ladies," Ash said, taking up a fresh deck, "same bets?"

Lady Tavistock glanced at Mrs. Tremont, who nodded tersely.

"Don't fret," Chastain said. "I intend to be generous in victory—generous to you both."

Ash dealt the cards, noting that Lady Tavistock had an ace showing. She chose to stand rather than take more cards, an encouraging sign. Mrs. Tremont had a nine showing and also chose to stand.

"And you, Chastain?" Ash said, holding the deck as if poised to toss him a card. "Are you feeling cautious or lucky?" Chastain had an eight showing, and—because the deck was fresh—nothing up his sleeve.

"Hit," Chastain said, tapping the table impatiently with his fingers. "Be bold, eh, Dorning?'

Be stupid was probably closer to Chastain's situation. Ash dealt him another eight.

Chastain glanced at the card, then sent Ash a puzzled look, then glanced at the card again. "Rubbishing cards." He flipped over his facedown card, showing a total of twenty-six points. With eighteen in his original hand, taking another card had been a classic beginner's mistake, and with no effort at all, he'd been goaded into making it.

Ash's hand totaled eighteen points as well. "I will be bold too," he said, turning over the queen of hearts, "and I will also apparently suffer for my lack of caution. I'm out."

"Nineteen," Mrs. Tremont said, grinning like a cat before a horse trough full of cream.

"Twenty-one," Lady Tavistock added, to a soft patter of applause. "But fear not, gentlemen. We ladies intend to be generous in victory. We'll give you both a fortnight to pay up."

Chastain sat back. "A fortnight? A mere fourteen days? But that's... that's..."

"Very generous," Ash said, collecting the cards while joy and relief course through him. "I can write out bank drafts to each of you ladies tonight for the full amount owed, and it will be my pleasure to do so. Chastain, if that suits, shall we drink a toast to the victors?"

A dozen conversations started up among the spectators, while footmen came around with flutes of champagne. Chastain helped himself to three glasses, drinking one and putting it back on the tray, then taking two more. Lord Wentwhistle passed him paper and pen, and between glasses, Chastain made out his markers.

Ash had brought the proper documents with him to the library and needed only a moment to execute bank drafts for both ladies, sums sufficient to pay both Ash's losses and Chastain's. The ladies were only too happy to pass him Chastain's markers.

Chastain was too busy swilling champagne and trying to look cheerfully indifferent to attend these exchanges, as Ash had expected he would be. The other guests shuffled toward the door, declaring the evening and the house party quite successful and the mezzanine emptied out as well.

Della slipped her hand around Ash's arm. "Well played, husband."

"Will you stay while I settle up with Chastain?" Ash asked.

Della looked him up and down. "Of course. You are well?"

"Well, but tired, and I don't want to lose my temper." He actually *did* want to lose his temper and leave Chastain with the bruises to show for it.

Della leaned near, which pressed her breast gently against Ash's arm. "Lose your temper just a bit. Clarice said to thank you. She lacks a means of removing William from the temptations that call to his worst qualities. Now she'll have a few years to bring him around."

Ash bent near, needing to dose himself with the soothing scents of honeysuckle and Della. "I would not lay money that Chastain will put those years to good use. I would, however, accept a bet that drink, a jealous husband, or a Captain Sharp will lay him low before those years are up."

"Somehow, I think Clarice would bear up well enough under the loss, leaning on Mr. Portly's sturdy arm all the while."

Della sounded relaxed and happy, and she was regarding Chastain with an attitude of pity tinged with disgust. Truly, the coin she'd spent at the table had been worth the reward.

"Portly," Ash said, "would you mind giving us a moment? I'm sure Mr. Golding can escort Mrs. Chastain to her room."

Sycamore came down the steps from the mezzanine and bowed over the marchioness's hand. Ash caught his eye, and Sycamore, to his credit, wished her ladyship good night.

The library emptied out, leaving only Ash, Della, Chastain, Portly, and Sycamore.

"Chastain," Ash said gently, "my wife now holds your markers. All of them, from every round of cards you've lost for the past two weeks. You owe her ladyship a fortune, and if you fail to pay her timely—because debts of honor are always to be settled quickly—she will ruin you. What say you?"

Chastain looked from Ash to Della, then to Portly and Sycamore. He reached blindly behind him and half fell, half sat in the nearest wing chair.

"*Lady Della* holds my vowels?"

Della brandished a bouquet of IOUs. "All of them, every single one, including the two you just made out to Mrs. Tremont and Lady Tavistock, whom you will not so much as look at, ever again."

Chastain's gaze went from Portly to the door through which Mrs. Chastain had just passed. "I believe I shall be sick."

Sycamore opened a window, tossed the contents of an ice bucket into the bushes, and passed it to Chastain. "A cheat, a fool, and an inebriate. One pities your wife."

"Clarice will kill me."

"Clarice," Ash said, "did not make one stupid bet after another. Clarice did not bully Lady Della into a sham elopement that became an abduction in truth, complete with an attempted rape. Clarice did not harass Mrs. Tremont into granting favors that ought only be given freely. Clarice did not threaten to spread unkind gossip about Mrs. Fairchild's daughter. Clarice did not paw at and bother Lady Wentwhistle's maids."

"And that litany," Della added, "is only a summary of the damage you've done in the past month."

Chastain tossed aside the ice bucket and pushed out of his chair. "It's not my fault! I would never have been driven to that little escapade with Lady Della if Mama hadn't forced me to offer for Clarice."

Of course Chastain would be tiresome about even this. "You, not your mother," Ash said, "came upon Lady Della in a bad moment. Instead of offering aid as a gentleman must, you took advantage of another's distress. You mocked my wife, threatened her, belittled her, and tried to force yourself upon her. I ought to call you out."

Real temper flared, the kind that could see Chastain measured for a shroud. Ash was tempted to have Sycamore drag Chastain out to the terrace, where anybody with a handy window could watch Ash reduce the baronet's heir to a bloody pulp.

"Don't show him any mercy on my account," Della said, tucking the IOUs into her reticule. "The least he deserves is to be gelded. I will write your mother a detailed letter, Chastain. I will explain to her my problems with nervous anxiety and exactly how cruel you were."

Della pulled the strings of her reticule closed with a decisive yank. "I will detail your debts and your behavior with the proper ladies and hapless servants at this house party. Lady Wentwhistle, if asked, will confirm my version of events, as will Mrs. Tremont, Lady Fairchild, and Lady Tavistock. Even Mr. Golding will likely have a few details to add about your unfounded allegations regarding the young marquess. I will explain to your dear mother how you have disgraced yourself on your very wedding journey."

"You can't," Chastain said, gazing at Della as if she'd condemned him to swing at Newgate. "You cannot tell Mama. She'll see me cut off without a farthing, and Clarice will have her pity, and this time Papa will not dare intervene. You simply cannot be so cruel."

"That is not cruelty," Ash said. Della's plan to write Chastain's mama a recounting of his crimes was pure genius. "That is simply putting truth into the hands of one who will use it to keep society safe from you. If you so much as stir from the family seat, Lady

Della will bring criminal charges for kidnapping and attempted rape."

"You're a commoner," Sycamore noted, "and your reputation among the people who work for a living at the various clubs, hells, and house parties is execrable. You cheat the trades, you cheat at cards, and you've already cheated on your wife. If I were your parents... well. One pities them."

"One does not pity you," Ash said. "You were born with every advantage, and all you've done is indulge yourself and prey on others. You would prefer being gelded to the fate I'd like to see you suffer."

"Portly,"—Chastain backed away from Ash—"you cannot let them do this to me. You cannot stand idly by while I am ruined by a lot of gossiping women and their... their bully boys."

Portly sighed. "Chastain, you brought this on yourself, and I tried to warn you. You are lucky Dorning hasn't simply set upon you in a dark alley and left you to die among the rats. You are being shown clemency, though how you will explain this situation to Clarice, I do not know. We saw you palm that ace. Half the guests had to have seen you attempting to cheat, and only Lady Della's quick thinking preserved your reputation from blackest disgrace. Make your apologies, and I'll escort you and Clarice home at first light. Your parents won't kill you as long as I'm underfoot to plead your case."

"I don't want to go home," Chastain replied, a hysterical note creeping into his voice. "I hate the place, and nobody ever calls there but a lot of dreary, muddy squires and their horse-faced daughters. The maids are all crones, Mama will make me go services, and Clarice will drag me around to call on half the shire. I hate Tidemarsh."

Della marched up to Chastain. "You'd best go with Portly, for between the Dornings and the Haddonfields, we will see to it that you will never again gamble in London. You will never again be admitted to a gentleman's club, where you can prey on unsuspecting young fellows just down from university. You sought to sully the honor of widows, schoolboys, and those like myself, who suffer simple human failings. Be off with you."

When Chastain simply stood before her, gaping and blinking, she served him a whacking good crack to his cheek, the sound particularly satisfying because it was followed by Chastain's whimpering.

"You..." he said, his hand to his cheek. "You *struck* me. You *slapped* me. You..." He sniffed, he blinked, a tear rolled down his cheek. "Portly, see me to my room."

Chastain tried to make a dash for the door, but Ash stepped in front of him. "What you tried to do to my wife was much more devastating than the single, well-deserved blow she just delivered. If I hear of you ever so much as glancing at another woman inappropriately, you will die slowly, painfully, and without the masculine organs you've indulged indiscriminately thus far."

Sycamore came up on Chastain's other side. "And if I hear that you are so much as playing Patience for farthing points with the footmen, I will take up where my brother leaves off, with compliments of Lady Tavistock and her step-son."

Chastain looked as if he truly would be sick, while Ash was feeling, at least for the moment, quite in the pink.

"Take him away," Ash said to Portly, "and see that he's off the premises before sunrise."

Portly nodded, took Chastain by the arm, and dragged him toward the door. "Come along, William. Clarice will be very disappointed in you, and you'd best reconcile yourself to doing a great deal of groveling over the next few years."

"Years? Years, Portly?"

"Decades, if you are lucky, but one doesn't hold out much hope you'll live to see a peaceful old age."

Sycamore closed the door behind them. "No, one doesn't, but I just can't seem to muster any sorrow when I contemplate a world without William Chastain in it."

"Damn your skinny arse," Ash said, crossing the library to drag Sycamore into a hug. "By God, Sycamore, you make a very fine second.

The bit with the ice bucket was grand, and the list—*you cheat at cards, you cheat the trades, you've already cheated on your wife*—Drury Lane lost a fine actor when you decided to run the Coventry." He scrubbed his knuckles over Cam's crown for good measure, then let him go.

"That was great fun," Sycamore said, brushing his fingers over his hair. "Serious, but fun. I predict by spring Chastain will have bolted for America. His father will either put him on remittance, or the colonials will do him in. I am off to bed, for this has been the most exhausting, interesting, trying house party I can recall attending."

Della kissed his cheek. "We leave for Dorning Hall after breakfast. Be packed, or we will wait for you."

He bowed, smiling bashfully. "You need not convince me to leave this place. I'll see you in the morning." He sauntered out the door, though Ash suspected Sycamore would not go straight up to bed. A night cap with the marchioness might yet await him.

And finally, at long last, Ash was alone with his wife. Della came to him, wrapped her arms about his waist, and gave him her weight.

"Did you mean it?" he asked, gathering her close. "You will put the whole business in writing to Chastain's mother?"

"Yes, and I will send a letter to my brother Nicholas too. He has no idea about my panics. Only George does, and he has kept my confidences."

A letter was a way to start, though Ash suspected the Haddonfields would find news of Della's malady a difficult surprise. Too bloody bad, because Della deserved their support and compassion, and her husband was determined that she should have it.

"Will you take me to bed, Della?"

∿

"I WILL JOIN YOU IN BED," Della said, stepping back to take Ash's hand and lead him toward the door. "This was hard for you, wasn't it?"

Ash had to consider his answer, because with Della only the truth would do. "Yes and no," he said. "The hard part was putting myself together and making idle talk until the appointed hour. The sitting on my backside, playing hand after hand of cards... That was simple. Not maiming Chastain... That was difficult."

"I wanted to kick him," Della said as they passed an oddly genial footman in the corridor. "I wanted to kick him in his breeding organs, but I'm only wearing slippers, and he might have retched on Lady Wentwhistle's carpets."

Ash paused at the foot of the steps to kiss his wife. "You are very fierce. I adore that about you."

"You are fierce too, Ash Dorning. Another man would not have passed Chastain's vowels to his wife."

"Chastain mostly wronged you and the other ladies. You deserved to hold his fate in your hands as he tried to hold yours in his."

They climbed the steps, and real weariness dragged at Ash. Not the megrims, blue devils, or melancholia, but the honest fatigue that follows strenuous mental exertion. When they reached their rooms, they assisted each other to undress, fell into bed, and cuddled up, as had become their habit.

Della wrapped her hand around Ash's half-aroused cock. "I would like to make love with you, husband, but I would also like to put a thought before you."

"I would like to make love with you too, so the thought had better be uncomplicated and briefly stated."

Della had already learned the exact grip and the loose, easy rhythm that drove Ash mad. He wasn't plagued by an ongoing sense of inchoate desire of late, but with Della's inspiration, he was rising to the occasion. He suspected as winter wore on, desire might be less in evidence, but as Della had pointed out, he could please her without himself being aroused.

He'd forgotten that. He would never forget it again.

"My thought is this," Della said, pausing to scoot down, get comfy, and drive him mad.

Ash had the oddest sense that this activity, about which most men could only dream, soothed Della in some way. She liked using her mouth on his cock, liked the trust it involved, and he liked—he *loved*—indulging her whims.

"Della, I will very soon be unable to think of anything other than *that feels good* or *please don't stop*."

She finished her frolic, giving him a final swipe with her tongue. "William Chastain is to be a father. The child will be Portly's, but still, William—a venal, self-absorbed, pathetic disgrace of an over-grown boy—will be a father in name. He might well become a father in fact, because Clarice is shrewd and practical."

"No woman should have to be *that* practical."

Della rose and straddled Ash's lap, then took him in her hand and seated his cock at her entrance. "I love this part. I love you too."

"I love you, and I love every moment with you." And Della had a point. The pleasure of joining his body to hers was always breathtaking, always miraculous. Della was in the mood to tease him, so Ash endured as best he could, playing with her breasts and praying for fortitude.

She set up a sweet, languorous tempo with her hips, never quite allowing him the depth he craved. "Does every child deserve perfect parents, Ash?"

She wanted to philosophize *now*? "Children deserve perfect parents, but no parents can meet that standard."

"Exactly." She wet her thumbs with her mouth and grazed them over his nipples. "There are no perfect parents, but just as you rose to the challenge at this house party, I think I could rise to the challenge of being a mother."

Ash's hands went still on her breasts. "Your panics made you doubt your ability to be a mother." Of course they would. When a woman's mind could race off with her good sense at the least provocation, parenthood was an emotional obstacle course. "You want to have children—with me?"

"I certainly don't want to have them with anybody else, and I thought we'd start with one and see how we manage." She shifted the angle of her hips, making coherent thought nearly impossible.

And yet, Ash knew he must think. He must comprehend, and he must gather up all his courage to love his wife as she deserved to be loved.

"Children, Della? With a man who stares out windows for hours and can't always satisfy his lady intimately?"

"A child," Della said, "with a man who will slay dragons, though his sword sometimes feels rusty and unreliable, his horse gets winded, and his shield occasionally becomes tattered. He knows things, that man, about determination and human failings, about compassion and appreciating the joys when they come along. He is wise and kind and loving, and he has absolutely stolen my heart."

Della quit teasing him and took him deep into her body, as Ash bowed up to wrap her close.

"Babies are awful, Della. They squall and stink and stay awake all night. They cry at nothing and drool and—are you sure?" A baby. A little soul full of love and wonder, somebody to cherish and treasure and delight in. Della's daughter or son, another Dorning, who might have the family eyes or might have Della's laugh. "Are you truly certain, Della?"

"With you," she said, pressing her cheek to his shoulder, "yes, I am certain."

"Then I am certain too."

Their lovemaking became something more then, a celebration of hope and joy, an exchange of vows beyond words. The pleasure reached past bodily satisfaction to encompass hearts and souls as well, until Della was replete and sighing in Ash's arms, and Ash was awash in a joy beyond anything he could have imagined on his best, happiest day ever.

EPILOGUE

The noise at Dorning Hall as the whole family descended was a cheerful echo of the mayhem Ash had grown up with—banging doors, barking dogs, children shrieking with glee as they slid down banisters. Though the family hadn't been all together for years, Ash had the sense this gathering was more than just a celebration of his recent nuptials.

He was being welcomed home as a prodigal was welcomed home, after a long, exhausting sojourn in a bleak foreign land. Willow gave him a dog and called it a wedding hound, a half-grown mastiff blessed with a quiet disposition and excellent manners.

Oak did a Michaelmas summer portrait of Ash and Della sitting on the porch swing where Ash had had his best talks with his father.

Hawthorne promised a pony to their firstborn child. Valerian dedicated a children's book on manners to Ash and Della, and Worth Kettering started an argument with Casriel at supper over whose turn it was to be godfather. Sycamore announced that it was his turn, and his elders were welcome to take their ill-mannered bickering some-place where they would not set a bad example for the children.

This provoked a silence, followed by toasts, followed by more bickering.

"Tresham sounds bored with the club," Ash said, passing Della her brother's latest letter. The brief Michaelmas summer had ended, and the days had grown short. Della had fit right in with the noisy, rambunctious Dorning horde, but she'd also managed to let Ash know that she was keeping an eye on him. He could slip away when he needed to, or—a new tactic—he could sit quietly with her while the family argued, sang, laughed, or played cards after dinner each night.

If anybody thought it odd that he was content to observe from a slight distance, they did not remark it. Ash could not say his mood was exactly ebullient, but neither was he sunk in despair.

Yet.

"The club sounds as if it's going into winter hibernation," Della said. "For Jonathan to have a chance to take up the reins, however briefly, has been beneficial. He can put to rest the idea that giving up the club was a great sacrifice. He has moved on to challenges better suited to his gifts."

Across the family parlor, Oak, Hawthorne, and Valerian each had one of Daisy's offspring on their laps, and a cutthroat game of Patience was occasioning much merriment.

"I thought we might take on the challenge of a trip to Lisbon," Ash said. "Winters there are sunny and mild, and we are entitled to a proper wedding journey."

Della set aside Tresham's letter. "Winters there are like spring and fall here. Is that what you're thinking?"

Ash had been thinking a lot, about imagination, melancholia, and the sheer glory of having so much loving family and a wife perfectly suited to him. "I would not want to go for long, a few weeks, if you're willing?"

"I will probably have the vapors the instant the ship leaves the sight of land."

"Very well. No Lisbon."

Della smacked him as Uncle Oak promised to send Uncle Valerian to the brig for peeking at a card on the edge of the table.

Della had, in fact, suffered the vapors just that morning, the incident occasioned by nothing more than Hawthorne and Margaret's children instigating a game of hide-and-seek with Daisy's brood and Casriel's eldest. Ash had taken Della up to their rooms and cuddled with her for a pleasant hour, and she'd come right.

"Does this mean we must bide here in dreary Dorsetshire for the whole winter?" Ash asked.

"I don't want to take you away from your family," Della said as Uncle Hawthorne told Uncle Oak to walk the plank.

"You are my family, and besides, this lot will be returning to their various abodes in another few days. I would like to have you to myself for a while, no pirate uncles, no nosy Haddonfields dropping around, just the two of us."

"I would like to have you to myself too, and Lisbon sounds delightful."

Lisbon was worth a try, and to Ash's great relief, his blue devils weren't as bad when he broke up the winter with some sunshine and sea air. Della did get the vapors on board ship—both directions—also mal de mer, or something like it, that persisted for a few weeks even on dry land.

In addition to periodic bouts of worry, Della in subsequent years endured four bouts of childbirth, Ash at her side through every hour of every travail. The prescription of wife and children did alleviate the worst of his melancholia, though some years were harder than others.

Della was his partner in exploration as they assessed the benefits and burdens of walks in nature (beneficial), gardening (some benefit), dancing (quite beneficial), improving tomes (useful as a soporific), and chocolate (much discussion), among other experiments. What worked one year was sometimes less useful the next, but then Della or Ash would have a new idea to try. Season by season, they weathered the passing showers, the storms, and even the occasional gale.

What did not change was their determination to share life hand in hand, through both the mess and the glory, in sickness and in health, in joy and in woe (and in that peculiar combination of joy and woe known as parenting), until both Ash and Della knew their love was equal to any and all challenges, and they lived lovingly—and mostly happily—ever after.

TO MY DEAR READERS

To my dear readers,

Ash and Della led me such a dance, but I hope you agree with me that their story was the right one for them, and worth the wait. No pressure, Sycamore... (He blows us a kiss.)

To my surprise, Sycamore's story is not the next in the **True Gentlemen** line-up. Daisy Dorning Fromm decided that she needed a real romance too (things with the squire haven't been a bed of roses). **Truly Beloved** comes out in January 2021, and Sycamore's tale will follow shortly after that—I hope.

But you don't have to wait until January for our next happily ever after. **The Truth About Dukes**, book five in the **Rogues to Riches** series, will hit the shelves Nov. 10, and has already earned a starred review from *Publishers Weekly*. This is the story of Constance Wentworth and Robert, Duke of Rothhaven. They each have difficult pasts which they must overcome together if they are to have the luscious future they deserve.

And yes, Stephen Wentworth's book, **How to Catch a Duke** (April 2021), is already up for pre-order because Stephen is precocious like that. (Stephen nods regally, the wretch.)

I am also getting together my thoughts on a new series, tentatively titled **Mayfair Knights**, which you should start seeing links for by the end of the year, and yes, I'm still working on my **Lady Violet Mysteries**, though I have no idea where that project will end up.

Do I have the best job ever, or what?

Happy reading!

Grace Burowes